White Clam

A Northwest Adventure

By

Gary K. Cowart

White Clam

A northwest Adventure

All rights reserved & retained by Gary K. Cowart
Copyright 1992 by Gary K. Cowart, Kent, WA. USA

This book may not be reproduced in whole or part, by
Any means without permission of author.

For information write;

G.K.Cowart
25052 104th Ave SE Suite C
Kent, WA. 98030

ISBN 10: 1468074768
ISBN 13: 9781468074765

Library of Congress Catalog Card Number;

92-075271

In memory of my special friend,

Sherry Lynn Hernandez

White Clam

PACIFIC NORTHWEST 1851

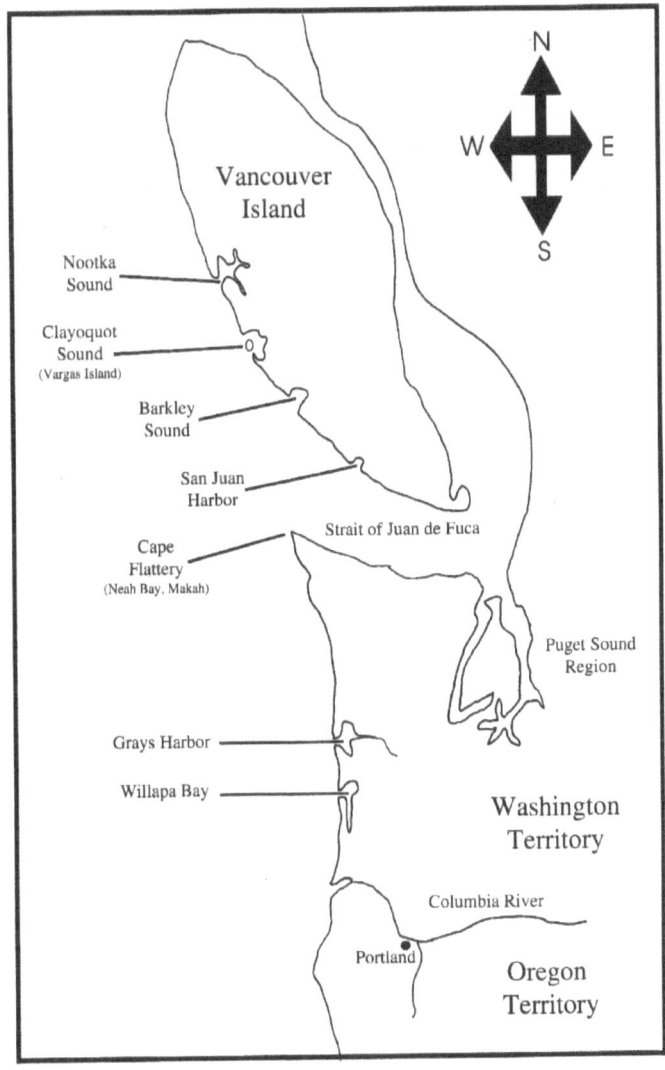

PUGET SOUND

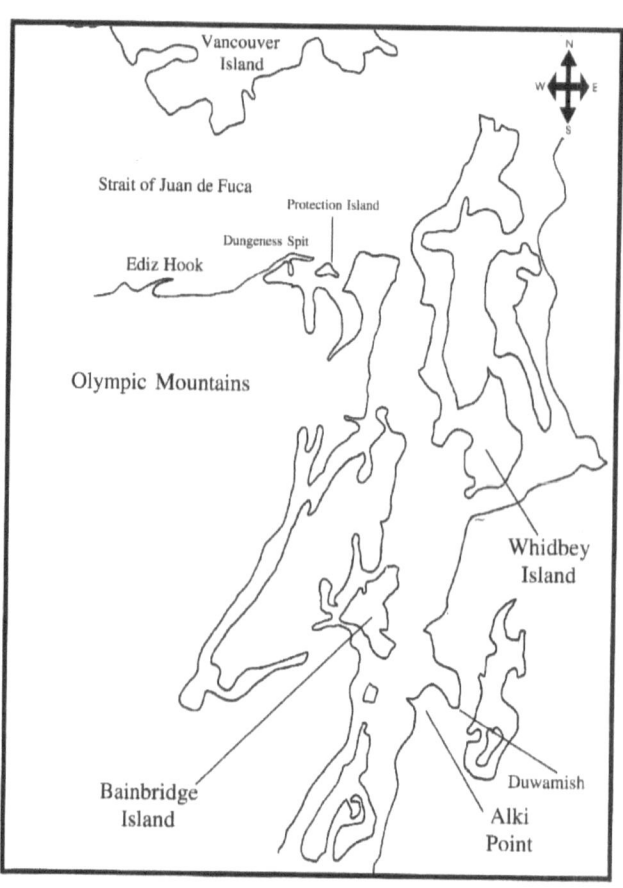

NOOTKA SOUND

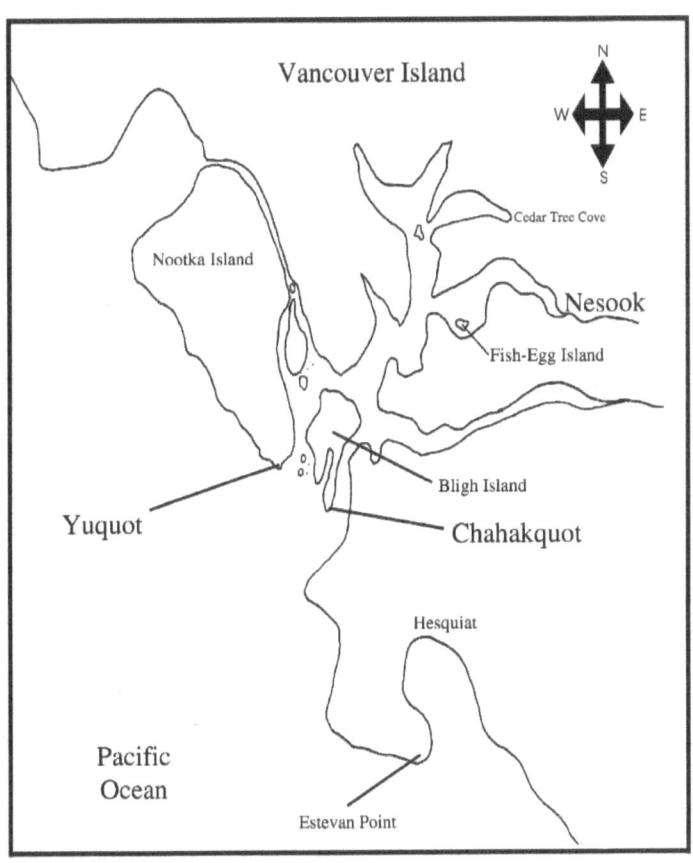

Prologue

The waters were absolutely still with no hint of wind. The dark silhouette of forest at the water's edge contrasted with the bright moon and stars. The raiding leader stood high in the bow of the first canoe not thinking of the beauty of the night, but wondering if the moon would give away their surprise. He felt little remorse for what was about to happen. It was his life. It was how he survived.

The three canoes moved swiftly toward the village shore as silently as possible. Each experienced warrior barely made a ripple as he plunged his paddle deep into the cold water. The attack's success hinged solely on surprise. The lives of the black painted raiders depended on the swift, efficient execution of the enemy warriors as they slept.

Now, as they neared their objective, the cold veined leader said a prayer to his god. Not necessarily to spare his own life, but to aid him in killing the enemy. He lived to kill. Animals, people, it did not matter to him. He only knew there would never be the peace in his life that other men cherished. When or where he died, it mattered not. He would simply kill again and again until that time.

The raiding canoes scraped the rocky bottom just north of the sleeping village. Outstretched arms projecting from a carved cedar welcoming figure stood in silent irony. Quietly the men got out and lifted the dugouts carrying them up the gentle slope of beach just far enough to keep the tide from re-floating them. The leader gathered his warriors and sent one group through the woods on a flanking maneuver and the rest with him along the beach for a frontal assault. Luck was on their side, for even the posted guard slept right along with the rest of the village. His life was ended quickly and quietly. Torches were lit, casting a morbid glow over the carved welcoming poles that stood high above the sand in front of each house. After the first house was entered, the screams of the horrified victims woke the rest of the village. Those villagers running out to join the battle were killed at their front doors by the waiting raiders.

The young village chief awoke to the screams of his people. Within seconds he had his wife and children up, running with the rest of the residents for the back of the long house. He assumed they would leave unmolested and hide in the safety of the forest. With that assumption the young chief grabbed his lance and whalebone club and started for the battle at the front of the great cedar house. His eldest son, a boy of fourteen, was torn between fleeing with his mother and joining his father at his place with other warriors of the clan. For a few steps he ran behind his brothers and sisters as they followed his mother. Then the boy hesitated, turned, and hurried to catch up with his father as he disappeared through the door.

As the young chief joined the battle his very presence created a momentary turn, causing the raiders at his door to give ground. His young teenage son was able to slip outside unnoticed. He stopped dead, appalled at the array of fellow villagers and raiders lying on the ground around him in varying stages of death. The young man could not deal with the bloodshed and stood locked against the planking of his father's house unable to do or say anything. He watched, horrified, as the raiding leader struck his father until the chief fell to his knees. The leader paused, noticing the boy, laughed at the boy's inability to move, and sent a crushing blow to the chief's head.

Watching his father's death sent the young man into shock. He slumped to his knees. The boy didn't even notice when the leader came to stand over him. He didn't see the leader's look of disgust, or hear the insult, or feel the blow that sent him into unconsciousness.

I

The young man made his way down the steep path as the darkness was beginning to fall around him. Ahead of him he could hear the laughter of many voices coming from the large log tavern in the clearing next to the banks of the Willamette River. A fine mist of half fog and half rain had been his companion for most of the day, and now the cold dampness spurred the young man's pace. Knowing food and warmth awaited him in the tavern his steps quickened.

The last dozen strides brought him up the rough plank cedar steps and on to a large front porch. As he extended a long slender arm toward the iron latch, the aroma of warm meat and potato stew welcomed the young man. His presence hardly caused a stir from the handful of motley characters sitting in the candlelight of the split log room. Newcomers were commonplace in the young settlement of Portland (Oregon Territory) in 1851.

The young man crossed the room with solid confident steps, set his pack down in the far corner of the room, and took a seat at the nearest table. Taking a damp towel from his pack the youngster wipe the raindrops from his short brown hair. The warmth of the large fire was already making him forget the day's wet and uneventful journey. The young man's eyes danced around the room as the cold began to leave his body.

The tavern was a pleasant enough place with open rafters of fir and a roof of cedar shingles. A half dozen tables and chairs, set side by side, stood away from the large stone hearth. On the other side of the room sat a grand finished bar with a neat stack of tin mugs at one end. Behind the bar stood various sized casks and barrels containing ale and wine. Above the liquor, in a place of honor, hung a vivid painting of a Boston Schooner, in full sail, battling a mighty pacific storm. A small fat man with a balding head was busy finishing some cleaning behind the counter. He picked up his towel, lifted a brass-hinged hatch at the near end of the bar, and squeezed through sideways. As the man neared the boy his expression became cheerful and his face showed a broad smile of bright shiny teeth.

"How ya be lad, what can I get ya?" said the round little man, as he wiped off the smooth top of the table.

"I'm fine, just fine," the young man replied as he stuffed his legs into a comfortable position under the table. "I need a bite to eat and a place to sleep for the night."

Chet eyed the innkeeper thinking him to be an honest man. The young man tended to trust people and looked for the positive in most he met.

"Well, you've happened along at the right time," the man said. "We've got beef stew and bread for twenty five cents and yer welcome to lie yer bed roll near the fire fer another two bits."

"Thanks," the younger man said politely, "that'll be just great."

With another broad smile, the little man turned and sped to the rear door where he yelled the order to someone in the next room. A few minutes later the younger man was taking his fill from a large bowl of steaming beef stew, followed by a pitcher of fresh cold milk taken from the root cellar.

The tired traveler paid for his meal and turned his attention towards the group of men settling in for a good night's sleep in front of the large roaring fireplace. He listened to their conversations, sizing up the group as to content and quality. As the young man began unrolling his blankets, he overheard one of the men talking about a schooner docked on the Portland waterfront and the name *Exact* caught his ear.

"She's a good enough ship," the thin little man announced, "and Capt'n Folger is as good as they come."

"Excuse me sir," the boy interrupted in a deep voice belying his years. "Did I hear you mention the schooner *Exact*?"

The thin, leather-faced man eyed the newcomer quickly, and approvingly. "Why, yes, son," the man answered. "Do you know of her?"

"I sure do," the young man grinned. "I've signed on board her starting tomorrow. I haven't seen her yet, but my dad knows the owner and got me a berth as a sailors apprentice and cabin boy. By the way I'm Chet, Chet Palmer."

"Lloyd Merrifield's the name," the thin man said raising a short strong arm toward the boy. "And I'm part of the gold expedition fresh up from the California strikes. I'll be sailing with you to the northern islands."

Chet took the man's hand. The boy liked the miner and felt comfortable talking to the stranger.

"... Say," Merrifield said after a few minutes conversation. "I've got some supplies to buy tomorrow, so maybe since we're headed the same way, we could go together. I would pay a fair price for a good breakfast, if you give me a hand with my gear."

"Why sure," said the boy. "I'd be glad to help."

"Good, then its a deal; we'll get an early start," the man said. He grasped Chet's hand firmly, and shook it.

With that, Lloyd bid goodnight to Chet and retired to one of the private upstairs rooms.

The conversation with the miner lifted the young man's spirits and as he lay his head down on the thick brown jacket, the homesickness that had begun on the trail the night before seemed not as important as it once had. The young man watched the flames in the fire a few minutes, thinking about the adventure he was starting. A farm boy going to sea - well, he wanted a change. Chet put his hands behind his head and stretched out his long slender frame. He missed his parents, but the thrill of a new challenge was a stronger pull. He had never had strong feelings for being a farmer and now was no time to have second thoughts.

The morning came early and cold, and Chet was thankful for the warm wool blankets he had brought with him from his parent's farm. It was still dark out but the boy could hear the sounds of many people working busily in the kitchen, and wonderful smells of breakfast began to fill the air. Lloyd Merrifield was already up and grasping his second mug of steaming coffee in both hands in an attempt to keep warm. A boy some years younger than Chet was busy re-starting the fire as the rest of the sleeping men, one by one, began to brave the cold, slowly getting their gear in order. Most of these men were teamsters who drove their wagons and four horse teams from Portland south to the many farms and settlements in the rich Willamette Valley. They carried trade goods to the farms and returned with lumber and food products needed in the city. Heaping plates of hash brown potatoes and scrambled eggs finally brought Chet out of his hibernation. The two new friends ate breakfast and were on their way by first light.

As Chet and Lloyd neared the waterfront, the town erupted into morning activities. Storekeepers were opening their doors and sweeping the rough plank sidewalks that lined the muddy streets. Wagon teams began to appear in greater numbers, hauling goods and merchandise to and from the warehouses on the waterfront. Only a few of these buildings were in total completion and less of them were painted. The smell of fresh cut pine and fir filled the air and not one weathered board could be found. Lloyd decided that they should find the ship first and purchase supplies after. When they arrived on the docks they asked directions from an old Chinook Indian, who used Pidgin English and sign language to show them the way.

"So, Chet. What made you decide on a life at sea?" questioned Lloyd, as they walked on.

"Honestly, I just wanted to get away from the farm," returned Chet. "I felt like I needed more of a change. More of a challenge, I guess. How about you?"

"Oh, you know I'm no sailor. I get on boats only if I have to. We're goin' to the northern islands, Queen Charlotte's, to see if there's any gold for the takin'. I'm just about done with my adventurous days. However, I am a little curious to see those totem pole Injuns."

The two continued on past a row of tall, masted ships and, following the instructions of the old Indian, they soon rounded a jutting pier where a trim, black, two masted schooner was moored. She lay at the dock like a sleeping monster floating on a smooth bed of glass-like water, disturbed only by an occasional seagull floating by from spar to spar. The ship's rigging was clean, with large, gray sails, neatly furled, and two long shiny white cutters atop the main cabin. One smaller boat hung above the stern.

On the dock near the gangway were two men in conversation. One was a stern looking man in naval blues, with bright brass buttons, and a dark blue skipper's cap. The other man, who appeared quite distressed, was very well dressed, obviously a man of some worth.

"No! Mr. Drake, again I must insist that no whiskey trade with the coast Indians will be allowed off my ship," argued Captain Folger. "You can trade jewelry, ironware, blankets, and any number of other items and make a good profit."

"You're right, captain," answered Drake, "but whiskey's what the Injuns want and they'll pay a higher price in otter pelts for it. I'm prepared to pay you handsomely to boot."

Chet thought the merchant was going to explode. His face was distorted and red, and his dark brown mustache twitched at the corners.

"I don't want yer money," yelled the skipper, "and I'll hear no more talk by it. Good day sir." And with that Captain Folger ascended the gangway onto the ship. Mr. Drake scowled deeply, uttered a threatening oath under his breath and headed back up the pier toward his waiting carriage.

Chet watched the carriage wind out of view down the bustling dock front street.

"Who was that guy?" asked the young man.

"His name is Drake. He's a merchant," replied Lloyd. "In fact he owns the store that's supplying the equipment for my expedition."

Chet pondered what he had heard. He felt the captain was reasonable, and trading whiskey was bad news. Trade with the northern tribes. Heathens, savages of the northern islands. The young man's excitement grew. His adventure was starting.

As the two boarded the ship, they approached a crewman who pointed the way aft towards the captain's quarters. The man and the boy found the captain still upset over his disagreement with Mr. Drake. Chet introduced himself and Lloyd Merrifield and the captain's disposition improved. Captain Folger told the boy of his duties aboard the ship and Chet perceived him to be a demanding but fair man.

A knock at the cabin door interrupted the conversation. A short stocky man with a dirty white apron and stocking cap entered the cabin. His shirt was sleeveless and he was missing his two upper front teeth, a loss which gave him a whistle when he spoke.

"Excuse me capt'n, will ye be needin' any noon meal today? If not I'll be goin' ashore to see about that fresh produce that's s'posed to be delivered this afternoon."

"No Albert, that will be fine," answered the captain. "This here's the new ward boy; before you leave, show him where he'll sleep and stow his gear."

With a cold stare, and a grunt of dissatisfaction, the cook motioned for the boy to follow him down the companionway toward amidships. As he turned, Chet noticed a faded blue anchor and blood drop tattoo on the stout man's left arm. Chet and the grubby little cook left the cabin. The two had traveled, perhaps, ten paces when the cook suddenly stopped and turned around.

"Nobody calls me Albert ceptin' the capt'n laddy. Bart's the name I go by and if you stay out of my business and do what's told, ye'll be just fine. This here's yer cabin next to mine and when I get back, be ready to learn yer duties."

Chet watched cautiously as Bart disappeared down the companionway and wondered why he was in such a foul mood, or if he was always that way. Some cabin, he mused. The door was made of some type of louvered hardwood and the opening was so narrow that Chet had to turn sideways to enter. The bunk was a narrow box-like affair, about six feet long, and built into the bulkhead. A small counter with pitcher and pan stood level with the head of the bed and at the foot was a wall with two coat hooks on it. The whole room was slightly less than five feet wide and the ceiling couldn't have been higher than six feet. Below the bunk were built in drawers, where he found a pillow and blankets in fair condition. Added to his own bedroll from home, he felt he would at least be warm, if not completely comfortable. Hanging from the ceiling above the middle of the bunk was an oil lamp of some years whose metal finish was tarnished and blackened. On the bulkhead at a position four inches above the edge of the bunk was an oblong brass mounted porthole some six inches wide and ten inches long. As he peeked out of the window he noticed the now all too familiar shape of Bart the cook working his way up the pier towards the business section of town and wondered how their relationship would fair. *Not well*, he thought. It didn't matter. Chet was confident he would survive. A knock at the hatch brought him back to reality.

"Chet it's me, Lloyd. I'm ready to go for my equipment," the older gentleman exclaimed.

Chet hopped off the bunk, almost hitting his head on the old oil lamp and quickly opened the door for his new friend.

"Mr. Merrifield." he answered, "I was just stowing my gear and getting used to my room. A little small, isn't it?"

"At least you have some privacy. You ready to give me a hand?"

"Sure."

Chet grabbed his warm woolen coat and the two of them made their way back up topside, down the wooden gangway off the stern of the ship and on to the bustling wharf. The gray chill of the morning was giving way to broken clouds and sunshine, promising a warm November afternoon. After a short detour for a filling lunch of broiled salmon and vegetables, the two continued on to Drake's store and warehouse.

It was a two-story building with a retail storefront on the first floor and offices and storage on the second floor. Lloyd and Chet walked in the front door past neat bins of rice, beans, and other foodstuffs. Rows of clothing, dry goods and tools lined the back of the store. At the far end of the room on a second level balcony was a railed stairway leading to an office enclosed in glass. The boy could make out the figure of Mr. Drake pacing back and forth, obviously in no better a mood than he was earlier on the wharf. He seemed to be talking to a man standing at the rear of the office who was only partially in view.

Chet and Lloyd finally reached the bottom of the stairway and started up. When they reached the office door, Lloyd sounded their arrival with a firm rap. After a few moments the door opened and Drake beckoned them in. Chet was surprised to find the room empty, but he did notice another door at the back of the room and figured that the other person must have left by that route. In the meantime Mr. Drake and Lloyd were talking of strange items called *Long Toms*, *Cradles*, and *Sluices*; things that sounded foreign to Chet, but obviously had some relation to the exploration of gold.

"Why don't we go down to the shop in back and inspect the equipment," suggested Mr. Drake, smiling for the first time.

With that, Drake went to the rear door and secured the fastenings. The three of them walked back out the front door and down the railed stairway. At the bottom the tall merchant led the way back to the rear shop where carpenters were busy finishing what looked like a long wooden trough. Lloyd explained to Chet that the contraption was called a sluice box and that it was used to process gold bearing dirt and separate out the precious mineral.

The miner was satisfied with the quality of the hardware he was purchasing and drew out a bank draft in the amount needed. Then Mr. Drake's men brought a freight wagon with a four-horse team to the back entrance of the warehouse and began loading the equipment for transfer to the ship. Besides the mining hardware, there were blankets, tents, cooking utensils, and other essential cold weather gear, including a small pot bellied stove, which was an item that Lloyd had done without in the early going of the California gold rush.

Finally all was loaded and the middle-aged miner joined the wagon teamster on the front seat while Chet sat in the rear with the cargo. It was well into the afternoon when they arrived at the pier and a warmer sun made unloading the mining goods a little more tolerable.

Chet was surprised to learn that Bart had not returned yet with the vegetables and dry goods from the farmers market. This good fortune enabled him to help Lloyd and the other miners complete the loading of their gear into the ship's hold. The hold was a dark and gloomy expanse, consisting of a large open area for cargo in the center of the ship, with forward and aft cubicles for passenger or other accommodations. In the farthest forward area, called the forecastle, were the crew's quarters and the anchor chain locker.

Just as the last of the wooden sluice sections were carried aboard, the boy noticed the figure of the little cook sitting atop a produce wagon winding down Dock Street towards the ship. In a moment Bart caught his eye and hailed him.

"Chet, over here boy," called Bart. "Come now and help with these crates."

Chet moved at a run down the gangway and sped over to the wagon. The cook was already down from the box seat loading crates of apples and potatoes on to a wooden hand truck. Chet found another hand truck and started loading sacks of beans and a crate of fall corn, taking care to see that his load was at least as heavy as the cook's.

After a few trips they had all the stores at the middle deckhouse, where the galley was located, with the exception of a large wooden barrel marked, *crackers*, that Bart insisted upon carrying himself.

The galley was a small affair with room for only one person between the counter and the huge black cook stove. The counter contained a sink with a metal hand pump, which was the only source of fresh water from the water tank deep in the ship's hold. The dining portion was a ten by twelve foot room dominated by a large table and benches that filled the whole room. Outside the aft exit was a breezeway that led to their sleeping quarters, with the captain and first mate's quarters beyond.

As soon as all the provisions had been put away and the cracker barrel tightly secured in the corner of the galley, the cook started the evening meal. Bart seemed almost pleasant while he cooked, and for all his gruffness, the old sailor was able to put on a feast unequaled on coast shipping. After Chet took Captain Folger's dinner to him, he sat down with the miners and some of the crew and had his fill of fish chowder, biscuits, and corn.

Of the six crewmembers, Chet thought only two seemed to be able seamen. One was a large jolly New Bedford man named William, whom everyone called Bill, and the other was a younger man of twenty-one, tall and strong, named Andrew. The rest of the crew were a collection of ex-prospectors and tavern rats that weren't able to make it in the gold fields and opted for the relatively easy and at least secure life on a coastal schooner. The first mate was a bright man by the name of Matthew English, a schooled sailor and an excellent navigator. He took Chet aside after the dinner mess and introduced him to Bill and Andrew. The boy found out that in addition to his kitchen duties, he would have a four hour shift learning the ropes and handling the ship with Matt's port watch in the afternoon and the captain's starboard watch in the evening. Chet wondered when there would be time for sleep, but did not complain. The ship would sail on tomorrow's tide, so he quickly turned in and was asleep in minutes.

"Time to turn out, Bart," yelled Andrew from the hallway.

Chet could hear the stirring and muffled oaths from next door. He pulled his sweater and coat on and was out in the hallway before Bart. When the old cook appeared, he greeted Chet with a gruff, "Come on," and the two of them set about making a fire. Soon the smell of hot boiling coffee filled the ship.

Within minutes the captain and the men of both port and starboard watches started filing in after their eight hours of sleep. After they put to sea, it would be the odd night that would find them getting eight hours of sleep in a row.

Breakfast consisted of coffee, oatmeal, and biscuits with strawberry jam. About halfway through the meal Matt English appeared, whispered something to Captain Folger and the two of them left the galley, crossing the gangplank to the dock. They shook hands with three bearded men and after a short discussion they shook hands again ending with the departure of the three strangers.

After breakfast the whole crew turned out to get the ship ready to leave that afternoon. Decks were cleared and cleaned, rigging was checked and tightened, booms were greased, and sails made ready. Chet had seen little of Lloyd since the previous afternoon, but when the noon meal was finished, he met with the miner, who confirmed a rumor that they had been hearing all morning.

"It seems as though we've had a slight change of plans, boy," said the miner. "A group of pioneer families, just off the Oregon Trail from Illinois, has tempted the captain with cash money to make a detour and drop them at their new settlement on Puget Sound."

"Where is this place?" asked Chet.

"It's a deep water inlet up in the Washington Territory. There's a map next to the wheel. I'll show you."

Lloyd showed Chet where the place was on the charts and since it would only be a two-day disruption, no one seemed too displeased, except Bart.

A little before noon the pioneer families arrived and started loading their belongings into the aft part of the ship's hold. They had very few items, mostly tools and clothing, and, of course, basic food staples as would be needed to make it through their first winter.

The leader of the group was a tall, slender man named Arthur Denny and he encouraged his members at every step. Dark circles surrounded the man's eyes and his brows seemed heavy. He coughed constantly as he spoke, but his words were focused and straightforward.

"Keep goin', everyone. This is the last stage of the journey. We've all but made it. Get your gear on the ship as fast as you can and we'll be on our way. No more walkin' from now on."

There were only a dozen or so adults and about that many children and all of their faces showed the wear of months on the trail. Chet wondered how the tiny group would fair in the wilderness. He had heard the tales his mother and father had told about their experiences and knew that the newcomers were in for some trying times.

Chet and some of the crew helped the men with the loading while the women and children retired into the ship's hold. They made makeshift beds and hung blankets from the ship's beams to form more private cubicles for each family. A central cooking area was set up, using a bed of ballast rocks and a sheet of iron plate, whereupon a cast-iron stove was placed. All and all Chet thought them to be quite cozy for their trip north.

After everything was stowed away, Captain Folger gave the word to let go the mooring lines and the sleek little schooner made its way quietly out into the current of the smooth flowing river they called the Willamette. Matt had the entire crew up the ratlines or on the ropes putting on sail, and soon the straining ship was making good time toward the Columbia River junction.

Chet took a hand at the foresail halyard and had his first lesson in seamanship. Most of the miners and families were on deck enjoying the crisp afternoon, including a young lady named Lucy Hill. Chet noticed her right off. The young lady's long brown hair flew in the wind and her eyes were so stunning they knocked him off guard. He was near speechless when she came up to him asking questions about this rope or that sail.

"I'm sorry Miss," said Chet, embarrassed. "I'm new at this myself. I'm just learning."

"Well, perhaps we can learn together," Lucy announced eyes sparkling. "You can teach me what you learn each day."

Lucy smiled at the young man and Chet wasn't sure he heard what she had said. Her beauty was such that he couldn't concentrate very well. She had soft facial lines, cream-colored skin and a feminine figure that was hard to ignore. The boy had girl friends in school, but none of the local girls had ever affected him like this one.

"Well, I'm not sure what kind of a teacher I'll be, but when I have some free time I'd like to spend it with you," said the boy.

In reality the young man knew he would take every opportunity to meet with her. But at that moment Chet heard Bart yelling for him so he said a hurried goodbye. As he rushed off, Chet realized he felt a little intimidated around the young lady, but he surely was glad she was on board.

Bart and Chet put out a fast lunch for the crew and the rest of the day was spent racing towards the Columbia, where at mid-afternoon the *Exact* hove to as a small boat came alongside. A rope ladder was thrown over the rail and a slender man in officers' garb ascended the ladder and talked briefly with Captain Folger. Chet found out later from Andrew that this was the river pilot. The sails were trimmed and filled again, and under the watchful eye of the pilot the schooner was swept out into the middle of the Columbia River on its way to the Pacific Ocean.

That night they anchored on the downstream side of a small island twenty miles from Portland. Chet was busy helping with the evening meal and had little time to talk with Lloyd or Lucy. As soon as the Captain and pilot were finished and the dishes cleared and washed, Chet was ordered out on deck with Andrew for the first watch with the understanding that Andrew would spend his two hour watch teaching Chet the names of the various parts of the ship. They started with the basic port and starboard, bow and stern, and then graduated to the names of sails and masts: mains, mizzens, jibs and so forth, and ended up with the really complicated rigging: stays, shrouds, halyards, cleats, bits and blocks. The rest of the time was spent tying knots. This was the most enjoyable time for the boys, and Chet not only learned to tie a bowline, fisherman's bend and a variety of hitch knots, but also how and where each knot was used.

All during the lesson various pioneers and prospectors wandered on deck for fresh air, a smoke, or conversation. As the watch turned over, Chet noticed Lucy coming his way.

"Are you a sailor yet?" she smiled. Her dark eyes almost floored him. His infatuation was growing. When Chet didn't say anything, she tried again. "Well, have you learned anything?"

Finding his tongue, the young man stammered, "Yeah...yeah, I guess so, but I think I've already forgotten more than I wish to admit." She was so attractive, he couldn't help but stare, and he hoped he wasn't too obvious. "Let's see if I can remember the names of the sails."

The young man struggled some remembering the nomenclature, but Lucy was impressed just the same. They walked and talked for nearly an hour, and when she occasionally took his arm, the thrill that ensued was indescribable.

"Lucy!" came a call.

"I think your mom's calling," said Chet.

"Lucy, time to come in!"

"No, that's Aunt Lola." Her smile turned serious. "My parents died last year."

"I'm sorry, Lucy," Chet said. "Wait. Don't go yet. I had fun talking. Can we do it some more?"

"Sure, maybe tomorrow," she said.

His heart felt pulled along with her as he watched her go below. He liked this girl.

Chet checked in with Bart, and, after stowing away some food items and tidying up the galley, he retired to his room. It was beginning to get cold and he was thankful for the warm blankets he snuggled under. Even though it was cramped, he felt safe and secure in his closet-like cabin.

The next morning was overcast and colder and the wind was from the southwest. As the galley crew readied breakfast, the rest of the crew went about lifting the anchor and setting the main and mizzen sails. Sailors scurried up the rat lines setting gaff top sails and a mizzen masthead staysail to take advantage of the favorable wind on this northern flowing stretch of the river. They passed the mouth of the Kalama River and just after noon they reached the headwaters of the Cowlitz, where the Columbia takes a westerly turn for the ocean. All day they passed sandbars and islands with trees on them, some of the islands quite large. The dark evergreen forest rose up from the banks of the river spreading outward for tens of miles and every so often a Chinook Indian canoe could be seen in the distance. Sometimes a fishing camp cook fire with its thin blue-gray smoke would be seen at the southern shore. An hour before dusk the pilot ordered the ship to anchor west of a small sand bar near the Oregon shore. Chet and the other crewmembers went aloft to furl and tie down the sails. From his perch in the main crosstree he could see three small craft heading toward them from the shore. The others saw the Indian canoes also and Bill hailed the deck.

"Ahoy Capt'n," screamed the burly sailor, "Injun canoes off the bow one half mile."

This started a mild panic among the settlers, for they had encountered Indians before on the Great Plains. Most of the women and children were already below decks and a few guns were loaded before the pilot and the captain assured the pioneers that this was not a raiding party. In fact, it was a trading party, which proved quite interesting to most on board. The canoes were fifteen foot-long dugouts with blackened gunwales, flat transoms, and pointed bows riding low to the water. Each craft contained two occupants trying to out-paddle the others. They were large men, well fed from eating the abundant sea life of the northwest coast, but they weren't very tall. They were wearing a combination of Indian and white men's garments. Their faces, round and rubbed with fish oil, sported long black mustaches. Their long dark hair hung down their backs. Few on board had ever seen such a sight, and as Chet dropped the last few feet to the deck, the first canoe glided alongside.

A few words were spoken in broken English and the Indian in the bow turned and removed a green grass mat, uncovering a mass of gleaming silver fish. He stood and struggled to raise one of the thirty-pound king salmon and the late afternoon sun glinted off the powerful, sleek body of the fish as it turned and twisted. Chet had never seen such a magnificent fish. He had seen some pretty good-sized trout before, but nothing compared to this seagoing big brother. Within half an hour all the settlers and the captain as well had traded for fresh salmon. All were going to feast tonight.

As Chet went to sleep that night, the whole ship was surrounded by the fragrance of broiled salmon, and he recalled how Bart had cut the mighty fish into steaks and cooked them, and he remembered the delicate flavor of that firm pink meat that seemed to melt in his mouth as he took his fill. He thought, *this sailor's life isn't so bad, plenty of sleep, plenty of good food and getting paid to boot.* He didn't forget Lucy's smile either, happy that the young lady was paying so much attention to him. With the image of her face in his mind he blew out the oil lamp, and fell asleep to the gentle creaking sounds of the ship.

II

The young Indian was aware that the fast moving dugout had been his home for the last week. With his eyes, hands and feet bound and a gag in his mouth, it was a wonder he was still alive. They had barely fed or watered him at all, and the constant lying in the same basic position had left him numb, requiring much effort to try to get into new positions along the bottom of the dugout. Also, the quick feet of the raiders would catch his sides if he got too comfortable, or encroached on their personal space within the canoe.

The leader meant to keep the boy alive as an attempt to shame the young captive and as an example to his own people of how not to act in battle.

The young Indian boy had been noticing the temperature drop this last day of the journey, and, combined with the frigid ocean spray, the cold only added to his misery. As the canoes scraped bottom once more the boy did not know that he had arrived at his final destination. He presumed he'd have to endure another night of torment on the dugout floor, and was surprised when he was grabbed by the hair, lifted painfully out of the canoe and dragged on shore. The rocky beach was hard on his sides and the boy was aware of talking and the movement of many people. He did not understand the language and lay numb, waiting in fright. He cautiously stretched his legs and arms a little for the first time in a week. As the hours went by, the boy thought he would be left in this place to die. He wished for death. He could feel the presence of occasional visitors and hear their giggles, but no one offered relief.

By this time cold was beginning to be a factor again, and the young captive felt it must be well into the night. He shifted his position once more and felt his seashell necklace fall away from his open shirt, exposing the silver eagle charm attached to the end. It was a gift from his father. He thought of a quick death again, and then heard a familiar sound, the leader of the raiding party's laugh. The leader was returning with his host. The boy's fear returned and he readied his body for more physical abuse, which wasn't long coming. Within seconds the boy felt the familiar blow of a bare foot in his exposed ribs. He couldn't even cry out with the gag in place. His hair soon ripped with pain as his head was pulled back. The young captive heard the laugh once more as he slipped into unconsciousness. The leader ripped the silver necklace from the young captive's neck and left.

III

At first light the ship was moving again, and the galley served a hot chowder and biscuit breakfast for the crew and prospectors made from the left- over salmon. The schooner was making good time and an ever-increasing number of small and large islands showing up. The pilot was now earning his keep as he guided the ship through the deepest and safest passages. Before mid day the *Exact* cruised into open water and the shore fell away on both sides. They were near the great mouth of the Columbia and the Pacific Ocean.

The ship glided down the slowly moving current under lightened sail, coming to a halt on the south bank of the Columbia near the village of Astoria. Captain Folger gave the command to drop anchor and ordered Matt English to pick three men and lower a boat to take the river pilot to shore.

"Move lively now," the captain growled. "We want to make the evening tide across the bar."

In the distance Chet could see the broad expanse of the mouth of the river, hardly able to make out the northern bank some four miles away. He watched as tiny white rolls of wave appeared and disappeared towards the west, not knowing that the waves over the bar were not tiny, but eight to twelve feet high in places. A sharp pat on the back brought him out of his daydreaming.

"Lad it's time to take the helm of your first ship," said Matt.

"That's great," returned Chet, excited at the prospect. "Let me yell at Bart and I'll be right with you."

The boy turned on his heel and raced down the companionway and, after a grunt of approval from Bart, he was back on deck just as the crew hoisted the cutter off its chocks. As they swung it out over the side of the ship Chet was joined by Lloyd and Lucy who made some comment about how the boys always got to do the fun stuff while the girls had to work or do nothing, but Chet promised her a full and detailed account of the adventure at his first opportunity. Lloyd cautioned him not to get drowned when the boat tipped over, and Chet could still hear him laughing as he climbed down the Jacob's ladder and into the cutter. The pilot followed shortly thereafter, and the two oarsmen pulled smartly away from the *Exact*.

Matt let Chet take the tiller and instructed him in the fine art of crabbing the boat toward the wind just enough to keep from being blown sideways off course. The wind was coming lightly out of the northwest and the small boom and sail were hoisted to gain more speed. Chet watched as the crewmen carefully set the mast inside the step, which was just a wooden box on the deck, and quickly set the stay lines and shrouds fast to the bow and sides of the cutter. Matt was already attaching the boom to the mast and all three men lent a hand to the halyard. Soon the small sail was filling with air. At last the second crewman took a long, wide, thin board and slowly shoved it through a slot in the amidships thwart, all the way down until it had almost disappeared, and retained it by two wooden pegs.

"What's that board for?" asked Chet.

"It's called a center board," the first mate said. "It enables the cutter to bite into the water. Without it the boat would simply drift where the wind blew it rather than where the helmsman steered it."

Chet remembered makeshift sails on rafts at home, realizing now why they were always so hard to maneuver.

Matt took the helm and quickly showed Chet how to lay down a tack towards the shore, and with the wind behind them, one broad reach was all it took to bring the cutter up to the dock without further change in tiller position. The pilot said his goodbyes and the fast little boat headed back towards the *Exact*, only this time into the wind. Chet was able to experience running the boat close-hauled changing tacks three times before they reached the ship. The crew of the cutter lowered the mast and stowed the sail as the shipboard crew hauled the cutter back up to the main deck. Captain Folger had all hands set sail, and, as the cutter had done, the schooner ran close-hauled on a west by northwest tack towards the north shore of the river mouth to Sand Island and Cape Disappointment beyond.

As the schooner neared the Cape, the captain turned due west on a starboard tack, close reach, for the Pacific Ocean. Gaff-topsails, a fore staysail and masthead staysails were ordered on, and, almost immediately, the schooner responded with more speed to battle the increasingly high seas. A two-foot swell was rising and it had started to rain. The sturdy ship with flying jib added dove relentlessly onward into three-foot seas and an increasingly grayer sky. Breakers began to spray foam over the bow, and the passengers in greater numbers left the deck for below. Chet was ordered to the galley to help Bart stow loose provisions and start the evening meal. Before the young man was finished, darkness had set in and his head was starting to reel. This was no river cruise now; this was real sailing! It did not take Bart long to notice the green expression on the boy's face. Handing Chet his rain slicker and hat, the old cook pointed him towards the lee rail outside the galley hatch where Chet eventually lost all he had eaten that day. After a few minutes, feeling cold, wet, and humbled, the boy thought he felt better and returned to finish his chores with his head still clouded.

"So ya thought ye had yer sea legs 'bout ya, huh laddy?" sneered Bart as he took pleasure in the boy's misery. "Lordy knows the lubbers down below will be pukin' there guts from here till' t'morrow, but don't be thinkin' yer'l be slackin' off, laddy, yer paid crew and crew has to take it."

Chet resolved to show the old cook that he was made of sterner stuff, and though it took a few more trips to the rail, he was able to finish the night's duties.

The crew was the only ones to eat that night, as none of the miners or other passengers felt the need. The port watch ate first and relieved the starboard watch, who retired to the forecastle after their meal. After the galley was cleaned, Chet joined the watch on deck. The cold sea air cleared his head and he joined Andrew at the helm. The captain decided they were well clear of the Cape and Peacock Spit rocks so he took the helm from the boys and close-hauled the ship towards the northwest. They sailed on for an hour, constantly trimming the sheets, cleating and belaying until Chet's hands were numb with cold and he could hardly grasp a line. After what seemed a miserable eternity, the ship's bell rang and the port watch was relieved. Chet staggered down the companionway to his quarters and opened the door. He stood there for a moment wet and cold, contemplating his thoughts of the night before. He struggled free from the wet coat and hung it to dry on a peg above the door. When he turned, the boy noticed a partially opened porthole and a damp bunk. The young man was dizzy and hungry but soon he forgot the cold as exhaustion took over his weary frame. Somehow he slept.

Chet woke to a beating on his door and slowly rose on one elbow. He was still feeling the ache in his stomach and head. *It just can't be time to get up yet,* the boy thought to himself.

"Hey, ya lubber, wake up. There's work to be done," grumbled Bart. "I get tired of roust'n ya out all the time."

The boy rose slowly and felt the damp stiffness in his bones. Chet didn't need to dress, for he was still wearing what he had worn the night before. He opened the door and made his way forward to the galley. Daylight was yet to appear, but Chet knew the gray clouds persisted. It wasn't raining, but there was a heavy, wet feeling to the air, and he could not make out any stars. As the boy stepped into the lamp lit galley, he noticed that Bart was already busy with the fire. Chet's head was starting to spin again, but he resolved not to get sick. Bart mumbled something about needing more dry wood right away, so Chet made his way to the main deck hatch and started below.

The under deck was strangely quiet and smelled of the sharp stench of human suffering that must have gone on most of the night. As Chet gathered the wood under the stairwell, he could hear muffled groans and moans, and the boy knew that not many passengers would venture forth that morning. When Chet returned to the galley, the smell of fresh coffee and the warmth of the stove renewed his will. He set about his chores with vigor. At 7:30a.m. The starboard watch was wakened and they filed in for a breakfast of chowder, hot biscuits, and coffee, after which they relieved the port watch, who had been up since 4:00am. Chet had a chance to eat a little and talk to Matt and Andrew before they went to their bunks and learned that the ship was just passing Leadbetter Point and the mouth of Willapa Bay on a starboard tack to the northwest.

The rest of that day the ship beat to the northwest, losing sight of the Washington coast on a long starboard tack. After a one-hour nap, Chet was feeling much better, and stood the afternoon watch. Soon the schooner changed course to the northeast and rode a favorable south wind, logging almost ten knots an hour. The skies were still gray, so Matt could not use the sextant to shoot the sun and they had to rely on Captain Folger's dead reckoning for their position.

Chet sensed a real thrill as the schooner cut through the green sea, rising and plunging into the waves. The rain had stopped, and as daylight started to fade, a few passengers made their way to the deck, Lucy among them. Chet was happy when she made her way back to the wheel deck and told him she'd had the strength to fight the seasickness when most of the others couldn't. The tall first mate at the wheel noticed the young girl, also.

"Chet, want to take 'er for a while?" asked Matt, somehow knowing that the boy felt the need to impress his female friend.

"Sure," Chet said, trying to hide his delight.

"Just keep 'er compass two points off the port bow and we'll ride back to the coast. I'll be up forward, so if you need me, just send Lucy or holler." With that Matt turned and shuffled down the ladder to the main deck where he started up a conversation with Bill.

"So, Luce, how ya feelin'?" Chet asked quietly. "To tell you the truth, I thought I was gonna die a few times last night."

"I feel fine," the girl exclaimed, "I felt a little bad last night, but most of the day I've been havin' to look after the rest of the family. Lola's feelin' better but Uncle Josh and the little kids are still under the weather. Say, that boss of yours, Bart, he sure is a mean old' sourpuss. I went to the galley earlier to get some salt crackers, but no one was around, so I found the barrel and was just startin' to help myself when the old' cuss walks in and just about bit my head off."

"Oh, he's not so bad. He never lets me near that barrel, either," Chet replied.

"Maybe he's got somethin' hid in it - pirate's treasure, gold, or maybe a loaded gun or somethin'. Chet, you gotta have a look next chance you get."

Lucy's imagination seemed to be getting the best of her, but Chet's interest had been stirred and the boy resolved to take a peek if the situation presented itself. Just then, Bart made his presence known by ringing the ship's bell and yelling an oath at Chet to start the dinner meal chores. Andrew was sent aft to spell Chet at the wheel and he said his goodbyes to Lucy. She in turn stuck out her tongue at the grizzly old cook's back.

That evening Chet thought of the cracker barrel, but the opportunity to look further did not materialize and he forgot the whole matter.

The next three days shown bright and clear, and even though the light winds continued and progress slowed to a crawl, the prospectors and pioneer families felt renewed, taking pleasure in what warmth the southern sun would give. Even Bart seemed to enjoy the carefree atmosphere, and set out some hand lines to troll for salmon. Lucy followed Chet whenever he had free time, and the two spent many hours going over the names of different lines and sails. Lucy even climbed to the main crosstrees before her aunt saw her and reminded the girl she was about to become a lady.

Captain Folger seemed to be the only one who was in a bad mood and the on deck watch was kept busy scrubbing this or that and doing general clean up and put away duties. The sails were constantly being trimmed to gain the most wind, and the crew was getting a good workout with no complaint. With the clear weather Matt was able to get a good reading from the sextant, and it confirmed the old captain's navigation. All hands were impressed with his accuracy.

The schooner made its way up the Washington coast past Grays Harbor and Destruction Island towards Cape Flattery, the northwest tip of the territory. On the sixth day out of Portland, Chet was scrubbing the galley table after the noon meal, when he heard a commotion out on deck. They had been hugging the coast all morning, when the lookout in the fore crosstrees sighted a large black object.

"Whale ho, I see a whale!"

Captain Folger rushed to the bow, and leaning against the knight's head, took out his glass and looked toward the northwest. Without saying a word, he changed positions and looked northeast, scanning the coast, and found what he was looking for.

"It's not a whale," the captain explained. "It's a coast Salish whaling canoe. Probably Quillayute tribe, and there's smoke on the shore north of here. They must have an encampment back of the beach."

The *Exact* was on a long port tack to the north, bringing it closer to the shore some three miles away. The Indian canoe was a half-mile further out and moving slightly faster than the schooner. Captain Folger decided to run the ship in to shore and give the passengers a closer look at the coastline and the Indians. An hour passed and the beach grew nearer. Chet could see the white tops of giant waves breaking on the beach. Further out in the surf were small islands, most a hundred feet tall and only fifty feet wide, with barren patches of earth growing only scrub pine and grass, but they were home to thousands of sea birds. Beyond the beach were cliffs with tall evergreen trees of enormous size. Chet didn't know then how important those stately trees were to the Northwest Indians, but he would soon marvel at the wonders of the giant cedar.

The Indian canoe had been steadily gaining and was only a hundred yards to port on a parallel course with the ship. The eight men in it were clearly visible, their half naked bodies glistening in the setting sun. Half of the men wore broad rimmed round hats that squared at the crown. The others were bareheaded with long, dark, flowing hair. Each man wore a curious vest of rough weave and each paddled relentlessly, never missing a beat. Chet thought he had never seen such a beautiful and graceful craft. It was narrow and long, less than half the length of the *Exact*, maybe thirty-five feet, the boy thought. The stern of the craft was raised slightly, and the bow projected a graceful six feet in the air, the top resembling the head of some dangerous, long ago sea beast. Except for a red and white design on the bow, the canoe was pure black. A large harpoon with wooden shaft rested on the head of the bow and coils of rope and wooden boxes filled the gaps between the men.

The day was turning to dusk and Captain Folger felt he had tacked toward shore long enough.

"Come about, Mr. English. Take her away from the coast."

Almost on cue the wind picked up and the pretty schooner turned to the northwest and picked up speed.

"There'll be no tradin' fer fresh fish today," said a disappointed Bart, as the Indian craft fell further behind and closer to shore.

Matt English set a course that would take them north but further out to sea and away from the jagged rocks and small islets that dotted the dangerous coast; too dangerous to sail close to at night. After the evening meal the rain that had been absent for four days returned, and by eleven the winds were gusting at twenty-five knots. All hands were brought on deck and the foresails and jibs were hauled in. A stout storm jib was run up and the main topsail was hauled in. The ship rode the storm with the main sail and the storm jib pushing it along at a rapid pace.

The wind and rain made for dangerous work, and after it was done, Andrew and Chet retired to the galley, where Bart had somehow made hot coffee for the wet and tired crew. Bill was telling one of his *Round the Horn* stories, where men's hands froze to stays and halyards, and all agreed that the relatively mild winters of the Northwest were a blessing. They soon disbanded for a few hours' sleep and Chet volunteered to close up the galley for Bart.

The old cook was almost pleasant in accepting, saying it was Chet's job anyway. It took the boy just a few minutes to clean up, and he was starting to leave when he spied the cracker barrel in the corner. He quickly stepped over to it and tried the lid. It was nailed shut. Chet walked to the aft galley hatch and checked the breezeway. Bart was nowhere to be seen, and the wind and rain made such a howl that no one would hear if he pried open the cracker barrel.

The boy shut the hatch and returned to the wooden drum. He reached for an iron utensil hanging above the stove and, as quietly as possible, pried the top of the lid open. Chet looked around again and then slipped his hand through the opening, deep into the crackers. Nothing. He reached as far as he could, and was halfway inside the barrel when his fingertips froze against a hard mass. There was something inside the barrel. Lucy had been right. Suddenly a tremendous fear gripped the boy, and he jerked his hand from the barrel, hammered the lid down quickly, and locked the galley.

As Chet walked toward his tiny cabin he felt a little silly and was ashamed of his fright. After all, there was probably a simple reason for the extra gear in the cracker barrel, but the boy couldn't think of one. Chet thought he might confide in Lloyd the next chance he got.

The crew and passengers of the *Exact* had been battered by wind and rain all night long, and at first light the captain and first mate could find no sign of land. They decided that the storm must have taken them north of Cape Flattery between the tip of Washington and Vancouver Island. They ran on a northerly course for another hour, and then swung the schooner around on a close haul to the east in hopes of entering the broad Strait of Juan de Fuca and the shelter of inland waters.

The wind kept gusting from the southwest and the ship made fair progress most of the day. Seasick miners kept to their quarters, only venturing to the galley for hot soup and coffee. The wet crew tried to stay as dry as possible. With the nasty weather outside and the crowded conditions in the galley, Chet was unable to corner

Lloyd alone and since the boy never saw Lucy, he decided to wait another day before telling of his discovery.

Late in the afternoon the rain subsided but the wind held steady, and as the starboard watch filed in for coffee after their turn at the sheets, Bill was saying that, "the old man must have us right down the center of the Strait, or we would' a hit land by now. Come mornin' we'll be seein' either Vancouver Island if we're north or the Olympic Mountains if we're south."

The wind had dropped in the middle of the night, and, as Bill had predicted, a forested coast appeared to the south in the early morning hours. No mountains were visible as the rain and low clouds continued, but the sight of land made all hands and passengers marvel at the navigational skills of the old captain. As the wind ceased, all hands were sent aloft to set more sail and trim for what wind there was.

The schooner sailed on the rest of the day, keeping the shore in sight. In the early afternoon the captain gave the order to come about to the south and the ship slowly made its way toward a sheltered bay. The skies to the west were clearing and a tiny stream of sunlight broke through the clouds. The anchor was dropped and the sails hauled in. Most of the passengers were already on deck when Captain Folger called for everyone's attention. He climbed on top of the main deck hatch and addressed the crowd.

"Because of the light wind and because we've been tossed around the ocean the last couple of days, I've decided to drop anchor and take the last three hours of daylight to regroup, make some repairs and let the crew get a full night's sleep." A cheer rose from the gathered group, as sailor and passenger alike were ready for a rest. "Now settle down, quiet please!" the captain said calmly. "Mr. Merrifield and his miners have volunteered to keep a watch tonight in two hour shifts. The crew needs to do some work for an hour and then you're free to do your pleasure. Mr. English will give out work details." Another brief cheer arose and then the group dispersed.

The sun was shining as Chet and Andrew finished straightening out the foremast crosstree rigging and tied down the fore gaff topsail. Everyone on deck seemed to be enjoying the sun, and Bart was running out three or four hand lines in hopes of catching dinner. The boy sat in the sling of the foremast yard and watched as the old cook lowered one line and then another. Chet wondered if Bart's luck would improve over his fishless vigil trolling on the ocean. Just as the young man was starting to climb down, the cook gave a yell.

"Fish on, ya lubbers," he screamed, "Bill give a hand ere'."

Bill came to Bart's aid and the two old seamen hauled hand over hand bringing up a large flat fish. The two eyes seemed grossly misplaced on the darker side of the fish. Bart reached for a spare belaying pin and with a crashing blow to it's head stopped the halibut from flopping any further.

Within minutes every spare fishing line was put into service with more men joining the sport, and after a couple of hours two dozen bottom fish had been brought on board. The women cleaned the rockfish and started fish chowder in the galley, while the halibut was cleaned and filleted into long thick steaks. It was a festival atmosphere and a meal to remember, with everyone enjoying chunky bits of tender fish and potatoes, corn on the cob, biscuits and buttery halibut steak. All praised Bart and the women cooks.

Darkness settled in and the stars came out, allowing Matt to shoot a fix and determine their position. Different groups of men gathered here and there, talking and having a nip of rum, while the women gossiped and enjoyed the calm evening. Chet found Lucy and hurried her aft to tell of the cracker barrel discovery.

"I told you so!" she exclaimed with pride. "The old geezer's hidin' buried treasure. I'll bet he used to be a pirate and is hidin' out on this boat till the coast is clear."

Chet thought for a second.

"I think he's hidin' somethin' too, but it's his stuff an' I don't know as we should be messin' into his affairs."

"Come on, Chet," Lucy begged. "He won't find out. We'll sneak in and find out for sure. It's not his cracker barrel, it's the boat's."

"I tell you what," Chet laughed. "Next time I'm with him I'll ask him why the barrel is always nailed shut. Meanwhile, we better let it lay. Why does such a good lookin' girl get so upset over nothin'?"

Chet's words caught Lucy off guard. She had never thought of herself as good looking.

Chet took the young lady's face in his hands, gently tipping her chin upward until their eyes met. Her beauty momentarily petrified him. Seconds seemed to pass then instinct took over. The soft touch of Lucy's lips against his caused surprisingly intense feelings in him. Chet's hands moved to her lush brown hair, and Lucy's hands found his shoulders. They parted for a moment then kissed again.

"I think I like you," said the young man, with lightness in his tone. "Even though you seem to have a mean streak."

"Me?" returned Lucy. "I don't think I'm mean at all," she laughed.

They embraced one another, each looking in turn to make sure their privacy was complete. Once convinced that no one was looking they continued enjoying their new found attraction for one another.

Chet was surprised to see it was already daylight when he woke up, and rushed to get his clothes on. The young man was still aglow from the events of the night before and still wasn't sure he was believing the deep feelings he had for Lucy. Hurrying to open the hatch, the boy started toward the galley, then stopped as he heard a loud snoring coming from behind the louvered door to Bart's bunk. *The old cook must have nipped too much rum,* the boy thought. Chet was further surprised to see Lloyd standing in the breezeway, smoking a pipe and being in no particular hurry to get anywhere.

"Where is everyone?" Chet asked.

"Don't you remember?" the miner returned, "the captain gave everyone the morning to sleep. Oh he's up himself, but when he found no wind to speak of, he decided to let um' sleep a little longer."

Lloyd was right about the wind; it was dead calm. The sun was yet to rise above the Cascades to the east and the sea was flat as could be. Chet took notice of the beach for the first time. It was not sandy at all, but was filled with smooth dark rocks; pebbles really, millions of dark pebbles. Driftwood was piled at the high water mark and giant cedar trees rose in a thick forest just beyond. The Olympic Mountains stood miles to the south and Chet wondered if any white man had climbed their snowy peaks.

The water around the ship was smooth as a table top, and the deep blue-green surface looked clear and cold. The boy could look straight down and see the rocky bottom thirty feet below. Long brown *bullwhip* kelp plants floated on the surface, and a family of sea otters played in the main kelp bed. The furry mammals floated on their backs and cracked shellfish for breakfast. They swam with ease and dove with a graceful, rolling motion. They were peaceful little animals, but their fine, dark fur brought a high bounty. Chet knew that the ship would soon be trading store goods for otter pelts when the schooner sailed north to Vancouver Island and the totem pole Indians.

"Well, guess I'll turn in for a little nap," the miner yawned, breaking Chet's concentration on the beauty around him. "I'll see ya later."

"Wait, Lloyd," the boy said. "I was meanin' to ask you about something. It's probably nothin', but I think ole Bart is hidin' something in the galley."

"What do ya mean, somethin'?" the miner mused, his interest aroused.

"Well I'm not sure. But it's something wooden, and he keeps it in a sealed cracker barrel, and he acts awfully suspicious."

"I wouldn't worry about it," chuckled Lloyd. "It's probably just his life's saving's. These old' coots have a way o' thinkin' everyone's after their money, an' they'll go to great lengths to hide their fortune. And more often than not, it's not enough to hide anyway. Most every miner I ever knew buried his stash. Old' Bart can't bury his on a ship, so he hides it in a barrel."

Chet, somewhat ashamed, had to agree, and the matter was dropped.

Within a few hours the ship's company and passengers began to stir and the captain gave orders to get under way. There still wasn't much wind, but the tide had finished its ebb and the ship was aided by the flow of water inland towards Puget Sound. Chet hoped that Lucy would make an appearance, but as the time passed her absence began to instill doubts. Had he said or done something wrong? After all, they had only kissed.

Chet hurried aloft to help set the foretop sail and from up there looking east, the boy could see the sandstone cliffs and green hills of a large island with the mainland beyond. He could just make out Vancouver Island to the north and the many smaller San Juan Islands to the northeast.

As the afternoon wore on, the wind picked up from the west and no tacking was needed. The *Exact* made a dead run east past Ediz Hook and later Dungeness Horn, two great sandbars that stuck menacingly out from the Olympic Peninsula. The wind held and it was almost dark when the anchor chain clanked down the side of the schooner. They were secured on the south side of Protection Island at the mouth of Discovery Bay. Matt informed the crew that tomorrow would put them in Puget Sound proper.

Chet had not seen Lucy all day and self-doubt ran rampant. He longed for her loving smile, the touch of her soft skin. He felt he was going crazy!

This night, Bart was in a foul mood, probably due to his hangover from the night before, and the old cook was nastier than usual at the evening mess. Chet cleaned the galley and stoked up the stove for the night. The boy felt grateful when he could finally join the watch on deck. It was a gloomy night, broken by the flicker of oil lamps hanging from the fore and main booms. The saltwater smell was strong. There was little to do other than some cleaning and straightening of gear. One man was picked as watch and the rest were given the time to themselves.

Chet couldn't stand it any longer and made his way down the main hatch, finally catching sight of Lucy. The young girl was busy helping her aunt, and, as usual her mouth was going a mile a minute. He was trying to look inconspicuous, afraid of his feelings, but when the older woman noticed the boy standing on the companionway, she gave Lucy a nudge. When the young lady turned and smiled, Chet felt the weight of a thousand tons fall from his back. She still liked him.

"Where have you been all day?" Chet said, with a degree of shortness.

"Not even a hello," returned Lucy, just as short. She was smiling, though, and Chet felt himself melting. The boy knew he was no match for her beauty.

"I'm sorry... I missed you." Chet paused, then started again. "Hello, Miss Hill, how are you today? Now, can we get out of here?"

Lucy said nothing more. Still smiling, she took Chet's arm and the two young people climbed the stairs up to the main deck. They found a quiet place near the starboard rail and looked out toward the small island.

"I missed you, too," said Lucy after some minutes. "I like you, Chet, but we have to be realistic. We only have one more day together and then I'll be gone and you will sail off to who knows where. I just don't want to be hurt."

"I like you a lot Lucy," said Chet, as seriously as he could. "There's something different about you. I don't want this to end here." He took her hand in his, but made no attempt to do anything further. "I won't be sailing forever. Just a few months."

Lucy laughed and seemed to let go of the emotional wall she had been putting up.

"I guess where I'm going there won't be a whole lot of eligible men around, anyway," the young girl said. " Still, though, I want to take it slow."

The two lovers talked and held hands for another hour until Aunt Lola came looking for Lucy. They stole a kiss and said their goodbyes.

Chet was up before Bart the next morning and daylight was just beginning as the grumpy old cook entered the galley. Bart only gave a grunt when he noticed the boy had already started a large steaming pot of coffee and had a large kettle of water boiling for mush. It was as though Chet had spoiled Bart's day by not giving him a chance to yell at him, and, as the crew filed in, Bart took it out on them. After the sailors had their fill, the captain made a rare appearance in the galley to have his breakfast and chat with Bart. Folger was in good spirits and paid some compliments to Chet that made Bart growl even deeper.

The men were already at the capstan hauling up the anchor when Chet raced on deck. As always, he and Andrew scaled the foremast to set the top foresail. As they unfurled the sheet, they watched the crew pull on the main halyard and marveled at their dizzy height where they could watch the small scurrying people below.

"Well I'll be danged," shouted Andrew. "I've been lookin' at that beach all mornin' from the deck and never once figured it for a sand bar."

Sure enough, as the boys looked across the fifty yards of water to Protection Island, the beach was not as it appeared from the deck. It was actually a sand bar with a two acre cove behind it and a narrow deep water entrance only ten yards wide. The back portion of the cove was covered with mud flats, tall grasses, and thick, chin high bushes that crept right down to the high tide mark. The entrance channel ran from west to east and was so narrow that at sea level the western beach and the sand bar looked as if they were one continuous stretch of land. Happy with their discovery at the moment, but wary of it's significance, the boys were content to keep the presence of the cove to themselves.

"Hey, Chet, why don't you name it, Palmer cove?" laughed Andrew as he hung from the ratlines. "It can be your claim to fame."

"Sure thing. Thanks for nothin'. What am I gonna do with a cove no one knows about?" returned Chet.

The schooner slipped away from the island on a westerly wind that lightly filled the sails. They made only four or five knots for most of the morning and noontime found them coming about to the southeast on a close hauled tack past Point Wilson, past Admiralty Head and on into Puget Sound.

They spent the rest of the day tacking back and forth between Whidbey and Marrowstone Islands. The crew grew tired of the constant trimming of sails and the increasingly worse weather. By four bells the ship was in a constant drizzle that soaked through every man's oilskins and dampened the heartiest soul. The visibility was down to less than a mile when Captain Folger hove to just southeast of Foulweather Bluff on the northern tip of the Kitsap Peninsula. The water was deep close in to the long crescent-shaped beach, and they found shelter from the cold wind, rain, and rising waves.

Chet spent the night with Lucy's family playing card games, laughing and trying to keep his mind off the time. The boy was sure he was in love, and his distress and panic grew as the time of Lucy's separation from him drew near.

The morning of the thirteenth of November, 1851, began as a dismal affair with a cold, steady rain and a brisk northerly wind that brought the tiny schooner to its initial destination, a small point of land jutting out into Puget Sound. Huge trees grew right to the waterline, while a small, unfinished cabin and a trickle of smoke could be seen on a grassy rise. The *Exact* anchored close in to the southern side and Captain Folger gave the order to lower the ship's boat. Chet and Andrew were picked for rowing duty, and the pioneers began the first of many trips to the beach with their goods and supplies. The women were in a state of shock from the dismal scene before them and most stayed on the ship until the last load was ferried over.

Arthur Denny, their young, twenty-one year old leader, saw that his brother, David, who, along with two other men, had staked this claim and built the cabin, was sick with fever and in low spirits. His attitude adversely affected most everyone except Lucy, who was as positive about the outcome as ever. The rain continued all day and the other women and children were miserable when they came ashore, all huddling together and crying.

The two sweethearts found a few minutes together while the captain and crew were saying their goodbyes to the pioneers. Lucy and Chet stood a few moments on the beach without saying anything. Chet wished he could tell her what he was really feeling, but he was afraid to get too mushy in front of the gathered group. Lucy didn't have those reservations, and she quickly grabbed his arm, pulled him nearer, and planted a big kiss right on Chet's rapidly reddening cheek. Then he kissed her lips.

"I'll miss you, Chet!" she cried in a whisper.

"Chet!" came a call from Matt. "It's time to go, son."

The young man gently cupped Lucy's face in his hands and kissed her, not caring what anyone thought. Everyone on the ship the past week knew their feelings anyway. Lucy pulled away with tears in her eyes and ran up the beach towards the cabin. Chet called after her, "I'll be back Lucy! I'll be back. I promise! He watched her run away and felt a deep emptiness begin to overcome him. The boy was surprised at how much he liked that skinny little girl. He didn't want to leave her, but he had to. Didn't he? His mind was in a muddle as he got into the ship's boat and began rowing with (the others) toward the *Exact*.

The boat slipped alongside the schooner for the last time that day and the crew wasted no time hauling it aboard, making it fast to its chocks. No one talked to Chet. They sensed his feeling of loss was a true one and not just another sailor's lust. The men raised the sails, exchanged long-distance farewells with the settlers on the beach, and headed north, back out into Puget Sound and into the growing darkness.

IV

The sky was clear and the *Exact* sailed all night making a steady five knots before the southwest wind. The crew worked flawlessly changing tacks often to keep the schooner well in the middle of the Sound and away from any unseen shallows that could run her aground. The ship passed Admiralty Head and Point Wilson, turning to port until the compass read 300 degrees northwest. As daylight broke the schooner entered the Strait of Juan de Fuca on a long tack toward Vancouver Island. They beat against the wind all morning, watching the hazy San Juan Islands pass to the northeast, wondering when the gigantic island would come into view.

The afternoon weather turned rainy and cold and Captain Folger turned the watch over to Matt English. Chet finished straightening up the galley from the noon meal and with a parting oath from Bart, joined the young first officer on deck. Bill was manning the wheel and Andrew was in the main crosstrees, his eyes straining through the clouds for a first sight of land to the northwest.

"Better get on your foul weather gear and a warm shirt," warned Matt. "Looks like we're in for more rain. It'll be cold and dark soon. Hurry back and you can take an hour at the wheel with Bill."

"Sure thing," Chet replied, as he sped aft to his room.

The deck was wet and the boy almost fell as he made his way to the after house. Once in the cabin, Chet took off his coat and put on a warm wool sweater, an extra pair of socks and struggled into the cold and stiff oilskin jacket and trousers. He squeezed his feet into his sea boots and topped off the affair with a knitted cap and gloves. Finally satisfied that he would not freeze, Chet ventured back topside and took his position at the wheel.

"Hold 'er steady, laddy," yelled Bill. "The wind has fair strength and the compass is right."

Chet felt the ship strain as he took the spokes in his hands. A sense of power and importance overcame him as the seaworthy schooner pounded through the deep blue-green spray. It was hard work at the wheel and more than once the older sailor had to help the boy back on course. After a few minutes Chet was outguessing the waves and needed less and less help from Bill.

"Hey, Bill, what are the Indians like where we're going?" Chet asked.

"Well, they're a strange lot as far as Injun's go. They're nothin' like the Injun's back home in New England. They live in big wooden houses with strange paintings on the outside and tall carved cedar poles dug in all over the place. They use spears and harpoons for huntin' and warrin' instead of bows and arrows, and they paddle around in those big black canoes. Damned if you'd catch me crewin' on one of those rigs. My bones would ache from the paddlin' 'fore we'd made a cable's length. I'll tell ye one thing though, they're no children when it comes to tradin' otter pelts."

"Land away, off the starboard bow!" came a cry from Andrew.

The few men on deck looked to the north and saw the faint outline of a huge mountain range backing away from the sea.

"Chet, keep her at 300 degrees until darkness falls, and then we'll dead reckon a new course for the night and hope we stay close enough to see the island in the morning," explained Matt.

The ship closed on the island for another hour and Captain Folger returned at darkness setting a new course that would run the schooner up the island's Pacific coastline without fear of closing on shore. Chet returned the wheel to Bill and went back to his cabin to change out of his oilskins before starting back to the galley to help with the evening meal. Bart seemed in better spirits, and with the warmth of the stove and plenty of hot coffee and chowder, the young man was glad to be back inside.

The ship was in heavier seas again and Chet felt a slight recurrence of seasickness. He was glad when he was able to climb into his cozy bunk. His bed back home never seemed quite as important or as secure as this tiny bunk was now and Chet would appreciate it even more in the weeks and months to come. He thought of Lucy a few moments, thought of her kiss; Chet prayed she was doing all right. Thinking pleasant thoughts, he soon fell deeply asleep.

Lloyd was the first miner in for coffee the next morning, and, as usual, he raved about the navigation skills of the old captain. First light brought them not more than a mile off the beach and sailing northwest at four or five knots with a favorable wind. Bart decided to have a treat for breakfast and sliced up some salted pork belly. Soon the smell of fresh crackling bacon brought the rest of the miners to the table. When the meal was over and the captain served, Chet had his fill of bacon, toast, and jam. As he was licking the last of the tasty morsels from his fingers, Andrew, who doubled as ship's sail maker, walked in with the top foresail and spread it out over the table.

Sometime during the night the buntline gave out and the sail had ripped, leaving the canvas in shreds. The gangly sailor had an array of needle and line and went to work, repairing the damage and giving Chet a lesson to boot. When the job was complete, the two boys climbed the foremast with canvas in hand and once again had the *Exact* in full sail.

They were closer to shore now, and from the crosstrees Chet could see the magnificent coast of Vancouver Island, with hundreds of small island boulders jutting skyward. Each islet was crowned with a tree or two and rimmed with glimmering green seaweed lining the rocks at their base. The sea fairly shimmered and sparkled when a stray beam of sunshine broke through the clouds; and those trees, those majestic trees two hundred feet tall and ten feet wide at the trunk! The forest readily beckoned Chet to enter, and he fantasized about what adventures a young man might have in their depths.

Chet stayed up in the rigging until an angry call from Bart finally brought him back to the deck.

"The capt'n wants us to inventory the tradin' wares down in the aft hold. Take this here paper an' pencil and follow me," the grumpy old sailor mumbled.

The two made their way down the main hatch stairwell and turned left toward the rear of the ship. Bart grabbed onto a dusty old lantern hanging on a crossbeam nail and steadied it with his left hand while striking a match with his right. The ensuing glow highlighted Bart's face and the boy thought the dim lighting did nothing to improve the old cook's looks. The hole where his two front teeth used to be didn't help either. All in all, Bart was just plain ugly. As Bart turned the oil valve on high, Chet noticed the blue anchor and blood drop tattoo on the cook's forearm again and decided he was glad Bart didn't read minds.

"Come on, let's git this thing done; don't know why we're tradin' this junk anyway. If the capt'n had any sense, he'd just giv'um cheap rum, let um' git drunk, and just take the furs for next to nothin'."

The young man remembered a similar conversation between Drake and the Captain back in Portland.

Wait a second, Chet thought.

He remembered the missing man in Drake's office and a chill ran down his back. That dark figure in the back of Drake's office was Bart! The old cook must have left by the back door before Chet and Lloyd came in. Chet was sure Mr. Drake and Bart were up to no good.

Shaking his head to come back to the present, Chet began helping Bart count cases of metal knives, nails, cookware, and blankets, while the old cook complained about the cost of the goods and how the Nootkas weren't worth the trouble. After compiling the list, they closed the locker door and Chet found the captain on the after deck discussing trading strategies with Matt and Lloyd.

"Ah, good, the list," said Folger, taking the paper from Chet. "Seems like we should have enough wares to take all the pelts they've gotten this season."

"Don't be too sure," returned Matt. "Remember, they have suffered greatly from smallpox the last few years and trading has become very bitter since the disease cut their numbers in half. In fact you might well find that there'll be a lot less pelts just because there are less Indians to catch um'."

"Matt may be right," Lloyd interrupted. "You may be wise to hold back some of your tradin' goods until you see how many otter pelts they have." The conversation lasted a few minutes longer and Lloyd was thanked for his input. All the while Chet had been standing near, waiting for an opportunity to corner Lloyd.

The two walked forward and Chet brought up the matter of the man in Drake's office and the fact that Bart was hiding something in the cracker barrel that might be liquor.

"That's an interestin' theory boy, mind you whiskey and tradin' can make for a mean situation. I tell you what, we may be way off base here, so let's just keep an eye peeled around Bart, and if he does have whiskey and if he means to trade it on the sly, the captain will hear of it from me. In any event, let's just take it slow in case nothin' comes of it."

Chet agreed and felt good that Lloyd gave him some credit without dismissing it as being a fool notion. However, the boy was starting to second-guess himself, finally deciding that maybe the whole idea was pretty far fetched at that.

V

The schooner continued sailing northwest for the next two days through the rain and clouds. Everyone on the ship was becoming excited to raise Nootka Sound and the Indians there. The *Exact* passed Barkley Sound, heading further north passed hundreds of islands, finally rounded Estevan Point and began the last run across Nootka Sound to Bligh Island.

On that last morning Chet awoke to find ice clinging to every line and railing of the ship and this made for sluggish going. Far to the north a cove was in sight and the smoke from warm fires could be seen from miles out. This was Friendly Cove on the southern tip of Nootka Island. The Nootka village there, named Yuquot, had a shaded background and a reputation for violence in past years. Captain Folger had decided to go to a smaller village on Bligh Island, a little further up Nootka Sound, where he knew the chief had a good reputation and there would be less worry about trouble. The village was called Chahakquot, which meant fresh water houses, and the *Exact* made a new easterly course away from Yuquot and toward the smaller village.

Soon the call for all hands on deck by Captain Folger directed everyone's attention to the nearing western arm of Bligh Island and Chahakquot village. Orders were given to come about on a last tack and men jumped here and there trimming sail and line. The decks were cleared and all gear stowed. Lines were coiled and all was made clean and shipshape. It was as though the captain was readying the ship for military inspection. Chet felt a little uneasy when Matt broke out two rifles and gave them to two crewmembers. The first mate also took a pistol for himself and the captain. Some of the miners donned their own side arms, so all on board felt comfortable with the ship's security.

As the *Exact* turned slightly to glide past the last small island before the cove, the order was given to shorten sail. The main sail, jibs and forestaysail were lowered and furled. Matt called Andrew and Chet to go aloft to take in the fore and main topsails. Chet chose the foremast and quickly went up the ratlines to the fore crosstrees. He let go the halyard and the sail fluttered down around the boom. The young man glanced back at Andrew on the mainmast and saw that the tall boy already had his sail furled and was tying the sail stops fast. Chet continued his work, and as they glided by the island with its rocky beach, Matt called for him to stay aloft. The foresail below him was the only sheet left pulling and as the schooner slowed and settled into the cove, the boy could hear the booming voice of Bill calling out the soundings as the ship neared the shore. The captain took the wheel, while the rest of the crew split between the foresail and the anchor.

In all the excitement Chet had not had a chance to look around, and from his favorite perch a whole new world opened up to him. The village literally spread before his eyes. Along the crescent-shaped beach stood an eighth of a mile stretch of huge wooden houses made of large cedar planks. Numerous smaller outbuildings, wooden racks and frames filled the spaces between houses. In front of the houses, sunk deep in the sand, were what seemed like a hundred carved cedar poles, most reaching thirty to forty feet in the air. Each pole had a different array of carved animal and human figures with many different heights, and degrees of relief. Some were more elaborate then others, with different colored paint and outstretched bird-like wings or horizontal animal shaped caps at the tops. Some were obviously old, weathered and gray in color, but still held that quality of wonder and beauty. At the waterline stood a fifteen-foot high solitary human figure carved out of a huge chunk of cedar. Long protruding arms stood out in a welcoming gesture.

One house in particular was extremely ornate with an underlying coat of whitewash paint and the most extraordinary visual design of red and black over the whole extent of the front face of the house. It was also the biggest house on the beach and Chet thought it surely must belong to the chief of the village. The beach itself was dotted with more canoes than the eye could count, and, like the cedar poles, they came in all sizes and degrees of elaboration. The most striking were the middle-sized whaling canoes, thirty feet long and six feet wide, with large raised bows painted with the same style of design as was seen on the main house. There were curious decks of planked cedar on stilts with benches for sitting and railings that looked like wooden patios where weary villagers could come and socialize near the water at the end of a long day. The Indians were a little shorter as a whole than the white men on board the ship, and their copper colored skin complemented their long, flowing, black hair. Most of the men had faces painted with red ocher or black charcoal. However, none of the women did.

As the ship neared the shore some canoes of moderate length were already in the water and moving rapidly towards the schooner. The men seemed to be wearing straw hats unlike anything Chet had ever seen before, tightly woven of dried grasses and bark and looking something like coolie hats worn by the Chinese immigrants who worked for the railroads. Most men were near naked, although some were wearing capes and skirts of bark. Others, probably men of wealth, were wearing decorated blankets of wool.

"Drop anchor!" screamed the wiry captain. "Drop that fore sheet, and don't let any Nootkas come aboard. We'll meet um' on the beach. Mister English, secure the ship and set the cutter over the side. Mister Taggert, take Andrew and Chet and bring up half the tradin' goods from the aft locker."

The boy didn't wait for a dirty look and holler from Bart, and quickly lowered himself to the deck joining the cook and the New England sailor at the main hatch. Within a half hour the crates of nails, blankets and hardware were loaded in the cutter ready for transfer to the beach. The captain hauled out a small sea chest full of beads and notions to use as preliminary gifts to the nobles, prior to any hard negotiations.

"Chet, you and Andrew lower the small boat and be ready to make any trips that might be needed between the beach and the ship. The cutter is too big to row back and forth for light jobs. You can follow us in and stay within shouting distance. Otherwise, you're free to look around."

"Aye, aye, sir," the young men returned, pleased with their choice of duty. They ran aft and pulled heartily at the block and tackle. Within a few minutes the boat was in the water and they were in the boat.

"Gentlemen," the captain called, leaning over the aft rail. "Bring the dory round amidships and take aboard Mister Merrifield and a couple of his miners." The two boys acknowledged the command and did as the captain said. Lloyd and the miners had volunteered themselves and their weapons as security for the shore party, allowing the men with the rifles to stay on board to guard the ship.

By now the ship was surrounded by hundreds of curious natives and Chet got a close look at the dugout canoes. The adze marks, marks left by a chipping tool, were visible on the insides of the canoes, giving them a scalloped look. There was a noticeable difference in the quality of workmanship, not only in canoes, but also in the Indian's clothing, which led Chet to believe there was a distinct upper and lower class of Nootkas. But to the white boy they all looked magnificent.

At last the trading party was ready to move and both boats made for the shore with their escort of Indian canoes. It came as a surprise to no one that they ended up adjacent to the large painted house in the center of the village, as it was indeed the chief's residence. The beach was cut along a deep drop-off, and, even in low tide, the water was of sufficient depth to allow all the craft to land right at the water line, making it unnecessary to get one's feet wet while disembarking. Chet also noticed a fresh water stream cutting a path through the sand and rocks to the cove. It passed to the far side of the chief's house and the boy had no doubt the deep anchorage and stream were the reasons this spot was chosen for a village. Not only did the creek provide fresh water, but also it was still sustaining a good run of salmon, although late in the season.

The crew went about the task of unloading the wares while Matt and Captain Folger met with the chief of the Nootka village. He was a handsome man of about forty and of good build, taller than most of his villagers. The chief was dressed in the same bark skirt as the rest of the males, and barefoot, but that's where the similarity ended. Atop his head was a carved wooden headdress in the shape of an obscure animal brightly painted with red and black pigments. He sported a long black mustache, something Chet had never seen on an Indian before, with a small ring of silver in his nose. The paint on the chief's face was more elaborate, with the addition of white and blue pigments to the red and black of the others. His vest was made of red and black wool with seashell buttons sewn in decorative patterns and his upper body was wrapped in a most beautiful wool blanket with rich yellow, green and black designs. The chief's name was *Standing Seal,* and he greeted the white men through a slave interpreter from another tribe named, appropriately, *Talking Boy.*

"Chief says welcome to village of Chahakquot, of Mowachaht Nation. Please accept our invitation to trade in peace with white captain of swimming house." Everyone seemed amazed at the fluency of the Nootka slave's English and knew the trading would indeed be easier with the language barrier broken down.

"Tell the great Nootka chief Standing Seal that we are humbled to accept his offer," replied the captain in his best diplomatic voice.

"May I excuse the most capable captain, but for your information sake, these people aren't Nootka as white men call them, but true name is Mowachaht. Nootka is the name of the bay, not the people." Talking Boy was quite the diplomat himself and the captain apologized for calling the people by the wrong name.

While the men were busy with diplomacy, Chet was able to wander toward the chief's house and get a closer look at the mural-sized painting on the front wall. The house was huge, almost fifty feet wide, a hundred feet long, and fifteen feet to the top of the roof. The picture depicted a thunderbird, a mythical avis clutching a killer whale in its talons. The door of the house was in the center of the killer whale's midsection. The walls of the house were made of thick cedar planks set horizontally between pairs of vertical poles and overlapped to allow for rainwater to drain down the sides. The roof consisted of more cedar planks of varying lengths and widths set loosely in an overlapping position to again ward off the almost constant rainfall.

Chet noticed that a group of curious children had gathered around him as he started back to the beach. Most were completely naked, although the weather was quite cold and damp. The children did not seem to mind and were quite unafraid, boldly coming up and touching Chet and making remarks the white boy could not understand.

In the meantime a new group of visiting Indians from a different village had joined the traders and were watching quietly as the Chahakquot Mowachaht vigorously bartered. They were from Cod Man's village, Standing Seal's cousin, and were led by a scar-faced Nootka named *Two Skins*. The leader was named for his half-breed ancestry. He was the son of a Kwakiutl slave girl, and for most of his young life he'd been a slave also, but his feats in battle and his taking of slaves gained him his own freedom and elevated his status to one of great importance.

As the trading progressed, Andrew noticed a signal flag raised on the schooner, and he called Chet back to the dory. The two young sailors rowed back out to the ship to see what was wanted. The crew on board was beginning to light the ship's lanterns, for darkness was setting in. Bart met the young men in one of his infrequent good moods.

"Boys, come on up and help fetch the vittles I've fixed to hold the men on shore," the old cook said with a touch of pleasantness. "There're two baskets and a cask of water and I've got another cask of water here."

Surprisingly, the old cook started down over the side with the cask on his shoulder, and the two youngsters just looked at each other in surprise. When Bart reached the dory, the two boys climbed to the deck and started for the galley.

"I guess he's goin' back with us," Andrew shrugged.

"Yeah, I guess he is," said Chet.

The boys entered the galley to pick up the baskets and water. As Andrew was turning to leave, Chet noticed some spilled crackers on the floor. His eyes turned and caught the cracker barrel with its lid ajar. Quickly, Chet moved to the barrel, lifted the lid and with one deep thrust of his hand he found the wooden mystery container was gone.

Chet didn't waste any more time, but went directly back to the dory with the basket of food and climbed down the ladder without saying a word. The boys shoved off and rowed to shore. Darkness was coming rapidly, and a large fire that had just been started illuminated the party on the beach. As the dory scraped the sand and rock, coming to a halt, Chet desperately looked for Lloyd in the large group of men surrounding the trading pit. Bart hailed Matt English and informed him of the food and fresh water. Matt in turn told Chet and Andrew to keep an eye on the food, lest it end up in Indian bellies.

A few moments passed and Chet finally caught Lloyd's eye on the far side of the fire. Lloyd was intrigued with the on-going barter, and when the boy waved to him, the miner's reply was a wave of his own that seemed to say, "I see you, but wait until this is over and then I'll talk to you." Disappointed, the boy sat back down on the bow of the dory and turned to check on Bart. To his surprise Bart was gone.

"Andrew, where'd Bart go?" Chet asked, with a surprised tone.

"Don't know. He just wandered off that a way with a group of Injun's. Why, what's a matter Chet?" asked the young sailor.

"Oh it's nothin'."

Chet turned to make a quick inventory of the dory and found the two baskets of food still in their place, but one of the water casks was gone and no one had been near the boat. Bart must have taken it and Chet doubted that it had water in it. Now Bart was gone and Chet wondered what the old cook was up to; it must have something to do with Mr. Drake and the whiskey. There had to be whiskey in that cask. He had to act.

"Say, Andy, can you watch the boat by yourself? I have to relieve myself somethin' terrible," Chet said, trying not to over act. "If Lloyd comes around tell um' that I need to talk to him."

"Sure, just walk down the beach a ways and you should get some privacy," chuckled Andrew. "And watch out fer them killer clams."

Chet buttoned the top button on his coat and moved out along the sand at the water's edge. He stumbled a few times and had to wait for his eyes to get used to the dark. The night was getting frosty and the boy was thankful for the wool sweater he had put on in the early afternoon. He strained for sight or sound of Bart and his companions, but all he could hear were the waves lapping at the rocky shore. He had traveled for some minutes and was passing the last of the wooden houses with their dim firelight streaming through the cracks in the cedar planks. Leaving the village meant running into more driftwood and slippery seaweed covered rocks, which slowed his progress. When the young man was just about sure that Bart may have been led into one of the great cedar houses, he heard laughter and whooping ahead. His pace accelerated, and as he rounded a large pile of drift logs, Chet caught a glimpse of the Nootkas with Bart. On the ground was a lantern that Bart had obviously brought and the yellow light flickered softly off their faces. The Indians were making merry with dance and chants and screaming, and all the while Bart was pouring from the cask, filling their carved wooden bowls. There was no doubt now that the cask contained liquor of some sort.

Chet crept toward the tree line and on his hands and knees moved behind the barrier of drift logs closer to the drunken group. The boy moved to within thirty feet of the gathering and peered over a log just in time to see the old cook cork the top of the cask. This act was not well received by the Indians, and their gestures became increasingly threatening. Bart had all he could do to control the situation and Chet was beginning to feel uneasy. The boy peeked higher over the log and noticed the Nootka men were not those he recognized as villagers, but, rather, the transient group from the other village that had just been passing by earlier that afternoon. Chet also noticed two forty foot canoes further down the beach, whose black shapes were hardly visible.

Chet remembered the leader of the group, Two Skins, and noticed the scar-faced warrior was not among them. Bart was desperately trying to communicate with the Indians, and, to Chet's surprise, the old sailor knew some Indian words, but in his frustration Bart blurted out some words in English.

"Tell your chief not to trade fer pelts lessen he gits whiskey. Understand, you savage? Whiskey."

Bart raised the cask and shook it for more dramatic effect, but all it did was arouse the thirst factor even more.

"There'll be another ship in three weeks with whiskey, so don't trade now," he pleaded.

So that was his game. Drake must have paid him off to keep Captain Folger away from the priceless pelts until the merchant could find a ship of his own. Things were getting ugly now, and Chet almost felt sorry for the grizzly old cook. Bart had no way of knowing that these were not Chahakquot Mowachahts, but unrelated Nootkas just passing through. They had no alliance to Standing Seal and in fact their leader was a ruthless warrior who was feared by most other Nootkas.

The group began closing in on Bart, and as the old cook sensed the loss of control, he drew a pistol from his belt.

"Back off, ya heathens," the old cook said.

The Indians did back off, not wanting any part of the revolver, knowing full well what it could do. Chet saw his moment. The young man felt that if he showed himself, both white men would have a better chance of backing down the beach to the safety of the village without any gunplay. The boy started to rise slowly, shaking a little as he rose. He stopped short of standing as a crashing blow struck him behind the head. A dizzy sound of gunfire, the smell of burnt powder and the sense of someone dragging him somewhere were his last conscious thoughts.

An aching in his neck and the cold pounding of the chipped floor of a canoe were all the feelings Chet could muster. A warm, wet, sticky sensation that filled the back of his head and the cold spray from the paddles being whipped backward were slowly bringing the Oregon farm boy back to reality. He had been taken captive and could fathom nothing else. Chet knew he was in real trouble, but at least he was alive. *For how long,* he thought. The white boy did not know that the scar-faced Nootka had followed him the whole way from the village and watched him as Chet was watching the events unfold with Bart.

Two Skins timed it perfectly. As he knocked Chet senseless, the Indian screamed and dragged the white boy into the lantern light. The old cook panicked and ran, leaving the boy and the whiskey cask behind. The Nootkas lost no time in grabbing the liquor and the boy, throwing both in the canoes and silently slipping away into the darkness. In a moment of conscience Bart turned and fired his pistol skyward in an effort to keep the savages from taking the boy, but the gesture was executed in vain.

Chet tried to move, but the cold and shock of the trauma made him immobile. He thought of jumping over the side, but remembered that Captain Folger once commented that a man could survive the forty-degree water for less than ten minutes and then needed warmth immediately thereafter to save his life. He was helpless, so he faked unconsciousness.

The Nootka warriors paddled for what seemed like two hours and Chet was wondering whether he could keep up his charade much longer, when the canoe's bottom hit ground with a thud. All six paddlers jump out of the craft, picked it up by the gunwales and went running along with the boy still inside. Chet could hear them splash as they ran and couldn't figure out why they were not reaching dry land. Finally they came to a momentary halt, dropped the canoe back into the water and continued running, dragging the craft along with them. Within minutes they were back in the canoe and paddling in silence again.

Another fifteen minutes brought the dugout to a final halt, and once again the warriors disembarked and carried the craft a few feet up the beach. The scar-faced leader checked his captive, roughly grabbing Chet's head by the hair. The boy let out a scream. Two Skins promptly bashed Chet's face back down to the canoe floor. The young man needed no faking now; he was out cold for the second time.

Hours or minutes passed, Chet didn't know. The white boy was gaining consciousness again and was in desperate need to focus himself as best he could. He lay there listening to a ruckus outside the canoe and knew the Indians must feel safe, for they were obviously drinking again. Their dancing and singing were very loud indeed.

Wondering where they might be, the boy lifted himself painfully on one elbow and surveyed his enclosure. Beyond the thwart directly behind him he saw an animal pelt, probably a bear skin. Discovering his hands were not bound, Chet slowly pulled the skin towards him. He slowly wrapped the warm fur over his body, cushioning his head wounds on the softness. As he half-slept, Chet knew he had to get away soon. The young man figured his life expectancy was fairly short with this group and the longer he waited, the worse would be his chances. The animal pelt warmed his body and he felt some of his strength returning. He soon realized that the partying was dying down and the silence outside the canoe gave him the courage to lift himself up once more and look over the side.

As near as Chet could tell, he was inland somewhere. The forest surrounded them and there were no waves beating against the shore. The clouds had cleared, allowing the slightest bit of moonlight through to guide his eyes. Chet slowly reached over the side of the canoe, touched the shallow water, and brought his fingers to his lips. The water was fresh all right. So they were by a lake, and that's why the Indians felt safe. Any pursuing rescue party would be unable to locate them off the salt-water beach.

A sickness came over him and he thought of Lucy. He missed her and wanted to see her again. He felt sorry for himself and wanted to cry. He had to escape.

As Chet watched, the last two warriors dropped to their knees. The campfire died out. The light was gone. They had all drunk themselves to sleep.

The white boy quietly rose up in the canoe. Dizziness came over him twice before he made it out of the craft. He bent back over the side, picked up the bearskin from the floor of the canoe and, staggering a bit slipped away. The young man followed the beach just above the water line away from the sleeping Nootkas, not sure if he were going inland or seaward. After about twenty yards the going got extremely complicated with fallen logs, brush and branches blocking his way, but though he was dead tired and his head ached, the boy knew his only chance was to get as far away as possible and hope that the Indians would not feel up to following him. After all, of what use was he to them?

An inner strength kept Chet going for hours, his legs and feet taking blow after blow from unseen branches and logs, and with few rest breaks he forged on. The boy kept thinking of Lucy to keep going. More than once Chet thought of tossing away the bear skin on his back, but kept it for its warmth.

Finally, as daylight was starting to break, he stumbled on the outlet stream of the lake. It was flowing away from this inland body of water at a very slow rate, with almost no detectable grade. Chet knew it must flow to the sea and decided to follow it. The water was cold, but it was only a foot and a half deep and some fifteen feet wide. As the young man found his second wind his, pace quickened.

The sky was lightening off his left shoulder and Chet knew he was heading south, which gave him greater assurance that he was heading seaward. The boy saw mountains on both sides of him, with only flat marshland in front. The forest stood thirty yards away on each side. Chet thought this shallow marsh stream must have been where the Nootkas dragged the canoe rather than carrying, and the events of a few hours ago were becoming less confusing.

The stream took a sharp bend to the west and then back to the south and, finally, the forest on either side gave way to a large pebbly beach and the sea. The stream was about twenty-five feet wide now and ran with smaller crisscrossing channels about one hundred yards further to the bay. The depth was only six to eight inches here, so this must have been where the Indians had carried the canoes while still splashing through water! How clever they were, knowing of the lake and using the stream to erase away any trace of their passage by. As he stood there in the water, Chet realized he could use the stream in the same way, and at a trot he made for the salt water. The beach to the east and west were also extremely wide for about a half mile. Chet felt that if he could reach the rocky area to the west and climb out without leaving tracks in the sand, he would be safe from even the best trackers.

As the boy reached the waves of Nootka Sound, he realized his extreme vulnerability, so he stayed in at least two inches of wave water at all times and spurred on by an overwhelming fear, he started west through the incoming tide. The bearskin was feeling extremely heavy, but dropping it now would give away his location for sure, so the boy struggled on through the light surf. Fatigue was his enemy, and more than once he wandered too deep and fell to his knees in the cold, biting water. And every time, he would drag himself to his feet and press onward.

The morning was full now and Chet prayed for the sight of the cutter. The boy thought at any minute he would look behind and see that hideous scar face coming after him. Almost unaware, Chet stumbled again scraping his knees on slippery, seaweed-coated rocks. He was there! The small boulders were right in front of him, and with his last reserve of strength, he pulled himself out of the surf. He climbed like a zombie and began to hallucinate. He looked back and saw the sea some fifty yards away, then dizziness overcame him, and he fell straight down between two boulders to a relatively soft patch of sand. With his last bit of energy, he pulled himself under the outcrop of a rocky ledge. Wrapping the wet bearskin around himself the young man fell deeply asleep, totally exhausted.

VI

The gunshot was heard back at the village and Captain Folger, Lloyd, and Matt looked at each other startled. Standing Seal was disturbed by the sound, also, and though he was not willing to suspend negotiations, he did relay his concern through Talking Boy. It was decided that Matt and one of the chief's warriors, Swimming Otter, should investigate the shooting. Both men moved down the beach with a few curious followers, and before long, they ran into the frightened cook. Bart was still holding the pistol in his hand and Matt took it from him as the old man recounted the events, carefully avoiding the mention of any whiskey. The old cook described how for no reason the scar-faced Indian dispatched Chet with a blow from a war club, and the last he saw they were dragging Chet's body toward the canoes; and seeing as how they were about to do the same to him, he had pulled his revolver, discharging a round into the air. Matt told Bart to return to the village while he and Swimming Otter continued up the beach at a run. The lantern was still burning, so they quickly found the site of the skirmish and the place where the canoes had been beached. The place was deserted. The Mowachaht warrior bent over an object on the ground, examined it briefly, and brought it to Matt.

"Two Skins is gone. The boy must be dead," the warrior said in Nootkan. "They were drinking bad water," Swimming Otter said as he handed Matt a wooden drinking bowl that reeked of cheap booze. Matt knew now the old cook was not telling the whole story, but his main concern was to find Chet. Although Matt didn't understand Swimming Otter, the Indian's expression was not very reassuring.

The investigators returned to the village to find that a deal for the soft pelts had been made. Perhaps the thought of trouble had made both parties give in a little, but, whatever the reason, the deal was done. Both Matt and Swimming Otter gave accounts of the skirmish in their own language. The young English speaking Indian translated each story. The chief was sympathetic to their loss, but he made no offer to help with a rescue.

"Two Skins is a notorious killer and there is little hope the white boy would still be alive," Talking Boy said in perfect English.

Although Matt, Lloyd, and Andrew wanted to take off after the renegades right away, Captain Folger felt that the boy was probably dead as the Mowachahts and Bart had concluded, but he allowed the three men to take the small boat and start after the renegade Nootkas.

"Soon as we've transferred the pelts to the ship and the extra goods back to Standing Seal, I'll send William and some o' the men after ye in the cutter. Probably won't be much afore three in the morning, so be careful and take weapons. I'll bring the schooner up at daybreak, if the tide and wind will oblige."

The three men left immediately, and their small sailing dory disappeared into the darkness. They hugged the shore and sailed in silence for the first fifteen minutes, still in shock over the loss of their friend. Matt was the first to break the quiet, and as a light wind in their sail kept them headed northeast along the coast, the young first officer related the story of finding the whiskey bowl. To Matt's amazement Lloyd added the story of the cracker barrel and Chet's insistence that Bart Taggert was the mystery man in Mr. Drake's office. Between the two stories it was concluded that the old cook would have plenty of explaining to do.

The three men continued to sail on through the night, taking turns trying to sleep, worried over the fate of their friend and not knowing that they had already passed the place where Two Skins had portaged to an inland lake. As day broke, they beached the small boat and took a break to stretch and eat some food. Matt unwrapped a spyglass from its leather case and scanned the early morning horizon without sighting anything human. They were beginning to believe the worst. The cold morning air and their aching backs helped them to decide to turn back and rejoin the cutter. In the meantime Captain Folger had decided he should bring the cutter aboard the *Exact* and let the weary men catch a few hours sleep. He'd sail the schooner up to meet the three men on the morning tide.

Two Skins awoke with a tremendous ache in his head and his body cramped. The sun had already risen behind the cover of clouds when the renegade leader remembered the white boy. Shakily, he moved to his feet and slowly walked the fifty feet to the dugout. The boy was gone! Two Skins stared into the canoe in disbelief. His bearskin was gone too. He grabbed a paddle, and unceremoniously began beating his band to consciousness, yelling and screaming all the while. The boy was gone and Two Skins did not want to get caught in this dead-end lake with the firepower of the whites against him. The renegade leader wanted to reach the sea and take his chances where he felt he had the advantage. If the boy reached his people, hiding by this inland lake would be a death trap.

The Nootkas paddled like mad men and soon reached the marsh stream at the end of the lake. They dismounted and retraced their steps of the night before, dragging the two canoes as they raced through the water. When they reached the final bend in the stream, Two Skins ordered a halt and crept low out over the sand dunes through the tall grass to see if the coast was clear. He looked east, then west, and saw no sign of the white boy or his people. The Indian stood up, turned, and signaled his men to bring up the canoes, while he cautiously moved toward the water.

The three would-be rescuers were making slow progress against the incoming tide and the light wind barely gave them two or three knots of headway. Andrew and Matt were trying to sleep while Lloyd was at the tiller, keeping the dory close to shore, and keeping a lookout for some sign of Chet. As they rounded a shallow point and started down a mile long straight stretch of beach, Lloyd fairly jumped out of the boat with excitement. There, just a half-mile ahead, was the band of Nootkas dragging their canoes to the water's edge. Lloyd kicked at Matt and Andrew. The other two men were awake in a flash and hitting the oars with a vengeance to gain speed.

"Matt, pass me the glass and I'll see if Chet is with them," Lloyd yelled as he stood in the stern, tiller between his legs. He searched the scene of the Indians milling around the canoes, unaware they had been sighted by the white men.

"No sign of the boy, Matt, but I'm sure that's the bunch. Whatta we gunna do?"

"I'm not sure," the first mate replied, as he redoubled his efforts on the oars. "Remember it was Bart that got um' drunk and they might not even of known what they were doing last night. Best thing we can do is try to talk to um' and see if they can tell us where he is, dead or alive."

"Well, son, that's of no concern now, for they've spotted us and from the looks of it, they're in no mood to stick around and chew the fat!"

Indeed the two dugouts and their occupants were moving strongly away from the beach, each man paddling with great resolve. Try as they could, without a favorable wind, the three white men could gain no ground against the sleek canoes. The Nootkas soon made a sweeping turn back to the northeast away from the dory, and the still unseen, but approaching *Exact*.

All the three could do was watch in silence as the black canoes moved further away on the horizon. Andrew pointed out that it might be better anyway to search the beach for any trace of the missing boy, so they gave up the chase and headed for shore. They pulled the boat up to the high tide line and decided to split up, after an initial search of the stream area. Lloyd would follow the stream inland, Andrew west along the beach and Matt along the beach to the east.

"Now be lookin' for any tracks in the sand and I'll be lookin' for any tracks in the mud upstream that might show where they camped," said Lloyd.

The three set off and combed their areas for the next hour. As Andrew reached the rocky outcrop at the end of the sandy part of the beach, he felt no need to go further, for he'd seen no tracks. Little did he know as he turned back that Chet slept less than twenty feet away. Chet had wanted to trick the Nootkas, but was tricking his friends instead. They all returned empty handed and frustrated, and as the three rested on the beach, the schooner made its appearance around the point.

Matt, Lloyd, and Andrew jumped to their feet waving and running to the water's edge, shoved the small boat into the surf and made sail for the ship. The captain saw them within seconds and the two masted schooner lowered her sails, hove to, and stood by to pick up her men. Captain Folger could tell they hadn't any good news for Chet was not with them. After hearing the morning's account, Captain Folger decided the boy was indeed dead and his body was probably washed out to sea. After a short ceremony with bible and ship's company, the *Exact* set sail, came about, and headed for the Queen Charlotte Islands. Matt and Lloyd told the captain about Bart's activities and Folger put the old cook under house arrest keeping him locked in the brig when not cooking.

As the ship sailed out of sight the boy slept.

VII

The anguished boy finally woke from his sleep and found he could not move. His head throbbed, his bones ached, he was thirsty, and his stomach was empty, but he was alive! The day was cold but the sandy area between the large black rocks gave some protection from the wind and the concave area under the larger rock gave him protection from the rain. Chet was still wet from his ordeal the night before. The young man had no strength to climb up the rock and look around, so he just scooped himself out a hole in the sand under the outcrop, and, after a few spells of dizziness, had himself a nice burrow. Chet climbed inside the dry sand pit and pulled the bear- skin over his tired body. The boy figured he was safe by now, but if the renegades did come back, he could care less; if they killed him, so be it. Right now he was fairly comfortable and warm and all he wanted to do was sleep.

The day and night passed without incident, as the boy alternated between waking and sleeping. The weather continued nasty, and the stolen bearskin proved to be indispensable. Chet shuddered when he thought of how many times he'd wanted to throw it away, but something in his mind kept telling him to keep it. If nothing else, Chet knew he'd have the satisfaction of knowing old Scarface was freezing out there somewhere without his warm bearskin. The young man's body felt better with the long rest, but every time he rose to his feet, the throbbing and dizziness would put him down on his back again. After awhile the boy felt he had to go anyway, for it was either stay here and die of thirst or move and be dizzy. He decided to leave the bear skin in the hiding place, and struggled to reach the top of the rocks. With much difficulty and resting, he was able to climb the short distance and make his way to the alder and fir forest back of the beach. The young man could see no sign of any humans, good or bad, but he decided to stay a few feet inside the woods, just in case. His dizziness lessened as he traveled the half-mile back to the stream, but the forest logs and branches took a toll on his strength and he finally moved out on the hard sand next to the tree line.

A few yards of travel on the hard pack quickened his spirits and then the young man came to an abrupt halt at the sight of footprints. Fear shot through him and panic almost swept him away, but then he saw it, that telltale difference. A white man's boot! The tracks in the sand that froze him were not those of Indians. They were, in fact, Andrew's tracks from yesterday, and though Chet didn't know that, he did know that someone was looking for him, and they were close. The boy quickly searched the horizon again for signs of the ship. He started to yell, but caught himself. There was no schooner in sight and the renegades might still be near. Chet knew he must reach the stream without delay and be on his way back to the village. The *Exact* might still be there, and the schooner was his only chance.

The discovery of the tracks renewed his strength, and he moved steadily nearer the stream. Within minutes the boy was taking long cool sips from the clear flowing water. He drank his fill, and then wasted no time in returning to the rocks, climbing back down to retrieve the bear hide. The boy folded it long ways, draped it around his neck, and started down the beach towards where he thought the Mowachaht Nootka village would be.

The young man struggled over the pebbles and sand for an hour, keeping close to the forest for safety reasons and always searching the sea every few minutes. He had no idea how far it was back to Chahakquot, and as the morning passed Chet hoped his friends would send another search party. The boy rested at noon and slept for another hour between two drift logs to cut down on the cold wind. Chet thought about trying to kill a sea bird with a well-placed rock, but then he had no way to skin or cook it, and Chet was not hungry enough, yet, to eat it raw.

The young man continued on that afternoon with his hopes of rescue dimming at each step. The night would come soon, and he was constantly hungry. Fortunately, there were plenty of fresh water creeks and streams all along the route, so the young man kept his belly full of water and that seemed to keep his mind off hunger. He also took time to strip off his jacket and shirt and wash the dried blood from his wounded head. Chet's hair was all matted and the cold water was painful on the healing cuts. His nose was still extremely tender and as the boy carefully washed it, he felt that, although it was probably broken, it seemed to be back in the right place.

As Chet started again he noticed that high cliffed banks rose above the sand and the beach was becoming narrower. The trees changed from alder and fir to madrona and vine maple, and because of the sandstone cliffs, there was no protective forest to hide in. If an enemy came now, Chet would be at their mercy.

With an hour left before dark, the boy decided it was time to look for shelter. In the distance down the beach he saw an especially large, weathered cedar trunk, with roots still attached at one end and washed clean of any dirt. It would be his best hope of shelter. One look at the sky left no doubt that a rainsquall or two would unload before the night was over, so Chet went to work digging a sleeping pit behind the log on the cliff side to protect against the weather. When that was sufficient, the boy selected a variety of straight driftwood branches and placed them over the pit in such a way that they rested on the cedar trunk. The tree was about five feet in diameter at the point Chet had chosen, so there was plenty of room to crawl in and out of the makeshift lean-to. He placed the branches tightly together and then filled the cracks with smaller branches and topped it off with a layer of dune grass. Darkness fell and with no moonlight to see by, the boy once again settled in for another night's rest. The gnawing in his stomach was paramount now, and Chet knew that he had to find some food soon.

The thought of killing one of the seabirds that scurried and pecked along the waterline did more to keep his mind busy than anything else. Chet went over many plans in his mind to capture one of the delicate little creatures, and the boy thought of how he could break one of the granite rocks that littered the beach and grind off a drumstick with the sharp edge. However, every time it came to the part where he'd have to bite into the raw, bleeding flesh, Chet thought that maybe he could last another day. The boy wondered how the Indians could live in such a place and how they found food.

A drop spattered on the sand outside his shelter and then another and soon it was raining steadily. His makeshift lean-to seemed to be keeping the majority of the heavy rain out and as Chet snuggled into his sandy bed, he was sure the bearskin would keep out the rest. It was peaceful under this bear blanket and the young man felt secure. He thought of Lucy and said a little prayer for her, hoping she was well.

Chet was awakened early in the morning while it was still dark, for the waves had risen with the wind and the tide was coming dangerously close to his log and stick shelter. He crawled out from under the bearskin and walked around the tangle of roots at the end of the big cedar. The waves were reaching almost to the log and the boy did not know if the tide had peaked or not. Chet felt he might be better off staying awake and watching the imposing surf, so he grabbed a stick and plunged it into the sand two feet from the log where the waves were breaking. This would give him a gauge as to which way the water was heading. Picking up the trusty bearskin, the young man climbed a few feet up the cliff bank. He spent a miserable hour there, but in the end Chet was sure the tide had turned and was going out away from his stick gauge. When the boy returned to his shelter he found the tide had reached under the log leaving the sand soaking wet. Disappointed, Chet lay on top of the cedar trunk on a flat area of the log and slept as best he could until full daylight.

The morning dawned bright and sunny, although still very cold, and the boy thought there might even be a light coating of frost on the madrona trees high above on the cliff. He raised on one elbow and noticed the gnawing in his gut was more intense now.

Chet felt a little ashamed that it had only been a couple of days since he had eaten. He had heard the crew on the schooner talk of men who lasted a month or more lost at sea with no food and water and had survived. The young man got up, still stiff and sore, tightened his belt a notch and looked around for something that might be construed as food. He saw a small brown lizard, or salamander more likely, standing on a little sandstone ledge a few feet up the side of the cliff. The salamander jumped from place to place and stood flicking its head in quick jerky motions as if to dare the boy to grab it. This was no food, and besides the salamander was too small, so Chet sat back down, wrapped the bearskin tighter, and looked at the ground. A myriad of broken shells and seaweed, red and green, lay randomly on the sand. The boy thought if he could find some clams or barnacles he might be able to stomach them raw, for, after all, people ate oysters raw. The green seaweed looked especially good this morning, but the red was too rubbery and had a texture not unlike octopus skin. *Maybe it was octopus skin*, he thought.

 Chet decided to move on to the next fresh water stream, for if he found any shellfish, the young man wanted plenty of water with him to wash it down. The boy made a short detour to the waterline, took the freshest green seaweed he could find and climbed onto a small boulder a few feet from shore to wash it in the crystal clear rain water that had been caught in a depression in the rock. The young man squeezed out the water and wrapped a big handful of seaweed in a ball and placed it in his coat pocket. Chet could not resist a little nibble and it wasn't bad, but it was salty and again the boy put off eating until he found a fresh water stream. At least he felt better and started west once again.

 Walking on the sand and small rocks was starting to take a toll on Chet's feet and ankles. With little support underneath, walking was becoming quite a struggle, and the young man felt the weakness in his legs more than he had the day before. The boy was walking in a trance at times and no longer attempted to put out any effort to search the horizon or look ahead for Indians. He followed the high water green seaweed path and fixed his eyes straight down. Once Chet saw the body of a huge crab, and when it didn't scurry away, he surmised it was dead. The ensuing smell when the boy picked it up confirmed the assumption.

Soon the boy hit a stretch of smooth boulders and jumped from rock to rock. The hard pan under his feet made it worth the increased output in energy. As Chet leaped on his way he almost missed the ring of barnacles around each rock and it was only because of the nearness of the next fresh water creek that he finally stopped and took notice.

Well this was the time, he thought, *I'm too hungry to wait any longer.*

Taking a good-sized rock and remembering the seabird slaughter plan, Chet smashed the rock down hard on a boulder a few times until there was a noticeable crack in it. A couple of more blows fractured off a nice sharp hunk of blade rock. The young man moved to the barnacles and hacked off a good many of them, cracking the shells and meticulously washing each piece free of any slime, goo, guts, or shell that might be clinging. Making his way to the stream, Chet sat down on the unfolded bearskin and neatly placed his barnacle meat on some fresh green seaweed. He brought out the dry seaweed from his jacket pocket, placing it next to the raw shellfish meat, rearranged it some, and when the boy had it looking as delectable as possible, it was time to eat. First, though, he thought a cool drink would set the mood. Once that was accomplished Chet sat back and took a morsel of semi-slimy barnacle and placed it on his tongue. With much gagging, eye tearing, and copious amounts of water from the stream he managed to get down one or two. The seaweed went a little better, and after another good washing down, Chet felt extremely proud of himself and thought again that he would live.

The lunch stayed down, and after a nap in the cold sunshine, the boy was on his way once more. The pace was slow and Chet was struggling with the sand again. As his head hung lower, he failed to notice the change in topography and the disappearance of the cliff. A gradual flattening of the slope appeared. A short time later the boy had to rest again. He fell back on the sand and lifted his tired eyes skyward and said a small prayer, thanking the Lord for getting him this far. Chet shut his eyes and fell asleep once more.

The young man awoke a short time later to find the weather turning nasty and the sunshine gone. Propping up his body and rolling over, Chet noticed the gentle slope behind him. He also noticed something else: berries, blackberries and lots of them. They weren't juicy or large, rather small and dry, but the boy gobbled them up just the same and they filled his shrinking gut. He followed the berries up the slope, finding only two or three on each branch. As the young man slowly climbed the slope he noticed he was above a point on the beach where the shore fell away to the northwest and there, not more then a quarter of a mile away, was Chahakquot.

The houses along the water were as Chet had remembered them and the smoke trickling up with a smell of broiled salmon in the air was encouraging, but his excitement was short-lived. As the young man's eyes made a long sweep of the cove, there was no schooner to be found and as he watched the few villagers who were outside doing their afternoon routines, a familiar fear overcame him. What if Scarface were here or what if they would no longer be friendly without the white men and their weapons? The fear overwhelmed him and the boy could not move or make a decision. He thought of waiting until dark and stealing some salmon from one of the community smoke sheds. If he could steal a canoe, Chet thought he might get to one of the islands off the cove and hide until the Nootkas gave up looking for him. Stealing enough food might enable the boy to paddle until he made Fort Victoria or at least to where he could hail a coastal schooner. The young man decided to watch the village and take his chance at night.

Trying to watch the village and stay awake proved to be quite a job, but as the afternoon grew on, Chet was able to pick out the closest canoe he thought he could handle. The boy did not see any of the ruthless Nootkas who had helped in his abduction. He did recognize one Chahakquot Mowachaht who was the whaler and warrior, Swimming Otter. The warrior frequented the second to last house and Chet assumed it was probably Swimming Otter's own house. That would be a good house to stay clear of and Swimming Otter would be a good person to avoid.

Chet watched as some of the women carried food away from a small stilted shed between Swimming Otter's house and the third house from the end. This would have to be the boy's main target and Chet lived his plan over and over again until he knew exactly how to proceed. Approach from the waterline and dump the bearskin in the canoe, make sure there were at least two paddles, one to paddle and one for a spare, and move on to the shed. He would remove his jacket and use the wool coat to bundle up as much fish as possible, return to the canoe, and quietly slip away into the darkness.

As the day waned, clouds began to pile up and the wind became extremely cold. The usually warm pelt was barely keeping the boy warm. Even before darkness a few snowflakes began to fall and as Chet shivered through the early evening the wind picked up and the snowflakes got bigger. The snow did not let up, and the young man kept telling himself it was okay, that it would serve to hide him better. There would be less chance of anyone being out for an after dinner stroll along the beach. He tried to feel positive, but deep inside Chet longed for the warmth of those massive cedar houses. The boy did not know if he could stand the cold while paddling in such weather, not to mention the chance of being capsized in this wind. Chet huddled for a while longer. When the young man felt that sufficient time had passed, he rose, shook the snow off the bearskin, draped it around himself, and started down to the beach.

Chet thought it must be around nine o'clock as he trudged through the two inches of snow on the beach. A new wave of dizziness hit him as he continued on towards the canoes. So far no one else was seen. As the boy was nearing the twenty-foot canoe, he heard grunts and laughter coming from further down the beach, but he just crept lower and reached the canoe unnoticed. He unwrapped the bearskin off his shoulders and dropped the half frozen pelt in the bow of the canoe. Luck was with him, for there was two four-foot paddles stowed neatly below the center thwarts of the dugout.

After taking a moment to clear his head, the boy cautiously moved up the beach on an angle towards the third house. Chet darted in and out among the canoes and totem poles, using their concealment to refocus and re-establish his will. As the boy passed the first house a sudden flurry of barking and yapping from the village dogs exploded. First one and then two or three more until finally all the dogs in the whole village were announcing his presence.

Chet was in shock and his only thought was to make it back to the canoe and make good his escape. The weather and his weakened state combined to cause the boy to fall over a wooden fish weir. He went tumbling head over heels, landing hard on the frozen ground. His body was numb and he heard voices and running feet muffled by the snow. Chet could not offer any more resistance, even knowing they would kill him for sure. He lay motionless a few feet away from the canoe while fatigue and shock let his mind slip from consciousness.

Swimming Otter ran from the doorway of his cedar house wearing nothing except a bark skirt around his middle and holding his whalebone war club in one hand and a torch in the other. Finding Chet, the warrior aroused the other villagers from their cozy fires and everyone stood around the human lump on the frozen beach.

"It's the white boy from the swimming house," remarked the shirtless warrior. "He is alive, but he's been beaten and is near dead."

"How did he ever escape from Two Skins with his life?" said a villager.

"Swimming Otter," roared a second native, "look here, it is the cloak of Two Skins is it not?" The Mowachaht elder took the bearskin robe, confirmed from its markings the suspicion as true and broke into a heavy laughter.

"The great scar faced half-breed has been outwitted by a skinny white boy," laughed the warrior. "No doubt the white man's bad water played a role in this, but it still lightens my heart. Does it not yours, my friends?" And all within hearing agreed and had good humor over Two Skin's loss.

"Bring the white one into *Whale Oil House* and send word to Standing Seal. We must keep this one alive," Swimming Otter said.

The Mowachahts did as the warrior said and Chet was carried into the warm cedar house and laid on a plank near the center fire. The boy's boots were removed and two of the women rubbed his feet and hands while a third, an old slave named Cattail Woman, massaged the general area of his upper body. Chet was moved onto another plank covered with shredded cedar bark to cushion him. He was placed closer to the fire where the women and some curious youngsters continued to care for him.

"Send word to the shaman," ordered Swimming Otter. "Tell him I will pay him well to keep this new slave alive."

Chet's clothes were removed. Dry skins, a cedar mat and wool blankets were placed over him.

Standing Seal burst through the covered doorway and his eyes searched for the white boy. Swimming Otter hailed him and the chief moved towards the group in the center of the huge house. Talking Boy, the Salish slave, was right behind the chief and looked on with interest as the two discussed the future of the white captive.

"He was planning to steal a canoe and paddle to his people in the swimming house. A noble deed," professed the warrior. "Two Skin's bear robe was found with him and that makes my heart glad."

Swimming Otter was more than happy to hear of any deed that belittled Two Skins' stature. The two had been adversaries all their lives and only the close family ties between the upper class of both villages had kept their obvious jealousy in check. Standing Seal, although amused at the turn of events, was nevertheless practical.

"From the looks of this one the half-breed meant him dead," commented the chief. "The winter season is upon us tonight so it will be many weeks and months before we will be visited by the scar faced one again. You may keep this one alive until such time as Two Skins returns and then we will bargain him back. I'm sure the scar faced one will take much pleasure in killing the boy. If his kind come by and are willing to pay before that time, then he can have his life. Until then the white boy is yours as my gift to serve your house. If the white boy tries to steal a canoe and leave again, he will be killed. Talking Boy, stay tonight and counsel the white slave in his own tongue. As soon as you have done this, return to me at *Sea Wolf House*."

With that, the mighty leader turned and left, stopping and making another half laugh, half grunt, as he closed the skin door cover.

The English-speaking slave had been listening intently and was way ahead of the chief. He welcomed having the newcomer in the village and could not wait to speak to the weakened white boy. Talking Boy hoped that in some way this white slave might be of some help to secure his own freedom. Although the Salish slave seemed passive, he was always planning ways of escape. This white boy and his bold plan of stealing the canoe might be what Talking Boy needed to pull off his own liberation.

The next moment another figure entered Whale Oil House with a flurry and made his way over to the white captive. He was dressed in a bearskin robe with red and black pigment in geometric designs all over his face. The newcomer wore a wooden cap in the shape of a wolf's head, with human hair, bird down, and feathers hanging from it. In his hand he carried a wooden rattle with a shallow carving of a contorted man-beast on either side. At his waist was a pouch containing magic powders, sticks, and feathers. His presence aroused a sense of respect and fear among the common people in the great house. His name was Salmon Wolf and he was the medicine man of the tribe.

"Salmon Wolf, this white slave has brought shame on my rival and I wish his spirit not to journey far from his body, but to return so that he may serve me and give my house pleasure," bellowed Swimming Otter. "You will be paid well if the white boy lives."

With that, the shaman started dancing around Chet, while the others in the room moved away. As Salmon Wolf danced, he took red powder and sand from his pouch, sprinkling it on the boy. The shaman raised his voice in grunts and chants, making a howling screech at times. After some minutes of this, the medicine man suddenly stopped and quickly moved to Chet's side, covering the white captive's face with the bearskin cloak. Grabbing two hollow cedar sticks from his belt, the shaman put them to his mouth and with a sucking motion placed the other ends at Chet's eyes. As Salmon Wolf sucked out the evil spirit, he pulled the pelt off the boy's face and to the amazement of the gathered throng the white boy was awake. Swimming Otter was beaming with elation and praised the great shaman, paying him handsomely in food and cedar bark goods for a job well done.

Chet was muddle-headed and still in a bit of a shock. As he was starting to come to, the boy had this sensation of someone jumping about and a cover being thrown over his eyes. He lay there awake, in fear of someone beating him again. Chet was aware that the medicine man was right next to him and he awaited the worst. Then the blanket was pulled back, revealing the huge cedar beams above his head and the surprised looks on the faces of the Indians around him.

It was just a clever sham, for the medicine man had danced around until Chet showed signs of waking, then made it seem as if he had performed a miracle.

The white captive lay soaking up the warmth of the fire, afraid to move, feeling he must be dreaming. Chet thought he heard someone speaking English to him.

"White slave, what is your name?" Talking Boy asked. "Can you hear me white boy?" he asked again, shaking Chet softly on the arm.

"Yes, I can hear you," the boy replied. "Are you going to kill me?"

The Salish slave thought this to be a proper response under the circumstances and set out to reassure the lad somewhat.

"No, I'm not going to kill you, not if you do as I say," the Indian said in a sterner voice then before. "So far luck is with you. Indians don't like white men; they bring disease and hardship. Kill lots of Mowachahts with pox. Your master (Swimming Otter) has spared your life for now, but he will bash in your head if you do not do as I say."

Chet was glad to hear that for the time being there would be no more trauma to his person. He was tired, sore, and hungry, but was afraid to ask for anything to eat for fear of upsetting anyone. The older Indian, Swimming Otter, interrupted Talking Boy and asking the younger to translate a question for Chet.

"Mowachaht who owns bear coat, did you kill him?" the Salish slave asked, holding up the scar faced Nootka's bearskin.

Chet, thankful that he had not and hoping for approval, answered quickly, "No."

The older Indian understood this English word and the scowl on his face confused the white boy. Chet got an indication that maybe he should have killed Scarface. Another conversation in Nootkan took place, and the English speaking Indian turned to Chet again.

"Did you escape from Mowachaht and steal coat?" he asked in a rough voice, while shaking the coat again.

Now Chet thought about lying, not wanting another beating, and he took a little more time to answer. Finally, the boy took a chance and answered, "Yes."

The broad smile that shown on Swimming Otter's face let Chet know that he had done an acceptable deed and guessed right that he and Two Skins did not like each other. The older warrior ruffled Chet's head like an approving uncle and reeled off a string of orders that sent half a dozen natives scurrying about.

"The master is pleased with you," Talking Boy said gruffly, "but you must always do as I say or he will kill you." The English-speaking slave was rough with Chet on purpose, wanting to establish his dominance and not let the white boy know he was just a slave also. Talking Boy felt that Chet could help him escape, but until the Salish slave had a plan and until he could trust the white boy, he decided to keep him unaware of the truth. "Are you hungry, white slave?"

Chet answered that he was and soon the women brought him dried fish, berries, and a beautiful wooden box of fresh water. The lad stuffed himself, but the women kept bringing more until Chet motioned that he was full. *Much better then seaweed and raw mussels,* he thought, feeling satisfied. Seeing that he was finished, Talking Boy came back over and sat beside him.

"I'm going to leave now to go to the chief's house. Do not try to leave or steal canoe again, or you will be killed. It is winter now and you would die before you went very far."

The Indian was almost decent this time, thought Chet, as he watched the Salish slave walk away. There was no way the white captive was going to go anywhere the way he felt. The Indian's words would be more meaningful later as the days passed and the weather got worse. For the time being Chet was just glad to be inside, out of the snow, and have the warm blankets around him. Two women and two men picked him up, plank and all, and carried him to a platform of cedar planks near the door. One of the men was very old and Chet thought he noticed a smile from the man. There were some fine wooden boxes and larger chests stacked on either side of the boy, obviously used to promote privacy. The old man settled down on the other side of the boxes and the other slaves returned to their own sleeping areas. The house was quiet now and no guard was over him. The sounds of sleeping filled his ears and soon he, too, felt secure enough to close his eyes and fall asleep.

VIII

Opening his eyes the next morning revealed a great-beamed roof of cedar. Dim rays of light filtered down through the cracks formed by pushed back planks over the fire pit. Chet had to think for a moment to remember where he was. A small patch of white snow lay on the ground below the smoke hole, but the women who were milling about, starting the fire and beginning their morning chores were rapidly eliminating it. The white boy had not seen the inside of the Nootka house the night before because of the darkness, and now he was amazed at how far back it stretched and how roomy it was. For the first time, too, Chet realized he was naked. Not knowing what to do, he decided to just lie there until someone said or did something.

Within minutes the old Nootka from the night before came through the door with some split cedar chunks for the fire. The old slave was wearing a cedar bark skirt and nothing else. His bare feet were wet with snow. Chet rose up on his elbow and watched the old man walk over to the left side wall, get something out of a large wooden chest and start back toward him, stopping on the way to exchange pleasantries with other household members.

Staring straight at him, the old man walked the last ten feet, and as he reached Chet's side, the boy thought he noticed another twinkle of a grin as the man spoke.

"How are you this morning, *White Clam*?" the old Indian spoke softly. "I have brought you a garment, and I'm going to show you how to put it on so you can go outside and relieve yourself."

Chet did not understand a word the Nootka had said but the tone was so polite he felt a response was needed, so the boy forced out a, "Good morning, sir."

"Good, White Clam, your mouth works wondrously, and your tongue speaks white even though it is pink like mine. Come, rise up and put on this garment so that you will not scare the young maidens with your manhood. They would surely scream violently watching your dangle pendulate around the room."

Again the boy could not understand a word, but was appalled at the obvious suggestion conveyed by gestures that he get up and stand naked. The boy drug the bark blanket up with him and the old man seemed to understand. Wooden Hand quickly covered the boy's embarrassment with the skirt and tucked it in tightly at the side. The old man then took the cedar bark blanket and wrapped it around the boy's shoulders, tying it with the string-like ends.

"Now, White Clam, we go to the relieving post."

The old Indian motioned for the boy to follow and headed for the door. Chet, with some hesitation, followed. In their naked feet and legs they stepped outside into the snow. The two walked around to the stilted storage shed between *Whale Oil House* and the third house from the end - the very shed that Chet was going to steal food from the night before. They stood in front of the nearest corner post of the storage shed, and the old Indian, speaking something in Nootkan, began urinating on the post.

"Go ahead, White Clam, relieve yourself on this fine post," the old slave said, motioning to the boy.

Chet understood the gesture and realized that he indeed was ready for the act. The boy could not remember how long it had been since he last partook of this particular necessity. Chet pushed aside his skirt and presented a long steady stream on the post.

"Good boy. You are white but your urine is the color yellow, like mine. And it smells so foul and strong that it will surely keep all the vermin of the forest away from this food house. In fact it may keep the great bear and the courageous wolf away as well. I can't imagine what your dung is like, but I will find a far away place for you when the time comes. As for now, relieve your water here where it is useful."

Chet wondered what the old man was babbling about, but he did understand that this was to be the place for peeing. Since his feet were freezing, the white boy was more then happy when they re-entered the house. After going inside, the old man went to the sleeping platform, and, knowing that the boy's feet were not toughened like the Indians', he pulled an old pair of deer hide moccasins from a chest. They were a little tight, but Chet was glad for the offer and thanked the old slave. Wooden Hand seemed to understand.

Swimming Otter finally made an appearance from the back of the house to eat breakfast with his relatives. Afterward the slaves were fed what was left. Chet was surprised at the order of things, guessing that the meal was served according to rank and importance. The master talked briefly with the old slave, and then left the house. When Chet had finished his meager breakfast and returned to his platform, he noticed his clothes and shoes sitting next to the sleeping plank, clean and neatly folded. The boy's first thought was to put them on for the warmth, but after thinking for a minute he decided to leave on the cedar bark clothing. After all, he would need his own clothes for any escape attempt, and if he wore them all the time they would quickly deteriorate in this environment.

Chet watched the old Nootka gather some equipment, some horn and wood wedges, a stone mallet, a metal chisel and an iron adze with a wooden handle. He gave the boy a cedar pouch with a rope tie and put a dozen wedges in the pouch, tying it around the boy's waist. Then the old slave picked up the other tools and made for the door, motioning for Chet to follow.

As the two slaves left the house, they were met by a third, Talking Boy. The English-speaking slave greeted the old man cordially. Their speech was pleasant and kind to Chet's ears, even though he understood nothing.

"Wooden Hand, it is good to see you this morning," said the young Salish slave. "How is my Haida friend? I see Swimming

Otter has given you the white boy as a helper. Has he chosen a name for the white slave?"

"Yes, he has. A name of great power." The old man paused.

The young Indian looked confused, for the Nootka didn't usually choose a powerful spirit name for slaves. "Well, what is this name of great power?" he returned.

"Now, don't be jealous, my son," Wooden Hand spoke, with another twinkle in his eye. "It is ... White Clam." Talking Boy stared, then both Indian slaves roared with laughter. Chet, not knowing what was said, tried to smile in tune with their laughter. Seeing this, they roared again.

"White Clam," laughed the young Salish boy. "Maybe it is powerful, for cannot the clam pinch the killer whale with its shell?" They laughed some more, and every time Chet joined in, it gave them that much more pleasure. They lightly patted the white boy on the back as a gesture of approval, and then their talk became more serious.

"Listen, old man, I want you to keep this white slave alive and in good health. I think he could be useful in getting us back to our own people. Every moon that passes brings more whites to this land, and maybe if we befriend this one, he could arrange our freedom or help us escape on the white sailing houses."

"This might be so," said the old Haida slave, "but I fear that Swimming Otter has a frightful plan for this boy. You remember his plans to raise a new pole in honor of his clan? Well, now that the master has made great wealth in the otter pelt trade with the boy's people, he plans to use that wealth to give a potlatch in the spring at the raising of the pole. Swimming Otter plans to make a special invitation to his rival, Two Skins that he cannot refuse. Not only will he try to humiliate the scar faced one with gifts, but also with the presence of the boy himself. Two Skins will want the boy's life, and if his temper is not held in check it could be a very bad situation."

"We can do nothing until the spring anyway," said Talking Boy. "There will be no more ships stopping until the winter weather has passed. We can only hope we have a plan and a return of his people before the potlatch."

During this conversation the tall boy stood shivering in his cedar blanket, wishing he had his trousers and jacket. The village was so peaceful and picturesque with the snow on the ground and the smoke rising from the huge houses. The beautiful painted poles stood in rows like guardian soldiers. Under other circumstances being here would be a welcome once-in-a-lifetime experience. Chet wondered about the concern on the faces of the two Indians deep in conversation. Finally, the younger turned towards him and spoke.

Talking boy told him his name in Nootkan, withholding the English translation and Chet recognized the gruntal tone from earlier when the old slave had spoken it.

"It is a suitable name for you," the young Indian said, "and remember my words of last night. If you try to leave, you will be killed, by us or by the weather. This man is Wooden Hand; he is a worker and carver of wood from the Haida tribe far to the north. He is a slave also and you will be his helper. If you labor hard you will be fed and clothed."

The English-speaking one turned to walk away, but stopped and turned back.

"If you leave, Wooden Hand won't stop you, but they will kill him if they don't find you."

For the first time the white boy realized he was considered to be a slave also, but in spite of Talking Boy's stern words, he read some compassion in the way he treated Wooden Hand. Remembering their laughter, Chet felt this young man might not be as bad as he pretends to be. Talking boy was obviously concerned with the welfare of the old slave, but why? As a Nootka he should not care. Maybe he had grown fond of the old man. Either way, Chet had a better feeling about the village as a whole and started to feel his fears easing. The younger Indian left and the old Haida slave and Chet started off into the forest behind the houses.

A short distance in back of the house the two slaves found some fallen trees that had already been worked. Fires had been set at one time to section the trunks into ten-foot chunks and the ends were chiseled and adzed smooth.

The Nootkas must not have saws, Chet caught himself thinking. *One iron saw and instruction in its use would bring many otter pelts in trading.*

As the old man set out the tools he named each one, and Chet tried to repeat the Indian word after the Haida slave would say it. They started working a log section where planks had been removed previously. Wooden Hand took some measuring sticks, and some charcoal and marked the cross section of the cedar log two inches below where the last plank had been split. He took a mallet, chisel, and wedges and set out to split off some planks. When the wedges were pounded all the way home, a two foot crack opened up and a spreading stick about four feet long was passed under the beginning plank. The old Haida then motioned for the boy to grab one end while he grabbed the other, and they pulled the spreading stick the length of the log, using wedges from time to time, finally lifting off a smooth plank two inches thick, ten feet long, and as wide as the tree trunk. Each plank took about an hour to split, and they worked the rest of the afternoon, Chet learning the nomenclature as they went. By the time darkness was near, they had seven ten foot planks of varying widths and thicknesses.

The two slaves stacked five of the planks on a prepared level piece of ground and placed heavy rocks on top to keep the wood from warping in the damp weather. The last two planks they carried back to *Whale Oil House*.

Chet had been cold most of the day and it was good to get back to the warmth of the longhouse. Only the hard work saved him from freezing, and the boy thought tomorrow he might wear some undergarments, shoes and his coat. In fact, since the cedar bark skirt was sometimes revealing, he might as well put on his shorts and undershirt now. Chet ducked behind one of the wood chests and quietly slipped on his underwear and re-did the bark cover. Feeling more secure, he came out from behind the screen of boxes and sat on the edge of the plank platform. The young man was ready for food and not having eaten since morning made him eager for dinner to begin. As near as Chet could tell, everything was about the same for dinner as it had been for breakfast and the busy cooks were well into their preparation.

Wooden Hand returned to the sleeping area and motioned for Chet to pick up one of the new planks they made that day and set it on the platform. The old man had some new tools, including rock scrapers, iron bars set in yew wood handles, sandstone, and some pieces of shark (dogfish) skin. The old man examined the plank and took some measurements with a smooth-sanded cedar stick. After some thinking, he took the stone scrapers and started a gross sanding procedure in circular motion. The old slave let Chet try it, and when he was satisfied the boy had picked up the hang of it, Wooden Hand pointed out an area equaling about one fourth of the plank on which the boy could concentrate. Soon they switched to the sand stone and the plank began to get a finished look to it. The old Indian checked for smoothness often and finally, he gave the boy a hunk of sharkskin. Chet held the skin in his hand and felt the gritty texture. He was shown how to wrap the skin in a chunk of cedar, with the scaled side out, and as he rubbed the grain of the plank, its surface became smooth as glass. Chet still didn't know what they were making, but he was pleased with his new skills.

The upper class was eating now and smells of fresh shellfish, clams the boy thought, filled the house. Talking Boy made an appearance at this time and disappeared toward the back right corner of the large house. A few minutes later the English speaking slave and his host, Swimming Otter, made their way down the center of the room past the eating people and stood directly in front of the two wood workers.

"How has the day progressed old one?" asked the master, while stealing an approving glance at the boy sanding the plank.

"We worked in the forest stripping these planks. The white boy learns fast and is eager to please, although he cannot take the cold very well and shivered most of the day," replied the old wood worker without taking his eyes off the work.

"Good, White Clam pleases me."

The warrior turned and yelled an order at someone in the back of the house. Chet was afraid to look up and continued working.

"Perhaps the cloak of the scar faced one would be better served covering the skin of White Clam," said Swimming Otter. "Talking Boy, tell him if he continues to work hard we will feed him and give him shelter. If he tries to leave we will kill him."

Talking Boy turned to Chet and told him in English what Swimming Otter had said. Chet was just glad to be alive and though the white boy was not happy with his predicament, he was feeling a bond forming between him and his Nootkan host. Since Chet wanted to stay alive, he might as well work. The boy's memory flashed back to the day before on the beach, and Chet remembered how he wished to learn how to survive in the wilderness. What better teachers could he have than the Nootkan slaves?

Two slave women appeared; bringing food for Chet and Wooden Hand, and the boy ate his fill of fish and dried berries. None of the fresh clams was offered probably none was left. One of the slaves was the short, round, middle-aged woman, named Cattail Woman, the same slave who had massaged his freezing body the night before. She smiled at the old man and was polite to Chet. She appeared to be friends with Wooden Hand and Chet felt a special bond between the two.

Swimming Otter returned with the bear pelt of Two Skins, gave it to Chet, grunted something in Nootkan and disappeared back in the depths of the house. Talking Boy said a few more words to Wooden Hand and started for the door, paused, looked right at Chet then left. Chet was confused by the actions of the younger Indian, feeling as though Talking Boy disliked him one minute and liked him the next.

The boy was excited to get his bearskin back. After a long drink of fresh water and a trip outside to the peeing post, Chet went back to his part of the sleeping platform. Seeing that no one was working, he snuggled under the blankets of bark and bear skin and was warm for the first time all day. His head no longer ached and the young man slept soundly the whole night through.

The next few days went much as the first, with the two slaves working in the woods during the day making planks and sanding them at night. The food was bland, but there was plenty, and at least no one starved. Some days there would be fresh halibut, flounder, or shark when the Nootka men went fishing, but mostly the slaves just subsisted on dried salmon, greens, tubers, and dried berries. Chet was picking up some words and was able to form a small vocabulary and more important to his long-range plans, he was picking up tips on survival. Wooden Hand and Chet met with Talking Boy from time to time and the white slave thought that the younger Indian, though still reserved, was warming up to him. The white slave did not see much of the other upper class Mowachahts and almost never saw Standing Seal, the chief. He did know that the upper class and the shaman had secretive religious meetings and functions not attended or seen by the common people. For the most part Chet kept to himself and slept when not working. He really only saw those who lived in his own house. Through bits and pieces Chet did realize that the people of *Whale Oil House* were working overtime making material goods as gifts for this potlatch party that Swimming Otter was giving in the spring. The white boy wasn't sure what this potlatch was, but he knew it was important to Swimming Otter. Everyone in the house, including the upper class, were doing all they could to process bark, wood, skins, bone, and food into materials to be used in the making of these goods.

Chet was amazed at all the things cedar was used for, and not just the wood, but the roots, needles, and bark. Chet thought that just a knowledge of this tree alone would give him enough skill to survive, for about the only thing you couldn't do with the lofty cedar was eat it. If he were going to escape, Chet would have to learn how to collect food and catch fish. The boy would have to learn what common plants and roots were edible. He liked woodworking, but the white slave welcomed the opportunity to get away with the women, gathering food. His survival knowledge grew each day.

The next morning Chet was surprised and glad to see that he and Wooden Hand would be staying in that day to work on finishing the cedar planks they had been gathering all week. The boy was set to work sanding the planks like before, but Wooden Hand was busy measuring an already finished board in preparation for sectioning the plank into four equal units. After marking the divisions by scribing with an iron tool, the old craftsman meticulously formed a `V' shaped notch along the length of the scribed lines.

The notching took all morning to complete, and, after a snack of fish for lunch, the old slave grabbed a small box from his sleeping place and he and Chet carried the plank outside. On the beach in front of the house Wooden Hand measured out three lines in the sand and had Chet dig one-foot deep narrow ditches where the lines were. Meanwhile, the old Haida slave set about starting a fire from sticks and tinder he carried in the box. By the time the ditches were dug, the old man had a roaring blaze going. The two slaves collected as many small stones as they could hold and put them in the fire to heat. They piled seaweed near the ditches and dipped a wooden box in the water of Nootka Sound, filled it, and returned it to the trenches. When the stones were pink with heat, the old man used long wooden tongs to pick up the rocks and distribute them into each of the three ditches, piling some of the seaweed over the rocks as he went. Water was added and steam began to rise. Without wasting time the old man grasped the plank and set it, notched side down, over the three steaming ditches. The ditches were aligned so the kerfs of the plank took the steam straight on and the hot water vapor served to soften the wood. Handfuls of seaweed were piled on top of the plank, over the grooved lines, more hot stones were laid on top, and then more seaweed. Water again was added, resulting in the kerf and grooved lines being heated with steam from top and bottom.

"White Clam, stay here and watch the steam. Add water as necessary," the old slave said as he sprinkled water drops on the seaweed and hot stones. Chet understood this command and took the wooden water box from the old man. Wooden Hand then walked back into the house and shortly returned with a wooden stud, about two by four shape and a *bender board* made of two cedar slats bound and spaced to allow the end of the plank to fit through the opening.

"Now, White Clam, we bend the box," the old craftsman exclaimed. By this time Chet knew the word for box and it was the first inkling he had of what they were making. When the kerf and grooves were soft, the old man sat the stud on the plank next to the first kerf and slipped the bender board over the end. While standing on the stud, he grasped the bender board and lifted the end of the plank, making a 90-degree angle. The soft wood bent without cracking and he quickly moved on to the next kerf. He soon had all three corners bent and joining the notches on the two plank ends made the fourth corner. After placing diagonal premeasured sticks on the inside, the whole outside was bound with cedar bark rope, and a perfectly square box open at both ends was the result. A top and bottom for the box would be crafted later.

Chet was amazed at the engineering of the box and the painstaking way the old craftsman made the corners fit so precisely. He had a growing appreciation for the Haida slave and thought him not a savage at all. The next few days were spent making five more boxes, and the remaining planks were used by Wooden Hand to make the tops and bottoms. This was very precise work, and after Chet sectioned the boards into their rough sizes, he was of no further use to the woodworker.

Late that afternoon as the white boy was watching the old slave trimming a box top to fit, Swimming Otter and his brother walked past with an array of fishing gear and nets. Chet watched the nobleman walk by and half smiled, nodding when he made eye contact, but got no response in return. The two Indians continued on to one of the small twenty-foot canoes and made preparations to launch. The boy went back to watching Wooden Hand, feeling a little bored and noticing the cold now that there was no physical labor to be done. Just as Chet was beginning to think of how nice it would be to be sitting in front of his dad's fireplace at home, a hail from the water's edge caught his ear.

"Old man," Swimming Otter yelled. "Do you have need of the white slave?"

"No, master," returned Wooden Hand. "Boy, go quick, your master has a use for you. Learn well what he teaches you, for it is a privilege you are getting."

Chet didn't understand all that the Haida slave said, but he knew that the upper classes did not always let common slaves hunt or fish, and only those of great worth were allowed to do anything but menial labor. The boy jumped up and ran to the canoe, where the master gave him a paddle and motioned the white slave to the middle of the boat. Water Bear, the plump brother of Swimming Otter, was already in the bow and Chet helped push the craft into Nootka Sound, jumping over the gunwale at the last second. The wet salt water on his legs sent a chill up the boy's back but the hard work of paddling soon warmed him sufficiently.

The canoe was soon cruising past the village and Chet was glad to be at sea again, even if only in a dugout. The boy watched the Indian in front of him and tried to mimic the short powerful stroke and return flip of Water Bear. The Nootkan made the most of his energy, never splashing the water with the paddle end, entering and exiting with surgical precision. After a few minutes Chet was able to stay in sequence with the Indian and not splash as much, but the young man did ease up on the strength of his stroke. His arm was already beginning to tire.

White Clam's struggles to learn and please did not go unnoticed, and although he disliked all whites as a rule, Swimming Otter was pleased with this new slave. Not only did the white boy shame Two Skins, but also White Clam's willingness to learn the Indian ways and his wearing of the Mowachaht clothing was already causing talk among the noble class. The more worthy the boy was, the more humiliation he would cause the scar faced one in the summer meeting.

"Brother, White Clam tries hard to copy you," Swimming Otter exclaimed. "I have decided to teach this one to fish and hunt. We will sing his praises at the fires of all our friends. When I raise my spirit pole in the summer and give gifts to Two Skins, we will have the joy of hearing the laughter of the people when they talk of how the white boy escaped death from the scar faced one and how he has flourished as a slave."

The fat Indian stopped paddling and looked back at his brother, lifting the brow of his cedar hat as he spoke.

"You know that Two Skins will demand the life of the boy because he stole his bear robe. Even though this will be a potlatch, it may be more than the scar faced one can deal with, and there may be bloodshed."

"If Two Skins kills the boy, we will kill him. His village can seek no revenge since they will be my guests and the boy is my property. Two Skins is a bad one and it is only a matter of time before he will do wrong to our people."

Chet wondered what all this talk was about, but he kept paddling. Eventually the two Indians quit talking and joined in with him again. They rounded a spit of land and headed close to shore next to an outcropping of rock that lifted straight out of the water. On top of the rock were nesting gulls that greeted the intruders with screams and flapping wings. The trio were not interested in them and, in fact, the gull was a bird that the Mowachahts neither hunted or bothered.

The water was about ten feet deep and there were patches of long green and red seaweed growing up from the sandy bottom. Water Bear took an eight foot cedar pole with a dip net lashed to the end and stood up in the bow, waiting. They were motionless for about five minutes before Swimming Otter quietly lifted his hand and pointed. One moment later the plump Indian with the cedar hat drove the poled net into the water and Chet saw a flash of silver as the tiny fish disappeared. Water Bear raised the dripping net up and turned it back towards the white slave, dumping it onto the floor of the canoe. A dozen eight-inch fish flopped and struggled, their silver and blue-black bodies catching Chet's eye. The Indians grabbed the fish, placing them in a special bait box filled with seawater and constructed so that it fit into the narrow constrictions of the bow between the sides of the canoe. After the lid was placed on the box, they headed for deeper water.

The sleek craft cut through the waves at a good speed and Chet thought that if he ever tried to steal a canoe again, he would have to paddle at night, because there would be no way the white boy could outrun Nootkas in pursuit. About a half-mile offshore the canoe came to a rest and the two Indian fishermen began to attach fine fishing lines, made of shredded cedar bark, to wooden floats carved in the shape of different animals and birds. The other end connected to a large yew wood and bone hook. The hooks seemed too large and cumbersome to be of any use, and Chet felt they couldn't possibly catch anything. The Indians tied smooth, oblong rocks to the line about two feet from the hooks, to be used as weights, and set the lines aside. Water Bear took one of the baitfish and promptly killed it with a whack of a cedar club, then tossed it to Swimming Otter. The master took a mussel shell knife and made a ventral cut along the fish's belly exposing the entrails, causing bleeding, but leaving it intact. He then slipped the bone barb through the operculum, past the gills and back out the mouth, turning the fish so it fit snuggly against the yew wood but leaving the barb exposed. After the other line was fitted in the same way, they were set aside, and the two Indians took a moment for what seemed like prayer.

"Great halibut spirit, thank you for giving your body to me and allowing this human to eat and live. Thank you for allowing me to send your spirit to the other world. May your spirit live for eternity and may your friends return to this place in greater numbers." As Swimming Otter finished his speech the two Indians tossed the lines in the water and let the hooks drop to the bottom. They tied off the floats and waited.

Chet was watching all this with fascination and thought how he could make some improvements on the hook design. The young man was sure of one thing though, a hook was another item that he would want to make and add to his collection of survival gear. After about ten minutes one of the floats was bobbing slightly and there was evidence of a fish on the line.

"Brother, set the hook and let White Clam make the haul," the warrior said calmly as they all watched the float disappear under the water.

The round Mowachaht braced his belly against the gunwale of the canoe, and when he was sure the hook was swallowed, Water Bear gave a terrific yank, setting the hook. Immediately, there was a strong tug on the line and the Indian motioned for Chet to come nearer and as the boy did, the fisherman gave Chet the line, frantically giving the order to haul it in. As Swimming Otter laughed, the boy pulled the line slowly aboard. It felt like it had a dead weight, not too heavy, but not putting up much of a fight either. Water Bear continued to coach the action and soon there was an eighteen-inch halibut flopping in the boat. The two Indians were noticeably annoyed with the small size, but Chet thought it was a fair sight.

The white slave was handed a club and ended the halibut's struggle with a few hard blows to its flat head. The two Indians then re-set the lines and threw them back over the side, hoping for a bigger fish this time.

The next half hour brought nothing but lost fish and stolen bait. They were down to the last fresh herring, as the clouds grew darker. The sky looked threatening and just, as it appeared Swimming Otter was giving up, his float took a dive and he gave the line a yank. It was a solid strike, and a big fish this time. The master gave his line to the slave boy and Chet knew immediately that this was no ordinary flounder. The white slave had to brace himself against the gunwale and strain at the line. This time he was not winning the battle, and as the cedar rope cut deep into his palms it was all Chet could do to keep even with the fish, much less pull it in. The two Indians were yelling their encouragement and Chet sensed that this was more than just another fish. The boy knew Swimming Otter wanted him to land the fish without help and he reached deep inside himself for strength, slowly gaining inch by inch on the heavy fish. Chet used his long legs to gain leverage and the canoe tipped dangerously, making the two Indians lean back to balance it. Suddenly, the dead weight gave and the slave boy gained by the foot. He was winning now and it renewed his strength.

The battle lasted half an hour. Finally, Chet saw the flash of the two huge eyes in their crooked sockets and the huge dark brown body. Water Bear took a long slender yew wood spear, and as he poised to lance the great fish, the boy relaxed for an instant. At the last moment the hundred pound halibut gave one last attempt to break free in a whirl of splashing fins.

Before Chet knew what had happened, he felt the bitter cold bite of the salt water engulf him. The young man sank below the surface on impact and his arms were so tired that he could not bring himself back up. It seemed like the end. All at once something ripped at his hair, his body shot out of the water, his mouth caught fresh air, and he was hung over the side of the canoe, doubled over at the waist and coughing.

Just as the huge halibut had jerked the boy overboard, Water Bear let go with the yew shaft and caught the huge fish behind the boney gill plate. Swimming Otter had grabbed the cedar line that Chet had given up and held the prize while his brother worked a loop of bark rope around the halibut's tail. The big Indian tied the fish off to the center thwart tail first and beat it to death with the club. After the priorities were handled, the two Indians paddled a few quick strokes to the boy and the master pulled him out of the water by the hair. The two Mowachahts were pleased with the turn of events and patted the slave boy on the back as much for praise as to get him breathing again.

After pulling Chet into the dugout they stripped him down to the bare skin, rubbing and massaging his limbs. Water Bear wrapped the boy in his shredded bark cloak and set him against the side of the canoe opposite the huge fish. The halibut was still in the water, tied by its tail, and because of its massive weight it would be towed home instead of hoisted aboard.

The dead drag of the fish made for slower going, but the two Nootkas allowed White Clam to rest until they rounded the spit of land and saw the village.

"White Clam, put on your wet garment and leave your chest bare," exclaimed the proud master, as he handed the boy the soggy bark garment. "You have strength again. Take this paddle now, and bring your prize home."

Shivering, the boy put on the dress and took the paddle but could not stop shaking as he dug the blade into the water. Both noblemen were making war hoop noises and the village was aroused. Soon a hundred people were following the path of the canoe along the beach and Swimming Otter paused in front of the chief's house, calling for all to listen. Hearing the commotion outside, Standing Seal left his warm hearth and joined the crowd by the half-beached dugout. Talking Boy was right behind and the gathering heard the brothers boast about how White Clam had captured the mighty fish, and how the boy was filled with great spirits. The crowd was in awe as Water Bear held up Chet's wet blanket and told how the boy jumped in the water to fight the halibut and killed the fish with his teeth. It was a good show indeed.

Swimming Otter invited all who wished to come to *Whale Oil House* and partake of the fresh fish. They continued on down the beach with the crowd following along and pulled the canoe out of the water. It took three or four men to haul the carcass up on the rocks and the slave women went to work skinning and filleting the huge body. Each chunk was wrapped in seaweed for roasting and a fire pit was already being dug, while fresh coals were brought out from the house fires. Unlike salmon, the white meat of the halibut did not dry or smoke well so it would be better eaten that night, and the whole village joined in helping with the preparations.

Talking Boy had come over to Chet and saw that the boy was still trying to keep from shivering. The Salish lad called for Wooden Hand and the old man took Chet back toward the house. The English-speaking slave then turned towards Swimming Otter.

"Great warrior, whaler, and master of the white one," Talking Boy interrupted. "Excuse me, master, but I had the old slave take White Clam inside to warm his white body that feels the cold so easily. He will be better when he feels the bear coat of Two Skins around his back."

"You are a wise one beyond your years, Salish slave," said Swimming Otter eyeing him suspiciously. "But you have pleased me and acted well. Go tell the boy he is in my favor, warm him with the bear skin from the scar faced one, and bring him back out wearing it."

Talking Boy turned and trotted to the house and found the other two slaves inside by the hearth fire. He found the bear skin on Chet's sleeping platform and took it to the boy. Wooden Hand was talking in Haida and seemed quite pleased with his protégé.

"Talking Boy, did he really jump in and bite the halibut to death?" asked the old man trying to look at Chet's teeth.

"Let's ask him," said the Salish slave.

Chet laughed with surprise when he was told what the two brothers had said and set about telling the truth about the fishing expedition. Talking Boy told the white boy how it was a great feat to battle the halibut as Chet did and no one need know the real truth, as it was Swimming Otter's story and would be fine the way it was told.

"Here, take this bearskin and come back out to the feast and enjoy your good fortune," Talking Boy said. "It isn't often that a slave is complimented this way."

Talking Boy knew that the good fortune would only be short-lived and that Swimming Otter was using the boy for his own selfish gains against the scar faced rival. But that was the Indian way, for wealth and power were related to rivalry, and shaming a rival, either by giving gifts to him or by exploiting his failures, was an excepted practice. Any way a man could gain wealth and power was usually worth the expense, even if innocent slaves lost their lives. It was a part of their culture that had evolved over hundreds of years.

When Chet returned to the beach, the fire in the pit was roaring and the great halibut was all but cut up. A large pile of sliced chunks wrapped in seaweed, over a hundred fillets, stood in readiness. Women were bringing baskets of dried bulbs and potatoes and wrapping them in cedar mats. Soon the fire was put out and the hot coals covered with a thin layer of sand. As the women laid the wrapped chunks of fish in the pit, Swimming Otter took great care to take the head, backbone, and tail of the huge halibut, and, while saying another prayer to the fish spirit, he tossed the remains back in the sea.

After the wrapped fish, potatoes, and bulbs were in the pit, the men covered the food with sand and started another fire on top of the pit. The sun had set now and other villagers brought out long cedar poles, split at one end, with shredded bark and spruce pitch wedged in the crack. They set these on fire and stuck them in the sand around the roasting pit. The long burning torches gave additional light to the gathering, and for the next hour there was socializing, gambling and game playing.

Chet sat by the fire with his bearskin wrapped tightly around him and took in the festivities. Every once in awhile a Nootka child would run up and stare at him and when the white boy showed his teeth the child would scream and run away. They must have put fear in the children with all the wild stories Chet thought. But at least he was the center of attention for something other then being the tallest and whitest person in the village.

Tantalizing aromas began drifting out of the pit and soon the men were busy putting the fire out. They carefully scraped away the coals and layer of sand, exposing the chunks of tender white fish. The upper class was fed first, as usual, dipping the fillets in small boxes of whale and seal oil, after which the common people took their fill.

Chet was the first slave offered any of the fresh fish and there was one whole fillet saved for him. He passed on the seal oil, but the potatoes were great and the cattail bulbs had a nice crunch to them, though little taste. The boy finished off with some dried berry cakes and a long cool drink of fresh water. It was the best meal Chet had had in two weeks. As he returned to *Whale Oil House* and his sleeping platform, the white boy felt confident that he would survive this ordeal and make it back to his people some day.

The boy lay down on the hard floor of planks and snuggled in the bearskin and cedar bark. He thought of Lucy, and his friends, Matt and Andrew, and wondered if they thought him dead. Well, not Lucy anyway, for she would have had no knowledge of his adventures the past two weeks, which was just as well. The young man thought of his mother and father in their cozy farmhouse in Oregon. He thought perhaps he was a little hasty in wanting to leave such a life. Farming didn't seem so bad right now. Chet shook his and tried not to second-guess himself anymore. What's done is done. For now, at least, the young man felt secure in the great cedar house and soon fell fast asleep.

IX

The first day in December was cold but partly clear with little rain and no snow. The village was buzzing with excitement, for on this day they would be packing up all their belongings and their food supplies and heading east, up the Sound to their winter village at Nesook. Chet was sorry to hear of this turn of events, because it meant they would be far away from the course of any coastal ship that might stop at Nootka Sound. He knew from talking with the old slave that the village would be gone for at least four months, so any plans of escape or rescue looked pretty dim until spring.

Nesook was at the head of a river valley that had high cliffs surrounding it, which formed a protective barrier against cold north winds and winter storms. The bay the river flowed into was part of Nootka Sound and was abundant with oysters, clams, mussels, flounder, and most of all, herring and sea otter. The river contained an early winter run of salmon, which would help keep the Mowachahts in fresh food.

That day the whole village was up at first light moving boxes, baskets and chests full of goods and food out to the beach. Swimming Otter was busy giving orders sending Chet and the other slave men up on the roof of *Whale Oil House* to lower down the roof planking. The planking was to be used in lashing pairs of canoes together to form a platform for carrying the cargo and also to be used to roof the winter houses at Nesook. Extra planking was taken off the side of the house also, but not all of it. The house frames at Nesook were smaller, and, therefore, less cedar boards were needed to cover the sides.

The villagers continued to work throughout the morning, and by early afternoon the first canoes left. Chet, Wooden Hand, and the other slaves carried the extra canoes to the back of the house frame, where they turned them upside down to protect them from the winter weather. In past years all of the canoes would have been taken on the journey, but with the loss of over half their population to smallpox the last two years, a surplus of material goods, including dugouts, remained.

The white boy was assigned to one of the large paired canoes next to the old slave and close to the master, which he now understood to be a place of great importance among slaves. The skill in paddling he had learned on the halibut expedition was put to good use immediately. Men, women, and children alike bent to the task of paddling the huge catamaran out into the cove, and after a few minutes they were setting a smooth pace and singing while they paddled. A light rain was falling and being on the water made the cold weather feel worse, so Chet tried to join in on the chorus to keep his mind off the freezing sting on his hands.

Not having eaten that morning or afternoon was starting to affect the boy's strength and after two hours of wet work, he was glad to feel the wind pick up and see the setting of a crude cedar bark-and-cattail mat sail. The canoers lashed a pole to one of the thwarts up front and hoisted a boom and sail up the pole. Since there was no centerboard, the wind had to be favorable and directly behind the craft. The catamaran configuration helped, but every five minutes they had to correct their course by crabbing with the paddles, and if the wind became a cross or head wind, the sail would be of no use at all. The boy thought he could show the Nootkas the error of their ways by designing a plank that could be lashed and used as a centerboard, but Chet knew his crude use of their language would not allow him sufficient dialogue to make himself understood.

Darkness had already fallen as they turned southeast into Nesook Bay and spruce pitch torches on the beach from the earlier arrivals made navigation to shore an easy task. Another fifteen minutes brought them to the river mouth and Chet was looking forward to an expected rest. He was not going to get it, however, for no sooner had they landed, than orders from Swimming Otter sent people here and there making more torches and unloading the cargo. The canoes were separated and the white slave, along with the other men, set about covering the winter house frame with planks from *Whale Oil House*.

The new house was older and quite a bit smaller, so the work of lashing on the sides went fairly fast. The smaller winter house had an advantage of staying warmer, and Chet would be thankful for that in the cold months to come. The house had no name but Chet called it *Little Oil House* for fun. When the work was finally finished, the family and slaves of Swimming Otter's house brought their belongings inside and sleeping areas were designated. Things were a little more cramped, but the white boy was able to have some privacy behind a stack of boxes. After putting on all of his white man clothes and an extra wool trade blanket from Cattail Woman, Chet felt warm enough to sleep. As he lay there, the young man realized there had been no food that day and he dreamed of having hot flapjacks, butter and maple syrup for breakfast. He could almost smell the hot butter melting over the cakes. Returning to reality, Chet knew that the dried salmon and berry cakes in the morning would only serve to keep him alive and not really fulfill his hunger for *real* food.

Swimming Otter and Wooden Hand left the next morning before Chet had awakened. Talking Boy, who stopped by for breakfast, told Chet that Wooden Hand and Swimming Otter had gone to the master's family stand of timber to pick out a lofty cedar tree for the carving of a new spirit pole for *Whale Oil House*. This was a big undertaking, and only the very rich could afford to make this commitment. Swimming Otter's family had been gaining stature and wealth the last fifty years and only the epidemic of smallpox had curbed its growth. It was a crushing disease for the Nootkas and reduced their population by almost two thirds, including the master's wife and only son. The raising of this pole would be the first in recent memory and a tribute to the warrior-whaler's family.

Chet noticed that the young Salish Indian was warming up to him and by now the white boy was fairly sure that Talking Boy was not Mowachaht. Chet was still not sure if Talking Boy was a slave or just a commoner who had gained status through his talent with language. In any case it was nice to know that the young Indian was not the tyrant he had made himself out to be and talk of killing had not been mentioned for some time. With his new position as favorite slave, Chet felt the courage to question the young Indian.

"Talking Boy," Chet started with some hesitation, "I've noticed that you don't seem to be Mowachaht. Your color and features are different and you treat the slaves with respect. Are you from another tribe?"

The Indian slave knew he had been found out, but since they were becoming friends, his original plan to use fear to get what he needed from the white boy seemed unnecessary and Talking Boy decided to tell the truth.

"You are correct, White Clam. I am not of the Nootka. I come from the Salish people many miles south of here. My talent as a master of ceremony and language upgraded my status when the white man's disease killed off noblemen of this tribe. Without that pox killer you and I would have long since been killed, I'm sure. The village needs bodies and slaves are treated better now."

The young Indian stopped and stared into the distance as though this melancholy conversation had brought out old wounds.

"How come you never tried to escape and go back to your people?" Chet asked.

"I have thought of it much and in fact I was hoping your presence here might offer a way to flee this land, perhaps on one of your white man's sailing ships," Talking Boy replied. "To leave by oneself would be foolish in this land."

The Salish boy seemed ashamed that he had not tried to leave before, but this life was not too far different from his own, and after the death of so many Nootkas and his rise in stature, he seemed to think less of leaving until Chet arrived.

"White Clam, you must not talk of leaving to anyone, for it would mean a quick death. Perhaps we can make a plan for this summer. You could come with me to my people, for they take no slaves and you would be a free man." The Salish lad thought of telling Chet of his fate when and if Two Skins ever made it back to Chahakquot or Nesook, but he decided that there was no use in making him fear for his life yet.

While Swimming Otter and Wooden Hand were gone, Chet was told to help Cattail Woman gather food, mostly shellfish and bulbs. Chet liked the plump middle-aged woman and she liked him. There were times when she would sneak the boy some extra food and the slave woman always was concerned about the way his head had been healing. She told him to relax in half Nootkan and half sign language and as soon as the tide was out they would leave to dig clams.

In the meantime Chet sat back and watched her as she was preparing some cedar bark for the making of baskets or clothing. From a large box of water Cattail Woman had taken a bundle of folded bark and removed the ties. The bark had been soaking all night and was soft and pliable. Grabbing the end of the long bark strip with both hands and folding it back and forth caused the several layers of bark to separate. She then methodically beat the length of bark until it started to shred. After about five feet of bark was shredded, the old woman took a sharp knife and cut the shredded length and continued to soften it by working it back and forth in her hands, rubbing in some animal fat and seal oil to soften it further.

All the while Cattail Woman talked to the white boy, repeating the Nootkan words and letting him say them in return. Chet was pleased with this language lesson and was eager to learn more. It was obvious that the Nootkas enjoyed it when White Clam tried to be like them, and the white slave was determined to learn as much as he could. Chet was not sure if he would ever be allowed to leave, but learning the language could help him while he stayed. The white boy knew his master liked it when he tried to be more like the Indians and Chet knew he was treated better when he did.

Even this bark shredding that seemed so simple a thing was of tremendous importance. It was the beginning of how the Nootkas made all their clothing, rope, fishing line, hats, and baskets. The boy thought that if it took months to paddle back to Oregon, knowing this one process would be extremely important. Remembering all the Indian canoes sighted during the trip up north on the Exact, Chet knew he would not feel safe in a canoe during the day. Any tribe might take him as a slave if he had no protection or weapons, so the young man would have to travel at night. By traveling at night Chet would miss any chance of hailing a passing ship, but the odds of finding one close to shore where he would have to paddle his canoe would be low anyway.

The thought of paddling down Vancouver Island with all its small coves, islets, and inlets didn't bother Chet, but the rugged Washington coast with its fifteen-foot breakers did. He might have to go back into Puget Sound and find a white settlement like Lucy's. The more Chet thought about Puget Sound, the better he liked the idea. It would be safer and, the boy had to admit, he missed Lucy.

The thought of having the young Salish slave as an ally presented new possibilities. An extra body at the paddles would come in handy and Chet thought that if Talking Boy could be trusted; maybe the two of them could just pull it off. The white boy needed a plan and would start formulating it as soon as possible.

"We go now, tanassis-check-up," Cattail Woman called.

She called him son and Chet thought that sounded all right, and he called her mom.

"Let's go then, hooma-hexa," the boy replied, watching for a reaction.

The plump little slave stopped in her tracks and turned with a big smile. She mumbled something and turned to pick up her gathering basket and digging stick, laughed a little, and motioned for Chet to follow.

All of the women were gathering their baskets and sticks and Chet was amazed at how they knew it would be low tide, for none of them had been outside all morning. Personally, Chet had never given the tide a second thought, but as the gatherers emerged from the house, sure enough the tide had receded and the bay was left exposed. The water was shallow everywhere and as they rounded the mouth of the Nesook river the mud flats stretched out for a hundred yards. Some of the other women and children were already at work, but there was no rush. Each family had its own shellfish area.

A few minute's walking through the squishy mud brought them to the clam beds. Chet took off his moccasins and let the cold mud ooze between his toes. There were almost no rocks on this beach, which was quite different from Chahakquot, where one-inch pebbles were dominant.

Cattail Woman had a basket strapped to her back and stopped to take it off. She put on her cedar bark hat and motioned for Chet to pick up the basket and follow her. Within a few feet a quick stream of water shot vertically from the sand into the air and almost hit the woman in the face. She fell to the ground and attacked the sand with her stick, using it like a shovel to scoop the sand away. After a few minutes she pulled out a long geoduck clam shell, smiled, and plopped it in the basket. Cattail Woman continued in this way for an hour with varying amounts of success.

"White Clam, come count with me," the Nootkan slave said as she picked up the clams. "Sah-wauk, att-la, kat-sa, mooh, soo-chah," Cattail Woman counted, one, two, three, four, five. The tide was already turning, but the Indian woman worked for another hour and got six more of the large geoducks.

"Boy, you must find a suitable stick for digging, and we will get twice as many tomorrow."

She pointed Chet in the direction of the high tide driftwood piles and picked up her stick, turning it around in a digging motion.

"Kom-me-tak, I understand," Chet said, and took off up the beach in search of a good piece of driftwood.

It was turning into a nice afternoon and as the white slave strolled up the beach, he noticed his surroundings in detail for the first time. The mountains seemed to be right on top of him, rising thousands of feet high. Their tops were already capped with snow, and the lush green forest was thick all the way above the snowline. The bay was picturesque, dotted here and there with small islets of rock and trees. Large kelp beds, where sea-otter families raised their young, were abundant. The smell of salt air and evergreen mixed in a pleasant, relaxing way.

Chet was enjoying this leisurely walk because it was the first time he had been able to be alone. The boy wasn't really as intent on finding a stick as he was to round a point of land to the west and see what could be seen. On the way the young man picked up and rejected several sticks, finally keeping a spruce branch that would serve as a walking stick. As he walked around the bend and out of sight of Nesook, Chet continued to search for a digging tool. Spotting a great collection of wood and debris at the high tide line, he went for a closer look. As the boy approached the largest log surveyed the jumbled wood, he thought of the two nights he had slept on the beach after his escape from Two Skins. Chet wondered where the half-breed was right now and the thought brought shivers down his back.

How could humans be so cold blooded?

The white boy knew the Nootka warrior meant for him to die and only the Indians' rush for whiskey and his own hard head saved him. He felt safe with Swimming Otter and knew that the master had no love for the scar faced Indian, but Chet knew the time would come when Two Skins would cross his path again. He just hoped his rescue would happen before such a time.

Chet continued searching for a piece of cedar wood for his digging tool, and thought he saw a suitable piece a few yards away, sticking out from behind a large log. The boy walked over and took hold of the stick and gave it a pull, but the wood didn't budge. He couldn't figure what would be holding it, so Chet straddled the log and looked at the other side. To his amazement, there, staring him in the face was the whole boom section of a topsail rig from a schooner.

X

The boy wasn't quite sure what he had found. It looked like the mizzen gaff-topsail or a masthead staysail of a schooner with most of the boom, crosstrees and upper mast intact. The sail had some serious gashes in it, but seemed in strong condition. There was abundant cordage wrapped around the wreckage and under the sand. There were also two wooden block and pulleys in a weatherworn, but serviceable state.

Chet had a whirl of thoughts racing through his head. He was not sure what to make of his find. The young man did know that he wanted to keep the discovery a secret from his Indian captors, so he set about excavating the wreckage, saving as much of the sail, cable, and mast work as possible. He found a small thicket in the dense evergreen forest just back of the beach and made half a dozen trips carrying the tattered rigging to his hiding place. The thrill of finding something civilized boosted the boy's spirits. For some time the white slave had been pondering the chances of escape. With his new Salish ally, Talking Boy, and the procurement of this schooner wreckage, Chet thought he now had the material and personnel for the beginnings of a plan.

The short winter day was coming to an end as Chet made his way back to Nesook and the warmth of the great house. He had picked up a five-foot plank outside the village and brought it inside with him. Cattail Woman greeted his return with a smile from her old round cheeks and a warm concoction of clam soup. The brew did not have much taste but the rubbery clam strips were nourishing and the broth was warm. *What I'd give for some hot apple pie with sugar and cinnamon*, the boy thought. *And a cold glass of milk.*

Chet daydreamed about white man's food for a while longer until he noticed that the chubby little slave woman was starting to work on her bark again. The boy sat there watching her take the long strands of bark and separate them into fine threads. She took two fine strands and knotted them together, placing the knot over her toe and twisting the threads to the right making a tight two-ply line. The white boy watched this intently, remembering the ripped sail and knowing stout line would be needed to sew the tattered ends back together.

"Old woman, may I try that?" Chet asked, motioning with his hands to make up for the lack of language. Cattail Woman gave him a silly look and giggle, but handed the boy some bark thread. With some practice Chet was able to make a strong string and was quite pleased with himself.

The other women in the house were also watching, and they were quite pleased as well to see White Clam try to do their tasks. The white slave was rapidly becoming one of their favorites, as he always had something nice to say or a helping hand to give. To such women who knew little respect, even these small courtesies went a long way in building loyalties, and the young white man would always be welcome at anyone's cooking pot in the cold winter days to come.

Chet almost forgot the cedar plank from outside and, grabbing it, he turned to the slave woman.

"Old woman...Mother," he continued. "If you would let me have some of that shredded bark, I will make you a special digging stick."

Chet was not sure she understood, so he went about gathering a few tools anyway and started making his clam shovel. The boy took a knife and notched the plank deeply on both sides a foot from the end. He split out the long ends of the plank, leaving a two-inch by two-inch shaft and a one-foot square blade. After two hours Chet had a makeshift wooden clam shovel with a fire tempered wooden blade, all from a single piece of planking. Cattail

Woman didn't know what to make of it, but she gave the bark twine to White Clam anyway. The white boy indicated he would show her in the morning how to use it and retired to his plank bed.

Colder winds blew all night, and as Chet wrapped up in the bearskin he thought he might look for some clay along the river in the morning and chink up the cracks between the siding planks to make his sleeping area less drafty. The cold didn't seem to bother the Nootkas as they still dressed rather scantily, but Chet had no intention of freezing to death just to try to prove he was as tough as anyone else, which he wasn't.

Lying there listening to the wind, Chet wondered if he could trust the young English-speaking slave. How badly did the Salish Indian want to get home? After all, this life was not too different from Talking Boy's own life on Puget Sound. For Chet, life in Nesook was a complete change, worth giving up his life to leave, but for Talking Boy it might not be worth the risk. And what of the wreckage? How could the boy make use of the masthead and sheet? Chet started formulating a plan, and he kept coming back to his original thought of stealing a canoe. But this time the young man took the plan one step further, thinking he could rig the torn sail and boom to an Indian dugout. With the cordage, canvas, blocks, and boom Chet thought his smaller stolen canoe would be more efficient than the crude sails on the large dugouts that would be sent after him. With increased efficiency and lighter weight the white slave thought he might be able to out-distance any pursuer.

Chet remembered the first trips on the small cutter with Matt. The boy opened his eyes and stared up into the rafters of the huge cedar house. The glow of the dying fires cast a dim shadow on the roof planks. He could barely make out the cedar slats in the darkness. But as his eyes cleared and his night vision sharpened, Chet noticed a small shingle-sized piece of cedar, blown and twisted by the wind, sticking down through the roof planks. *That's it,* he thought. The shingle reminded him of the centerboard. At that moment the young man relived the journey from Chahakquot and the thought he had of designing a centerboard that could be lashed to the side of a dugout. That would be his advantage over the Nootkas. He would be able to use his centerboard canoe with any wind. The prevailing southwest wind would only allow the Indians to paddle when heading south while Chet could sail close hauled.

He was almost too excited to sleep. Chet decided to make an attempt to see Talking Boy in the morning and start broadening their rapport. He also decided to keep any plan of the escape to himself for the time being.

By this time White Clam had become a familiar sight to the Nootkas, and it was of no surprise that his comings and goings were almost unnoticed. This morning his travel to the house of Standing Seal was something new. The white boy brought his newly made clam shovel on the premise that he wanted Talking Boy to help translate its proper use, but all the while Chet was intent on winning the Salish Indian's trust.

"Good morning, Talking Boy. I came to show you my shovel. It's a diggin' stick," Chet tried to explain.

The white boy motioned with leg and hand, but he could not make himself understood.

"It's for diggin' clams in the sand," he finally said in English.

With all this commotion some of the other Nootkas gathered around trying to figure out the crude wooden tool, shaking their heads and looking puzzled.

"White Clam, this stick is no good for digging. It is made of cedar. It is too wide and weak. It will break," the English-speaking slave returned.

"Well I was hopin' you'd come along with me this mornin' and help me try it out with Cattail Woman."

"You don't need me, White Clam. Besides, I don't dig clams," answered Talking Boy in a show of disgust for menial labor.

"It would be a good chance to do some talkin'," Chet said with a gleam in his eye. "We could talk about Puget Sound."

The young Indian recognized this name to be the white man's word for the large inlet that led to his people's territory.

"Perhaps it would be amusing to watch this new wooden tool after all," the Indian said, and turned to put on his bark clothing. "I will find you on the beach after the water has left."

The young slave didn't know the English word for tide but Chet understood what he meant and returned to Swimming Otter's house.

The white slave spent the next two hours helping Cattail Woman with her rope making, storing some of it for his own use. After helping Water Bear make some roof plank repairs, Chet was off to the beach with the women. The rain started shortly after they arrived at the clam beds and within a few minutes Talking Boy showed up with a broad smile on his face.

"All right, white one, let us see how the clam stick works," chuckled the Salish slave.

Cattail woman started her methodical search and soon found a water jet streaming upward, signaling the clam below. The white boy wasted no time in attacking the sand with his shovel. The first three thrusts in the soft sand netted great volumes of excavated material, but the fourth shove with his moccasined foot gave way to a tell-tale *crack* and the right side of the shovel blade split cleanly, leaving a one inch wide area where there were four inches before.

"I told you so," laughed Talking Boy. "You were doing well for a few moments."

Cattail Woman was not pleased with Talking Boy's laughter. She wanted White Clam to succeed. Eyeing the broken shovel the old slave took out her iron knife. Cattail Woman took the shovel from Chet and buried the blade in the sand with one push of her foot. The stocky slave woman then placed her iron knife blade on the intact side of the shovel blade, one inch from the shaft and struck the knife with a mighty blow from her digging stick. The other side of the shovel blade broke to match the side Chet had broken. The result was a thinner shovel blade four inches total in width with a long two-inch wide shaft.

"Now the stick is good," Cattail Woman smiled as she held it up, and went to work scooping out the clam hole.

The new design worked well and Cattail Woman was quite pleased with it.

"White Clam is a smart boy."

The two young men helped the women gather clams until the tide started to flood. Then the two played more then they helped, wrestling each other in the mud, and stripping off their bark clothing for quick runs through the waves. Chet was enjoying his new friend and both boys forgot all about their talk of escape. By the time they returned to the village, the white boy was chilled through and after washing the sand off in the river, Chet and Talking Boy went into Swimming Otter's house to warm up by the fire.

Water Bear had just returned from fishing with his catch, three plump rockfish for the cooking pot. The young men asked him if they might be able to go fishing with him the next day. Water Bear knew Swimming Otter wanted Chet to help with the supply of fresh food during the winter encampment, so he agreed to let the two slaves go, but only after they had stored up a supply of firewood. Chet pulled on his pants and bark poncho, borrowed an old cedar hat and shoulder strap basket from Cattail Woman and the boys set out for a load of driftwood. The Nootkan hat shed the rain like an umbrella and Chet stayed much warmer with pants on. Inside of an hour they had a good pile of wood stacked under cover. Chet wanted to make one more trip and asked Talking Boy to follow him.

"You know I think it's very possible that if we are careful and make right choices," Chet started, "there is no reason why we could not escape from this place."

The white slave stopped and sat down on a drift log, slipping the basket off his back.

Talking Boy turned and threw a pebble into the sea.

"My river valley is a beautiful place," he gazed as he spoke. "I am with you, White Clam, but we must wait until spring or the sea and winter cold will swallow us for sure. Standing Seal and Swimming Otter will return all the people to Chahakquot in two, three moons at most. We must leave then, it will be too dangerous to stay further."

"March," Chet thought to himself. "I thought we could steal some dried fish and essentials like rope and line and clothing just before we left. And a canoe," Chet added. "We must have a good fast canoe with extra paddles."

Chet picked up a pebble and joined the Salish slave in tossing rocks seaward.

"We can learn a lot about fishing in these inlets from Water Bear. He is a good man."

"We will need lots of reed mats for shelter. It will still be cold and wet when we leave, and White Clam does not like the cold," added the young Indian with a chuckle.

The white boy took a stick in his hand and threw a rock in the air, swiping at it with the stick.

"You need to start calling me by my Christian name. It's Chet. Can you say it?"

"Chit."

"No Chet, et, Ch-et," schooled the white slave.

"Ch-et, Chet, Chet, that's easy," repeated the Salish slave, picking up another pebble. "Try to say my real name. Its Wikseyah."

"Wik-se-yah, what's it mean?" returned Chet while taking another swing at the rock, with the stick, and missing badly.

Talking Boy took up a healthy driftwood branch himself and tossed a pebble in the air. He swung with all his might and struck the rock soundly with a piercing *crack*. The stone flew high in the air, past the waterline, splashing some twenty feet past the beach.

"It stands for *Great One*," the young Indian grunted.

Talking Boy had just lied. It didn't stand for anything. It was just an old mystical Salish name, little used, and mostly forgotten. He didn't think the white boy needed to know the truth, and besides, Talking Boy thought his high rank back in his own tribe deserved a great name.

Not to be outdone, Chet searched the woodpile for a bigger stick, and choosing just the right rock, he gently lifted it into the air, taking a mighty swing. *Ka-whack*, the stone flew swiftly to a spot ten feet further than Talking Boy's, sending up a larger plume of water when it splashed.

"Great One, huh, let's see ya beat that one!"

The battle of the rocks and sticks continued for some time and proved to be a great amusement. Each young man tried to outdo the other and the fish and sea birds in the bay must have thought something strange was happening with the in flood of rocks. As they took turns smacking stones, they talked of Talking Boy's home to the south. Chet thought that his river valley must be very close to Lucy's homestead. Talking Boy also said that it was halfway between the mouth of the inlet and the white settlement at the foot of the Sound. The young Indian must have meant Olympia, even though he had never been there. The Salish slave recounted to Chet how he once lived with the white men, on the Nisqually one year, and how he learned their language.

The late afternoon sky was darkening and the two young men decided to return to the village before the rain got worse. They said their goodbyes and parted as true comrades for the first time. It was decided that they would not call each other by their given names in front of the other villagers, for fear of someone becoming suspicious.

XI

The three men slipped the cedar canoe silently into the water and let the river's current carry them seaward. Water Bear corrected their direction occasionally with the thrust of a paddle blade. The rain that had been falling for two days continued at a steady rate, beading up, and then running off their conical bark hats. The sea birds were still asleep and the darkness was quiet. The salt smell was not as strong with the freshwater rain. It was still two hours before daylight and Water Bear, not being one to sleep in, wanted an early start on the morning's fishing. The two young men wanted to stay in bed, but a measure of hot spruce root tea and words from the large Nootkan stirred them out of their warm furs.

The air was quite warm for the end of December, but the wet kept their hands very cold while paddling. Chet was glad he had worn his trousers and undershirt. It was hard to imagine the Indians staying warm with just a bark skirt and bearskin robe.

Water Bear was after plump rockfish and brought extra line and hooks for the two slaves. They also had plenty of fresh clam strips for bait. The three paddled slowly out of the river mouth, for the early morning sky showed no moon and the darkness was near total. They were going to fish by using pine knot torches stuffed with cedar bark and pitch. It was a technique Water Bear liked because he'd been successful with it in the past. The light was supposed to attract the fish, but it was doubtful that bottom dwellers would see any torchlight through sixty feet of water. Just the same, it was a new adventure and offered another lesson in survival that would be of use to both Chet and Talking Boy.

The canoe glided close to a small island in the bay that was not much more then an outcrop of rock with a steep drop off. A collection of evergreen trees rested on the crown. The island was only discernible by the sound of the waves breaking gently on the beach. Water Bear took a large clamshell full of hot coals, and with some dry tinder started one of the torches on fire. Steady blowing by the big Indian soon had the torch blazing.

"Take this line and do as I do," said the fisherman as he placed the torch in a notch at the back of the canoe. The boys tied on iron weights, baited the bone hooks with the clam meat, and slowly lowered all the lines over the side until they hit bottom. Raising the hook slightly off the sand and rocks, the three settled down into comfortable positions. Turning away from the torchlight, Chet could see the small island outlined against the blackness. The light had disturbed some gulls, and they fluttered about not sure if it was time to search for herring or stay in their roost.

"I should be settin' next to the fire," Chet complained in English. "You fellows never get cold."

"Quiet," shushed the big Indian in Nootkan, cocking his head as if to listen.

"Yes, Quiet! White Clam, you might scare the fish with that white man's talk," chuckled Talking Boy.

"Quiet, both of you!" Water Bear's voice was stern this time, and both slaves knew something was wrong.

The big Nootkan was not concerned about the fishing. With a quick motion he plunged the crackling torch into the water where it fizzled out. They stood there motionless for seconds, Chet straining to hear any sound other then the waves lapping at the island.

"Haul in your lines," the older Indian whispered. "Talking Boy, take the coals and the other torch and be ready to light it when I say so."

They got the fishing gear stowed away and silently the large Nootkan paddled the dugout towards the seaward side of the island.

Chet closed his eyes, and continued to strain with his ears, letting Water Bear do the paddling. Then he heard it. *Clunk*, silence. *Clunk, clunk,* more silence. It was wood on wood. Someone was paddling towards them in a canoe. From the sea, not from Nesook. The big Indian turned the canoe around and pointed it back towards the village.

"Taking Boy, light the torch, and hold it high above your head."

The young Indian did as he was told. Opening the shell of hot coals, Talking Boy placed the torch directly on them, blowing hard until the tinder and pitch caught hold. By the time the Salish slave lifted the torch into the air the fire was blazing brightly. Chet and Talking Boy could see nothing but the glow of the torch, but Water Bear, with his back to the light could see, and he was frightened.

"Great Raven, protect us. White Clam, Talking Boy, paddle for all you're worth. We must warn the village!"

Talking Boy threw the torch aside and all three put their shoulders to the paddle with a will.

"Master, what is it?" asked Talking Boy, gasping for breath.

"War canoes, four of them," returned the older Indian. "A raiding party."

The three fishermen sent the cedar dugout racing at a rapid clip. Chet did not understand what Water Bear had seen, but he needed no encouragement to paddle fast. The water sprayed over the bow of the canoe and the white boy was soon drenched. A loud voice broke the silence.

"Hello, the canoe, we come as friends!" cried the pursuer. "We are from Yuquot and seek Nesook and Standing Seal. Wait for us friend, and show us the channel."

"Keep moving," cautioned Water Bear in a hushed tone. The large Nootkan turned and called back. "Who are you? Identify yourself."

"Water Bear, is that you? Do you not recognize my voice?"

So the pursuer knew them. Chet eased up on his stroke a moment, thinking all was right.

"Water Bear, it is Two Skins," the voice called.

Two Skins! The white boy knew that Nootkan name and a chill of fear ran through him. The half-breed would surely kill him. Swimming Otter was gone, and without the master, Chet had no hope of protection.

"Keep pushing hard," the large Nootkan whispered. "Something is not right. Two Skins should not be here at this time of day."

There was just a faint light beginning to show over the high mountains to the east, and the white boy could make out the cedar poles placed to guide them in to the mouth of the river. He was also glad to see that Water Bear was not buying Two Skin's story.

"Two Skins, it is indeed Water Bear. I will announce your coming to the rest of the village!" the big Nootkan called out.

Water Bear lowered his voice and urged the two young slaves to paddle faster than ever. Every moment counted now, for he knew their only chance was to have enough warriors awake and ready to meet the raiding canoes.

The canoe flew up the river and Chet felt aching pain at each stroke. His hands, unused to the paddles, were starting to blister.

Chet was not totally sure what was going on, for all the talk had been in Nootkan. All the white slave knew was the scar faced Indian was behind him. Chet knew that Swimming Otter took great joy in the way the white boy had outwitted the half-breed, staying alive and stealing his bearskin. The white boy was even wearing Two Skin's bearskin at this moment.

The houses were in sight now and the raiding canoes were still far behind. Two Skins had evidently decided that there was no use in pressing the matter, but Water Bear was going to take no chances.

"Talking Boy, tell White Clam to go to our house and wake everyone. Have the women and children flee to the woods behind the village. Oh, and tell him to stay in the woods with them. He must not be seen. You take the next house and I will get Standing Seal."

The Salish Indian yelled the instructions in English to Chet, and told him to use the Nootkan words, I-yah-ish, Ar- smootish-check-up, meaning, many warriors coming!

The white boy now knew the gravity of the situation and leaped off the instant the cedar boat hit the beach. Before Chet got to the door of their house, he could hear Water Bear screaming at the top of his lungs that the great Two Skins was arriving for a visit - a bit of diplomacy that would prove fortunate.

The scarfaced one heard the announcement. So did most of the village. Within seconds the Chahakquot warriors were running out of their houses, weapons in hand. Still fuzzy from sleep, they weren't sure what was happening, but they were alert enough to know that all was not right.

The half-breed scoundrel saw his chance to save face and had his war canoes stand off the beach waiting for a formal invitation to come ashore as was the custom. The surprise had been foiled and there was no use in starting an attack with thirty warriors pitted against an alerted village of four hundred people. Two Skins was clever enough to know that if he pretended to come in peace Standing Seal would go along with the ruse to save bloodshed. Diplomacy played a large part in Nootkan culture.

Chet ran through the house shaking and waking everyone. He could not remember the words Wikseyah had told him, but the people new instinctively that danger was on them and acted accordingly. The men drew daggers, grabbed spears and took their harpoons. Some even broke out long yew wood bows with decorative cedar and feather arrows. Chet had not seen bows and arrows before, for the men kept the string weapons in boxes. The women and children fled to the rear and out to the relative safety of the woods.

Chet was frightened, and started to follow the women, but then he felt a growing shame and decided his place was with Water Bear and Standing Seal. The white boy looked around for a weapon, finding only his wooden clam shovel. Thinking it would make a good club, he returned to the front of the house.

The scene was tense, but under control. Everyone knew Two Skins was not here just to visit, but the game was played out with great caution, weapons at the ready. Chief Standing Seal looked magnificent, stripped almost naked in the dim light, and was the perfect picture of the Indian warrior. Chet had never thought of him as dominant physically, but the scantily clad chief would make one think twice before starting a fight.

"Mighty chief, may your humble servant, Two Skins, come ashore to talk and dine? My men have paddled hard and reached you at this early hour to ask that any of you who wish can join us in a party to the south."

What a jerk, Chet thought. No one shows up at five in the morning to chitchat. From their facial expressions and the quick half-looks at one another, he knew the rest of the villagers felt the same way.

"You may come ashore, my Mowachaht brother, and talk," said the chief in his strong, eloquent voice. "But the bay begins to swell with herring, and soon they will come in numbers great enough to rake. I will need all my people for the harvest and the spawn."

That was Standing Seal's out. He had just given credibility to Two Skins' being there and let the half-breed know that Standing Seal's people could not go on any bogus raiding party, all in one short speech.

In the increasing light Chet saw the lead canoe shoot forward, the scar faced Indian in the bow noticeably searching the crowd. Two Skins was not looking for Chet, but was searching for his old rival, Swimming Otter. Just then a burly hand grabbed the white boy around the mouth and gently pulled the would-be warrior back into the shadows of the house.

Water Bear had slipped away from Standing Seal's side as soon as he spotted the tall, skinny slave returning to the beach. The big Nootkan nudged Talking Boy along with him, and the two Indians made their way over to where Chet was standing. The only reason the white slave had not been seen by Two Skins was because of the darkness and Chet's bark clothes. He looked like a Nootka. In the last few weeks the white boy had unknowingly transformed his dress and physical appearance to that of an Indian. The trousers below his bark skirt looked a little strange, but in that light he passed as a savage.

"I thought I told you to hide in the woods," Water Bear whispered in Nootkan, still holding the boy tightly.

"It is dangerous for you to be seen," exclaimed the Salish slave softly in English. "You could cause us great trouble."

The large Indian released his grip on Chet enough for the white boy to talk.

"I just wanted to help you fight that cowardly snake," Chet said, turning to look at Water Bear. "I have a score to settle with that creep, remember."

Talking Boy told the big Nootkan what Chet had said and the older Indian let go and laughed under his breath, patting Chet on the shoulder.

"You are a good white slave, but we should have named you Stupid White Clam, for you have put us in a difficult position." He turned to Talking Boy. "Tell him to go to the woods and stay hidden until Two Skins leaves. It will probably not be until Swimming Otter returns tomorrow."

Quite pleased with the boy's bravery, the big Mowachaht warrior smiled at Chet as he left and returned to Standing Seal on the beach.

Chet grabbed his blanket and some mats to make a shelter. He also took some of Cattail Woman's fine bark line and a bone needle. The young man placed everything in one of the shoulder strap baskets and told Talking Boy that he would be near the large drift woodpile out on the point. Chet asked the young Indian to bring food when he could.

The white boy made his way out the back of the house where the women had removed the planks to make good their retreat. Chet was glad he had the extra mats and pulled one around him as he walked into the woods. The rain was more intense, and the boy wasn't sure if the continuing darkness was from the thick clouds or the lack of daylight. The brush was thick with fern and vine maple, making the going a bit rough. Every step made him wetter and colder. He already missed the warmth of the cedar lodge and hoped that the scar faced one would leave soon. Chet was at least secure in the knowledge that the Chahakquots were in no way obligated to turn him over to Two Skins if they could help it.

Although the distance through the woods to the point on Nesook bay was shorter then going by way of the beach, the thick undergrowth doubled the usual time in getting there. The boy caught sight of the beach just short of the driftwood pile. After making sure no one was in sight, he walked on the rain-hardened sand to the thicket just off the beach where the hidden sail and rigging was stored. All was as he had left it.

Chet stood there with the rain pounding off the umbrella hat and could not decide what to do next. The white slave decided that whether he was going to be here a long time or not, he would need some shelter. Besides, the work would keep him warmer and keep his mind off his misery. Chet noticed a small clearing between three of the bushes in the thicket and moved the short distance towards them. Taking the wet mat off his shoulders, the young man turned and placed the bark and reed material over the three clumps of brush and using some of the shredded bark line he tied the shelter down on all sides. Except for the fact that the mat sagged in the middle and was going to eventually fill with water, it was an effective means of keeping a four-by-six foot area dry. A nice driftwood branch would serve to prop up the middle and allow the rain to drip off.

Chet placed the pack basket under the mat shelter and returned to the beach. It wasn't long before he found a suitable hunk of wood for the mat tent, and one for use as a club just in case. With the stick in place and the lashings re-tightened, the shelter was repelling the rain. The wind was another story. The brisk breeze off the bay was hardly detoured by the bushes, so the white boy made a trip over to the rigging and dragged the badly ripped canvas back to his temporary home. The boy already thought of repairing the sail when he took the line and bone needle back at the long house. Now Chet positioned the triangular sail with the masthead corner draped over the tent with the base along the ground in such a way as to afford protection from the wind and still have the ripped areas of the base to repair at his leisure. Chet took the other stick, and cleared small protruding branches and ferns from the area under the tent. The white boy leveled the ground as best he could by hacking at the clumps of grass and filling in the depressed areas. He added a layer of soft moss and ferns, spreading out the remaining mat over them. He stuffed some more moss under one corner for use as a pillow, and after a few more lump removals, Chet found he had a comfortable bed.

The boy figured it must be no later than eight o'clock and decided to try his hand at mending the sail. He quickly found that his hands were too raw and cold from the morning's activities to be of much use pushing the bone needle through the canvas. He might as well get some rest. The young man was wet clear through, but decided that he would stay warmer with the dry wool trade blanket on top rather then stripping and wrapping up in it. He laid his head down on the bark mat, and pulled the gray blanket over himself. Initially Chet felt some warmth, but that soon changed to misery.

The rain came down with no let up. He knew now why Talking Boy had no desire to leave until spring. The boy also doubted how badly he wanted to go. That warm wooden house with its smell of cedar and stench of fish sounded pretty appealing right now.

Chet pulled his knees closer to his chest and put his hands between his legs. *Yes, that was much warmer. Still wet, though. Kind of like, wettin' yer pants,* he thought. But he was definitely warmer. He watched as a large brown slug, with black antenna, slimed its way past the shelter, leaving its trail of mucus on the blades of grass. Chet noticed other slugs, too. Some were huge and some were tiny. One big one was spotted like a leopard, only with greenish-brown spots. For a moment he wondered what was happening back at the village. For a while longer Chet thought about Lucy, and with her face in his thoughts, he soon fell asleep.

Standing Seal felt that he had succeeded in showing Two Skins that there were no ill feelings. Now the chief wanted the scar faced one out of the village as soon as possible. The chief feared that

Two Skins might happen upon Swimming Otter and Wooden Hand by accident as they returned from their expedition.

Rain still fell from the sky when the two leaders emerged from the house. The steady drizzle, aided by a gusty north wind, stung their faces. The cold was noticeable to the Indians now, and many were glad to see Two Skins saying his farewell. The raiders paddled their canoes rapidly downstream. Standing Seal sent Water Bear and some others to follow at a distance just to make sure they did not leave in the direction of Swimming Otter. The chief sent two slaves a few minutes later in the opposite direction with orders to bring back the Chahakquot warrior immediately.

It was late in the afternoon before Water Bear returned. With all the excitement, everyone had forgotten about Chet, and it was Talking Boy who reminded the chief that the white slave had been sent into the forest to hide.

The Salish slave was allowed to go find White Clam and take him some food. Standing Seal thought it best for the two young slaves to wait until morning before they returned, for his warriors would be a little jumpy on guard that night, and the chief wanted no accidental bloodshed.

The rain and wind had turned into a full-blown storm, and the young Indian was glad to find the shelter Chet had arranged. Talking Boy reached the driftwood pile and had been calling for some time before the white boy heard him. Chet was cold and wet. Even though the white slave was glad for the dried fish and berry cakes, his heart sank at the thought of staying out for the night. Even as wet as Chet was, his mouth was dry and he took a long drink of fresh water from a bark container. Talking Boy was dazzled at the sight of all the sailing gear, and agreed to keep the find a secret. The young Indian was impressed with the little shelter Chet had made, but knew the white boy was depressed by the weather.

Talking Boy tried to cheer Chet up but it was no use. The young Indian made some improvements to the mat shelter and dug a shallow drainage ditch all around to stop the flow of rainwater that had been seeping under the old mat Chet had been lying on.

Talking Boy laid down a new mat he had brought with him and settled in with the white boy.

Chet could not believe how fast the Indian slave fell asleep, but Talking Boy had been awake since early that morning, when they had left with water Bear to go fishing. The Salish slave had brought a dry trade blanket with him also. With two blankets over them and the warmth of their backs next to each other, Chet felt that he would survive. The white boy rearranged the wet bearskin so he could have his bare back touching Talking Boy's back. The extra heat seemed a godsend. Chet kept nudging closer until there was almost no space between them, and finally he fell asleep.

As the night continued the cold took a deeper bite and, while the two young men slept, the rain turned to snow. The wind was relentless and the drifting snow started to pile against the canvas wall. The sturdy bushes of the thicket, along with the cedar branch, held the mats up, but it was shaky at best.

Chet woke up feeling the cold, but at least the wet was gone. Now they only had to worry about freezing. Chet remembered that he had not repaired any of the rips in the canvas, but his fingers were so numb the boy doubted whether he ever would.

The hours passed slowly and Chet fell in and out of sleep. The white boy had a new problem. He had to pee, but the young man was so cold there was no way he was going to get up. Cold, hungry, thirsty, and ready to pee in his pants, Chet had never been so miserable. Would it ever get light out? He thought the top of the mountains would surely be silhouetted with the dawn any moment.

Finally, when the white boy had almost convinced himself that letting go of his urine would make him warmer instead of wetter, there was a slow stirring next to him. Talking Boy had solved his dilemma. The young Indian was getting up to pee himself. And it was daylight, though still snowing. Not a word was said as the white boy stiffly rose to join his friend outside. Steam rose from the yellow hole in the snow he made. It gave Chet the illusion of more warmth.

"White Clam, I'm freezing. It must be safe to go back now. Grab a blanket and let's go. We can come back for the rest later."

They both wrapped a trade blanket around themselves and trudged out through a foot of snow. Chet could not stomach the fish Talking Boy offered. All he could think about was getting back to Nesook and comfort.

Chet felt very ill when he entered the long house. He wasn't sure but he thought he might be a little feverish. He was freezing and just stood there, not quite knowing what to do. Some of the women noticed White Clam shivering and called for Cattail Woman. She fussed over Chet like any mother and brought him over to the breakfast fire. Within minutes she had small stones heated for tea. The white boy drank the warm liquid from a wooden bowl carved in the shape of some mythical fish. His body was shaking relentlessly and he had no control over the shivering.

Chet felt sick and could not think of eating anything the round slave woman offered. She understood and gathered some spare blankets, along with some shredded bark and made a bed next to the fire. Chet forgot his modesty allowing the women to take his underclothes and wrap him in the dry blankets. He lay there next to the fire, shaking, with his knees drawn up to his chest and his hands between his legs. Chet's head began to spin as the fever started to take hold. The young man was becoming very sick as the long exposure to the wet, cold weather finally caught up with him.

XII

Chet wasn't aware that Swimming Otter and Wooden Hand had returned. The master was beside himself when he learned of the failed raid. As Water Bear recounted the event, Swimming Otter's anger grew. Most were convinced that Two Skins was only meaning to kill Swimming Otter and his family, but the master dismissed that, arguing that the scar-faced half-breed had more ambitious goals on his mind. Standing Seal would not be easily convinced, but it was clear that something must be done to eliminate Two Skins.

The two slaves who had been sent to tell Swimming Otter to return had reported to the chief, and Standing Seal arrived at the warrior's house just as the brothers were leaving for his.

"Swimming Otter, it is good to see you home," the chief smiled. "We have had some anxious hours and the village feels safer with your return."

"Master, my brother has told me of the events of yesterday. Please come to my hearth. We must talk."

Swimming Otter extended his hand toward the back corner of the cedar house and the chief led the way. The three men sat down by the fire and Water Bear dismissed all present, leaving them in privacy.

"Standing Seal," Swimming Otter continued, "my brother tells me that you, and the village as a whole, believe that Two Skins came to kill me and my house alone. Let me beg to differ. This half-breed has designs on greater bloodshed. He would take your cousin, Cod Man, if his warriors did not feel a loyalty to the old chief. He would have that great village of Yuquot if there were fewer warriors indebted to Cod Man. Two Skins did not come here like a snake in darkness to kill just me. He came to take our people, our lands, and our waters. You must understand that eliminating him is in your best interests. This is not just a grudge any more."

Swimming Otter paused waiting for a reaction from the chief, planning a stronger comeback when Standing Seal disagreed.

"Rest your tongue, my friend," the nobleman said, while placing his hand on Swimming Otter's shoulder. "I agree with you. There is no need to convince me."

The stunned warrior could not believe his ears. Swimming Otter had never had Standing Seal's agreement on matters concerning Two Skins before. This was so unexpected that it left him speechless. He could only sit there in disbelief and listen to Standing Seal agree with him. What a truly great and perceptive leader!

"I was warned some time ago by Cod Man himself as to the ambitions of Two Skins," the chief went on. "My old cousin has many spies and they told him that the scar-faced one had designs on being the chief of a village, but we both thought he would go elsewhere. When Two Skins left, it would solve the problem of the two of you. I never thought he would come after my village, but his dislike for you has made Two Skins take grave steps. By the way, the scar faced one thinks he has divided us by telling me you have similar thoughts, and to watch out for you."

"I hope I have always shown my loyalty," exclaimed Swimming Otter, still in shock. "But why did you not tell me of this before?"

"I did not tell you before because you would have pushed for a confrontation. Our people are few; we need all the men we have alive. At that time it was not worth starting a war over, but now we have a different situation. It is time to make plans. It will be done at the potlatch and Cod Man will only slap us verbally. He will not interfere beyond that."

The stately chief rose and threw a twig into the fire.

"It will be best to keep any plans to ourselves. Let the people think what they must, but only those that need to will know. I don't want any spies spoiling our surprise," said the chief.

Standing Seal turned to go and stopped.

"How is White Clam? He must not die from his sickness. He will play an important role at the potlatch."

"His body is weak, like all white men," said Water Bear, "but his heart is Mowachaht. He will be fine."

The next two weeks were spent getting ready for the sacred winter festival. It was a time when all the nobles would ready their best clothes and finery for the secret society meetings, dances, and ceremonies. These societies were based on common spirit totems and family lines. The common people and slaves could not attend these meetings, but their presence was tolerated at the many dinners and dances. It was a time when the Shaman, Salmon Wolf, was at his peak spiritually. It also was a time when people feared him most and superstition ran high. If you had crossed the Shaman, made him upset in any way, or owed payment to him, he could easily put a curse on you. At the same time if the shaman or one of his apprentices had failed in a spiritual or healing act for which they were paid, refunds could be demanded, or even the conjurer's life taken in repayment.

Chet was having a hard time of it. He had lost twenty pounds of his already skinny frame, and, if not for the caring of the rotund Cattail Woman, the white slave surely would have died of lung fever. She was at his side constantly shoveling hot food and drink down his unwilling mouth. Cattail Woman emptied his waste box for him. She would rub him violently on the back and chest as the Shaman would dance and gesture to drive away the evil spirits. Standing Seal sent Salmon Wolf many times at his own expense. Chet was grateful for the thought, but wished the Indian holy man would just stay away. Sleep, warmth, and nourishment were what the young man needed, and finally, after two weeks he felt his strength coming back. It was a good omen to conclude their sacred religious winter ceremonies with a healthy White Clam. Of course, the Shaman took full credit and the loving slave mother got none, but no one was happier to see the white boy rise up than she.

Chet also knew that his old mentor, Wooden Hand, spent many hours by his side. The old man was caring and carved him a special wooden spoon shaped like the concentric rings of a clamshell. The handle was carved like a small totem pole with various figures telling the story of his meeting with Two Skins and the battle with the Great Halibut.

Talking Boy had kept a vigil also. The young Indian was concerned that his white friend would not live, and with White Clam's death their plans for freedom would end. When Chet could eat again, Talking Boy went fishing every morning for fresh rockfish so the boy wouldn't have to eat dried salmon and herring oil. The Salish slave returned to the hidden shelter and brought back the mats and other items Chet had taken with him that rainy day. Talking Boy also hid the sailing gear in the thicket and erased all signs of their being there.

"White Clam you look better this morning," the young Indian grinned. "If you feel like it, I will take you outside. It is cold, but sunny. It will give you new life."

"Yeah, that sounds good. I think I can stand up and walk now," said the boy.

After some hesitation, the round slave woman agreed to let Chet go out.

The Salish slave helped Chet to his feet, and, after some initial dizziness, the boy was able to take some solid steps. Cattail Woman had long since bundled the boy back in his own clothes, knowing he needed the extra warmth. The two Indian slaves helped him put on Two Skins' bear robe and each of them took one of Chet's arms as they made their way to the door.

As soon as the three stepped outside, the warm sunlight hit Chet with blinding light. The many days inside had conditioned the boy for semi-darkness and bright light would take some getting used to. He sat down on a cedar plank bench between two hunks of drift log, and after the slave woman was sure the young man was all right, she returned to her daily chores.

Chet wondered if there was news of Two Skins and if anything was being done about the attempted raid. Talking Boy said that Standing Seal would discuss it with Cod Man in the spring, but as far as the chief was concerned, it was between Swimming Otter and Two Skins and the matter was closed for now. What the young Indian and most of the village didn't know was that the secret society meetings served as a venue for discussions on how best to confront the scar-faced one. The two friends were disappointed that no return raiding party was being formed, but Chet and Talking Boy decided they needed to escape before any bloodshed commenced so that tempered their disappointment.

As soon as Chet could focus his eyes, he knew that things were different in the village. There seemed to be an abundance of gulls and other seabirds in the air and on the ground. Their endless screeching was deafening at times. Talking Boy told him that the last few days had brought increasing numbers of herring to the bay, and with them increasing numbers of sea lions, and sea birds. Many of the men were now out with their dip nets and rakes, testing the bay for the upcoming herring harvest.

The villagers were excited about the return of the herring, for it meant having fresh fish. It also meant that the next month would bring the herring spawn and the small rubbery eggs they relished raw.

"White Clam, if you feel up to it we could get a small canoe and join the men in harvesting the herring run," said Talking Boy.

Just then one of the canoes was poling up the river, riding deep in the water, with none other than Water Bear leaning to the bow pole. He called some of the women over and soon they were scooping large handfuls of bright silver fish into waiting baskets.

"Look at all those fish," said an amazed Chet.

Water Bear caught Chet's eye and the overweight fisherman made his way over to the boy and greeted him in Nootkan.

"Good to see you up again my sickly little white friend. Do you like herring?" he questioned. "We'll eat well tonight."

The big Indian smacked his lips and gave Chet an approving pat on the back.

"See you later, White Clam. I don't think I'll wait until tonight, I'm hungry now."

Water Bear turned to go and Chet went back to watching the village routine. The sun did feel great and he felt his strength coming back to him with each passing minute. After an hour, Cattail Woman came to get him and Chet was able to walk back to his bed. After some tasty roasted herring, the boy, exhausted after his morning activity, fell asleep for a long afternoon nap.

Chet awoke to Wooden Hand's nudge and his head seemed extremely clear. The air inside the longhouse had a fishy smell and as the boy looked around he could see the women stringing lines everywhere with fresh-gutted herring hanging to dry. The men and children were stuffing themselves with the small silver fish, dipping the roasted flesh in seal oil or in the freshly rendered oil from the herring.

"Time to eat, boy," said the old man as he offered some of the oily fish. "It will make you strong again."

He placed one of the herring in his own mouth and ate it with a smile. Chet watched him chewing it, bones and all. Then he tried it. The fish was salty and oilier than the fresh roasted white meat he'd had for lunch. It wasn't bad, but after eating a few, he lost his taste for them and finished his meal with some dried berry cakes.

The Indians never lost their excitement for the little silver fish. Chet watched as man, woman, and child consumed great quantities of the fish well into the night. Feeling much better now, Chet walked around greeting his housemates as they gorged themselves. He took an extra bite of this or that as he made conversation, and after a long, cool drink of water, Chet felt quite full himself. The master saw White Clam and called him to the back of the house. Chet had not spoken to Swimming Otter since the first day they arrived at Nesook and the warrior was pleased at his recovery.

"You look fine, White Clam. How do you feel?" asked the master of the house, as he sat with fish oil running down his cheeks and dripping from his fingers. "We have run out of herring. You must go with us tomorrow and catch a monster herring. You always bring us luck when you go fishing. You are a good slave."

Swimming Otter was in a good mood and Chet was glad to see him again. The young man felt secure and protected with his master at home.

"I'm feeling better, master. The fever is gone, and, although I feel a little weak, I have been able to stand and walk without being lightheaded."

After seeing the warrior's confused look, Chet realized that he had answered in English and quickly said, "Feeling much good," in Nootkan.

That brought a smile to Swimming Otter's face. He approved of every effort the boy made to do and talk like the Indians.

"Tomorrow, go fish, Talking Boy," continued Chet in broken Nootkan.

The master seemed pleased and gave his permission for the boy to go fishing tomorrow with his friend. They said their good nights and the white boy returned to the front of the house checked on his slave mother and then retired to his bed. It felt good to feel good again and Chet promised God that he would never take a warm bed for granted again.

With the exception of the lookout guards changing in the middle of the night and at daylight, no one in the whole village was in any hurry to get up the next morning. The low sun promised another shiny day as it rose slowly behind the eastern peaks. The sky was cloudless and cold, a touch of frost was on the ground, and a thin rim of ice had formed on the banks of the river. A glorious day indeed.

The white boy was feeling well and was careful not to wake the household as he rose stiffly and walked outside. His tattered socks were growing huge holes inside the old moccasins, but Chet knew he needed the extra protection of his old clothes and would continue to wear them under the bark and bearskin until the weather turned warm again. He found the same plank bench as the day before and sat down watching the gulls pecking at the sand and each other. The seabirds would rest for a while, digesting their herring breakfast, then fly off down the river to the bay for another helping.

The screaming of the sea gulls was becoming more tolerable and almost pleasant at times. Chet was melancholy and thought of his friends and parents. The young man wondered whether he would ever leave this place. It was beautiful but it was not his culture. He thought of Lucy and wished the young girl was around to raise his spirits.

The boy tucked the bearskin robe tighter around himself and sat watching the sun scale the last obstructing peak. The warm rays of light felt good on his face. The frost quickly melted away, turning the sparse grass from white to green. As if on cue, the village awoke and people appeared to start their daily activity.

His peace broken, Chet got up and returned to the house for a bite to eat. Smoked salmon was the only item on the menu, for all of the herring had been eaten the night before. The men were planning to harvest the run in earnest now, and before Chet had finished eating, Talking Boy came by to see if the white slave felt like joining the fishing party.

"It's great sport, this herring fishing, and there're so many fish, even I can catch them," the Salish slave laughed. "Standing Seal gave me a small canoe and an old herring rake left over by a family killed by the pox. You feel up to it?"

"Sure, I've been up already, but I'm wearin' my pants and shirt this time," Chet said.

Wooden Hand had been sitting nearby, and since the young men had been speaking English, he asked Talking Boy what they were saying. On learning the subject of their conversation the old man asked if he could go along to help so that he could get extra fish for Cattail Woman. The younger men were happy to have him along and the three of them were off to find the canoe.

They headed up river to one of the last houses in line, where no one was living. The house was smaller than most and in need of some repair. Most of it was walled and the roof was eighty percent in place. The family who lived there had died two winters ago. Wooden Hand did not like being near it and would not go inside. A small sixteen-foot dugout was sitting bottom up on a cedar post rack along the side of the house. Underneath it, still in a neat arrangement, were ropes, paddles, and other gear.

They flipped the canoe over and off the rack. Chet was surprised at how light the craft was. The paddles and rope were placed in the canoe, and, after an inspection for cracks and dry rot by Wooden Hand, the three men pulled and pushed the dugout to the riverbank. Talking Boy returned to the house for the herring rake, and as he came running back to the beach, Chet thought, *what a strange tool for catching fish.*

The rake was a narrow hardwood pole, about seven feet long, two inches thick and thinned to a flat half inch thick for the last two feet. The upper shaft had two handholds made of cedar twine, wrapped tightly around the pole about two feet apart. Each was made of ten rotations of twine and was used to keep the fisherman's hands from slipping when raking the herring. The thin, flat end had a long row of needle sharp spikes made of whalebone protruding past the wood. Chet had no idea how this would catch any fish but he kept an open mind. Most of the new Indian methods he had been introduced to seemed weird at first but worked exceptionally well.

Chet took the bow, Wooden Hand amidships, and Talking Boy the stern. They pushed the canoe into the river and headed downstream to the bay. By now everything that could float was out in the bay with slaves and nobles alike taking as many of the silver fish as they could carry. The gulls were out in force and a fat herring or two in the beak almost always rewarded their constant dive-bombing as they flew off. It was a wonder they never lost their catch, for, while in flight, they would always maneuver the herring so as to swallow it headfirst.

There was a new animal to be seen in the bay, also. Large barking sea lions well out of range of the harpoons, were feasting on the herring, too. The white boy stopped his paddling and looked at the crystal clear water. The rocks and sand on the bottom were clearly visible.

All of a sudden a black mass blocked his view. A dark living current flowed beneath the dugout and the boy had to blink twice to make sure he was not seeing things. The moss green backs of the herring were packed so tightly together it looked as though there was no space at all between fish. They moved and turned as one. As the white boy continued to look downward, the water suddenly broke into a rippling, splashing mass of fish. Startled, Chet watched them literally jumping out of the water.

Wooden Hand laughed.

"King salmon," he shouted in Nootkan. "Chase herring, eat many, scare rest."

Chet had never seen such a sight. Canoes were everywhere. He saw men sitting in the bows of their craft, stroking the water with the odd looking rakes, and flipping a half dozen fish at a time into the middle of the dugouts. The fish in the water were packed together like sardines in a can, and it was no wonder the rakes worked well.

The old Haida slave motioned for Chet to put his paddle down. Wooden Hand grabbed the rake and crawled up just behind the white boy and thrust the pole downward into the muddy mass of fish. The old slave struggled as the sharp teeth of the rake found flesh, and as he flipped the rake out of the water, four or five herring wriggled to the floor of the canoe. A few more passes with the pole and the old man was ready to let the younger ones do it, but he had brought in at least two dozen fish from five minute's work.

Chet took his turn next and his first try only netted him one herring. There was a trick to it, Wooden Hand told him. A steady backward motion with a quick flip. The fisherman couldn't be lazy if he expected to get the most for his effort. The next two tries were better and Chet impaled seven more herring. This was more then Talking Boy could handle. The young Indian had never had to be much of a food provider, so the ease at which the herring were caught was to his liking.

"White Clam, trade me now," he called. "It's my turn, and besides you should be getting ten at a time."

"Hold on, let me take one more scoop."

Chet was still feeling a little weak from his illness, so he felt that steering the canoe would be an easier assignment. The white boy took one more sweep with the rake and just as the whalebone points entered the water, the sea began to boil with fish frightened by something below. Chet pulled with all his strength, intent on getting more herring on the spiked teeth, but just as he started to raise the pole there came thud on the end of the stick as if he had hit a brick wall. A split second later a huge silver streak broke water in back of the rake. Its glistening body twisted and large amounts of water splashed as it rose in the air. The fish was bleeding from half a dozen spike holes along the side of its body. With his last bit of strength, Chet brought the rake up and with it a handful of herring. But more important, his follow-through hit the thirty-five pound salmon in mid-air, knocking it off course and into the dugout.

Those near enough to see all this action sat in disbelief. The old Haida slave could not believe his eyes. Water Bear and Swimming Otter a hundred yards away gave out savage cries of joy when told what the commotion was all about. It added to their already increasing admiration for the boy. White Clam was quickly becoming a good omen and a fishing legend. Imagine, a king salmon caught with a herring rake.

Chet just sat on his haunches, not quite believing what had happened either. The King salmon was huge as it flopped and wriggled between Wooden Hand and Talking Boy. Finally, the old slave came to his senses and grabbed a yew wood club. With a couple of well-placed blows, the old man killed the mighty fish before it could flip out of the canoe. It took both Indians to lift the beautiful fish for the curious who paddled by. The white boy was exhausted. He just smiled when praise and congratulations were sent his way.

Swimming Otter and Water Bear came by after a few minutes and the master boasted about White Clam for all who would listen. Even Standing Seal and Salmon Wolf, the shaman, swung their canoe over to praise him. The latter made sure the chief was reminded how he had brought the boy back from the dead twice. Salmon Wolf also took credit for amplifying the powers the boy obviously had.

Things soon calmed down and Talking Boy remembered that he had not had a turn at the herring fishery, so the old slave traded places with him. Chet and Wooden Hand seemed content to let the Salish slave have his sport, and just paddled the canoe for the rest of the afternoon.

The amount of the catch continued to amaze Chet. The village literally caught tons of the herring over the next week. They never seemed to tire of the oily fish and gorged themselves nightly. They roasted it fresh, dressed and strung it to dry, put it in watertight baskets to boil out the oil, and buried it in pits to ripen for a particularly nasty dish of half-rotten fish that only a native could get downwind from. All this served to keep Chet out of *Little Oil House* as much as possible. The stench was such he started sleeping right next to a wall plank that he had moved slightly so as to keep his nose in a cold fresh breeze all night.

It was well into January, Chet thought, and the thrill of the herring run was finally dying down. The villagers spent less and less time raking the schools and more time on other projects. However, there was constant talk of the herring spawn and the Nootkans, to a man, relished the thought of eating those wonderful little fish eggs. The Nootkans were totally out of the delicacy they had preserved last year. Chet knew how much they liked the dried eggs in seal oil, but as he didn't, the boy could not share their enthusiasm.

Chet was glad for the large salmon, and for a while he had fresh fillets nightly. Chet chose to freeze his catch for days rather than smoke it all at once a practice the Indians did not understand or think very tasty. Eventually, the white slave did smoke the remainder of the pink meat in fear of its spoiling, but he stopped short of drowning it in herring oil as the Nootkas would have done.

Swimming Otter's household had made many gift items, putting up lots of herring and salmon for the upcoming potlatch in the spring. The master's thoughts had turned back to the great pole of his totem and the large cedar he and Wooden Hand had selected weeks earlier. Swimming Otter had commissioned four slaves to go with the old wood carver and cut the tree down. Chet and Water Bear would go along to keep them in fresh fish and game.

The night before they were to leave, the white boy was asked for the first time to take a turn as night watchman. The Indians had not forgotten the scar-faced one and were still deploying men after dark to keep a lookout. Chet was given a large copper plate and a war club of whalebone with instructions to beat them together at the first sign of any would-be enemy. The resulting noise would surely be enough to wake the village.

The White slave was given a small one-man canoe of about ten feet in length and paddled the short distance down-river to the bay. Making shore on the opposite side of the river from the village, Chet easily pulled the light canoe into the bushes, and sat down in it, hiding the dugout and himself from view. He wrapped the bearskin around him, as he had done so many times the last three months and wondered what he would have done without it. He surely would have frozen to death those first cold nights walking back to Chahakquot. And those first days in the snow cutting planks and making boxes. How did the Indians survive the cold? Maybe it was the fish oil and bear grease they were always rubbing on themselves after meals. *Oh well, who knows?* he thought. Chet was always so cold and the Nootkas never seemed to mind it much. The boy decided to keep this smelly old robe forever. It had become his security blanket.

Chet thought about Andrew, Matt, Bill, Lloyd, and the schooner. How he would love to see that old girl sail into sight! And Bart, good old stupid Bart. Chet wondered if they ever found out it was Bart's trading whiskey with the Indians that got him captured or if the old cook was even alive.

"They probably wouldn't even know me now," he said to himself.

Chet's hair was long and greasy. His hands were constantly dirty and he had not seen the white color of his feet for almost three months. The young man knew he stank, but so did everyone else. The only time the Mowachahts jumped in the river was to chill their bodies and beat themselves with sticks in some religious ritual that Chet never understood. He had tried to wash with leftover hot water from dinner a few times back at *Whale Oil House*, but the household had given him such strange looks he stopped the practice.

"Yes," he said aloud. "I'm sure I'm quite a sight."

The young man settled in for the night and thought of as many happy days as he could to stay awake. He caught himself dozing off a few times and got up to take thirty minute strolls up and down the beach, taking care to walk quietly and stay out of sight. The strolls were as much for keeping warm as for staying awake.

"I wonder if the other guys really stay awake all night?" Chet said to himself.

Well he was determined to stay awake.

Well past midnight Chet got his second wind and that, along with a vivid imagination, made it easy for him to last the next few hours to daybreak. The boy almost had himself believing that he might once again help save the village, for Two Skins would surely pick that night to try his bloody deed again. Ah, to see his face when old Scarface was foiled again would be delightful!

But the legend of White Clam would have to wait for another time, for this turned out to be just another peaceful January night. As darkness blossomed into daylight, a cold rain started, and the brave white boy headed back to Nesook and a warm plank bed. Chet was greeted by a few early risers on his return and reported to Standing Seal that all had been quiet. By the time the white slave reached the smelly confines of *Little Oil House,* the rain had turned to a downpour. As he took his bed, Wooden Hand reminded him of the planned trip to cut the great cedar. The old Haida said they would not leave until later that day, when the storm passed. Chet barely heard him as he drifted into sleep.

XIII

After a long nap Chet was awakened and fed by Cattail Woman. There seemed no end to what the old slave woman would do for the white boy. All he had to give her in return was respect and attention. His deeds, his increasing popularity with the tribe, and his open relationship with the old woman served to raise her status in the village, at least among the other slave women. Cattail Woman had packed a strap basket for Chet with two wool trade blankets, a sleeping mat, cooking box, ladle, and the rest of his smoked salmon. She threw in as many dried berry cakes as she could round up, for the slave woman knew Chet was a picky eater and would not enjoy the smoked, or ripe herring in oil that the other men would be eating. He thanked her and gave her a hug.

"Wooden Hand, White Clam, it is time to go," came a call from Water Bear as he walked toward the door.

Swimming Otter followed his brother and softly took the old wood carver aside.

"You do this thing for me old Haida and I will pay you with your freedom to work for others. You will be able to eventually buy your own freedom. I'm counting on you for this and trusting you."

The master grabbed the old man by the shoulders and gently shook him in a gesture of approval.

Chet put on his bearskin robe and reached for the old cedar bark hat. He waved goodbye to the assembled household and followed the old carver outside. Water Bear had two thirty-foot canoes loaded with tools and gear - large mats for temporary shelters, boxes of herring, cedar poles, planks, and two dozen alder logs, each four feet long and eight to ten inches in diameter. Of course there was plenty of fishing gear, including a harpoon and lots of rope. Water Bear also carried two long and very thin wooden boxes under his arm and stowed them in a special place behind his thwart in the stern of the canoe.

Talking Boy had joined the group at the beach to say goodbye to his white friend.

"Stay warm, oh great fish killer," he laughed as Chet approached.

"I will," the boy returned. "Cattail Woman has given me two trade blankets and I'm wearing every stitch of clothing I had from the ship underneath my robe. Say, what's in those boxes Water Bear has? "

"Those tall skinny ones?" Talking Boy asked.

"Yeah, the ones in the back of the canoe," said Chet pointing.

"Those contain sealing bows and arrows," the Salish slave answered.

Chet seemed confused. Talking Boy saw his troubled look and elaborated.

"They are used for taking seals and otter. Water Bear will show you how to use them, I'm sure."

The young men said their goodbyes and Chet climbed into the canoe with Water Bear. Two slave men the white boy was acquainted with pushed the craft out into the river and hopped in. Wooden Hand joined three other men in the next canoe and followed them down river. After half an hour Nesook was out of sight and a new destination lay ahead.

The two black canoes headed northwest out of the bay towards some property held by Swimming Otter's family. There was said to be a nice stand of old growth cedar two hundred feet high, not too far from shore. It was the place where a hundred years before, their ancestors felled trees that were used for the very beams that held the roof of *Whale Oil House* off the ground.

The big canoe moved swiftly through the mist and it wasn't long before Water Bear started a song to keep time with the stroke of the paddle blades. It was surprising how easy it was to keep the thirty-foot dugout moving at a good clip. Chet had become quite used to the paddle after the last two weeks of herring fishing, and his hands had calluses where blisters used to be. The boy also traded some of his fresh salmon for a couple of strips of seal hide that he wrapped around his hands. The makeshift gloves and all his wool clothing made this journey much warmer then the trip from Chahakquot.

They settled in to a steady pace and kept in as straight a line as possible to the north, passing small islets and tree lined coves. Chet noticed different sea birds along the way and one in particular. It looked like a stork, with tall skinny legs that bent backwards at the knee, and its beak was long and pointed. When the bird was swimming it dived under the water for great distances, exhaling large bubbles that rose to the surface like water boiling. It was when one of these birds dived particularly close to the canoe that Chet turned and asked Water Bear its name. Both canoers stopped paddling for a few beats as the rotund fisherman leaned forward to try and understand what the white boy was saying in Nootkan. Before Chet could answer there came a deafening scream from the second canoe. Chet turned and looked, thinking the worst, but instead saw the bright shiny teeth of the old Haida slave grinning as he paddled by, screaming an oath. Water bear wasted no time screaming in return. In fact they all screamed, even Chet, and the race was on.

The surprise tactic gave the second canoe the advantage, and for the first five minutes they kept a slim boat length lead. Chet and the others in his canoe rose to the occasion and soon, aided by Water Bear's power they started to gain. The dugout inched closer and closer as the minutes went by. The race turned to a matter of pride, with the Indians good-naturedly calling each other names while joking back and forth. The white boy pulled with the others as hard as he could, but fatigue was setting in. Chet hoped someone would break and give in, but even old Wooden Hand was matching him stroke for stroke.

Finally, the two dugouts came even and the men in Wooden Hand's canoe found renewed strength. The two black canoes raced on, dead even, for another minute, but the strength of Water Bear won out. Chet watched out of the corner of one eye as his canoe pulled slowly ahead. When the white boy felt he could go no further, the second canoe dropped off the pace and slowed to a stop. Wooden Hand had had enough and raised his paddle. Slumping forward in exhaustion, the old man laughingly admitted defeat and talked of younger days when he would have outlasted them easily.

Thankful for the end of the race, both canoes drifted as their riders rested. Water Bear allowed Wooden Hand's dugout to lead on, and soon they were back into a steady pace. Chet didn't have to worry about being warm anymore. In fact, he took the bearskin off and draped it over his knees. The exercise was more than enough to keep him warm.

The party had come almost ten miles by nightfall, but Water Bear pressed on. There was no moon and the old slave was the only source of navigation. Though the canoes pulled closer to shore so landmarks would be visible, the men could barely make out the forested beach.

By the time Wooden Hand's canoe headed for shore a light rain had started falling. The boy pulled the bare skin back on his shoulders and placed the worn conical hat on his head. They beached the canoe and Water Bear fired out a string of orders to the assembled men. Chet understood enough to know he had to gather dry driftwood for a fire while the others unloaded the temporary shelter materials from the dugouts. Using dry tinder and kindling he brought with him, the old slave had a small fire started before Chet returned with his first load.

The other men were constructing a cedar pole framework behind the fire, above the high tide line. The slaves buried the ends of two poles in the sand and lashed a twelve-foot pole between them, about six feet off the ground. They then took seven other twelve foot poles and lashed them to the cross pole at two-foot intervals. Next, they tied long mats, beginning at the back bottom, over the leaning poles and overlapped them to keep out the rain, thus forming a twelve by twelve foot lean-to. The slaves took one last mat and wrapped it around and over the north side of the lean-to. This made an effective wind break and would keep the group drier and warmer. The men chose their places and placed their blankets and personal gear under the shelter. Chet picked the spot right in the middle, next to the fire. The Indians boiled water for tea and ate the ripe herring they had with them. The white boy had his salmon and berry cake and a long cold drink of fresh water from a seal bladder container.

Some of the men started the gambling game Chet had seen many times before, but the young man spent his time feeding the fire and bringing in a good supply of wood. One by one the gamblers settled in to sleep and finally only Chet was left awake. The white slave put on a hefty load of wood and snuggled as close to the fire as he dared. Chet felt quite comfortable and for the first time, outside of the long house, he actually slept a few hours at a time. The young man got up to relieve himself and re-stoke the fire once around midnight and then stayed asleep after that.

The next morning was a typical winter day in the Pacific Northwest, rainy with blustery winds and not too cold. The party had actually traveled too far, so Wooden Hand, with the tree cutters, took one of the canoes to search for the correct beach. After an hour's time the group returned, and having found the chosen cedar, they broke camp, paddling the short distance to the new beach. It was a small cove with a fresh water creek at the deepest end. Just beyond the cove stood a small islet and a large kelp bed, home to some hundred or so sea otter. The beach was rocky like Chahakquot, and the tall cedar grew right to the high tide line. These closest trees were large, but their trunks were curved and weathered. They had too many branches and were not fit for most uses. The tree Wooden Hand selected grew about a hundred feet inland. It was a younger tree, set in a thick forest of giants. The sparse light made this tree grow upwards quickly with few branches on the lower hundred feet. Its base was broad and flared to six feet in diameter, but it thinned to three feet in diameter a few feet off the ground. For most of its length the cedar's diameter remained constant and had only narrowed to two feet through the first hundred feet of ascent. The old slave would start by placing a cut at the five foot level and cut it again at about the eighty or ninety foot level, after it had fallen.

It was decided that the party would make camp next to the tree. The forest provided protection from the wind and rain and the fresh water creek meandered within a distance of thirty feet. All the group helped in carrying the goods and tools in from the beach. After a couple of trips a well-worn path through the giant green ferns led the way. A temporary shelter was set up as before, and a flat area in front of the lean-to was cleared for a fire pit. As soon as the camp was in order, the men pulled one of the canoes up into the woods completely out of sight and the other one was left at the edge of the forest. Cut tree branches were placed to conceal it. Before they returned to camp, each man carried as many fist-sized rocks from the beach as possible. The rocks were thrown in the fire pit and a fire started. Chet and one of the other slave men from *Whale Oil House* were sent to gather wood. The boy took a basket and headed for the beach for driftwood, while the other man headed into the forest for dry cedar branches. Water Bear and Wooden hand set to work on the tree with the other men.

By the time Chet returned with his first load, the cutters were well on their way to constructing a scaffolding, four feet high, around the trunk of the tree using the remaining cedar poles. They used planks for the footing on top of the scaffold, which enabled the workers to walk completely around the great tree at the cutting level. After two hours the scaffold was complete and the wood pile sufficient. The rocks that had been carried from the beach were heated to a glowing orange.

At last all was ready to begin and the old Haida slave went to the great tree spreading his arms around the trunk as far as he could. Grasping the bark with his fingers, Wooden Hand began chanting and praying to the spirit of the cedar. Chet noticed the group took this ritual dead seriously, and made no movement while it went on. The old man jumped down from the scaffold and took his adze, dancing and chanting all around the tree. When he was satisfied, each man came forward, touched the tree, and prayed.

Chet was standing alone now, and at the urging of the old man, with a wink, a smile, and a nod of the head, the white slave went forward to speak to the tree.

"Mighty cedar I don't know your spirit, but I bet he knows my God. Please, Father, let this tree die with dignity so that it may serve these people, your children. Let it fall true and straight and may no harm come to any one of us."

Chet turned and walked away from the tree noticing that Water Bear seemed pleased with his prayer, even though the big Nootkan couldn't understand it.

Wooden Hand used his iron tipped adze to rough out the size of the initial cut and two of the Indian slaves began chipping away at the bark. He also roughed in a bottom line, and two feet higher, a top line all around the tree. The other two slaves started removing the bark between those two lines but did not cut into the sapwood.

While those four slaves were at work, Water Bear, Wooden Hand, Chet, and Flying Gull, the only common man in the party, began to lift and place the twelve four-foot alder logs in a row ten feet apart, and parallel to one another along the line of fall. It was Wooden Hand's intention to drop the great cedar, so that its length would fall across these logs. This would enable the wood workers, while keeping the fallen tree off the ground, to strip the bark and sapwood. It would also serve to aid in pulling the great cedar to the beach by allowing the tree to roll on top of the alder logs. When the logs were in place, Flying Gull went to join the first two slaves. The common man would work with and supervise the first two slaves, and Wooden Hand would work with and supervise the other two. The men would work in half hour shifts, from morning to night, until the tree fell.

Chet was in charge of keeping the firewood supplied, when not with Water Bear fishing for the group's only fresh food. When the first shift change was made, the tree bark was halfway stripped between the two parallel lines, and a small shelf and notch formed at the initial cut area. Before going up the scaffold, the old slave broke out a pair of long wooden tongs cut from a single yew branch and picked up a hot rock from the fire. Carrying it to the tree, Wooden Hand placed the hot rock in the cut notch. The wood began to smoke and burn. The old man repeated this procedure until he had three rocks crammed into the notch. The old slave took a hemlock branch and dipped it into a basket filled from the stream. Wooden Hand used the bough to keep the tree wet where he didn't want the burn to extend. After the rocks cooled, the resulting charred wood was easily chipped away before a new set of hot rocks was put in place.

A new cut was started on the back of the tree opposite the first cut and the same procedure followed. In addition wedges were used above the burned notches and driven down at forty-five degree angles splitting off bits of wood, and making the notch more of a wedge shape. The process was slow and tedious. After hours, the cuts were no bigger than one good lumberjack could do with a sharp double bladed axe in a half hour. So it went the rest of the day, rotating shift after shift.

Water Bear, satisfied that the tree was lined up properly and that the work was progressing well, decided to take some fishing gear and check out the cove for whatever might be dwelling there. Chet had a substantial supply of wood to keep the fires going, so he joined Water Bear on the woodland path to the beach. The large fisherman threw his gear into the dugout at the edge of the forest and stood for a moment scanning the horizon. The boy thought he might be concerned about unwanted neighbors still hanging around the area. Why else would they hide the canoes?

Water Bear walked out onto the beach still searching the sea, then turned around and looked back toward the camp. The smoke from the fire was barely visible, and what smoke there was blended quickly with the low hanging clouds. At a distance no one would be able to pick up the fact that a fire even existed. Happy with the situation, Water Bear turned to Chet and smiled.

"We'll go fishing now, White Clam," he said. "While the others work."

The boy understood the Nootkan words well enough and walked up the sloping beach to the canoe. He began taking the tree branches off the dugout. The young man had never taken time to notice the carved figure on the bow before. The Indian carvings were so unique and this one was accented by red, white, and blue-green paint. The geometric designs raised up out of the wood, and were extremely pleasing to look at.

Water Bear gave Chet a bark rope, of good size, that was made fast to the bow. The white boy pulled on the rope but the thirty-foot canoe would not budge.

"Wait, White Clam," called Water Bear as he walked to the stern of the craft. "If you wait for me to push, the canoe will move much easier. Sometimes that boy is a little stupid," the big Indian murmured to himself.

Water Bear gave a great shove and Chet pulled hard on the cedar cable. The black canoe creaked and slowly began to move down the rocky slope. As the bottom moved from dirt to the wet round rocks the process speeded up. The brightly painted bow neared the water and the boy, not wanting to get wet, dropped the rope and sped to the back of the canoe where he helped shove it the rest of the way into the water. Water Bear, knowing that the white boy was weak when it came to wet and cold, let Chet jump in the dugout and the big Nootkan alone pushed the craft further into the waves until the canoe was able to carry its own weight off the bottom. The dugout was quite easy for just the two of them to paddle and they spent a few minutes exploring the cove. Finally, the large fisherman found a suitable area and baited two lines with some extremely ripe herring. It was so rotten Water Bear had to tie it on the hook with fine threads of bark. Chet was happy he was twenty or so feet away where the rotten smell of the bait box was minimal.

After tying on some weight, the lines were dropped to the bottom and Chet took one of them. The boy took off his bearskin and propped it in the bow. He stretched his legs out and settled back on the robe, his cone-shaped hat tipped forward. Water Bear made himself comfortable also, but the large Indian kept alert and searched the horizon every few minutes. If any unfriendlies did show up, Water Bear wanted to have time to paddle far enough away so as not to endanger the rest of the work party. If overtaken by an enemy, he and White Clam would just beach the canoe and hide in the woods.

They did not have to wait long for the fish to bite. Within minutes the round fisherman had a nibble on his line, and with the skill of many years he jerked the line at the right instant. Up came the fish without much fight, and soon a flopping fifteen-inch sand flounder was wriggling on the dugout floor.

Not much of a fish compared to king salmon, Chet thought, but tasty just the same.

Water Bear brought two more of the fish up in the next few minutes and Chet, holding his empty line, was beginning to feel left out.

Why can't I catch any fish? he thought. *Are they all over there under the back of the boat? I always catch the biggest fish, usually.* The white boy wasn't feeling quite as cocky as he had fifteen minutes earlier and was beginning to think that the crafty fat Indian was playing a joke on him, when a sharp tug on Chet's line caught all his attention. *This might be the big one!* The boy let the fish take the bait until he was sure the hook had been swallowed, and then gave a jerk. There wasn't much dead weight on the other end of the line, but Water Bear's fish had not been large ones either, so the young man still felt optimistic.

"I got one!" Chet screamed as he reeled in the line hand over hand. "I think it's pretty good sized - big one," he turned and said in Nootkan.

That got the big Indian's attention, for it was true that White Clam had the big luck. The boy pulled frantically, fearing the fish might get away. With a mighty last jerk the fish broke water and flipped into the canoe. It was another flounder all right. Its ugly eyes were set on the same side, the brown side, of its head. The white underside was only visible when its powerful muscles flexed and twisted round. Chet stared at the fish as it lay in all its savage bloody beauty - all seven and a half inches of it.

"A big one," Water Bear repeated. "A BIG ONE!" he laughed. "You call that a big one?"

The fat man was beside himself with laughter. Not in Chet's three months with the Chahakquot Mowachahts had he ever seen an Indian laugh so much. Water Bear would quiet down, then look at the fish, then at Chet, and laugh some more until he fairly choked. Chet almost wished the big Indian would choke.

This went on for what seemed like an eternity. In fact Water Bear and the boy both caught more fish before the laughter ended. Chet's other fish weren't any bigger, so there was nothing to save the white boy's ego.

The rain started after a late afternoon haze appeared and with it darkness rolled over the mountains. The two fishermen decided it was time to return to the others. The men would not go hungry on this trip, for Chet and Water Bear had a good eighteen flounders in the bottom of their dugout.

It was high tide when they returned to the trailhead; so the two needed no help getting the canoe up to the edge of the forest. The tidewater was already there.

A tired group was waiting for the fishermen when they arrived at the camp and Chet noticed his woodpile was half gone. One of the men was still tending the hot rocks in the notch of the cedar tree and the live wood glowed to a flame every few moments. The progress looked painfully slow to Chet. *What he could do,* he thought, *with an axe and bucksaw!*

The men were hungry so they quickly set about cleaning the flounder. Wooden Hand made some thin cedar stakes and they skewered the fish and roasted the fresh white meat next to the fire. There were two fish for each man except Water Bear, who got four. There was little meat on the flat fish, but they welcomed it just the same. As they ate, Water Bear recounted the events of the fishing expedition making great mention of Chet's *Big One* to the laughter of all.

Chet was sitting by the fire licking the oil off his hands and watching the rocks smolder on the tree, when an idea hit him like a lightning bolt. He crawled over to the old Haida slave and tapped him on the shoulder.

"Wooden Hand, you want rock tonight?" he struggled in Nootkan.

The old man thought this was a strange question, but then he thought White Clam was strange anyway.

"I want rock tonight," the white boy struggled again.

The old slave looked at Water Bear and shook his head.

"Sometimes I think White Clam has lived with strange spirits. What do you think he wants to do with these hot rocks tonight?"

"You know the boy is stupid at times," the fisherman said. "It might be that white skull of his. Two Skins clubbed him pretty hard. Maybe his brain is damaged."

The other men laughed when they heard this, but Chet could not follow such eloquent Nootkan and just smiled, not knowing what was said.

"Let's see what he does with them," Flying Gull whispered low not wanting Chet to hear what was said. The boy didn't understand it anyway.

"All right, you take them as long as they are back by morning," Water Bear said in all seriousness.

Chet understood that he could use the rocks, but instead of reaching for the hot rocks and make some use of them that would entertain the waiting Indians, the boy jumped up and ran to his bedroll. The group was confused. They looked at each other and then at the white boy. Why was he digging a hole?

"Wooden Hand is right. He must have lived with strange spirits," exclaimed Flying Gull.

They watched as the boy dug a pit in the soft forest floor under the shelter. He was careful not to disturb the sleeping places of the men next to him. The boy saved the excavated dirt in a neat pile then stripped some small branches from a cedar bough piling them next to the mound of dirt. Next, he came back to the fire, grabbed the tongs, and to the generous applause of the group for finally doing so, took the rocks, one by one from the fire and placed them in the pit.

"Is he going to cook something?" said one of the slaves with a puzzled look on his face.

"That's it," said another slave, "he's going to roast something in the pit."

"Yes," said Water Bear. "It looks like he's going to roast himself."

They all laughed again.

After spreading the rocks over a four-foot area of the shallow pit, Chet covered the pit back up with dirt and spread out some of the boughs of cedar on top. That done, he lay down on top of the closed pit. The Indians looked at one another, saying nothing, but knowing what was going to happen.

At first, Chet could feel the warmth, and he smiled at them. But soon the white slave jumped up with a big, "ow." The rocks were too hot and were burning the bottom of his pants.

"I told you he was stupid," was Water Bear's only remark, as the others laughed.

"And I knew it would be entertaining," boasted Flying Gull.

Ignoring them, Chet added some more dirt and boughs to the bed place and soon had achieved what he wanted. With the mat in place the boy had a nice warm bed under him that would last for hours. Chet snuggled down contentedly, knowing that as long as there were fire and rock he would not freeze again. That night the boy spent his best night out of doors. The young man cuddled under the bearskin happy with his new found warmth, remembering all the times in his life when he had been cold and how good it felt to be in a nice warm bed. Chet fell asleep within minutes.

A heavy rain was beating down as the boy opened his eyes. The warmth underneath Chet had long since faded, but at least he and his belongings were dry. The men were stirring and no one had to remind Chet that driftwood was needed to replenish what was burned the preceding night. Wooden Hand was busy heating water for tea and motioned for the white boy to return the rocks to the fire. The boy dug up the stones and placed them back in the fire pit. Rain was coming down hard above the group but the large branches of the cedar trees kept it from saturating the camp. The drops that fell off the boughs were larger but less frequent than if they were out in the open.

Water Bear was nowhere to be seen. Chet headed for the beach, walking down the path, his moccasins squishing water out of wet moss at each step, rain beading off his bark hat. He soon saw the large Indian standing next to the canoes. The fisherman was working with the fishing tackle and was getting ready to go fishing.

"White Clam, glad you are here. Come help me push the canoe towards the water."

The big fellow motioned with his hands as he talked so Chet would understand better. They worked the heavy dugout to the beach. Water Bear grabbed a small wooden box from the canoe, opened it, and showed the boy its contents. Chet recognized the goods immediately, having used them himself on many occasions.

"Tell me white slave, are these of any good use?" the Nootkan said as he turned the box over, letting a dozen iron hooks fall in a tangle, into his left hand.

The boy did not understand but said, "hooks," in English, pointing at the shining bits of metal.

"I traded for these with one of your white men. I think we will try them today. We will drop many lines at once. Catch many fish. Go now. Fill the wood pile and call to me when you have finished."

The Indian smiled and pushed the craft into the water.

Chet made for the nearest pile of driftwood and started loading sticks. He stopped to watch as the sleek canoe moved away into the cove. It was a truly beautiful craft to watch, with its classic lines and its mysterious painted bow. *Water Bear did not have to worry about anyone seeing them today*, Chet thought. Not only was the rain thick, but a cold fog also hugged the bay. The tops of the trees were not visible and the smoke from the fire would be impossible to detect. The young man put both arms around the load of branches and headed back to camp.

Flying Gull's team was already chipping away at the huge trunk as the other two slaves and Wooden Hand ate. Chet took time for a cool drink and a couple of smoked herring, but passed up the putrid fermented herring the Indians so relished. After working another hour, the white boy had the pile of wood bulging again and seeing that the tree burning was well under way, Chet told the old Haida slave that he was going to join Water Bear. He took his bearskin robe and put it on, for the sedentary business of fishing would not keep him warm like wood gathering did.

The moss on the forest floor was becoming even more saturated with moisture and stepping on the soft green mat made Chet feel he was walking on large wet sponges. When the boy reached the beach, he searched for a glimpse of the black canoe. On the far side of the cove, about a hundred feet off shore, the white boy saw a faint dark shadow, motionless on the calm water.

Chet started along the rocky beach towards the fresh water stream at the head of the cove. Even though wet and cold from his morning's work, the young man's heart was light because he was already looking forward to his warm bed that night.

As the white slave neared the stream the beach became sandy, and he walked closer to the saltwater where the footing was solid. The canoe became more and more defined the closer Chet got, and he could see the fat Nootkan sitting in the back of the canoe, hunched over. Water Bear was motionless and he was not facing forward, but facing backward, which was a strange thing to be doing since Indians almost never faced backward in a canoe. Water Bear also had a strange stick object in his hand, resting on his lap. The big man was studying the water behind the canoe and as Chet came closer the boy sensed something was afoot.

"Ahoy, Water Bear, what's goin' on?" the boy yelled in English. The big Indian said nothing but made a definite motion with his outstretched hand for the boy to be quiet and stay still. Chet took a few steps further and stopped. There about twenty feet from the back of the canoe was a trio of sea otters playing in the gentle waves. They were diving and swimming, but only staying above water for a split second at a time. Finally the biggest one rose to the surface, swimming on its back, sporting a shellfish on its chest. Chet remembered watching the playful animals from the

Exact while at anchor in the Strait of Juan de Fuca. The furry otter lay there on its back cracking open a shell with a sharp rock it had carried up from the bottom. *What a peaceful playful scene,* the boy thought.

Chet had momentarily forgotten Water Bear until quick movements from the Indian made him realize what was happening. The large Nootkan pulled back swiftly letting go the string on the bow and the arrow went true to its mark. The otter had no chance as the shaft pierced its flesh above the right arm and into the lung. Choking and gasping in its own blood, the creature rapidly fell still and floated on top of the waves as the Indian paddled towards it.

"And Bill thought they didn't have bows and arrows," the boy whispered to himself as his mind drifted back to the galley conversation they had about northwest Indians.

Water Bear had given a cry of joy upon slaying the otter, but Chet could not help feeling sorry for the gentle animal. Killing fish and clams was one thing, but killing mammals, even for food, just didn't appeal to him. Many times at his parent's farm, the boy was made to skin and butcher livestock. He enjoyed eating meat, but the killing of the animals was not to his liking.

When the dugout was paddled ashore Chet waded out and climbed aboard. Otter was not the only prey Water Bear had had luck with that morning. Already a dozen flounder and one large sculpin lined the floor of the canoe. The otter lay on top of the fish. It was about four feet long with a fourteen-inch tail. The fur was glossy black except for a white patch on the forehead and a white tip on the tail. The eyes were closed and the long black whiskers stuck straight out from its face. Chet tried to seem happy for the big fisherman, but inside he felt sick seeing the bloody mess before him.

"White Clam, see the otter. It is of good quality and will bring many trade goods. I also found a good spot for fishing. Grab the paddle and let's go back out to the place between the two rocks," the Indian said, obviously in good spirits. "After we catch some more fish we will go after another otter. The white man's hooks work well. Look, I have rigged a double line for each of us."

Water Bear held up a bark line tied to a small, triangular shaped affair made of two twelve inch strands of line and a twelve inch piece of cedar. From the ends of the stick dangled two leaders with the iron hooks attached. Tied to the middle of the stick was a slightly longer line with a heavy rock bound to it. The rope triangle with the stick base, two hooks and a stone looked strange to the boy, but the configuration hauled in the fish.

Within two hours they had forty bottom fish, mostly flounder, with some sculpin and rockfish thrown in. During the morning they were also getting bites from crabs on their lines, but the elusive creatures would fall off the hook just before they could get them into the canoe. This was just a nuisance for Water Bear, who had little experience with crab, probably because the bulkier whalebone hooks made by the Indians were too big for the crab's mandible. But the fine iron hooks seemed to snag the crustaceans and only at the last second did they try to get free. Chet, unlike Water Bear, was hoping for a good sized one for his dinner, and, to his delight one of the last pulls netted a nice ten-inch crab.

"We have enough food for the whole village," Chet said.

Water Bear seemed to understand and smiled rubbing his stomach, in anticipation of the coming night's feast.

"Lets try for another otter," the big hunter said with a twitch of his eyebrows.

Water Bear took out the long narrow box behind him and drew out the crabapple wood bow. The wood was very hard and the length was almost four feet when unstrung. A half dozen cedar arrows, whose shafts were sanded perfectly round, filled the rest of the box. The large Mowachaht fisherman-hunter motioned the boy towards mid-canoe and set about teaching him how to use the weapon.

The Nootkans, as did all northwest coast Indians, held the bow in a horizontal position, rather than the traditional vertical position of the plains and east coast Indians. The shaft of the arrow was feathered with eagle plumage when possible, otherwise with gull. The point was made of lightweight bone, so the whole arrow floated. A flint or granite tipped arrow would sink and with it would go many hours of highly skilled work.

It was well into the afternoon and the otter colony had forgotten the loss of their cousin earlier, for the far islet was once again busy with silver-black swimmers. The little animals had no fear of man and were incredibly tame, which allowed the experienced hunter to paddle within a few feet of the playful mammals before they would dive to safety. Water Bear broke out a second bow, and much to the boy's dismay, wanted him to try and kill an otter also.

Chet climbed forward over the ripening bodies of various dead sea life sprawled on the dugout floor. With bow and arrow at their sides the two hunters paddled towards the rocky islet, and right into the middle of the feeding otter clan. Water Bear motioned for the boy to pick out a target to the south and he would do likewise to the north. The white boy's heart was not in it, but the thrill of the hunt was too strong and Chet found the bowstring coming back, an otter in his sights.

"Aim just above the head and over the chest," Water Bear said in Nootkan.

The big hunter picked out one for himself, only ten feet away. Bow strung, he turned to watch as Chet let the arrow go and before it struck, the big Indian had sent his own arrow true to its target. The boy's arrow hit three feet in front of the otter and submerged for a few seconds before floating, feathers first, to the surface. Water Bear was two for two. The two-year-old otter was so close it would have been difficult to miss. The rest of the colony dived to safety and rose a fair distance away. Water Bear put the struggling sea otter out of its misery with a sharp whack on its head from his whalebone club and hauled it aboard. The crack of the otter's skull made the white boy sick to his stomach, but Chet kept his revulsion hidden.

"Not a bad shot, White Clam," the hunter smiled, "we'll practice some more tonight. Right now there is much work to be done."

They dug in their paddles and swiftly sped across the cove to the beachhead. The booty was too much for the two of them to carry, so Water Bear carried his otter and Chet carried some flounder and his crab. Darkness was still an hour away when they reached camp and Flying Gull sent his two slaves with baskets to carry back the rest of the fish. There had been some progress made on the tree burning and Chet thought they must be more than half way through by the time dinner was started.

The white boy was not too fond of the way the sculpin's spiny dorsal fin looked, so he let the Indians take all of them. Chet picked three nice flounder and a rockfish, cleaned and filleted them, and wrapped them in seaweed. He dug out a shallow pit next to the fire and placed the fish in to roast. The Mowachahts, as was their want, almost always boiled their fish. Chet added his crab to their boiling basket. The young man hoped the hard shell of the crab would keep out the fish taste and let him enjoy the tender meat.

The slaves were cleaning and cooking Water Bear's fish while he was busy skinning the two otters. Since the white boy was waiting for his own dinner to cook he sat down and watched the big Nootkan dress the dead mammals. Water Bear had taken one of the spare planks and had converted it into a cutting table. He made a vertical cut up the center of the ventral, or belly, surface from the anus to the sternum. The big Indian cleaned out the innards and placed them in the wastebasket with the fish guts. Indians always threw the waste back into the sea. Water Bear carefully cut horizontally around the feet, leaving the tail attached, and on around the head, scalping the fur with ears, eyes, and nose included. He peeled away the pelt in one piece, cut the meat in chunks, and threw all of it in with the boiling fish except for a couple of chunks Chet kept for himself. The boy quickly fished his crab out of the basket before more hot rocks and the otter meat were added.

Chet took the rest of the rocks in the fire to use for his bed then picked up a driftwood branch to use as a skewer. He stuck the otter meat on one end and pushed the other end in the soft ground so that the meat hung over the fire. As the men began to dip into the boiling basket of fish and otter stew, Chet cracked crab. The flesh was tasty but he longed for some real butter to go with it. The fish was fully baked by this time and the boy ate his fill of the tender white meat. The smell of roasting red meat started to remind him of days long gone. It had been so long since Chet had eaten anything but roots, berries, clams, and fish, he had forgotten how good red meat smelled cooking.

The meat roasted slowly and Chet watched as the juices sizzled and the steak began to char. After letting it cool, the boy took a bite of the meat and found it to be quite good. It was still raw just below the surface; so the young man had to eat and roast, then eat again. A berry cake and some fresh water ended the meal, which was one of the more diverse and enjoyable ones Chet had experienced since his captivity.

Water Bear was enjoying his meal too and there seemed no end to the amount of food the man could put away. Chet was sure they had caught enough to warrant some leftover fish, but only a dozen strips of otter were left for him to smoke above the fire and turn into jerky. The big Indian, although full, had to get back to his skins, and set about scraping the inside of the pelts with a sharp rock. He pierced holes through the head, tail, and the four legs and stretched the skin over the cleaning plank until it was smooth. Fully extended, the pelt measured five feet by two feet and drying it in this manner would allow the fur to keep its flat shape and glossy appearance.

As Chet watched the skinning he thought of many articles of clothing the pelt could be used for. A nice pair of furry gloves would do well indeed. A fur lined jacket, or perhaps some fur-lined moccasins would make life easier, but the pelt was worth more as a trade item to the Indians. The thought of warm fur made him remember his bed.

Chet rushed to the fire and got the hot rocks, one at a time, into the bed pit, and covered them with the right amount of dirt. He sat down on the warm bed and listened to the Indians talk. Wooden Hand had determined that by the end of the next day the great cedar should be ready to fall. That meant maybe only one more night here. Chet hoped he would be in camp when the tree fell. It would be a sight to see, but his whereabouts would be up to Water Bear. Chet never knew what the big fisherman had planned from day to day. It was still early, but the cozy warmth of the rocks under ground lulled and relaxed him, and Chet was soon under the blankets and fast asleep.

After the morning chores of firewood gathering and a bite of otter meat to eat, the white boy joined the big fisherman for the daily routine of fishing. It was a cold, clear day with frost on the ground and the sun in the sky. The water was flat and there was little or no wind. They took the canoe out of the cove and headed for the islands that rimmed the expanse of the Sound to the south. The smoke from the fire was easily seen today, but there was also unlimited visibility for the big Nootkan as well, which would enable him to detect any unwanted visitors in plenty of time. At any rate Water Bear didn't seem concerned about the clear day and they made for the outermost island.

The fishing went well and by noon slave and master made a landing on the island's sandy southern shore. Water Bear built a small fire and they roasted fresh fish for lunch. The sun, although not really that warm, gave the illusion of warmth, and the large Mowachaht decided to take a nap in the rare sunshine.

"Master, tide out, I get clam for dinner," Chet said in broken Nootkan. The big Indian just grunted approval, knowing there would be little luck in finding shellfish. The white boy set off down the beach in search of a suitable digging stick. *This would be a good test,* the boy thought.

"I'll pretend this is the way it will be when I escape, and if I don't find food I'll starve," he said to himself.

Chet scowered the beach for signs of shellfish, but soon came to the realization that this was not a good clam beach. The one back at Nesook was long and shallow. This one was short and had a deep drop-off a few yards from shore. The sand was different also. It wasn't as fine and the color was lighter.

The boy searched the beach to the north but things did not improve. The sand turned to rocks and finally to black cliffs, with wind-battered evergreens rimming the edge in various stages of stunted growth. The lack of food gathering made Chet think twice about his escape and the boy knew it would be well into spring before he dared make the attempt. Chet was, however, confident in his fishing skills and success in that endeavor made him feel better.

By this time the cliff looked inviting, and the young man searched the rocky crags for the best route to the top. The boy started up the cliff, keeping to the outcrops with the most trees and shrubs. Using the branches as handholds, he slowly made his way up the steep face. After fifteen minutes Chet found himself sixty feet high on a small ledge with no safe path to continue. The cliff had beaten him, but it was such a nice sunny day he did not mind. Just being sixty feet up gave the boy a great view.

Chet was a little confused as he looked around. The expanse of the Sound to the south split to the southeast and to the west. The former headed back to Nesook and the latter was the channel back to Nootka Sound and the Pacific Ocean. They were in a dead-end finger of water and it was no wonder that Standing Seal was concerned about which way Two Skins was going to go. If the half-breed had turned north into this channel it would have been hard for Swimming Otter to escape his notice.

Chet looked east along the sandy beach and could see the black canoe and the sleeping form of Water Bear lying in the sparse grass, some hundred yards away. It was getting late so the young man slowly started his descent. Chet stopped half way down to take another look at the view. As he glanced toward the mouth of the split channel, grasping a spruce branch for support, his heart almost fell out of his chest. There to the south, just breaking out of the western channel was a two masted schooner, stretching her main and foresails to the wind.

The white boy could not believe his eyes.

"Ahoy, sail ho!" he yelled, waving his arms, not realizing he was too far away to be seen.

No one saw him, but someone heard him.

Chet raced down the last part of the cliff and ran down the beach yelling to his Indian companion.

"A ship, Water Bear, a ship!" he cried.

The big Indian had seen the sails after the boy's first cry and watched as the schooner sailed on to the east towards Nesook. Chet, full of hope and all smiles, ran up pointing to the ship disappearing into the east channel, but his enthusiasm was cut abruptly short.

Before the white slave knew what happened the big Nootkan grabbed the boy's neck and slammed his face to the sand. The grit burned Chet's eyes and he could not breath, as his head was pressed harder to the stinging ground. The white boy felt a rope go around first one hand, than the other, with a knee pressed to the back of his neck so he could not resist. *What was happening? He thought Water Bear was his friend. Why was he doing this? He was willing to fight for the village. He had great medicine. The people had come to love him. He was good luck and he was a good slave.*

Slave! Then Chet remembered. He was, indeed, still a slave. No matter that the white boy laughed with his masters, and felt secure in their presence. When it came down to it he was still just a piece of property. Chet was unceremoniously picked up and dumped in the canoe. Water Bear said nothing and shoved the dugout back into waist deep water, turned it around and jumped in. They headed back to the cove as fast as the big fisherman could paddle.

Chet was hurt emotionally, and as he worked himself to a sitting position, the white slave looked back at the Indian he considered a comrade and tried to make eye contact. Water Bear would not look at him. The boy only wanted to give him a look of understanding. He was not bitter. Chet truly understood that Water Bear had to act this way. The young man also knew that there would be no getting back to his people without escape and this just deepened his resolve to do so.

The canoe moved slower with only one paddling, and the darkening sky brought on a chill from the light north wind. The white boy stared at the shoreline, intent on not showing his usual weakness for the cold. The half-breed's bearskin was at his feet, and Chet hoped that Water Bear would take time to throw it over his shoulders before heading back to camp. As the dugout's bottom scraped against the rocky beach, Chet was surprised when the big Nootkan reached for the rope and untied the boy's hands.

"There will be no more screaming at the floating houses. If you try to steal a canoe again I will not hesitate to kill you. Now get out and help me beach the canoe," the Indian said in a gruff monotone.

Chet did not understand much of what Water Bear had said, but from the tone of his voice Chet knew whatever it was was not good. With an expressionless face the boy jumped into the shallow water and helped push the dugout to the high tide line. The two gathered the day's catch, and after picking up their gear, they silently made their way into the forest.

XIV

The *Exact* was finally weighing anchor again after six weeks of freezing weather. The schooner had off-loaded its cargo of miners and equipment on Moresby Island, the southernmost of the two largest islands in the Queen Charlottes. Hoping to get back to Portland before the winter set in, the crew had worked around the clock, but an early arctic storm, with its cold wind and freezing rain, encased the ship in a spider web of ice. Two weeks of snow further complicated matters and the frozen ropes and cables snapped in places, leaving the ship's running gear crippled. Fresh water was in short supply and the crew had to melt snow for drinking because the supplies on land were frozen solid. Days passed and the ship's men and captain became more and more on edge. The first week in January brought southwest winds and balmy forty-degree temperatures. After a slow thaw, the rigging was able to be repaired. Captain Folger was in no mood to stay the winter in Skincuttle Inlet, and neither was the crew. All hands toiled long and hard to repair the rigging, anxious to see the Queen Charlottes behind them. The Hudson's Bay store and white settlement there amounted to just a few buildings. The Haida Indians were always a nuisance, lurking near the ship, making threatening gestures, and looking for something to steal. Guards were posted nightly. The food available was limited and the crew were using up their profits to buy what food and goods they needed. When the fair weather held after the rigging was fixed, Captain Folger decided to make a run for the northern tip of Vancouver Island.

The ship seemed deserted with no miners or settlers on board, and Matt had the crew working the schooner hard. After leaving the inlet, Bart was released from the brig during the day and allowed to cook and walk about the deck. He was not warmly received by any of the crew, and hardly talked to by anyone at all.

Lloyd Merrifield was the only passenger. The miner had taken advantage of the eight-week delay to get his claim squared away and decided to go back with the Exact to report to his partners. Lloyd was also concerned about Chet and wanted to find out if there had been any news of the missing boy. In all, only ten men were on the ship as she beat down the Canadian coast ahead of the weather.

Three days of hard sailing brought the schooner to Cape Scott, the northern tip of Vancouver Island. It was now the last days of January and Captain Folger, at the insistence of Matt and Lloyd, was going to make a detour back to Nootka Sound to search for the lost boy. Before they had left Chahakquot, back in November, Lloyd had persuaded Standing Seal to point out the location of the winter village at Nesook on one of Captain Folger's charts. The ship's crew would make one last attempt at finding the boy before sending news of his probable death to his parents.

Three more days of cold, rainy weather brought the craft into Nootka Sound, past the deserted village of Yuquot, and on to the southern tip of Bligh Island, where Chahakquot stood. They anchored in the cove and lowered a boat to take on much needed fresh water, and to search for anyone who might still be around.

Matt and Lloyd, armed with pistols from the captain's locker, headed towards the huge house frames, while Bill, Andrew, and two crewmen filled casks with fresh water from the creek that split the village. It did not seem like the same place they had seen two and a half months before. The village was a ghost town. The cedar plank sides of the houses were gone and the wind raced and whistled through the emptiness. The great wood beams and totem poles stood quietly like the last remnants of some lost civilization. The two men didn't speak, but searched in silence, and, after finding no one, they returned to the boat.

The water barrels were loaded and the party returned to the ship. Captain Folger decided to spend the night in the cove, and get an early start up the Sound in the morning. One guard was posted and changed hourly, so the men got a long, secure night's sleep. They wanted no trouble from renegade Indians, so they slept with guns at their sides.

"Wake up ya worthless lubbers!" yelled Bill as he clanged the ship's bell. "All hands rise and turn out."

The sleepy crew stumbled on deck and headed for the galley where the old cook had been preparing a hot meal of coffee and porridge.

"Hey Bart, how you gonna' feel when we find old Chet and we let him become your boss?" laughed Andrew.

The old seaman just scowled and swore under his breath. Bart had never meant the boy harm; it was just business. He stood to make a fair amount of money from Drake if the Indians got hooked on whiskey. The old cook's only intention was for them to keep their pelts and hold out for the liquor that Drake's ship would bring in the spring. How was he supposed to know that the boy was going to follow him and get killed? Besides, Bart had broken no law, and as soon as they reached Portland, the captain would have no legal recourse to keep him in the brig any longer.

Outside, it was a clear, cold day and the sun shown brightly. The anchor was raised and the schooner moved up Nootka Sound under shortened sail. The detail of the upper Sound on the charts was limited, so the ship proceeded with caution. Two men were always in the bow taking a depth sounding every few minutes and the schooner was kept in mid-channel at all times. A mistake now could cause the ship to go aground and might prove disastrous if they were unable to free her. Being off the normal sailing path, and with hostile Indians around, their prospects would be bleak indeed.

"Give me a sounding!" yelled Captain Folger, cupping his hands to his mouth.

"Six and a half fathoms, capt'n," answered a crewmember, as he pulled the line in and cast it out again. "Six and a half steady."

It took all of the morning and into the afternoon, sailing at a slow pace, to reach Nesook Bay. The sun was shining and it was a balmy fifty-five degrees. The seas were calm and the crew had a touch of spring fever as they turned toward the eastern channel and, unknowingly, away from the boy they sought. The *Exact* could not get within a quarter mile of the river mouth because of the shallow water, but the crew saw many Mowachaht canoes in the bay, and the smoke from their cooking fires let the men on the schooner know that the village lay to the east of the long sandy beach in front of them.

As soon as they sighted the ship's tall fore and main masts, a few of the Indians paddled hard for the village, and the rest came towards the schooner. Their red and black painted faces, bark hats, and clothing assured Matt and Lloyd that they had found the right bay. These were Standing Seal's people.

Andrew had climbed the foremast some time before and called down a warning as the ship neared the sandy shoreline.

"Shallows ahead, one hundred yards," he bellowed.

"Captain, three and a half fathoms," yelled the crewmember in the bow. "Make it less than three, now."

That was enough for the old captain. No use in taking her any closer. "Strike the sails Mister English, let go the anchor, and keep them Injuns off the ship. I don't want any trouble."

A group of five dugouts were already snug against the side of the schooner and the Nootkans in them were trying to trade their catch of fresh fish for anything that could be deemed useful.

"Captain, I think we should lower a boat and find that English speaking Indian right away before it gets dark. If he has any news we can act on it and get back here before dusk. I don't like the thought of being so far up this narrow sound and being outnumbered fifty to one," said Matt.

"I agree," added Lloyd. "These folks were kind enough before, but this place is a lot more isolated. No tellin' what they might do, and it's best to plan for the worst."

"Well, if we're gonna' do it, let's keep our position as strong as possible," said the captain. "Break out the rest of the firearms and have every man carry a piece, including Bart. Half the men will stay here with me and the other half will go ashore. Take some of the leftover trade goods as a present to the chief, and get back as soon as possible."

By the time the schooner was secure and all the men armed, two or three Indians had tried to climb aboard and were repelled gently. The captain traded for some of the fresh seafood, while Matt, Bill, Lloyd, and Andrew made the small boat ready. Bart had been released from the irons in the main hold and was shocked when a rifle was placed in his hands. The old cook learned the reason for the journey so far up the Sound and headed for the captain.

"Er, ah, excuse me captain," Bart said, stammering and unable to look Folger in the eye. "I'd like to volunteer to go with the shore party, if it pleases the captain. I'd like to make up for the wrong I've caused. I never meant the boy no harm. How was I supposed to know he would follow me that night?"

"It's all right with me, if Mister English doesn't mind," lectured the captain. "I'd just as soon you be traded for the boy if he's there, but bein' a Christian man, I suppose I couldn't do that. Now go away with ya, I got a ship to guard."

"Thank ye, captain," Bart tipped his wool cap. "You'll be glad ye counted on me."

The old cook hurried off to help with the boat, and, after some initial complaints, he was allowed to go. Bill and Andrew took one set of oars, while Matt and Bart took the other, and Lloyd handled the tiller. With the chest of trinkets securely stashed, they rowed towards the river mouth and Nesook beyond.

The small craft made its way past the cedar channel markers and up river to the village. Standing Seal was already forewarned and stood at the riverbank with Talking Boy and Swimming Otter by his side. The white men recognized the English-speaking slave and were glad to see they would have an interpreter.

"You will make no mention of the white slave," the chief said sternly, "they must not know we have him until after the spring potlatch, for only then will we trade for his release."

"Yes, master," the young slave replied, keeping his eyes straight ahead.

Talking Boy had to think fast. The Salish slave knew he had to give the white men some indication that Chet had survived, but he had to be cautious or Standing Seal would know too much had been said. The Indian boy was nervous. What could he say? The white ship was the best escape plan for both of them. If Chet had been in the village, it might have been worth the risk to tell the white men where he was being held. In exchange for that information, the sailors might take Talking Boy as well. But Chet was gone and Talking Boy did not know where. It would be too risky to start more trouble now. He would just have to be cautious and see what might happen.

"May we have permission to land?" came a cry from Lloyd at the back of the small boat. "We bring gifts to Standing Seal."

"Slave, what did he say?" questioned the chief.

"White men have brought you an offering in good faith so that they might have a council. They ask permission to land."

Talking Boy chose his words carefully, hoping to force the talk towards Chet without Standing Seal knowing the young Indian was doing it.

"By all means let them come ashore. I will take their gifts and listen to what they have to say." Standing Seal folded his arms, trying to look as strong and important as possible.

"Chief says come ashore," the Salish slave returned.

The men dug in with oars one last time and drove the keel up on the sandy beach. Lloyd took control of the pleasantries and opened the box of trinkets. Most of the villagers stayed well back of the group, for they knew that this was not a trading party and they were well aware that the presence of the white slave was to be kept a secret.

"Tell your chief to accept these tokens and ask him if he has heard news of our missing comrade," said the old miner.

Talking Boy was still not sure how to let them know that Chet was alive, but he knew he had to think of something soon.

"Master, they are inquiring about White Clam and whether you have heard news of him. What should I say?"

"Tell them he is probably dead, and we have heard no news since they were last here. Thank them for the gifts and tell them I have some fresh salmon for them to take to their captain."

Standing Seal motioned for one of his slaves and gave an order to fetch some freshly smoked salmon fillets.

Talking Boy knew he had to say something now.

"Chief says thank you for the presents and he has some news for you. We have heard rumors that the white boy lives."

There, he'd said it. Talking boy hoped their reaction would not give him away. He was lucky, for Lloyd and the others showed no joy in the words, just surprise.

"Where is he, where have they taken him?" asked Matt.

The young Indian steadied himself for his next deception and turned to Standing Seal.

"Master, the white men say that they have heard a rumor that the boy lives and is with a clan of Mowachahts."

Talking Boy was scared to death at what the chief might say next. Would Standing Seal take offense and attack the white men or would he order them away? Whatever the chief might do, the white men would not understand his fury.

Standing Seal turned, looking at Swimming Otter and said nothing. The Indian boy felt a wave of fear pass through him.

"This is a problem, my Salish slave," the noble chief said calmly. "I wonder how the word has gotten out, and if Two Skins has heard the same rumor."

"Perhaps they are just trying to fool us. How could anyone in this village have told?" Swimming Otter added. "Besides, Two Skins would have mentioned the white boy when he was here last."

"Master, perhaps I could tell them that we could meet with the other clans in the spring and find news of the boy," Talking Boy interrupted. "We could also tell them that a trade could be arranged, if we find him alive. We would bring him with us to Chahakquot in the spring. The white men could return at that time, after the potlatch, and repay us."

Talking Boy was proud of himself for thinking so quickly.

"Perhaps this may work, for I don't want them searching for the boy elsewhere," Swimming Otter said.

"Yes, good work Talking Boy, tell them your story," said Standing Seal.

The Indian boy was relieved. He turned and told Chet's friends what had been made up and they seemed encouraged. Talking Boy added that Standing Seal was a man to be trusted, and if anyone could get the boy back, he could. Talking Boy also made it clear they should bring many trade goods, for the white boy's freedom would not be purchased cheaply.

"I say we search the village fer him right now with the barrels of our guns. I don't trust these savages," argued Bill angrily.

"I know you mean well, Bill," said Matt, "but if the boy were here, don't you think they would trade for him now? By goin' off half cocked we might jeopardize his safety. Let's be realistic and keep our heads cool. Remember there are a lot more Indians than we have bullets."

"Well, at least there's a chance that the boy's still alive," commented Lloyd, "and at least I can offer a reward for the boy's rescue. Standing Seal may be able to get the boy back, unharmed, where we might just end up startin' an Indian war. I think we have to trust this chief."

"Don't worry about that there reward, Mr. Merrifield," shouted Bart. "I figure most of this problem is due to merchant Drake's all-fired greed to trade whiskey. Mind ya, I'm no pure Johnny either, but I'm sure we can convince him to put up any trade goods, as needed, fer a reward."

"He's right," added Andrew, "and there's not a captain on the coast that wouldn't make a detour to save a good Christian lad."

"Then it's settled," said Matt. "We'll return to Portland and wait out the winter for the first schooner to leave in the spring. If Bart and Drake can help get the boy back, I'm sure things will go easier for them with the authorities."

"Tell the great chief that we appreciate his intervention on the boy's behalf," the miner said, "and if he can return our friend to us, we will pay him many blankets and iron tools. Also tell him that one of us will return before three moons with another ship at your summer village of Chahakquot."

Lloyd stopped speaking and waited while the happy Salish slave recounted the white man's decision. Talking Boy had pulled it off. His cool deception allowed Chet's friends to, at least, be aware that the white boy might have survived and that if they returned in a few months, they could gain Chet's safe release and, hopefully, the freedom of Talking Boy, too. As Lloyd and Standing Seal shook hands and parted, both were pleased with one another. The Salish boy took great pleasure in what his manipulation had accomplished. He still had to keep Chet alive, though, and with the coming potlatch that might be difficult.

The men pushed the schooner's boat into the river and started back to the ship. Bart kept commenting on how he knew the boy was still alive all along, both to keep the thought strong and to help save his own miserable hide. There was still a good hour of daylight left as they reached the ship, and, after a brief report, Captain Folger decided to take advantage of the running tide and remove his vulnerable schooner from the shallow bay and away from the Indians. With the new knowledge of the depth of the channel, there was no reason for a slow pace, and every sail was brought out full. The sleek schooner put ten miles between itself and Nesook before, dark and never stopped. Fair winds, clear skies, and a full moon allowed the ship to reach the wide deep waters of Nootka Sound, and by morning they were on the ocean again.

Swimming Otter took no chances and along with two husky slaves launched a small dugout to follow the ship and make sure it did not sail northeast to where Water Bear and White Clam were. Standing Seal was so impressed with the amount of ransom offered for the white boy, he half wished the boy were there to trade for now. The white men's visit changed his mind about the expendability of White Clam and the chief intended to make sure no harm came to the white boy.

XV

Chet's wrists were sore from being tied for the hour it took to paddle back to camp and as he came into the clearing the boy wasn't aware of the excitement in the air. Wooden Hand was close to felling the tree, but the white boy could see little joy in that now. Chet had seen a ship and that, plus his rough treatment at the hand of Water Bear, was all the young man could think about.

The boy was heart broken. Not only was his chance for freedom smashed, but also his loyalty to his Indian master had been questioned. Chet could not understand why the Nootkas would not have at least traded for his release. Maybe they still could. After all, Standing Seal and Swimming Otter were at the Nesook village and his release could be taking shape as he sat there. This thought made Chet feel better as he set down the fish and rubbed his sore wrists.

Water Bear said nothing about the ship, mostly because Wooden Hand did not give him a chance. The old Indian had tied a cable high up the cedar tree and the extra strength of the white boy and the big Nootkan nobleman might be just enough to start the tree earthward. The two newcomers took up positions on the rope, and, with the four slaves, pulled with all their might. Flying Gull and Wooden Hand continued to chop away at the huge cut, and soon the great tree started to groan and rumble with a deep cracking sound.

The old woodworker yelled out instructions on where to run when the timber fell and cried for them to pull hard once again. After three days the combination of the pull and the adzing was finally too much for the huge tree to withstand. The men scattered to each side of the drop zone and the big cedar came crashing down with a deafening roar, branches cracking and trunk straining in a cloud of dust that did not seem possible in the rain soaked forest.

The first one hundred feet of the tree hit the log path exactly on target, right where Wooden Hand said it would. The carved portion of the pole would cover about eighty feet, with at least ten feet below ground at the final positioning. A fire, which would separate the portion to be carved from the top half of the tree, was started at the hundred-foot level. It was getting dark now, and all the men carried or dragged wood for a stockpile to keep the fire burning throughout the night. It wasn't until a suitable amount had been gathered that the men turned to their dinner preparations.

While the slaves were cooking, Water Bear took Flying Gull and Wooden Hand aside, explaining what had transpired that afternoon. Initially, Chet had felt better being in camp with the excitement of felling the tree, but now the other men avoided the boy, too, and after a few minutes it was clear that everyone knew the ship had passed by. The white boy was allowed to eat dinner, but then suffered more torment when Water Bear bound his hands behind his back and tied the remaining rope to a tree. Chet was made to sit away from the others, with Wooden Hand being the only one who dared talk to him, and that was only a few words of encouragement that the boy did not understand. The old Haida Indian brought Chet the bearskin and draped it around him, knowing the young man would need the warmth.

It was a long night for White Clam. Between the gnawing of the rope at his wrists and the cold Chet could not fall asleep for more than a few minutes at a time. Even when he did sleep, the coming and going of the slaves tending the fire would wake him again. At least it wasn't raining. Better to be uncomfortable and cold, than to be both cold and wet to boot.

Everyone was up at the break of daylight. There was much to be done on the tree this day. Flying Gull untied the white boy and ordered him to collect firewood. The common man was cold in his conversation, but there no longer seemed to be a concern that he would run away. Chet tried to stand, but his legs were so cramped it took two or three attempts to make his feet. Chet's hands were almost frozen and his wrists felt raw. The boy took a few moments to warm them, wrapped the bearskin around his body, and set off for the beach. Wooden Hand stopped Chet, took him by the arm, smiled, and told him not to do anything foolish.

"Make sure you come back, White Clam," the old Haida said. "This will soon pass."

The slaves worked without rest stripping the tree bark and limbs from the downed cedar. Water Bear was nowhere to be found and after the woodpile was stocked, Chet was given the job of feeding the fire at the hundred-foot cut off point. The boy liked this job and refused relief for lunch, choosing to stay and eat as he worked. The young man wanted to be there and be the one who burned through the last of the log. Not only was it a challenge, but also it kept his mind off all that had happened. Burning the log with a vengeance helped steel his resolve to make a successful escape in the future.

By noon long, usable strips of bark had been removed from almost all the tree trunk and stored in large rolls. The last of the bark was hacked or pried off, and soon all that remained was the separation of the bottom and top halves of the trunk. Chet refused to let anyone else help in chopping the last inches of burnt wood free. He attacked the tree with such violence that the other slaves were more than happy to stay away from him. Finally, the huge trunk twisted and groaned, settling to the right a few inches, straining the last attached wood fibers to the limit. A dozen more hacks with the adze and the two halves separated.

The white boy leaned against the stripped trunk, exhausted. The others had been breaking camp, and whether they actually cared or not, the boy felt he had proved himself as good as any of them. Chet walked back and gathered his things together, stuffing all he could into the strap basket. The group would be returning to the village that afternoon, as there was nothing else to be done on the cedar until after the herring spawn. After the herring egg harvest the whole village would return to Chahakquot, but along the way they would stop at the cove and every man, woman, and child would help drag the hundred-foot log to the water. It would then be towed to a place near the summer village, where Wooden Hand and the other slaves could complete the totem pole in secrecy.

The men loaded up the tools, gear, and shelter mats, taking the load to the beach in one trip. The second canoe that had been hidden in the brush was dragged to the water's edge and loaded with half the gear.

Within minutes Water Bear appeared at the head of the cove with the first canoe. The men on the beach could see another smaller canoe following close behind. Chet was glad to see his Salish friend in the bow and Swimming Otter in the stern.

Earlier that morning the two had left Nesook on their way to the cove to warn Water Bear of the ship's coming and to check on the totem pole's progress. They met the big Indian half way, learned of the sighting, and returned with Water Bear. The larger canoe beached and was immediately loaded. The smaller canoe landed and Talking Boy leaped out.

"How are you doing, my friend?" said the Salish slave, sensing that Chet had had a rough night.

"I'm fine. Just a little confused and feeling sorry for myself," the white boy replied.

Swimming Otter dropped his paddle and came toward the two boys.

"Tell White Clam that he must not try to escape, or hail a passing ship. I alone will decide when and if his freedom will be bought. If he agrees, his life can return to the way it was. If not, we will bind him at night, and supervise his activities by day."

Talking Boy relayed the message and Chet assured Swimming Otter that he had no wish to cause problems and only wanted to serve his master as before. He added that he had only hailed the ship because he thought that was what they would have wanted him to do. The master smiled and was satisfied. Talking Boy thought of telling his friend about the visit of the *Exact*, but thought better of it. The Salish slave still thought that perhaps the best chance for his own escape was with White Clam alone and not with the white boy's friends.

A string of orders were given, and the canoes were launched. Wooden Hand rode in the small canoe with Swimming Otter, and Talking Boy took the old man's place in the second canoe. Chet took his place in Water Bear's canoe, but try as he might, the white slave could not get the big fisherman to make eye contact. This puzzled Chet, for he still liked Water Bear and just wanted to get him back to his jolly self.

Darkness fell shortly after they left the cove. The three canoes traveled on in silence, with most of the men too tired to talk. There were no races or good-natured antics on this late evening voyage, just the monotonous dipping of paddles into the cold dark sea. They reached Nesook at midnight, setting off the beating of copper shields by the lookouts until it was verified that they were friendly. The noise woke the entire village, but most were back asleep by the time the dugouts reached the upstream riverbank in front of *Little Oil House*. A few people, Cattail Woman among them, greeted the returnees. The old woman had hugs for both Wooden Hand and Chet. The long house smelled strongly of herring, and, if not for the warmth, Chet would rather have been outside. He said his goodnights to the old couple and Talking Boy, and curled up next to the crack between the wallboards where the young man could breathe reasonably fresh air. *Things will be better tomorrow,* he thought.

The next few days were spent in preparation for the herring egg harvest. The spawn would be occurring any day now. The tiny fish had moved further out of the bay, towards a small islet with deep sandy shores. There the herring would spawn by the thousands, releasing eggs by the millions. The talk of the whole village was about the great feast they would have on these rubbery round eggs. The way the villagers talked, Chet was convinced this was their greatest delicacy.

The white boy was ready for something different. All the Indians had to eat, day and night, was the rotten herring, dug out of the putrid pits in the ground. Cattail Woman tried her best to find roots and berry cakes for the boy, but they came at a premium. Chet could not stomach the rotted fish; in fact he could not get past the smell without gagging. The white boy had to make do with clams, or the occasional flounder he might catch. Chet prayed that the herring spawn would provide a meal he, too, could relish. What he would give for a beefsteak with roasted potatoes!

Preparations for the spawn harvest included the search for hemlock trees. These trees had low growing branches that were ideal for trapping the sticky eggs under water. The women were not haphazard about cutting the branches. Only those of a certain size were taken and in such a way as to ensure the rejuvenation of the tree. By taking branches carefully, a continued supply of boughs could be provided in the future without having to travel far from the village to locate new trees.

Chet and other slaves were employed in transferring the bundled branches in canoes back across the river, where each family stored them until the herring spawn started. Everywhere, people talked of the coming fish-egg time. Not only was it a time for feasting, but it also signaled the end of winter and the beginning of spring. Right after the spawn, the villagers would return to Chahakquot for the salmon and whaling season.

"Talking Boy, how do the villagers know when the herring start to spawn?" asked Chet.

"What is the most visible animal in the bay the last month and a half?" returned Talking Boy.

"That's easy, herring," said the white boy smugly.

"No, you can't see the herring, they're under the water. Look down the river, to the bay, and tell me what you see," ordered Talking Boy.

Chet looked out over the bay and saw nothing unusual. Just the cloudy sky and the screeching gulls flying here and there. Could that be it?

"You mean the sea gulls."

"Yes," the young Indian smiled. "The birds are the key. When the herring leave for the spawning island the birds follow. No more dive-bombing, no more screeching, just quiet. Of course all the other animals that feed on the fish go too, but you don't notice the eagle, the salmon, and the sea lions as readily as the gulls."

Talking Boy was right. Chet had gotten so used to the thousands of sea gulls, he forgot how their appearance signaled the coming of the fish. Now the birds would signal the departure of the herring. The boy found it hard to imagine a Nesook without birds.

With all the people ready for the spawn harvest, the last week in February was spent doing almost nothing. Even though their personal food supplies were dwindling, they continued to eat only the rotten herring, seal oil, and the occasional river salmon caught in a weir trap. The herring were still plentiful in the bay but no one seemed to want to go fishing.

Water Bear still avoided Chet as much as possible. The big Mowachaht could not allow himself to become too fond of someone else's slave. Water Bear's avoidance meant that he liked the white boy too much. A master had to have a colder heart. Talking Boy explained all this to Chet, and he felt better, but he still wished the big Indian would take him fishing. Swimming Otter had never allowed him to take a canoe out alone and wasn't likely to do so now.

Things were getting desperate for Chet, as the young man could not stomach the herring any longer. He lost weight and became ill. Wooden Hand and Talking Boy, at Cattail Woman's insistence, finally approached Swimming Otter, who, once was aware of the boy's plight, allowed the old Haida slave to take the boy fishing.

That afternoon they caught a dozen flounder in an hour, using Water Bear's iron hook set-up. The next afternoon they moved to a rocky islet and caught rockfish. The fresh, tender white fillets, baked in seaweed, gave the boy his strength back. But what the white slave really wanted was fresh salmon.

That night the old woodworker and the white boy went back to the abandoned house at the edge of the village. The two slaves found the old sixteen-foot canoe they had used before for raking herring. Swimming Otter gave new permission for Chet to use the dugout for fishing. Also, at the back of the house was a cedar salmon weir that Wooden Hand took back with him to repair. The weir was a long, narrow, cage-like affair that was placed upstream, where the river narrowed. It was weighted down with rocks, with the wider end facing the sea. A salmon traveling upstream could enter the wide mouth of the trap and continue swimming until it caught itself in the narrow end. The careful placement of cedar slats, pointing backward, near the end of the trap did not allow the salmon to turn around. The doomed fish then would just swim trapped in place until the fishermen came and took it.

Chet was allowed to fish for himself every afternoon from then on. No one, especially Swimming Otter, wanted to see him die of malnutrition. They made it clear that if he was not back before dark, they would hunt him down and kill him. The white boy was so thrilled at the chance to eat fresh food again, he promised never to disobey, and meant it - at least for the time being.

That next afternoon Standing Seal, Talking Boy, and a group of prominent villagers left for a week long visit to the winter village of Cod Man's people. Chet didn't realize that the trip would serve to strengthen the case against Two Skins. The official reason for the visit was to announce the coming potlatch to be given by Swimming Otter that spring. Swimming Otter was left in charge of the spawn harvest while Standing Seal was gone.

With his chores finished and goodbyes said to his young Salish friend, Chet grabbed the salmon weir and a ten foot cedar pole and began poling up the river to a place which, earlier that day, Flying Gull had told him would be good for trapping winter run salmon. The area was about a mile upstream, just before the first set of rapids. The mountainsides closed in on this part of the river, forming a deep canyon, and the white boy felt a thrill upon seeing the wildness of the place. The huge trees grew right to the water's edge, and were so thick that a person could barely see ten feet into the shadows.

Chet tied the dugout to a tree branch extending from the bank. He took off his moccasins and his tattered socks. Placing his feet in the ice cold water was not pleasant, but the young man wanted to keep his footwear dry. Picking up the weir, the boy carefully walked out to the middle of the stream feeling his way carefully, for the rocks were smooth and slippery, and the last thing Chet wanted to do was fall in the ice cold river. After wedging the trap between two exposed rocks, he placed a heavy rock inside to anchor it. The boy checked the trap door for ease of opening and returned to the canoe. Warm rays of sun came out, briefly, as Chet drifted back to Nesook, and he thought it a good omen. In a short prayer, the white slave quietly gave thanks for his survival and mentioned that a nice salmon would surely be welcome.

Sunshine greeted the people the next day, and Chet flew through his chores, gathering wood, carrying water and doing other menial things. Almost forgetting to eat, the young man hastily set out in the afternoon in the canoe to check the salmon weir. The twenty-minute trip was even more beautiful than the day before. The sun actually felt hot whenever the tall mountains allowed the light to touch the winding river. As he neared the rapids, Chet felt himself lose some of his enthusiasm. The trap mouth was visible now, and the boy had expected to see a thrashing, and spraying of water that would have let him know the trap had caught a fish. However the weir looked as empty and quiet as when the white slave had left it the day before.

Chet almost felt like turning back without looking closer, such was his disappointment, but he knew he must check the trap thoroughly. He beached the dugout and waded towards the trap; glad he had checked when he got closer. There at the back of the weir, and gently swimming at pace with the river, were not one, but two healthy, sea running, winter salmon. They weren't as big as king salmon, but would be just as tasty. The white boy looked around the bank for a club and shortly afterward had the two twenty inch beauties cleaned and sitting in the bottom of the dugout. That night Chet feasted on fresh salmon steaks and Cattail woman helped him fillet and smoke the rest.

The last days of the month brought with them the much-heralded event. The village awoke one day to near silence. The gulls had all but gone, and Swimming Otter pronounced the beginning of fish-egg time. There was a flurry of activity as whole families packed the largest canoes with bedding, temporary shelters, food, and the hemlock branches. Only a few of the oldest people would stay at Nesook, along with two young warriors as lookouts.

Chet had packed his fishing gear, smoked salmon, extra clothes and blankets. The white boy was excited about trying some new food for once, but knowing the Mowachaht palate, as he now did, Chet decided to take no chances and was determined to continue fishing for his food. There was no extreme rush to leave, other than the social aspect of the event. Just as when they went to the clam beds, each household had its own areas for harvesting the spawn. Some families had year round wooden shelters on their particular beaches, but most used temporary bark mats for protection from the weather.

Swimming Otter's forty-five foot canoe, with twenty-five people aboard, including Chet, Wooden Hand, and Cattail Woman, finally pushed off the muddy banks of the Nesook River, and headed downstream to the bay. A flotilla of medium-sized dugouts with supplies, family members, and slaves, followed behind. The entire village fleet extended over two miles, as it snaked its way between the shoals and islets towards Fish Egg Island, six miles away. The usual songs sprang up as the Indians paddled along at a leisurely pace.

"White Clam, I will show you a good place to fish for flounder when we get to the island," commented Cattail Woman as she rested on her paddle. "I don't think you will like the fish eggs any better then the herring. However, you might like a special seaweed that grows there."

The group of canoes paddled on for two hours and as they rounded a sand bar near the southern shore of the Sound, Chet saw the telltale signs of the island being near. Seven fat sea lions were lying out on a rocky outcrop from the beach a hundred yards away. In the distance a flowing white mass of seagulls and other birds were taking off, landing, and dive-bombing for herring.

Fish Egg Island was about a half mile wide by one mile long, and it lay about two hundred yards off the southern shore of

Nootka Sound. The long sandy beach was well protected from the elements, with deep drop-offs a few yards from shore. These beaches afforded the massive schools of herring ample depth to congregate and have fine, protected sand in which to spawn. The extra addition of kelp beds, just off shore, offered the schools of fish some protection from predators. They also gave the Nootkans a second way to harvest the eggs. The sticky spawn eggs that flowed with the current away from the beach would collect on the kelp by the thousands.

As they neared the island's southern shore, the different family groups split, heading toward their respective beaches. Chet could see no geographical landmarks that would help separate family areas, but everyone else seemed to know where the invisible lines in the sand were.

Swimming Otter yelled a command to pull hard at the paddles, and the huge dugout knifed its way onto the sandy beach. Everyone filed up to the bow and disembarked on dry sand. The unloading began right away; slaves and commoners taking their belongings to the same campsites that had been used for years. Some had poles or small house frames already standing, so all they had to do was stretch mats over the framework. Others, usually slaves, had to make lean-tos from scratch.

Wooden Hand brought mats and a half-dozen poles, enough to make a small but cozy shelter for Chet, Cattail Woman, and himself. The old slave woman brought lots of baskets for storing eggs. As was always the case in food gathering matters, a percentage of the harvest went to the household head, or master. The old slave couple were counting on Chet to help them gain a little extra this year, since he would be able to collect much, and, more than likely, eat little.

While the two older Haida slaves were making their camp, Chet rushed off to gather firewood. It was more a premium to him then the rest of the Indians and the boy quickly got the best stockpile of wood. Cattail Woman just laughed at the amount of wood Chet thought he needed. When the white slave started bringing rocks back, she thought the stones were for weighting down the hemlock boughs. The old wood worker had to tell her the stones were for White Clam's bed and cooking only. Cattail Woman would have to get other rocks for the tree branches later.

By late afternoon the tide had ebbed and the first hemlock branches were placed in knee-deep water. The resulting flood, or high tide, would submerge the boughs in six to ten feet of water, allowing the herring to swim over them and deposit their roe. Chet carried the branches for the old woman and she stuck them deeply in the sand so they would not wash away. Some boughs Cattail Woman weighted down with rocks. When the job was finished, they returned to the lean-to where she and Wooden Hand had their dinner of fermented herring. Chet had leftover flounder, smoked salmon, and root bulbs.

There was a festive atmosphere the rest of the night with the men gambling and the women and children playing their cedar stick games. Chet heated rocks for his bed, and the younger children watched him, thinking the white slave was going to roast himself. While all this was going on, the tide came in and with it the enormous run of herring.

Ever so often Chet could hear the boiling of the water, as some predator from the deep would streak upward through the mass of fish, causing them to break the surface. There seemed to be no rest for the weary fish. *Not much of a life*, the boy thought. Living only by the luck of numbers, allowed to live only because others died and filled predator bellies. If the herring beat the odds and died a natural death, the bottom fish ate their bodies. They were bred to be eaten one way or the other.

The children were finally convinced that Chet was not going to roast on the bed of rocks and left the white boy to enjoy his sleep. The old slave couple turned in earlier than most also. One by one the gamblers and game players grew tired, and by midnight all was silent. Chet woke later to the sound of raindrops pounding the mat roof. He scooped a little more dirt away from the rock pit below him, and the renewed warmth lulled him back to sleep.

By early dawn the rain was beating steadily on the sand and the fire had long since died. Chet was glad he had placed a stash of dry wood under the lean-to. The women were already up in anticipation of checking the egg harvest. Some were wading deep into the water pulling up egg-laden branches and stripping the boughs of their bounty. The eggs were eaten raw on the spot, but the biggest spawn was yet to occur, and most, including Cattail Woman, left the branches alone to collect more eggs during the next tide change. However, eggs that were adrift or on seaweed were collected for immediate consumption.

The rain brought an end to the merriment. The Nootkans stayed close to the shelters that day to keep dry and to eat what few eggs were harvested. The eggs were small, round and translucent. There was practically no taste, save for the salt from the water. Their texture was rubbery, and after handling a few raw ones, Chet decided he was glad he had plenty of smoked salmon along for the trip. The Indians thought them grand and as the tide rose higher in late morning, few of the early eggs were left to be found. The villagers ate them raw, with herring oil, steamed them in seaweed, or mixed them in a cooking box with water, and the ever present, rancid, fermented herring.

Chet decided it was time to go find the fishing spot Cattail Woman had mentioned. The only problem was the need of a canoe and there were no small ones. The only dugouts that Swimming Otter's family had journeyed with were over twenty-five feet long, and no one else had anything on his mind but herring roe. So without anyone available to help in paddling a large canoe, the boy decided to take a water container, fill it at the only spring on the island, and go exploring. He put on his cedar bark rain hat and went looking for Swimming Otter.

"Master, go walk up island, all right?" the white boy asked in struggling Nootkan. Chet had found the master at his small, wooden shelter in the middle of the family group. Swimming Otter was in good spirits and he always enjoyed it when the white slave spoke in Nootkan. The tension about the return of the *Exact* had all but gone away, and the trust Swimming Otter had in the boy was returning. Water Bear was with his brother and the big fisherman still would not look Chet straight in the eye.

"Brother, you have been with White Clam more than I. What do you think he is up to now?" Swimming Otter asked.

"It is always a surprise," returned Water Bear. "I think he only means to walk the island for adventure. I don't think he likes the fish eggs. He cannot cause any trouble now. I say let him go."

Chet watched the conversation between the two brothers and wondered if he was understood. The white slave had no way of knowing that few Indians ever left the beach on Fish Egg Island. They were all very content with the egg activities. The boy was pleased a few moments later when he was given permission to go.

"White Clam, here, take this with you. You may find a salmon or a duck for your dinner," said Water Bear as he handed the boy a salmon spear.

It was the first time the large nobleman had spoken to the boy in weeks and Water Bear was rewarded with a full smile from the white slave.

"So-har, Mar-met-ta, kom-me-tak," the boy said in Nootkan. "Salmon, duck, I understand."

Chet examined the spear as he walked away. It was made of a six-foot long shaft of cedar with a three-piece bone spearhead tied on the tip with spruce root twine. The white boy felt better now that Water Bear was civil to him again and was almost whistling as he headed toward the stream. The young man thought following the creek should find him some game to spear. If not, he could always follow it up to its source on the hill in the middle of the island.

The rain had died down some but refused to completely subside. Wearing the bark hat and poncho kept him amazingly dry on top, but the squishy, water-soaked ground soon made his feet miserably wet.

The stream was a small affair, not very wide, and maybe ten feet across at the widest points. Chet followed the grassy bank up a slight grade for a short while until the ground leveled again and the swift creek turned into a wide, marshy clearing. A hundred yards further was a steeper grade and a heavily forested hill at the center of the small island.

The marsh was a series of many different channels dotted with grass-covered peat islands. The grass was tall, and the ground was spongy. Slow moving waterways less then one foot wide separated most of the little peat islands, so the boy could hop from grassy mound to mound without much difficulty. There were some deeper, wider ponds among the peat mounds, and as Chet made his way toward the hill, he tried to look for signs of fish in one of the many holes along the banks. The continuing rain made that almost impossible, for the raindrops on the surface of the pond made seeing a difficult target even harder.

After giving up on finding any good-sized trout, the boy turned his attention to the many wild ducks that were wintering on the island. The ducks were more visible, but more elusive. Every time the boy jumped from mound to mound to get closer to a few birds, they would sense him and swim off. Finally, Chet decided to wait on the largest peat island for the ducks to come to him. He kept very still.

Within five minutes a group of four mallards swam and pecked and bobbed ever closer. The white slave crouched in the tall grass, as quiet as could be. The thrill of the hunt and visions of roasting duck filled his thoughts. Killing ducks wasn't as troubling as killing otter and he had no inhibitions in stalking this game. Calculating the distance and strength needed to launch the spear, Chet moved his feet into position to leap and throw. The ducks swam closer and the boy readied himself as the raindrops dripped off the conical hat rim in front of his eyes. With a quick lunge and a powerful throw the young man let the spear go toward the nearest mallard. The duck was in no danger, for the spear hit the water miserably far to the left and short. The mallards took to the air.

Disappointed, but not surprised, Chet rose up and walked along the peat mound toward the spear stuck in the mud. It was a good thing the throw was short and not long, for he could barely reach the end of the shaft without having to go into the water. The white boy soon broke it loose of its hold and washed the spearhead until the mud was gone. With his loss of interest in hunting complete and the wooded hill just a few leaps away, the call of adventure and exploration beckoned. In a few minutes Chet was scrambling through the trees and soon found a game trail heading upwards. Deer droppings at his feet momentarily gave him renewed hope of a successful hunt, but reality sank in. Short of a deer rounding the bend and dropping dead in front of him, the white boy figured his chances of killing anything that day were about as good as finding Lucy sitting on that rock next to the path.

The spunky, little girl wasn't there, of course, but Chet decided to rest on the rock anyway. The path had taken him around to the southwestern side of the island and the dense forest was broken by a rocky crag and drop off in front of him. The boy was surprised to notice the wind picking up and the weather clearing to the west. Patches of blue came and went and then a beam of sunlight broke through. Eager to get some of that warmth, Chet moved from the rock across the trail to the broad, rocky crag. The sun's heat was already causing water vapor to rise off the granite surface of the ledge, prompted the boy to remove the bark hat and let the warmth fill his face.

The low position of the sun in the sky warned him against staying too much longer. Chet moved closer to the edge of the drop off and looked at the hillside below. There had been a rockslide at one time, as many smaller pieces of granite and gravel sloped away from him ten feet below. The boy picked up a good-sized rock and lazily dropped it, watching as it bounced its way down the rubble pile, coming to rest just where the brush started again. He looked at the spot for a moment, and then stared hard, cocking his head slightly and squinting. Something shiny was reflecting the sun.

His curiosity aroused, Chet began looking for a way down the ledge to the rock floor below. The young man thought he could make it down the left side if he chose his footing carefully. With little difficulty Chet was able to descend the cliff and move along the rockslide. As he neared the brush, the boy found he had lost sight of the exact spot where the rock came to rest. Chet sat down on a small boulder and meticulously scanned the brush border, checking each rock, one by one. As his eyes moved from left to right, he noticed a rock that looked different, whiter than the others. To the left of it was a shiny object. The boy stood, walked closer to the unusual rock, and then stopped, gasping, as he recognized the round object for what it was. A skull, a human skull. Chet kneeled slowly and touched the hard white object, then turned it over. Looking around, he noticed other bones among the rocks at his feet.

Turning his attention to the shiny metal object, the white boy began digging at the earth and soon exposed the long metal blade of a sword. It appeared to be made of brass on the cutting edge, with a silver inlay pattern covering the blunt side. Chet tried to pull the blade free but could not. After further digging, he exposed the handle and finally freed the long sword. Scratching dirt off the handle the boy thought it was made of brass, too, but after further cleaning the soft gleam of solid gold left little doubt as to its composition.

Chet stood there, dumbfounded, holding the priceless sword. A passing cloud blocked the sun and brought the boy back to reality. He must be getting on his way. Chet looked at the bones once more, then turned to climb the rockslide and stopped in his tracks. The boy had been concentrating so hard on finding the shiny object earlier, he had not noticed the cliff behind him. Ten feet below the rocky crag was a small cave. The mouth of the cave was wide, and had obviously been further widened by the recent landslide. As the boy reached the cave, he saw there was still enough daylight to see inside. Chet stepped into the gloomy interior. The ceiling was low and the white slave had to stoop over as he walked along. The light became dimmer, but he continued on toward the back of the cave and suddenly stumbled across another discovery.

He'd been stepping slowly in the increasing darkness and had stubbed his toe on a solid object in front of him. Chet knew it wasn't a rock from the dull thud it made. Hardly noticing the pain in his toe, he bent over, felt around with his hands, and with his eyes becoming more used to the dark, made out the shape of some kind of a chest or box. The boy's hands found thick handles on the sides, but when he tried to lift the object up it would barely budge. Failing that, Chet took one side handle with both hands and slowly dragged the heavy box into the light near the open mouth of the cave.

The wooden chest was covered with dirt from the partial cave-in and rockslide. After a few moments of brushing the loose dirt away with his hand, Chet uncovered an old wooden sea chest, complete with metal strapping, metal hinges, brass lock, and handles. There was also a brass plate inlaid on the lid, which contained an inscription in a language Chet did not understand. However, at the end of the writing in bold print were the numbers, 1792. *That must be a date*, the boy thought. Almost fifty years old! There must be a connection between the sword, the chest, and the bones of a dead man outside.

The boy's head was spinning and his thoughts were running a mile a minute. It surely was not a Mowachaht chest. They had no written language. Chet knew he had seen language like this before, but could not remember where. He tried to read the words again, "Jose' Francisco de la Bodega y Quadra de Madrid Espana, 1792." They made no sense to him, but now his curiosity got the best of him and Chet looked around for a rock he could use to break the lock.

The boy grabbed a good-sized hunk of rock and brought it crashing down on the brass lock. He was surprised at how easily the metal tore away from the wood. Pausing a moment to catch his breath, Chet slowly began to lift the old lid. The hinges gave out an eerie squeak as the chest displayed its contents. The boy wasn't sure what he had at first. It looked like a box of brown bricks. He took a deep breath and blew the dust away from the top bars and a dull yellow color appeared. He frantically scratched at the top bar with his fingernail and the bright shine of gold dispelled any doubts as to what was in there. It was a fortune in crude gold bars.

"Dear Lord, what do I do now?" the boy said under his breath.

He shut the lid and sat on top of the chest. The sun was setting now, but there was no longer a cloud in the sky, and Chet knew he would still have a good thirty minutes to get the three quarters of a mile to the beach before dark. The boy also knew he could not take any of the gold back with him or tell anyone about it. The

Nootkans would not know its value, but would surely find some practical use for it and not let the boy keep it. The white slave just had to leave it and hope no one else would find it before he could return to claim the fortune.

Chet covered the chest with small chunks of rock and dirt without moving it back into the cave. It was still under the ledge and if there were a further rock slide, at least he would not have to dig deep into the old cave to find it later. The young man almost forgot the sword. It would be a great weapon to have, but there was no way the boy could take it with him. Chet thought of hiding it in his bark skirt, but decided to bury it next to the chest. He climbed the short cliff, found his spear, and hacked out a blaze on the nearest tree as an added marker of the right location. It might be years before he could return to this place, and Chet wanted all the help he could get to find it again.

The trip back down the game trail was an exercise in memorization of landmarks. Every thirty feet Chet hacked a tree with his spear until he reached the marsh. The boy leaped and pole-vaulted on the spear shaft from peat mound to peat mound, until he'd traversed the swamp, then ran down the center of the creek bed all the way to the beach. With his feet soaking wet and face flushed, Chet entered the temporary community, trying to look as casual as possible.

The tide would be at its lowest level of the day in less than two hours and all the villagers were making preparations for a torch light harvest. The water was boiling with the spawning fish, and this was the moment the Mowachahts had all been waiting for. Chet went to the master's shelter to return the spear and found the head of the household painting fresh red ochre on his face and combing seal oil through his hair. The white slave had not seen the men paint their faces since the winter ceremonies and always found the practice particularity distasteful.

"Master, here is spear, no good luck," the white slave said in Nootkan.

Swimming Otter couldn't be bothered and just grunted for the white slave to take the spear and go away. He had fish eggs on his mind and really didn't care whether White Clam had any luck hunting or not. All of the Indians had been waiting in anticipation for the coming harvest and the feasting that was about to begin was foremost on all their minds.

Chet returned to the lean-to and sat down on his mat. He wrapped the bearskin around himself and took out a healthy piece of smoked salmon for dinner. The older slave couple were patiently waiting for the low tide. Wooden Hand smacked his lips in anticipation of stuffing himself with the herring roe. Chet was finishing his salmon and taking a long drink of cool water from the stream when the first torches were lit. The villagers couldn't wait any longer. *They were just like kids on Christmas day*, Chet thought, *waiting for church to get over, so the presents could be opened.*

A few hardy souls braved the deep, cold water and took out branches and seaweed. Within half an hour everyone was doing it. Cattail Woman lit her torch and handed it to Chet. They made their way to the beach, with the old wood worker following, and soon Cattail Woman was waist deep in water feeling for branches with her toes. There were fish eggs floating everywhere, even sticking to the sides of the woman's clothing. She found the branches in short time and tried to lift the first one, but could not. Wooden Hand moved out to help her. The white boy stood in his bare feet in shallower water several feet away, holding the torch and baskets. The two old Haidas lifted the first branch and Chet was amazed at the bounty of eggs massed on the bough. Within a short time they had all the baskets filled to the top with spawn-encrusted hemlock, and there were many more branches to get.

Chet could see many people eating the eggs raw, so the boy thought he might try one. He eyed a nice pearly egg floating by and picked it up. It was smaller than a pea and felt rubbery. After some deliberation he plopped the morsel in his mouth and chewed down on it. The resulting squish proved to be fairly harmless to his palate. Aside from the oil and salt taste, there was no other taste. Just a rubbery, fishy, oily squish in his mouth. If this was all there was to it, he surely was disappointed. *Well,* he thought, *no use swallowin' this,* and with an unceremonial spit, the crunched egg made its way back to the sea. Wooden Hand and Cattail Woman watched this from a distance and just shook theirs heads.

The three slaves had many eggs in the baskets and many yet to claim, so they returned to the lean-to and started a fire, much to Chet's delight. The old woman who usually let the eggs dry on the branches, decided to start water boiling. Boiling in the fresh water would preserve the spawn as well as drying in the sun. It would also make the eggs lose their stickiness and fall to the bottom of the cooking box so that the boughs could be reused.

Chet was given the job of boiling the eggs and packing the cooked roe in boxes with seal oil. It was a sticky job, but the boiling was better then walking around in freezing water. The Indians worked hard for about two hours, stripping the boughs, placing them back in the sand, collecting egg filled seaweed, and all the while nibbling at the abundant spawn that floated about.

When the flood tide retreated, and the empty boughs were placed back in the sand, the real eating began. They seemed to prefer the roe dipped in herring or seal oil. There was no lack of eggs and Chet watched as all, except himself, consumed huge amounts of the rubbery dish. The eating went on until the wee hours, and, as the old couple enjoyed their spoil, they instructed Chet on how to wrap and store the eggs on the seaweed, how to smoke the eggs on the branches, and how to make spawn cakes and store them in baskets. The fishy smell threatened to overwhelm him and he was thankful for the outside location. The white boy could only imagine the stench of the long house with rotten herring and rotten egg both. The way they put up the roe, Chet knew it would not be long before the little eggs began to ferment.

With all the excitement about the herring spawn, Chet had temporarily forgotten the day's discovery. Now it was starting to sink in. The sword alone must be worth a thousand dollars. There must have been a hundred and fifty pounds of gold in the chest. At least a hundred thousand dollars. He was rich! He could buy a castle if he wanted to. He was rich beyond belief and the boy could do nothing about it except wait and hope he could stay alive long enough to spend it. Spending money was something Chet had done very little of in his short life and the prospect seemed like great sport.

It must be after midnight, the boy thought. Most of the villagers were still going strong, playing games, gambling, and gorging themselves. Chet never knew people could eat so much at one time until he met the Mowachahts. The young man kept the fire going late into the night, too excited to sleep. Thoughts of the gold danced through his mind over and over again.

Reaching for the last stick of firewood and feeling exhaustion overcome him, the boy took his bear skin and snuggled down on the mat. He always slept best in the morning anyway, and no one would be in a hurry to get up soon. Chet thought for a moment about Lucy and how excited the young girl would be if she knew of the gold. The boy thought he would share some of the fortune with his good friends. Chet thought again of the strange words on the chest and wondered where he had seen words like those before. It must be a pirate's treasure chest, what else could it be? The sword must have killed the man Chet had found, but who would leave a priceless object like that lying around in a dead man?

Then the boy remembered the rockslide. Maybe some of the slide wasn't that recent. Visions of the pirate, or thief, or whatever he was, struggling with the heavy chest up the hillside, played in his mind. Chet could see the man sitting in the cave, exhausted, and being too tired to move, when an earthquake or muddy rain loosened the rocks above the cave mouth, sending them toppling down on the human and the treasure. Subsequent slides over the years, including the recent one he noticed, could have moved the bones and sword further down the bank. Finally, the white slave could no longer keep his busy mind awake and fell deeply into a sound sleep.

That afternoon the harvest was repeated, and the boy was so sick of fish eggs he wished the hordes of herring would up and disappear. Within a few days they did. But now the villagers had the big job of transporting all the bounty back to Nesook. Chet was part of a group of slave men who took the master's large canoe, loaded with nothing but eggs, back to Nesook and returned the same day for the household and more eggs. The trip back and forth between Fish Egg Island and Nesook was a tiring one, but it assured Chet that he would be able to find his way back to the island and the gold at some future time.

XVI

The sunny weather held for a few days, enabling the eggs and seaweed to be sun-dried. The dried sheets were stored in baskets and boxes. Some of the eggs were dried and mashed together in small cakes for further use, and all the while the feasting on the fresh, oiled eggs went on.

Chet caught another salmon in his weir trap and supplemented his diet with greens and flounder. The rains started again by the end of the week and the last gasp of a winter storm dumped a few inches of snow one night that quickly melted by sunset the next day. Standing Seal and the group of nobles had been gone eight days, and the white boy was growing eager for the return of his Salish friend. Chet had a new reason for escaping now, and although he thought it best not to tell the young Indian slave of the treasure, the young man did want to start finalizing a plan of escape and make a list of essentials they would need.

The constant rain kept most of the Indians inside, and the cramped quarters and fishy smell made living in *Little Oil House* almost unbearable for Chet. After his morning work the white boy spent most of his time in the old abandoned long house. He found many useful items left in the old building and started stockpiling a few things such as mats, baskets, water containers, cordage, and boxes. In particular Chet found one good-sized box that would hold and conceal the chest of gold, if he were ever able to recover it.

One afternoon Chet managed to slip away to the beach where the schooner wreckage was hidden and he found everything to be undisturbed. The young man was trying to figure out how he was going to get all his gear together for a quick escape. He knew it was well into the month of March and that the weather should start getting better. Chet also knew that when the Indians returned to Chahakquot, he would lose the chance to take the sailing gear with him. That gear was his key to outdistance any pursuers. Then there was the gold. He might have to leave it behind, because there would be little time to stop and pick it up. It would be a risk to stop at all, but the white boy would wait and play that by ear. Chet had overheard some of the men saying they might not leave for Chahakquot until another month, so the boy still had time to plan. Another month would put him into April. The weather should be good by then. He wished Talking Boy was back so they could plan their escape.

The next two days were spring-like and the white boy felt better as the days grew longer and warmer. There was a freshness in the air and the Nootkans felt it, too. Chet knew that the Indians used the spawning time not only as a feasting festival, but to celebrate the time of year when winter turns to spring as well. Even though, in the far Northwest, winter would still make itself known for weeks to come, the people felt as if life had been renewed again.

Chet was encouraged, and took advantage of any opportunity to prepare for the escape. He had turned into a scavenger of sorts. Every loose piece of rope, twine, basket, or tool the white slave could find lying around, he would take and stash in the abandoned house. A few times Chet would get caught taking something that belonged to a neighbor and get yelled at, but taking someone else's things left lying around was not all that unusual for the coast Indians. In fact, some thought the white boy was becoming more like an Indian because of it.

Chet was also checking his weir every chance he got, and the basket trap was proving to be a great asset. Every salmon that was caught was smoked and most of each fish was stored in a large box back at the deserted house along with the other gear. The young man also stored some smoked herring and fish egg cakes for Talking Boy. Chet was careful not to let too many people see his comings and goings at the old house and Wooden Hand was the only one who knew he went there often. The boy told the old slave that he just liked being in a place of privacy, and since Chet knew the Haida slave was superstitious about going in the house, he did not worry about being discovered.

It had been two weeks since Chief Standing Seal had left for the meeting and feast with Cod Man at his winter village. Swimming Otter had not let on, but he was getting uneasy about the passage of time. The party was supposed to have been gone only seven to ten days, so when the nobleman heard the shouts of the villagers announcing the return of the great chief one afternoon, Swimming Otter was greatly relieved. He had been thinking the worst and now he would know for certain if his secret plan to kill Two Skins would be allowed to progress without interference from Cod Man and his people.

Chet was up river with his salmon trapping when Standing Seal and the party returned. Talking Boy looked for his white friend, having good news to tell him, and was disappointed when Cattail Woman told him White Clam would not be back until just before dark. Standing Seal, Swimming Otter, and the two heads of the village, along with Water Bear and other nobles, went into secret conference.

"My dear friend, it is good to be home," said the tired chief. "I have much to tell you, but first tell me of the spawn."

"See for yourself, master," returned Swimming Otter, as he pointed to a slave coming in the room with a large tray of eggs swimming in herring oil.

The two began their conversation between gulps of roe, and all the men who had not been at the meeting with Cod Man listened with sharp ears.

"My friend, there is good news of sorts from Cod Man's village," Standing Seal started. "Two Skins, after he left our village of Nesook that day, took his men and traveled to the south. There he attacked a small Mowachaht village, killing most of the old people, all of the men and boys, and sparing only those women and girls he wanted for himself and his men. Cod Man had forbade him to attack those of our own people and thought Two Skins had raided further south to the Makah people. He had left many of his men at the village and returned to Cod Man just prior to our visit. One of his lieutenants, whom he'd promised great spoils if he killed Swimming Otter, became enraged when the village was attacked, because the man originally came from there. Fearing for his life, the lieutenant said nothing other than voicing some initial disapproval and would not take part in the massacre because he still had relatives living there. Instead, he chose to hide, and when the lieutenant returned to Cod Man, he told all. My cousin, the old chief, was planning to banish the half-breed when we arrived, but Two Skins had placed a spy among those at Cod man's village. This spy warned Two Skins of our plan at the coming potlatch, using the white boy to provoke him. The scar faced one stormed into the meeting with a white man's fire gun. He shot at the old chief, but the bullet hit a slave, killing him. In the confusion Two Skins and his men made their escape, but not before vowing to kill Swimming Otter, myself, Cod Man, and White Clam. It was said Two Skins was extremely enraged when he heard of the boy living with us and wearing his robe."

Swimming Otter was in shock, but overjoyed. It was now open season on his old rival. If the half-breed showed his face again, there would be no politics to stand in the way. In fact, Swimming Otter thought he would reward handsomely the man who could bring Two Skin's head to him.

"I have other news for you all," the chief continued. "The great Gray Whale has followed warm water from the south early this year. It is my wish that we quit this place and return to Chahakquot as soon as possible. Tomorrow, if practical."

"That should not be a problem," said Swimming Otter. "We have three more hours of sun today and the people can pack tonight. I will send Water Bear and Wooden Hand within the next two hours to make the great cedar tree ready."

"I had almost forgotten about the new totem pole," Standing Seal said.

"It is close to the sea, only a hundred feet, and we should be able to move it quickly," assured Swimming Otter. "It will take most of the adults in the village to move the great tree, such is its weight. I have already alerted each family and agreed on payment so we are ready to move it any time." He turned to Water Bear. "My brother, find Flying Gull and have him round up Wooden Hand and the other slaves, including White Clam, and get them ready to leave as soon as you can."

Water Bear did as his brother asked. He found Wooden Hand and gave him instructions. Wooden Hand knew the where about of each slave on the wood cutting team, and sent word to them. Talking Boy volunteered to pole up river and bring White Clam back.

The Salish slave took a small canoe and started after his friend. In the meantime Chet was doing what he liked best, catching salmon. The boy had caught a big twenty pounder, cleaned it, and with a piece of flint and iron that he had stolen, had started a fire to cook some of the fish. He had been able to get some cedar shavings smoldering and had blown the embers to life, and by the time he saw the dugout heading up the river toward him, the white boy had a good fire going and a thick salmon fillet roasting next to it on a stick. Talking Boy hailed his friend from the river, and pushed the canoe toward the bank with the cedar pole.

"White Clam, it is good to see my slave brother again," smiled Talking Boy. "I have much good news to tell you."

"Sit with me Talking Boy, and have some fresh salmon. I caught it myself, in the weir trap," Chet explained.

"We don't have much time for eating right now. They are waiting for you back at Nesook. Standing Seal has ordered us back to Chahakquot as soon as possible, and Swimming Otter wants you to go with Wooden Hand tonight to help ready the great pole," the Salish boy said.

"Leave now? We can't leave yet! I thought we would be staying another three weeks. I wanted us to escape just before the village moved, when the weather would stay good."

"Don't worry, my friend, there is no need to escape now. That is my good news," exclaimed Talking Boy.

The young Indian slave went on to explain to Chet all that had happened in Cod Man's winter village, particularly about the meeting and the attempt on Cod Man's life. Two Skins had been banished and there would be no confrontation at the potlatch.

"What do you mean no confrontation?" the white boy asked.

"I was afraid to worry you before, but Standing Seal and Swimming Otter were going to use you to shame Two Skins in front of all the Mowachaht people. They hoped the scar faced one would lose his composure, like he did this week, and try to kill you. They would be prepared to kill him to save face, but you could have been sacrificed in the process. But there is no reason to politically trick him now. All are against him and he can be killed on sight without offending his Nootkan relatives."

The Indian boy saw that Chet was a greatly shocked.

"No wonder Water Bear treated me the way he did when the ship came by. They meant to let me die all along," the white boy said.

"That is not so," Talking Boy interrupted. "The masters all admire you and think of you highly. It is true they would have used you and you might have died, but they were prepared to protect you as best they could. It is not their way to show emotion toward slaves and they are supposed to not blink when a slave is killed. In the old days, before the pox, they used to kill slaves for fun. Water Bear is a good human being and it was hard for him to treat you bad. He had to do it because that is what is expected of him."

"All right, so what if Two Skins is not a threat anymore. We still are trapped here and leaving this place today will not allow us time to escape with all the food and gear I have hidden. And what about the treasure?"

Chet stopped. He'd forgotten about not telling his friend about the gold.

"What is this word, `treasure'?" the Indian slave asked.

Good, Talking Boy didn't know what the word meant, Chet thought. He could lie and save the explanation for a better time.

"Oh, it just means the collection of sailing gear out at the beach," the white boy said lamely. "Anyway, we still need to get away and now it will be harder without all the sailing stuff."

"No, you don't need to escape any more. That is my other good news. I didn't get a chance to tell you before, but the ship that came was your old schooner, and they will return in the late spring to pay a ransom for you. They think you were being held by another group of Mowachahts and they know Standing Seal will negotiate for your return. I don't think they will have any trouble raising the trade goods."

"So, that was the *Exact,*" Chet said. "It was so far away, I could not tell for sure.

"I told them you were alive and they're coming back. I feel much better. I just hope they return soon."

"Hey, but what about you? That doesn't mean that you can go."

"I know," Talking Boy said, "but I was hoping there was some way I could be included. Maybe you could buy me also. My family would help pay you back, or I could work off any payment."

"We will think of something."

Chet felt good about his own good fortune but he knew getting his Indian friend aboard the schooner would be next to impossible. Most of the white sailors were not fond of Indians at all. Even though Talking Boy was not Nootkan, and didn't paint his face with ochre and grease, he was just as savage looking to white men as any other Indian. The white boy knew his friend would not be welcome on the schooner under any circumstances. Chet knew for a fact that Captain Folger would make no payment for an Indian slave. The white boy thought there might be a chance to smuggle the Indian boy aboard the ship, but with Talking Boy being the only interpreter, it would be hard to get him aboard un-noticed. Chet decided not to worry about it now, for it would be weeks yet before the ship would return, if at all.

There was still the possibility that no ship would return for him. Just because he was a captive didn't mean that anyone would be in a hurry to sail a ship back with no other purpose but to purchase his freedom. It wasn't economical, ships cost lots of money to run. Chet decided to have a back-up plan to escape if no ship appeared soon. He didn't think he could last another winter with these people, so he would have to leave well before the end of summer. He knew how quickly the weather could turn in the Northwest country.

Chet wolfed down the rest of his salmon fillet, offering some to his friend, but Talking Boy thought it very bland without some type of fish oil to dip it in. They took the weir back with them, along with the rest of the salmon, and started a leisurely trip back down the river. Both boys steered more than paddled, letting the current take the dugouts downstream at the river's pace. The weather was beautiful, making their spirits merry and though the two mostly talked, they did turn to a game of canoe ram before the journey ended. First one would paddle ahead, toward the nearest bank, while the other stayed mid-stream, drifting. Then the canoer at the bank would have to position himself in such a way that after taking three strong strokes with the paddle, his canoe would meet and ram the second dugout without missing it ahead or behind. After awhile they got very good at the timing and were taking turns ramming each other with great force and enthusiasm.

When the boys returned, they found the village alive with the activity of moving. People were packing boxes and baskets, others were lashing the big canoes together, and still others were packing away the gear to be left at Nesook over the summer. Chet and Talking Boy put the extra canoe, bottom side up, in its perch, next to the abandoned house. They put the salmon weir under the dugout, and, after a glance inside the house, with Chet wondering what would become of his food stash, the boys went off to find Swimming Otter. They found the warrior in front of *Little Oil House* directing the family members and slaves, giving instructions on how to load the canoes.

"Master, I have brought White Clam to you," said the Indian slave.

"Good, Water Bear will be leaving shortly. Tell the white boy to take all of his personal items, for he will not return here," ordered Swimming Otter.

Talking boy relayed the order to Chet, who understood most of it anyway, and turned back to the nobleman.

"Master, if it is all right with Standing Seal, may I join Water Bear and Wooden Hand on tonight's trip to the cove where your pole lies?"

Swimming Otter knew Talking Boy could care less about his brother and the old Haida slave, and what he really wanted was to be with his friend, White Clam. Just the same he didn't see the harm in it and since Swimming Otter was feeling good about the plight of Two Skins, he gave his permission. Both boys showed restraint, but were happy, and rushed to ready their gear.

When Chet entered the long house, Cattail Woman already had his things in order. She also had his smoked salmon packed in seaweed. The boy asked her what he could do with the fresh fish carcass and the old slave woman quickly cut off the head, tail, and skin, leaving the pink meat. The slave woman skillfully cut the remaining meat into strips, as she had done for the boy in the past. Chet was given the discarded parts to throw in the river, and when he returned, Cattail Woman had the pieces of flesh packed in a small basket with instructions to smoke it that night so it wouldn't spoil. She gave the boy a hug and told him that Wooden Hand was waiting for him on the beach.

Chet had no idea he had accumulated so many things. The young man had a hard time carrying the boxes, strap basket, fishing gear, blankets, bear robe, hat, mats and now the spear. The old Haida slave saw him from a distance and came over to help him.

"Ah, White Clam, you are worse than an old woman," mumbled Wooden Hand. "Why do you need so many blankets and clothes? I suppose I should be grateful you didn't fall in love with the rocks from the fireplace, for we would be carrying them, also. Sometimes I don't know why I like you."

"It must be my handsome face," laughed Chet, handing over some of the load.

209

The old slave didn't understand his English words, which was just as well. He shook his head and begged the boy to hurry, for Water Bear was ready to go.

Talking Boy was already at the canoe standing next to the big fisherman. The four of them were going ahead to the cove where the cedar tree lay. They were to build a marker fire to guide the rest of the village and to begin clearing brush along the path the log was going to be dragged. Water Bear looked at all the bedding and wasn't surprised.

"I hope we have room for all of White Clam's things," the large Indian said. "He's got more food and bedding for himself then the rest of us put together."

The big nobleman took the stern and Talking Boy the bow, with Wooden Hand and Chet in the middle. They shoved the thirty-foot canoe into the river and headed away from Nesook. The late afternoon sun hung in the sky with no clouds for company, keeping the day longer then usual for that time of year. It also kept the white boy warm and little clothing was needed while he worked the paddle.

The black dugout made its way at a slow pace, helped along by a seaward run of the tide. They passed a small islet, not much more than a big boulder with a lone evergreen on top, occupied by five or six sea lions that got skittish as they neared. The big brutes never did hit the water but the dominant male kept his eye on the canoe every second. Their thick fur was completely dry, evidence of a long sunning, and they looked more like bears, than sea mammals.

The peaceful voyage continued in silence. As the sun went down, the wind died, also, leaving the surface of the water without a ripple, broken only by an occasional branch or floating seaweed. From time to time a gentle swell lifted the canoe lightly, and the continuous paddling was almost trance-like. The moon and stars took the place of the sun and there was light enough to easily find the silent cedar cove. The four men pulled the heavily loaded canoe well up on the beach and went to work setting up camp. Chet, as usual, went on the wood search while Wooden Hand started the fire. Water Bear and Talking Boy set up a small mat shelter and soon they were all preparing their sleeping places.

After the camp was set up and the signal fire blazing, Chet and the others were hungry. While the Indians were deciding on what they were going to eat, the boy remembered the small box of fresh salmon strips tucked in the bow of the canoe. He didn't disturb his smoked fish and took only the fresh back with him to the fire.

Rotten herring smell filled the air, as the three others were dipping with gusto when the white boy returned. Chet thought he would roast his fill of salmon now and sit up smoking the rest when the others retired. It didn't occur to him to offer Water Bear or Talking Boy any salmon, for he had not seen any one of the Nootkas or slaves grow tired of the herring or its roe for almost two months. The glut seemed never ending, so Chet was startled when Water Bear began to speak.

"White Clam where did you get the salmon?" asked the big fishermen.

His tone was the same old Water Bear that Chet had grown to like and admire.

"It looks fresh, how much do you have?"

The white boy was shocked that the big Indian talked without giving the impression he was upset, and such was Chet's joy that he offered a few strips to the nobleman. It was nice to have Water Bear his old jolly self again. Maybe Talking Boy was right and only in the presence of other family members or other people's slaves would Water Bear act mean to the boy. After Wooden Hand and Talking Boy saw Water Bear dip his fresh salmon steak in the herring oil, they asked for portions also. Within minutes all the salmon had been eaten and all four were full, happy, and friends again.

Chet was glad the fish was gone. He was so tired, it would have been hard to stay up and make a rack for smoking the strips. The young man lay with his head at the open part of the lean-to, and looked up at the stars. The moon had already set in the southeast, and the big dipper was right in the middle of the night sky. The boy tried to remember the names of other constellations and single stars, but could only guess to himself. Astronomy had never been his strong suit in school. Chet wished he had listened closer to Matt English when the first mate was telling which stars to guide by. If Chet had, he might be able to escape by sailing far out to sea and find his way back to the Oregon Coast by the stars. Even though the white slave might not need to escape now, he could always follow the coast of Vancouver Island south to the Strait of Juan de Fuca, then into Puget Sound and civilization. Chet drifted into sleep thinking about it.

XVII

It did not seem to the boy that he had slept very long before the first villagers started to arrive. It was very early in the morning and darkness held a firm grip. The clear night sky of a few hours ago turned cold and cloudy. Chet could no longer see any stars. Most of the natives milled around and started more campfires to keep warm, but some slept in the beached canoes. Talking Boy was up acting as host, going from fire to fire conversing and playing up the festival atmosphere. Chet was surprised to see the villagers so soon. The original plan called for leaving Nesook in the morning, but Standing Seal must have decided to get an earlier start. Nothing could begin before daylight, so the white boy curled up in the bearskin and tried to get some rest.

More canoes arrived throughout the early morning, and by daybreak the largest family canoes, lashed together with their mat sails flying, reached the secluded cedar cove. The increased population of the beach made it hard to sleep and Chet was already sitting up watching the landings as Swimming Otter's dugout catamaran nosed unto the rocky shore, with Standing Seal's just behind. The master was quick to get on land and found his brother, Water Bear awaiting orders.

"My brother, have the family members and slaves start clearing the path to the cedar pole. Standing Seal is eager to reach Chahakquot, as his spies have seen the gray whale off the mouth of the Sound again."

Water Bear gathered all the family, including Chet, and headed towards the forest. Swimming Otter waited for Standing Seal to reach shore, as only the chief could order the others to work. After a short speech by the chief, where he discussed Swimming Otter's payment to each family, the whole village of men, women, and children, with the exception of the very old or the very young, headed toward the downed cedar.

Chet helped Wooden Hand attach a long hawser, or tow rope, to the base of the pole. The bark rope was three inches thick and one hundred feet long. It took four of them to carry the heavy cable from the master's canoe, and tying the knot was no easy trick.

With the arrival of the rest of the villagers, the work began in earnest. One hundred men took up positions on the rope, which stretched almost to the beach. Twenty men took up positions behind the log, ready to push. The rest of the men, women and children stood on either side of the pole in groups of ten, ready to lift up on cedar posts placed between the alder log skids. Chet, and another slave were assigned the job of bringing the alder log skids forward as the pole traversed each one. When everyone was in position, Swimming Otter gave the signal to begin and three hundred fifty people lifted, pushed, and pulled at once. The huge log lurched forward a few feet. Everyone adjusted to the new position and the cedar pole lurched again, freeing up the last alder skid, which Chet and his comrade brought quickly to the front of the pole.

For two hours the people worked, bringing the log toward the beach, until the men pulling on the rope were standing in water. Chet now knew why they had pushed up the time schedule. The arrival of the log at the beach coincided with the high tide. As the huge totem pole neared the water's edge, more men left the rope and helped lift on the sides. The smooth topography of the beach made the going easier and Chet was kept busy moving the alder skids. When the men in front were waist deep in water the thick cable was attached to Swimming Otter's catamaran. The totem log was already displacing water at its base and as the double canoe filled with paddlers, the rest of the villagers, those who could find a place, pushed on the log. Another fifteen minutes found the huge pole finally floating, and with the tide turning, no time was wasted attaching the rest of the master's canoes, about six of them in single file, to the front of the catamaran. A special towing hitch for towing dead whales was used to attach all the canoes together, and allowed for equal distribution of forces. With the help of the outgoing tide, the long procession started for Chahakquot.

All eyes were fastened on Water Bear, who along with Chet, Talking Boy, and Wooden Hand were in the lead canoe. The big Nootkan was the key and everyone paddled in unison with his strokes. With Swimming Otter in the stern of the catamaran, the half dozen family canoes, slowly, made their way out of the cove, dragging the heavy log behind them. Standing Seal and the rest of the families went ahead to the summer village, promising to unload their belongings and return to help with the towing.

Raindrops spattered on the saltwater as the day progressed, and the gray clouds got thicker, turning on a cold shower by noon. Chet was growing tired of the paddling. It seemed like no one would take a rest, but for all their work, the pace was extremely slow. The cold rain made his aching body suffer all the more. The white slave's fingers were cold and his feet were numb from the cramped confines of the bow. Wooden Hand and Talking boy paddled on, singing a whaling chant, and keeping pace with the relentless Water Bear. The nobleman soon shouted an unfamiliar word in Nootkan and Talking Boy told Chet to stop paddling and rest for a while.

The boy welcomed the first rest break, while the others continued. He could hear the men and women in the catamaran singing and chanting behind him. Chet felt no guilt after the three hours of heavy work. His cold hands could barely open the box containing his smoked salmon, and after a few morsels of fish and a drink of water from a seal bladder container, the white boy settled down for a few minutes sleep.

The rest break was short lived, as it was soon Talking Boy's turn. Chet's aching muscles were stiff as he got back into the rhythm of the paddle. The rain was coming down even harder now, as the boy's movements became trance-like. He was going through the motions without putting much power into each stroke. *How could these people do this so easily*, he thought?

All through the afternoon everyone traded rest breaks while singing the whaler's song and pounding the sea with their paddles. Shortly before dark, relief arrived. But it was only relief in the sense that more canoes and men joined the tow. The new canoes attached to the main towline behind the catamaran, but no sense of increased speed was apparent. Swimming Otter lit a torch and wedged it so it showed above the bows of the lashed canoes, allowing any others to find them on the dark waters of the Sound. As more dugouts came, the boy's strength of will was renewed and he pressed on through the night.

Chet's body was running like a machine and he had no knowledge of time passing. In darkness the chanting was more important, as it was the only way the group could continue paddling in unison. Chet was thankful for the short rest breaks, but the relentless rain had soaked all his clothing and gear and sleep was impossible. He satisfied his hunger and thirst and rested his eyes, but he never fell asleep.

Daylight broke as they passed to the northeast of Bligh Island. Twenty hours of paddling and twenty miles of progress. One mile an hour. A man could swim that fast. Still there were ten more miles of twisting channels and islets to go around until they hit the cove where Chahakquot stood. Standing Seal himself joined the tow by midmorning, shouting words of encouragement to the weary people. It worked for a while, but even the sturdiest whalers, like Water Bear, were showing the wear of the journey.

Chet had never been so tired in his life. He thought duty on the *Exact* was bad, but this was an experience he never wished to repeat again. Talking Boy was saying how the whalers, in one canoe, would paddle for days sometimes without rest to tow a large Gray in from twenty miles or more at sea. The white boy was happy to hear that most slaves weren't allowed the privilege of whaling. Besides, the young man already knew he would be helping Wooden Hand and Flying Gull with the work on the totem pole and would not have been included in any whaling trips out at sea, in any case. Chet couldn't wait for that work to start.

Concentrating on those thoughts, he adjusted the wet bearskin robe under his knees and dug in the paddle as hard as he could.

There was almost no one chanting any longer as the second day of paddling worn on. The thought of paddling through another wet night was beyond Chet's comprehension. He wanted to quit and sink to his knees, crying like a baby. *I can't go on any longer*, he thought, and turned to look at the big Indian in the stern. Water Bear stared right through the motionless white boy and gave out a blood-curling scream. Chet didn't react. The big Nootkan could kill him for stopping, but the boy was too tired to care. He could paddle no more.

It took several moments before Chet realized that his master was screaming for joy, and not out of anger. The big fisherman had spotted the dim light of a beach fire at Chahakquot as they rounded a small islet in the bay. Everyone was paddling harder and singing again and no one seemed concerned that the white boy was staring into space. Chet felt a bit guilty when he realized that the trip was almost complete, so the boy sucked up all the strength left in him to keep paddling for the last mile.

Water Bear's was the first canoe to hit the beach and it took a few minutes to adjust their legs to solid ground after thirty-two hours in the dugout. Water Bear disconnected the cable and the group carried the canoe up to the high tide mark. They rushed back to help with the next canoes in line and shortly thereafter, the master's catamaran with the main tow hawser was beached. The remaining canoes behind Swimming Otter let go of the cable in midwater and joined the gathering on shore.

Since the tide was going out, and to the relief of all, the beaching of the log would be delayed until high tide the next afternoon. The men gathered the cable and pulled until the log was securely fastened to a mortuary pole in front of Whale Oil House. Satisfied that the cedar pole would not break loose in the night's tide, Swimming Otter ordered the planks unlashed from the two large canoes and placed around the family house. His was the only house not rebuilt, as the other families had replaced their planks prior to rejoining the tow. It was a pleasant job and was completed within an hour. Chet was glad when Talking Boy said good night and he was free to rest.

Cattail Woman had a fire going at the hearth nearest to Chet's sleeping platform when he finally came inside. Other women had similar fires going and hot wild herb tea and soup had been started. Everything the boy owned was wet, and the old slave woman had him strip down to his shorts and place his wet clothes on a fish drying rack next to the fire. He hung the heavy bearskin from the rafter beams and watched as the water dripped from it in big noisy drops. Shivering, Chet sat down by the fire and grasped his carved wooden cup of tea. The warm liquid tasted good. The white boy was joined by a wet Wooden Hand, who broke into a big smile when he was given some warm herring soup. They watched as the slave woman opened a watertight basket and pulled out three dry wool trade blankets she had painstakingly packed. It was the most welcome sight the boy had ever seen. He took the blanket and gave Cattail Woman a hug. Chet wrapped himself up in it and let exhaustion take over. He fell asleep next to the warmth of the fire, too tired even to dream.

Many hours later Chet was amazed that no one was up when he went out to relieve himself on the old peeing post. It had to be well along in midmorning, yet only a handful of villagers were even awake. The clouds and rain were still around, but there was a sense of being back home, and the boy daydreamed that soon a schooner would appear, ending this nightmare he was living. Chet picked up some firewood and returned to the house. He had forgotten how big *Whale Oil House* was and how much better the air smelled there. Two months of smelling nothing but rotting herring at Nesook had left him with greater respect for fresh air. As the white slave looked around the interior, he rediscovered the huge roof beams of the house. They made the totem pole log outside in the bay seem small in comparison, and he wondered how these massive cedar logs were ever put in place. Chet remembered the trouble they had building their log cabin in the Willamette Valley, and those logs were like toothpicks next to these roof beams.

Chet wrapped the wool blanket back around himself, checked his clothes and found them still wet, and re-kindled the fire. His body still ached as he bent over to blow the coals back to life. After the embers caught hold, the young man built the fire up and went back to sleep on the warm earth next to the hearth.

Everyone in the house slept until late afternoon, at which time Water Bear made the rounds waking the household. It was almost high tide and the optimum time to beach the totem log. Most of the rest of the village was already awake, having spent less time and energy towing and were now gathering to help beach the log. Although Chet did not realize it, a careful accounting was being kept as to who was helping and how much labor was being spent, as payment would be made at the potlatch later on in the spring.

When Standing Seal and Swimming Otter arrived, a canoe and ten men were dispatched to hook onto the log and keep it off shore, while another hundred men pulled the log a quarter of a mile past the last house in the village, to a spot of seclusion. At this private location the totem pole could be carved, out of sight, with only the workers and Swimming Otter able to view the pole until its completion.

The trip down the beach took about fifteen minutes and the hundred or so men and young boys pulled the log ashore. In groups of five or six they waded into the water on the seaward side of the log and placed cedar poles under the log. Chet and the other four wood worker slaves assigned to Wooden Hand were given two-foot wedges of cedar, and each man was placed about fifteen feet apart along the log. As the men on the poles lifted, the eighty-foot log rolled a few feet up the watery incline of the beach. Chet and the other wedge holders placed their chunks of wood so the log could not roll backwards. After the poles were repositioned they were lifted again and the wedges moved forward. Slowly the log was rolled, a few feet at a time, out of the water and up the sandy grade of the beach. The large team of men worked for an hour rolling the log up the sand dunes and over some waist high shrubs that sprang back after being flattened, finally resting at the base of a cliff. Another half hour of lifting each end onto large cedar blocks left the pole completely off the ground and hidden behind the screen of brush.

Swimming Otter thanked the gathering again for all their help and as the throng of men left, he walked along the great log surveying every inch. The master dismissed all the slaves but Wooden Hand, and he, Flying Gull, and Water Bear sat down to discuss the placement and pattern of the totems.

Chet spent the rest of that day fishing with Talking Boy. They only had two hours of daylight left, but the time was well spent. The young men found an old canoe to use and paddled over to the nearest rocky shoal, where they caught four good-sized rockfish apiece before dark. That night they dined with the old slave couple on a fish chowder that Cattail Woman made out of some roots she had dug and the fish the boys caught.

"White Clam, I'm pleased you have become a good fisherman, because you will be the main supplier of food for me while the pole is being carved," commented the old Haida slave, as he wiped the fishy stew from his lips. "Talking Boy, tell him in white man's language so he is sure to understand."

The Salish slave told his white friend all that Wooden Hand had said. Chet was to help the old wood carver in two ways. Since the totem pole was now the family's main priority and the old man was the only experienced carver, Wooden Hand would have to spend all of his daylight time working on that project and would have no time to fish or gather food for himself. The old slave had asked for and received permission for White Clam to fish in the mornings and help with the work on the totem pole in the afternoon.

The salmon Chet caught would be for the exclusive use of the old man and the boy. Chet would not have to give a percentage of the catch to the master, as he had done before. This didn't seem important to the boy, but it gave great prestige to the old man. Most slaves had enough to eat during the year by getting leftovers or being able to keep part of what they caught. This time of year was different, for most of the common men would be whaling soon and could be gone for days or weeks at a time. There would be a shortage of men to provide fresh fish and game to each household until a whale was killed, and any extra fish that Chet might catch could be used as a trade commodity to the families of those men.

Chet was just happy to be doing something he liked. After Talking Boy left, the white boy went over to the basket that contained his fishing gear and went through it, making sure that all was in order. The half dozen iron hooks that Water Bear had given him a few weeks before were starting to rust, so the boy cleaned and sanded the hooks with dogfish skin and soaked the hooks in seal oil. He borrowed some bear grease from Cattail Woman, formed a little block of lard with the hooks inside, and wrapped the whole thing in seaweed. He hoped that would keep the iron hooks from rusting.

Chet had two hand lines already set up and borrowed Wooden Hand's line as well. There was plenty of seasoned herring for bait, but the boy hoped that he would be able to get some fresh herring, via a dip net, from one of the other men. Chet also decided to fish for flounder on the sandy bottoms, rather than run the risk of losing hooks in the rocks.

The bearskin robe was still wet, but his other two trade blankets were dry, so he spent some time arranging his possessions on the sleeping platform and made his bed in the old place between the big storage boxes. Chet was happy to have all the extra space again, and since he was still tired from the last three days, turned in early, knowing there were long days of work ahead.

The next few days were transition days for the town of Chahakquot. The women put the houses in order and the men prepared for the whaling season. Standing Seal sent two of his strongest young men in a fast dugout to scout the Pacific Ocean at the mouth of Nootka Sound looking for evidence of the large sea mammals. The Nootkans would kill any type of whale or porpoise but preferred the larger humpbacks and gray whales that migrated from warmer waters to the south. Whaling gear was seen on the front decks of every house, and special whaling canoes, used for no other purpose, were being removed from their resting places at the back of the houses. However, none of this gear would be used until Standing Seal had made the first kill.

Whaling for the Mowachahts was more of a manhood ritual than a way of procuring sustenance. It was only the chiefs and those of noble blood who could kill a whale, and usually only common men could command a seat in the special whaling canoes. Slaves were almost never allowed in the whaling dugouts and women never were. In fact, Two Skins, though freed, was the only slave that Chet ever heard of who was actually allowed to kill a whale, and that was only because of his great feats in war.

Most of the slaves were employed, as Chet was, in the business of catching fish. The boy learned the first day that this was not the season for flounder. He was able to catch some smaller fish, but the young man watched as a dozen other canoes worked the cove for salmon. With rakes and dip nets the men would secure a number of fresh herring or eulachon, an oily little fish found in schools near the shore, and bait their hooks. The line, made of whale sinew and very strong, was attached to their paddles, and as the canoe was moved around the cove, the trailing bait was in constant motion. This motion attracted the aggressive salmon, which took the hook violently.

That first morning Chet watched as one of the slave men kept losing huge fish off his line. Catching the man's attention, the white slave was able to trade the Indian slave two of his prized iron hooks for an old cedar dip net, some whale sinew line, and one of the silver salmon the man had already caught. The trade worked out well for both men, for Chet later saw the other slave land two salmon with the iron hooks.

In the meantime the white boy rigged a line of his own, but found the technique harder than it looked. He was able to hook the salmon, but not keep them hooked for long. After awhile Chet stopped and fished for flounder once more. While doing so he studied the men's technique once again and saw subtle changes in fishing methods he had not noticed before. There was a certain way the slave fishermen used the paddle to help land the salmon and not let it throw the hook. After another failure, the boy succeeded in getting a salmon on board. With this success Chet felt he had a good morning's work done, and rushed back to *Whale Oil House*.

Chet walked past harpoons, line, lances, seal skin floats and more whaling gear as he made his way through the door of the house to find Cattail Woman. She had been busy that morning herself, picking fresh greens and digging roots. The white boy left her to prepare the fish and the slave woman said she would help him repair the old net that night. Chet grabbed some smoked salmon from his personal supply and ate as he walked down the beach towards the pole carving area. As he continued, Chet noticed the many other poles in front of the houses, and thought that Standing Seal's pole was the only one that would come close to being as big as this new one. Unknown to Chet, the chief had already made sure the dimensions would not exceed those of his pole. Wooden Hand had specific measurements to follow.

The white boy moved past the scrubby thicket that surrounded the long cedar pole and saw Flying Gull and Wooden Hand at the base drawing animal form outlines on the pole with sticks of charcoal. The boy recognized the two slaves adzing the base of the pole as two of those who were on the original tree-cutting expedition. They were preparing the bottom ten feet of the log by chipping away the sapwood. This was the part of the log that would be under ground and needed the sapwood cut away so the solid old wood that was more resistant to decay would be exposed. They were also getting ready to split the great log in two halves, to decrease the weight and guard against cracking. Chet knew that the slaves would work in half-day shifts, or more, if needed, adzing and chiseling the areas that Wooden Hand designated for removal.

Flying Gull, the common man, had at one time been a carver's apprentice, but all the experienced men had died the last three years from smallpox before the young Indian man could learn much of the craft. That's what made Wooden Hand so valuable. Even though the old man was a slave, Swimming Otter knew the old one was once a master carver with his own people. The Haida were not only a fierce warrior group, but also their art and woodcarving were the most refined of all the Northwest Coast tribes. That was why Swimming Otter promised the old carver new rights now and maybe his freedom later, when the pole was finished.

Chet strolled into the carving area and approached the old slave.

"Wooden Hand, food and drink," the white boy said in his improving Nootkan.

"White Clam, how did the fishing go this morning? Well, I hope," said the old man as he took the smoked salmon and seal bladder water container.

"Fishing, good," the boy replied.

Chet noticed that the two Indians had drawn about ten feet of outlines on the bottom part of the pole and charcoal covered both their hands. He was mystified how they were going to take a thick log and turn it into a magnificent carving like the ones that dotted the village beach already. Wooden hand left Flying Gull to finish a drawing on his own and took the boy to the other end of the pole.

"The chief is becoming very jealous of this pole, White Clam, so we must shorten it by ten feet so it will not be taller than his own. We need to make it end here."

The old man took a piece of coal and made a mark transversely across the log, about ten feet from the end. He gathered some dry tinder and within minutes had a small fire started under the log.

"You must be very careful not to let the fire burn beyond the black mark," cautioned Wooden Hand. "Take this old adze and chip away a flat spot on top of the log, above the fire and behind the black line. You can put hot rocks on top and the burn will go quicker." Chet told the old slave that he understood, and after gathering a supply of wood, along with a few rocks, he set about chipping the log. The old adze was the same one Chet had used earlier in the winter when they were making bent wood boxes. It had been sharpened since then and its metal blade worked well on the sapwood. After ten minutes the white slave had flattened out a small area, and using some wooden tongs, he placed two of the glowing hot rocks on the log.

The rest of the afternoon was spent burning the log with rocks and chipping away the blackened material. The white boy was careful not to let the fire get too big and used seawater from a watertight basket to keep the fire from burning below the black line.

While the slave Indians were continuing the sapwood removal, Flying Gull and Wooden Hand got started on removing sapwood around the outline of the base figure. From time to time the boy would purposely wander down that way supposedly picking up driftwood for the fire, but mostly sneaking a peak at the work. He didn't see much progress that first day and had his doubts as to how the project would fair.

By the time it got dark, the burn was about three quarters through, counting the top and bottom burns together. The thicker middle part was still left, and the boy asked if he could return after dinner to continue the fire. The sun had come out the last two hours of the afternoon, promising a balmy, clear night, so Wooden Hand saw no reason why not and gave his permission.

There was some excitement around the evening fires that night as Standing Seal's scouts had returned with news of multiple sightings of whales within a few hours' paddling from the village. Since only the chief could kill the first whale, everyone was confident that Standing Seal would be successful in killing a whale quickly, thus allowing the other nobles a chance to fulfill their manhood as well. Once again, talk turned to the feast they would soon have of whale blubber, which Chet perceived to be as relished as the herring roe, but on a bigger scale.

Great feasts were in the future, but for now the chief and the other whalers would fast until they reached the whaling waters. Standing Seal had been in solitude most of the day, praying to the spirit of the whale. The other whalers jumped into the cold water of the bay and beat themselves with sharp branches until they bled. It was all part of the manhood ritual, and Talking Boy even told of old chiefs who made their villages fast until a whale was caught. Chet was glad he didn't have to join in on the fun.

Plans were made for most of the family whaling canoes to leave early in the morning. For the first time in years, slaves would be needed to fill extra seats in the canoes of many households. Those picked welcomed it for the extra status it gave them, not to mention their own small share of any kill that their master made.

Chet was glad he did not have to go with them. The thought of paddling made him cherish the fire tending. The young man was also glad that Talking Boy would not be going either. The two boys would be able to fish together, but when Chet asked if the Salish slave could join him at the pole that night, Wooden Hand strongly reminded him that no one but the actual workers or the owner could see the pole until its completion.

All of the whaling families joined a meeting that night at Standing Seal's house, where Salmon Wolf, the shaman, was to do some ceremonial whaling chants. *Sort of a blessing of the fleet,* Chet thought. Prior to that, the village heads discussed the defense of the town while they were gone. The threat of Two Skins was still on the minds of most, and lots were drawn by families to see who would provide the nightly lookouts. Standing Seal gave a horrifying speech about the ruthlessness of the half- breed in order to enlighten those male slaves who didn't feel obligated to fight for the village. However, most slaves knew they had a good life in this village and were more than willing to defend it against the murderous foe.

Growing bored with the whole affair and wishing to be off by himself, Chet said his goodbyes to the old slave couple and went back to *Whale Oil House*. He took his robe, spear, and adze, picked up some salmon to snack on, and left for the thicket. The fire was almost out when he got there, but by adding a few sticks and blowing on the coals, the white boy got the blaze started again. Chet enjoyed these simple responsibilities and liked working where he could see accomplishment with time. The young man took most jobs as a challenge and not as menial labor. Besides, it helped the time go faster, and as he chipped away at the burnt wood, Chet dreamed of the day when a schooner would next sail up the Sound and take him away.

What the boy didn't know was that no schooner would be coming soon. The success of the gold strike in California was peaking, turning the town of San Francisco into a major city - a city that needed wood, raw logs, and lumber to build stores, houses, wharves and the gold mines themselves. Ships were abandoned and scuttled in the city harbor, when their captains and crew ran off to the gold fields to seek their own fortunes. What schooners were left made the round trip to Oregon and Washington territories bringing back the precious logs needed to feed the boomtown.

Back in Portland, Lloyd and Matt were having a hard time convincing any ship owner to go out of his way to find a boy who was probably long dead anyway. The old cook, Bart Taggart, told a hearing about Drake's involvement in the whiskey scheme, but the crooked merchant's lawyer got him off with nothing more than a slap on the hand. Nor would Drake make any commitment to put up trade goods for the boy's release. It didn't look good for Chet, but his friends were determined to try one last time, even if it did take longer to return than they had hoped.

Unaware of any of these events, Chet was confident of freedom soon and his mood was light as he tended the fire. The young man thought about the surprise his friends would have when he sailed back to Fish Egg Island and picked up the chest of gold bars. He thought again of the treasure and his good fortune in finding it, and the strange writing and where he had seen it before. The white slave remembered a time when Matt and the captain were working over an old chart in the captain's cabin one night, when he came in to serve them their dinner. It was just before they entered the Strait of Juan de Fuca.

Wait a minute that was it! The captain had an old Spanish chart of the coast. That's where Chet had seen that writing before, on the chart! That meant he had probably found some Spanish gold. Maybe pirate treasure. *What if the pirates returned?* Chet felt a little uneasy thinking about the treasure being gone when he returned. If he returned.

Two more hours brought him close to the burn-through point, so the boy rolled a hunk of driftwood and some large rocks under the log so it wouldn't fall to the ground when it burned through. Finally, around midnight the unsupported ten-foot end fell into the fire, sending up a shower of sparks that could be seen by any lookout that night. Satisfied with his accomplishment, the white boy smothered the fire, then returned to the house and fell asleep wrapped in dry blankets and a dry robe for the first time in three days.

XVIII

The next week was spring-like and every day was much like the next. Chet had plenty of success with fishing, joined by Talking Boy when the spoiled slave would get up early enough. By the end of the week, the totem pole actually began to take shape. The second day after Chet had burnt through the upper end was spent finishing splitting the log in two. After the log was split, all the slaves, including Wooden Hand and Flying Gull, attacked the backside, smoothing and hollowing it slightly. Then the pole was turned right side up, and the actual work of deep carving began.

Chet's main job now was to keep the log wet, for with the warming sun the cedar would crack easily if not kept saturated with water. The boy always kept his spear and the old adze with him, and he was allowed to use the adze to cut, chip, and form parts of the design himself. The shapes were gaining depth and form fast and Chet was amazed at the precise manner in which the old Haida carver went about his business. Although Wooden Hand was mostly the main carver, he was constantly moving from slave to slave, checking on how they were progressing with the depth and design of each cut the old man delegated to them. Wooden Hand was extremely patient with Flying Gull, showing the young man how and why he made each decision pertaining to a certain cut.

The base was worked first, setting the size and shape of each symbol or character depicted. The position of each character on the pole and what they were doing determined the story line that Swimming Otter wanted to tell about his clan and family. By the end of the first week the pole was ahead of schedule and progressing well. In fact, the totem was the only thing going well in the village.

Earlier in the week two of the whaling canoes had returned with some women who had escaped from the village to the south that the murderer, Two Skins, had pillaged. Their stories were gruesome and their wounds many. The next day more canoes returned to re-supply and take back-up harpoons to the chief. Although many whales were around, none had been taken, and Standing Seal's frustration was reported to be at a high level. If the chief did not make a kill, no one else would either. That night, Talking Boy came over for a dinner of fresh fish and dried herring spawn cakes, and told of Standing Seal's family and slaves' concern for their own welfare. The last time a chief could not take a whale, a lot of slaves were sacrificed to save face and no one was allowed to eat for days. Chet was concerned for not only the slaves, some of whom had become close fishing friends, but also for his own welfare. An unhappy chief would not take trading for a white slave lightly. The cost for his freedom might soar. As the boy fell asleep that night he said his own prayers in hopes that God might take pity on these heathens and help them for the white boy's sake. It was a prayer Chet would remember all too well for the next few days.

The white slave had not been sleeping long when he felt the force of a hand over his mouth through the cloud of sleep. He struggled initially, and then a familiar voice came to his ears.

"It is all right, White Clam. We just don't want you to wake the household."

It was the voice of his old friend Water Bear. *What was he doing here and why was he being held so tightly? What was going on?* Wooden Hand woke also and whispered the same questions of the big Indian.

"Quiet, White Clam, and I will let go," Water Bear said.

Chet held still, listening to what the master's brother had to say.

"We have come back for White Clam," he said to Wooden Hand and Chet. "It has been determined that every time the white boy has been with us when a harvest from the sea takes place, it has become fruitful. We are having no success with killing a whale so far, and the elders have decided that the boy's spirit has been offended because others have gone to manhood and he has not. The shaman has agreed that White Clam has a strong spirit and may help us. It also might be that too many slaves are with the party this time and there was talk of killing some. However, it was decided that we should try White Clam's presence first, before sacrificing a slave."

Water Bear's face was completely black from a recent painting. Chet's heart was pounding as he rose to go with him knowing he had no choice. Chet was told he could only take his hat and robe along. Wooden Hand pleaded that he be given some smoked salmon, but Water Bear refused. Luckily, Chet had been eating well the last week. They moved outside the house and the boy said goodbye to his old friend. The sun was just starting to show a faint light above the eastern mountains when Chet and Water Bear entered the canoe and headed out into the bay.

Chet was still in shock from being awakened so rudely, and was just beginning to get his bearings. He had not been given a paddle, but was placed in the bow where the harpooner, Swimming Otter, normally sat. The position was quite roomy and the young man sat on the whaler's tackle box, curling up his feet under the bearskin robe. The special whaling canoe was different from the others, mostly because of its neatness and attention to detail. Every item used was in a certain place and every one of the eight men in it had specific jobs when it came to the hunt. Alongside the tackle box Chet was sitting on were the harpoon and killing lance. He took note of neatly stacked coils of rope and seal skin floats, (both deflated and inflated), boxes of food and fresh water under the seats, and spare harpoons.

The dugout was not as large as some of the other family canoes, but with its shorter length and at least seven men paddling, it flew through the water. Chet remembered when he was on the ship, and they had seen a canoe off the Washington coast that was traveling as fast as the *Exact*. Those must have been whalers, too.

Two hours put them well out into Nootka Sound and heading for the leeward side of a small islet where the great Pacific mixed with the mouth of the Sound. A trickle of smoke could be seen drifting in the breeze, and soon he could see a collection of men with less than happy faces standing on the beach.

Water Bear steered the canoe towards the middle of the collection of dugouts on the small shore. Swimming Otter was standing in the water and helped Chet, almost grabbing him, out of the canoe. The white boy was unceremoniously whisked toward where Standing Seal was waiting. Without a word of greeting, the boy was placed before three harpoons that lay on the ground. The village head was in bad spirits, and the white boy noticed that his almost naked body was bleeding badly about the back. The chief had obviously been beating himself violently, and Chet knew this was desperate business now. Salmon Wolf felt the pressure too, and started dancing and chanting, shaking some kind of rattle at the boy. The chief, who had never before spoken directly to the white slave, looked him right in the eye and asked the boy a question.

"White Clam, which of these harpoons looks right in your eyes?" said the great chief with the sternest of voices.

Chet didn't understand the words totally, but guessed that the leader wanted him to pick which weapon to use. Since the boy knew his choice would possibly determine the fate of an unnamed slave, if not his own, he took time to study each weapon. They all had iron points and wooden shafts, but one had more ornamentation then the others. It looked older and had obviously been used more than the other two. The iron point was rusted, but its strength and the sturdiness of its shaft won the boy over. Chet was not sure why he chose it, but the boy did, and he even became dramatic about the choosing. Just as if Chet knew the chief needed the encouragement, the boy turned to Standing Seal, and with all the courage he could gather, chose his words carefully.

"Tyee," the white boy said, picking up the harpoon of choice, hearing at the same time gasps coming from the assembled crowd. "Ma-mook-su-mah mah-hack, wocash Tyee."

"Go fish for the whale, great chief," said Chet as he handed the harpoon to Standing Seal.

With all the gasps and whispers from the crowd of whalers, Chet at first thought he had done something very wrong. Even the chief's face was in shock as Standing Seal took the harpoon White Clam held before him. As the boy stood there for endless seconds, waiting for the worst, Standing Seal just looked down at the harpoon in his hand. Slowly the chief's head rose, and as he stared at the white boy, his faced turned from sober to smiles. Standing Seal raised the old harpoon overhead, shouted out a scream, and cried out.

"Yes, it is time old one! It is time to use you again. Let us go now, and kill Mah-hack!"

There was a combined yelling and screaming from the men as they ran to their canoes. Swimming Otter grabbed Chet and shook him approvingly, and Water Bear gave him a clout on the back of the head, much like a proud father would do. The boy didn't know it, but he had not only picked the right harpoon, he had picked Standing Seal's father's harpoon. The weapon had not been used since the old chief's death, and no one had even touched it since, except Standing Seal himself. Chet's ignorance allowed him to pick up the priceless harpoon, taboo to everyone else, and hand it to the shaken chief. The choice must have pleased the chief, for Standing Seal took to the water like a man possessed.

One of the master's crew was ill and stayed on the islet, allowing Chet to take his place in the canoe. In fact, most of the men looked sickly and underweight, for they had been fasting for a week. The white boy was beginning to appreciate the seriousness of whaling to these men, and as he sat in the canoe, right in front of Water Bear, Chet remembered his prayer of the night before. His first instinct was to tell the Lord that this wasn't what he had had in mind, but the boy thought better of it and simply added to the prayer.

"Father, whatever is right in your eyes, is all right with me."

The dozen magnificent canoes spread out over the sea, staying in hailing distance of one another along a line almost a mile wide.

Standing Seal would not sit and Chet watched him from a hundred yards away, as the great chief stood naked against the cold wind and spray. The white boy's own master was in the bow of their canoe with Water Bear as the steersman. Three rows of cedar plank thwarts were used as benches for the six crewmen. Chet was on the port side in the last row, where Water Bear, just behind him, could coach the boy in what he was to do, which was mostly paddle until his guts ached.

It wasn't long before a scream from the south alerted every dugout along the line that the great beasts had been sighted. The chief's canoe turned to meet the prey and Swimming Otter fell in line right behind. The southernmost canoes were herding two gray whales northward, allowing Standing Seal to strike the first blow. The water spouts shot ten feet into the air as the unsuspecting creatures headed towards their approaching doom.

The leader's canoe had gauged the distance and speed, and with their own canoe close behind, Chet caught glimpses of the chief as he stood in the bow with the harpoon in his hands. The young man could see the huge creatures slowly rising and falling in the waves as they made their way northward, their gray speckled backs glistening in the bright sunshine. The lead dugout was closing now and the air filled with nervous anticipation. Swimming Otter turned back and looked at the white slave as if to say, *I hope you have brought us luck once again.* For seven days they had tried and for seven days they had failed. As the minutes passed, Standing Seal's canoe inched ever closer to the gray whale.

"He is almost there," cried Swimming Otter, turning back once again. "Pull hard my men, pull hard, and maybe we can catch the second whale before it dives to the deep."

Just then the chief's canoe fairly collided with the first whale trying for as close a shot as possible, and Standing Seal drove the shaft and metal point deep into the side of the great beast, while the canoe was rocked skyward. This time the line held, and the black canoe sped away, towed by the wounded whale. Large sealskin sacs, inflated like balloons, and attached to the main cable, were tossed behind the whale to keep him from diving and to tire him out.

In the meantime, Chet's canoe was closing on the other whale. Swimming Otter yelled a request to his chief and Standing Seal screamed his permission to attack the second whale. The chief had drawn first blood, and Swimming Otter wanted the next kill.

There was no time for Chet to be scared, for now he was paddling like he never had before. The white boy was thankful he hadn't paddled the two-hour trip out to the islet, or he would never have been able to keep up with the rest of the crew. They neared the large body of the second whale, and the smash of its giant flukes on the water shook the tiny craft. It seemed confused and out of rhythm. Perhaps it already knew the fate of its mate, but it was doing nothing to escape. Water Bear steered the canoe close in for the attack, while his brother stood in the bow poised for the lunge of the harpoon. Swimming Otter aimed a mighty thrust and sank the harpoon home. Immediately, a gush of red spray hit the crew and Chet gagged on the monster's blood, which caught him opened-mouthed, and gasping for breath. It must have been hit deep in a vital organ, for the waterspout continued to run red as the bleeding animal tried to swim away. The sealskin floats were launched and the paddles were brought in as the canoe was taken for a short ride well behind the splashing flukes.

The other canoes caught up quickly, most speeding on to help with Standing Seal's whale that was still vital and running. Two dugouts stayed with Swimming Otter, and within fifteen minutes the mighty beast that had been swimming in circles ceased to move. The dugouts closed in and converged at the monster's head, and the master took a long iron lance and finished the kill with a deep plunge to the heart, turning the sea an even brighter red.

A young noble in one of the other canoes got Swimming Otter's attention and asked permission to attach a cable. With the master's approval, the young Indian stripped naked, and while clutching a long knife, plunged into the freezing water. Chet, already sick to his stomach, could not even envision this frigid deed. The Mowachaht boy swam right to the whale's mouth and sliced a gash through the top and than the bottom flesh of the huge jaw. The Indian boy then passed a length of rope through the slits and effectively tied the jaws shut so the body cavity would not fill with water and sink the whale to the bottom. More sealskin floats were attached to the body to keep it buoyant, and the young Indian attached a line to the tail flukes for towing.

Chet was glad to see the young man get out of the water and bundle his bluing body up in a bear skin robe. Watching him, the blood and the realization of all that had just transpired began to sink in and Chet started shaking uncontrollably. Whaling was another experience the white boy knew he never wanted to be part of again. Chet felt extremely uncomfortable being on the open sea around whales in such a small craft and he hated the killing. Water Bear saw him shaking and just patted him on the back.

After the cable was made fast to the canoe in such a way as to get an even pull, the other two canoes attached in single file. The lead canoe set the stroke and the other paddlers joined in. Even with the circle of floats around it, the whale pulled as slowly as the totem log had a week before.

Chet sat for some time trying to gather his wits, but no one said anything about his not paddling. When the top speed was reached, slow as it was, and the rhythm set, each man took turns eating food for the first time in a week. They offered some to the white slave, but he refused. Gradually, the warmth of the sun lessened the horror of the slaughter he had just witnessed, and his mind drifted into daydreams about being back with his own people - and Lucy.

Three hours passed and the group of three canoes was almost at the islet where the sick crewman had been left behind, when they heard a shout and sighted Standing Seal's convoy coming up fast behind them. The chief's whale had finally succumbed to the chase, and with the aid of many sealskin floats, and crews of nine canoes, the happy fleet was making good time.

Chet had long since pulled himself together and was paddling again. No one spoke to the boy as the group exited to the islet for more food and a short rest. He was left to himself, but it wasn't because they didn't like him. They were in awe of him. His power was great and no man doubted it now. The chief made no comment to him either, but everyone knew it was the white boy who had picked the harpoon that made the difference.

The two whales were lashed together and the whole column of canoes was attached in single file, with the leader's canoe nearest the dead beasts, and Swimming Otter's dugout second. The tow went on through the night, and, as daylight broke, the town lay only a mile to the east. The lead canoe broke away from the column and paddled with top speed to wake the village and give them the good news. Chet, in the meantime, had experienced an easy tow. Since the regular crewmember had eaten and felt better, and since the man shared in the celebrity status because White Clam had taken his seat, the whaler wouldn't think of letting the white boy paddle. There was no other paddle, so Chet slept between the legs of the crewmembers all night long.

Shortly, canoes launched from Chahakquot came into view and hooked onto the towline ahead. Dugouts of every size, loaded with women and children made a big difference in the pull. Others who did not come in canoes, climbed ladders to the top of the long houses and chanted a greeting to the great chief.

It was quite a sight and Chet took it all in. He was pretty sure no other white man alive had ever witnessed such a spectacle. Men, women, and children were beating sticks and paddles, chanting and singing words of praise to their returning chief. The white boy felt strangely at home.

As soon as the whales were beached, the chief walked over to the whale he had killed and cut a prime chunk of blubber from the whale's back. Standing Seal cut a small piece from the large chunk of blubber and ate it raw. Each of his crew did the same, picking their own share of the kill. When the crew was finished, the whale was attacked by Standing Seal's household, who began to systematically strip it clean.

Swimming Otter's crew took their shares with less formality, but with just as much pride and enthusiasm. The other crews from the other families that helped tow the prizes home would get their share later that day. The rest of the blubber and meat would be cooked immediately, and the whole village would feast on a community dinner. The household chiefs picked the best parts of the whale and anything left over was fair game for the rest of the village, according to rank.

Chet was offered a part of the blubber and accepted. He than shared his portion with the man whose seat he had taken. Talking Boy, who found his white friend in the crowd, told the sick man, diplomatically of course, that he was deserving, for if the whaler had not given up his seat to White Clam, the hunt would not have been successful. The man and his family were grateful for the prize, and talked over and over about the great kindness of the white slave.

"My white friend, you are a hero," exclaimed an excited Talking Boy. "Did you not fear death when you touched the forbidden harpoon."

"No...no, I just pick the one that looked right. I didn't realize until now that it was so special."

Chet just wanted to find Cattail Woman and have her take the oily blubber off his hands. He finally saw her and called for her to come over. She and Wooden Hand were the only reasons Chet had kept any of the gross-looking whale fat. When he gave it to her, the old slave woman beamed with pride and was the envy of the other slave women. She had never had a large chunk of blubber of her own to boil before, and gave the white boy hug after hug. Hearing the shouts and cries, Flying Gull and Wooden Hand had left their totem carving to come to the village, so they helped the old woman carry the heavy blubber to *Whale Oil House.*

The butchering was starting to make Chet sick to his stomach again. The beach was red with blood and with a hundred natives cutting into the whale's entrails; the boy thought it was time to make an exit. He decided to climb the cliff above the village and watch the activity from a distance. The wind was favorable and would not carry the stench towards him as long as he stayed south of the village. Chet told Wooden Hand where he would be and grabbed some food, a blanket, water, and his spear.

The boy walked down the beach towards the last house and climbed up the sandstone cliff via a small foot trail. The morning sun was bright and the warmth felt good on his back. Fresh air in his lungs made his stomach feel better and cleared his head. Even though he was hungry, his old staple of smoked salmon just couldn't fill his longing for real food. Once again, hotcakes and syrup were all he could think about.

Boy, what he'd give for a real breakfast! Chet found a grassy spot where he could look northwest and watch the activity down on the beach.

The villagers were well along in the dismantling of the two giant whales. Men and women with sharp knives were cutting the skin and underlying blubber into long strips, one foot wide. They started at the dorsal line of the back and worked down to the belly. Other women were starting fires to heat stones for boiling the blubber. Drying racks were set over the fires to smoke the whales' meat, which would be cut up after all the blubber was taken off.

Already, large wooden boxes were being dragged outside and half filled with water. The long strips of blubber were further cut into shorter chunks and tossed into the boxes. As stones from the fire got hot, they were thrown in the mix of blubber and water, and the resulting heat started the water boiling. Since the whale oil was lighter than water, a layer of oil began to form at the top of the box. Oil was then skimmed off with wooden spoons and placed into sacks made of whale bladders, and stored for future use.

Chet was not surprised to see the eating begin as the people did their work. The Indian lust for overeating in times of plenty was beyond belief. Blubber and meat were eaten raw or boiled. Even little children would cut a piece and roast it in the fire a few minutes, then swallow it rare. Chet was amazed at how blood red the whole scene looked, and decided it was time for a nap. Even though he had slept most of the night, it had not been a warm, comfortable sleep, so when the boy curled up on the bearskin robe with the blanket over him, the warm sun soon lulled him fast asleep.

The feasting went on for two more days, almost nonstop, with eating, gambling, and dancing going on into the late hours of the morning. Some of the older girls tried to entice Chet to join in the dancing. They had tried it before, and he knew they wanted more than dancing from him. They were looking for a mate. Being a normal male, he had to admit he was tempted. Two or three of the girls were quite pretty, particularly when they smiled at him. But just as temptation would tug harder at him, visions of Lucy filled Chet's mind and he'd always politely refuse the girl's requests.

With so much food to eat, there was no need for the boy to worry about having to fish, so he just slept in until Wooden Hand decided it was time to work. The Indians had little desire to work on the pole when there was feasting going on, but Swimming Otter was in a hurry for the totem to be finished. So even though they grumbled about it, the work went on.

By the end of the week the village returned to a normal routine. Some of the families sent canoes whaling and once more men began fishing in the bay. Talking Boy and Chet spent as much time together as they could, mostly in the mornings while fishing, or later at night. The totem pole was coming along quickly now and the rumors were spreading from the slaves on how elaborate the work was becoming. Nothing more had been said about Chet's part in the whale hunt, which surprised him. Talking Boy said it was because he was another man's slave. Swimming Otter could brag about White Clam's deeds all he wanted if it was a deed that brought prestige to the household, but when his slave was used to help a chief, bragging about one's slave would take away from the pride and power of the chief. There were other rumors saying that Standing Seal was pressuring Swimming Otter to give him White Clam and Wooden Hand after the warrior's pole had been raised and the potlatch completed. There was little doubt the white boy had power and the chief wanted control of it.

Two days later there was no doubt at all. Chet was using his adze, along with the other slaves, roughing in the last of the figures near the top of the pole. Flying Gull and Wooden Hand were doing some initial refining at the base, when Swimming Otter and

Standing Seal came into the thicket. The white boy was surprised foe he knew that traditionally, only the workers and owner of the pole could see it before it was finished. However, the friendship between the chief and Swimming Otter and increasing tensions between the two caused Swimming Otter to offer the chief a chance to view the work - and at the same time, Wooden Hand would be given to Standing Seal as an offering of loyalty.

Standing Seal was pleased when Swimming Otter told the old Haida slave that his work was well liked and he would be given to the chief as a gift in the spirit of the potlatch. Now, Wooden Hand would be given his own slaves and would be treated as a common man, keeping payment for woodwork done, for others. His first job would be to erect a larger and more magnificent pole for the chief over the summer.

Wooden Hand was polite and thanked them for the praise, but the white boy knew the old man had greater rewards envisioned. Chet knew the Haida wood-worker had dreams of dying in his home islands to the north, with his own family around him. The young man could see the hurt in the old man's eyes the rest of the afternoon, and Chet started to fear for his own future as well. If Wooden Hand's skill served to keep him here, then maybe the chief's belief in White Clam's powers might be strong enough to keep him from freedom as well.

Later that night the boy found an opportunity to talk with Wooden Hand, and the old man seemed in better spirits.

"At least I will become a rich man, if not a totally free man," the Haida slave laughed. "I would rather earn my freedom and take Cattail Woman home with me to the place of our birth, but I feel this chief won't see it that way. White Clam, maybe you can take me with you when you are purchased back by the whites."

The old man was teasing, but Chet wished there really was some way he could take him along. The white boy knew that, even if the man was worth little in goods, the old prejudices against Indians would keep a deal from being struck. Because of those prejudices, Chet was worried about getting Talking Boy aboard the ship, so how was he going to get an old slave aboard, also?

Chet told himself not to worry. All he could do was try to see what happened if the opportunity arose. The young man did make another vow along with the one about taking warm beds for granted, and that was freedom. Chet never once thought about his own freedom as he was growing up and the boy vowed, now, never to forget it.

IXX

"It ain't fair, I tell ya. It just ain't fair," grumbled the old cook as he walked out of the Territorial Hall.

Old Bart had just been testifying at a hearing to try and force Mr. Drake to help pay for Chet's release if the boy was still alive. However, the laws of the United States and its territories did not apply to lands claimed by the British, and there was no law that prevented a U.S. citizen from selling whiskey in British Columbia.

Matt and Lloyd followed Bart out of the hearing room and onto the street. The old sailor had really tried to help, and now, not only were there no ships going that far north, there was nothing to help convince a skipper to stop there in the future. The *Exact* had left Portland prior to the hearing, stranding Lloyd there, and leaving Matt, Andrew, and Bart without employment. They stayed, hoping to find a ship to crew in that would be heading farther north than Washington, but no ship could be found. The men decided to get some lunch and had started toward a nearby eatery, when Andrew came into view. The young man ran towards them yelling and waving.

"Hey, guys, I got some news that you might be interested in," said the boy, as he gasped to catch his breath. "There's a sloop of war at the wharf that's come up from San Francisco. The captain is on his way to Puget Sound as a show of force to protect against Indian raids from the north and to talk with the British about some disputed islands in the Strait."

"What good would that do Chet?" asked Lloyd.

"Well that's what the captain wants to talk to us about," returned Andrew. "You see, he needs some civilian crew to sign on for the three month tour of duty, and he couldn't find anyone young enough in California willing to stay away from the gold fields that long. The captain said he might be willing to do some exploring if the British gave their permission. By the way, he needs a cook, too!"

The men all turned and looked at Bart, wondering how far the old man would go to help save their lost comrade.

"Well, I don't particular like the fuss and all, about navy life, but if it's only fer three months we might as well check this here capt'n out. 'Sides, I'm broke anyways."

The old cook put his hands in his pockets and started for the waterfront. Then he turned his head back toward them.

"Well, ye comin' or not?" Bart asked, as he sent a stream of tobacco juice to the ground.

The *USS Intense*, was a clean little sloop, smaller and faster than the *Exact*, but with her five imposing cannons, she packed a large punch of firepower. Four shiny twenty pounders, two on a side, and a nine-pound bow chaser would scare any raiding canoe the northern tribes might send out. The trim black ship was freshly painted with white shutters surrounding the windows and gun ports. The crew included a squad of six marines with muskets, four sailors, and three officers, the latter being composed of the captain, a marine lieutenant, and a naval ensign.

The ship could sail well enough without anyone else but the marines were new additions with no previous sea duty and they had spent most of the trip up the coast being sick. The two naval officers, marine lieutenant, and four sailors were working beyond their limits, so hiring four seamen and a cook made good sense.

When the four men arrived at the sloop, they introduced themselves to the ensign and stated their business. A young seaman was sent to fetch the captain, while Matt and Andrew took the opportunity to look around the deck. Shortly, a tall, good-looking man came out on deck wearing a navy blue jacket with brass buttons and shoulder bars.

"Good afternoon, gentlemen. My name is Captain Scott, Jordan Scott."

He extended his hand smartly to Lloyd, and then to each of the other men, ending with Bart. Captain Scott was in his mid-thirties, had a good build and a suntanned face, and seemed extremely intelligent.

"This young man says you may be interested in signing up for some Indian duty."

"Those three, maybe," said Lloyd. "I'm afraid I wouldn't be of much use."

The miner went on to tell the story of Chet's fate, leaving out the part about Bart being the one who was trading whiskey. The captain was very attentive and listened without interrupting.

"That is an extraordinary tale....Here's what I think I can do for you. First of all, my mission is to protect Puget Sound and its growing community over the next three months. During that time I have been given authority to pursue any raiding Indian group back into British waters for as far as my judgment deems necessary. If the occasion presents itself, I see no reason why this ship couldn't make a detour to the village in question and at least find out whether the boy is still alive. I will also be meeting with the British about a land dispute, so perhaps they will give us permission to enter their waters to search for the boy. Now, remember, I can give you no guarantees, and the mission is for three months only. After that, it's back to Portland. I will give you my word to try. None of this crew has ever sailed north of the Columbia River, so your experience means a lot to me. You help me and I will do my best to help you."

The captain sounded sincere enough, but they all agreed to sleep on it. It was only the first week in April and they had a few days before the *Intense* would leave port. The men went back to their boarding house and talked things over. Bart wasn't real hot on the idea but Andrew wanted to give it a try.

"There isn't much else we can do around here, anyway," the young sailor pointed out. "Bart has no money and Lloyd is even starting to run short. It's either this or forget all about Chet. I don't care what you guys do, but I'm gonna sign up for three months and see what happens."

"Now settle down, son," said Lloyd with a fatherly approach. "There is another thing we can do. We can wait till my partners and I send a re-supply ship back to the Queen Charlottes in July or August. Any of you who still want to go, can do so then. As for me, I've got to get back to California. We can leave word for each other here at the boarding house address."

"Waiting till August still doesn't do us any good now," commented Matt. "I can get a mate's berth any time, but I kinda like the thought of maybe seein' those shiny black cannon used on that son of a gun who clobbered Chet. Besides, I've worked on a dozen ships and that Captain Scott seems like a decent man. I guess I'm for signin', too."

The other three men turned and looked at Bart, who was still half-hoping they would forget the whole thing. The old cook sat there and squirmed a few seconds, but finally spoke.

"I ain't gonna stand fer no military fuss and what have ye, but I guess I'm with ye, too."

"Good," said Lloyd, "then no matter what, we can meet back here around the middle o' July. If the boy is found to be alive, I should have some goods together to trade for his release."

That settled, the men retired to their rooms and had a good night's sleep. After breakfast the next morning, Lloyd booked passage on a lumber schooner that was leaving that afternoon for San Francisco. The two sailors and the old cook made their way back to the *Intense* and told Captain Scott of their decision.

"That's great, men, welcome aboard," the young captain said. "Take this voucher to the outfitter's shop at the end of the pier and he'll set you up with a new suit of seamen's clothes for each you. I don't foresee getting anyone else to sign on, and my sick marines are better, so I see no reason why we can't leave just as soon as you get your affairs in order."

Bart grumbled at the thought of having to wear a uniform, but after looking at his torn and dingy clothing, Matt and Andrew convinced him that a new blue shirt and dungarees wouldn't hurt his image. The outfitter was able to give them sizes that fit all right, even though Andrew's pants were a little baggy. They stopped by the boarding house, and settled up with the owner. Lloyd was there packing his gear also. The four men shook hands and said their final goodbyes. Lloyd was full of confidence for them and wished the sailors luck as he hurried to catch his schooner. Matt carried his two sea bags and Andrew, who had little in the way of material possessions, carried his small bag and helped Bart with his sea chest.

Back aboard the sloop, the three men were introduced to the crew and officers and were told that there would be no formal military courtesies while at sea, but Captain Scott expected them to stay clean shaven, dress in an orderly manner and use respect in front of civilians. Before he signed the final papers, Bart had to be reassured that he wouldn't have to stand inspection or scrub decks, after which he retired to the galley. Matt and Andrew were assigned to a battle station and gun crew and were shown where to string their hammocks.

The rest of the sunny afternoon was spent getting acquainted with the ship and crew, and the two civilian sailors soon found that only the captain and the boson's mate had more experience than they. The ship was picture perfect, with shining brass bells and fixtures everywhere. The cannon caused the most curiosity, and Andrew was excited to find out they would drill with paper shot at least once on the way up the Washington coast.

Bart came up with his usual excellent meal for the evening, and the whole crew raved about his cooking. The seaman who had the cooking duty before was Bart's biggest fan. The boson, whose name was Carpenter, and the Ensign, named Jarrell, met with Matt and Captain Scott on the aft deck after dinner to go over the charts of the Strait of Juan de Fuca and Puget Sound.

Matt's experience and knowledge were quite evident, and the captain teamed him up with the young ensign's watch, making Matt the mate. The boson would be the mate of the captain's watch, and, with the help of the marines, the ship could be run on a four hours on, four hours off basis at night. Switching to two watches would allow the sailors, who had been working long hours, a chance to get a decent amount of sleep while at sea.

The next morning was a glorious spring day and the trim little ship looked smart as she pulled away from the wharf. The speed of the sloop was evident from the beginning, and only Matt, who had worked on some real scows, appreciated the change. With a clear day and moonlit night, they were able to navigate the river and make the mouth of the Columbia by midmorning of the second day. There were no problems passing over the bar, other than some seasickness experienced by a couple of the marines.

The *Intense* turned north, caught a brisk southwest wind, and flew up the coast at over ten knots an hour. After the sails and rigging were trimmed, the crew busied itself with various cleaning chores. Some of the men cleaned the decks and coiled rope ends, while others painted and polished. Even Matt took a turn at swabbing the aft deck, something the mate hadn't done in years. Both Andrew and Matt didn't mind this extra work, for it gave them a sense of pride to have a clean, trim ship, a luxury not seen on merchant vessels.

Within a couple of hours the sloop was shipshape, and the bosun piped the company to attention. Captain Scott took the roll and found only one marine sick in bed, and Bart excused for galley duty. He read from a list of announcements and then dismissed the men into their gun crews for gunnery practice.

Since the marines and sailors were well trained on the retractable twenty pounders, a decision was made to put both new men with Ensign Jarrell on the nine-pound bow chaser. This cannonade was fixed to the deck, next to the bow rail, with an iron stand and brass swivel. Its round sides were trimmed with brass, and the thick, black breech was polished to a high shine. Ensign Jarrell swung the barrel around and named off the important parts of the artillery piece, explaining the loading and cleaning procedure to the two newcomers.

On the gun deck, Lieutenant Mykleburg, the marine officer, commanded all four guns. He had the crews simulate firing, cleaning and reloading, while moving from gun to gun giving suggestions and pointing out mistakes. At the same time, Matt and Andrew were learning how to swing the barrel of the nine-pounder around, clean and reload it. After half an hour of practice, Lieutenant Mykleburg ordered Carpenter to break out the powder charges and paper blanks. The twenty-pound cannon balls were not to be wasted in practice.

Andrew was excited, for he had never witnessed the firing of a cannon before, and felt like a little kid as he made his way to the ordinance locker.

"All right, we're gonna see some action, now!" said the young sailor.

The regular crew was less enthusiastic, knowing that practicing to clean out the long guns was easier then actually doing it for real.

"Stand by the port battery!" snapped the Lieutenant.

The men took their positions and the crew chiefs held the lanyards ready. The Marine officer turned and waited for an approving nod from Captain Scott at the wheel, then the order was given.

"Fire as you're ready!" called Mykleburg.

The forward gun leaped off the deck a few inches as the crewman pulled the lanyard. The cannon spewed black smoke and orange flame, accompanied by a deafening roar. Seconds later the whole ship seemed to shake as the aft gun was set off. The crews pulled on the block and tackle, bringing the guns back in position, and hurried to swab the barrels and reload. In less than a minute, the forward cannon fired a second time, followed by the aft ten seconds later.

The pungent smell of burnt gun powder filled the gun decks and spread lightly forward, allowing Matt and Andrew not only the sight and sound of battle, but some of the odor as well. As the newcomers watched, the starboard battery repeated the display with excellent timing and no mishaps.

"Stand by the bow, Mr. Jarrell," came a call.

Matt and Andrew nervously loaded the shiny nine pounder under the watchful eyes of the young ensign. After some slight delay, the officer turned and gave the ready signal.

"Fire the bow," returned the marine lieutenant.

Ensign Jarrell aimed and locked the cannon. Then with a quick pull of the lanyard he sent the paper blank reeling ahead of the ship in a tumbling, fiery ball of flames. Immediately, he barked at the two civilians, who were enjoying the sight, to snap to. Embarrassed, the two newcomers quickly and without a mistake, swung the cannon around and reloaded, impressing the officers and men who were watching.

"Stand clear!" the young officer shouted and the bow gun reported a second time. "Well done, men," said the ensign, smiling. "Just remember, men, you can't take time to watch your shot in battle. Otherwise, you did well."

Captain Scott was pleased also and issued an order for a measure of rum at the evening meal to all who had a taste for it. The gun crews had all performed well, and as the sloop raced northward, the men cleaning the blackened cannon had a well-earned sense of pride.

Andrew was especially fond of polishing the brass of the forward nine pounder. He was infatuated with the carronade and stayed at the gun polishing it long after Ensign Jarrell had inspected the cleaning job.

"Hey Matt, how'd you like to aim this beauty at the old Indian that took Chet?" asked the young man, as he grabbed the breech handles and aimed at a make-believe figure off in the distance.

"I'd like it, just as long as he didn't have somethin' to shoot back in return," laughed the mate.

The *Intense* continued to make good speed up the Washington coast, staying well out of range of the treacherous breakers and rocky islets near the shore. Bart continued to impress the men with his meals, and the last of the marines finally became healthy again. The end of the second day at sea brought them around Cape Flattery and into the Strait of Juan de Fuca. Matt warned the captain of the shoals on the Washington side and told him of corrections that needed to be made on his chart. Since it was already dusk, with cloudy skies, they chose not to chance an anchorage for the night, but to sail on.

"Mister Jarrell, set a course for mid-water. Mister Carpenter, get your men aloft and shorten sail. We don't need a lot of speed tonight," ordered the captain. "Don't want to run into the eastern shore before morning, do we, Mister English?"

"No, sir," replied Matt.

With the shortened canvas, the ship slowed to a snail's pace, and lookouts were placed forward and aloft all nightlong. By eight bells the wind had all but stopped, and the sloop drifted in the ghost-like waters. At midnight a light fog rolled in, making the ship more isolated from the shore on either side. The sails hung limp with no wind to fill them, and the cordage dripped with moisture from the fog. Matt assured the captain that no wind was a rare occurrence for these waters and, sure enough, by morning a light breeze was pushing the sloop along at two knots.

After a breakfast of hotcakes and maple syrup, the crew straightened up below decks, and by noon the fog had lifted, revealing a beautiful day with a light wind. Able to get his bearings again, Matt suggested they head for Dungeness Spit and make anchorage before dark.

Carpenter, the bosun, piped the men to the shrouds. Topsails and staysails were set aloft and jibs and forestaysail set forward. Even in the light wind the sleek ship picked up her bow and cut for the Washington side of the Strait. Officers and men alike commented on the beauty of the Olympic Mountains and the forested shore. Matt and Andrew knew the scenery would get even better when they entered Puget Sound.

Making better time than expected, the sloop of war passed Dungeness Spit late in the afternoon and headed for Discovery Bay and Protection Island. The shoals of the bay were not well charted, so the *Intense* anchored in the same general area at Protection Island as the *Exact* had five months before. The crew welcomed the chance to anchor again, and after the rigging was secured, some of the men set out long lines with baited hooks. By the time darkness fell, a fair amount of fresh flounder had been taken. Dinner was even better that night, with fresh tender fillets of white fish, boiled potatoes and butter. To top it off, the old cook had found some canned blueberries and made a large fruit pie, which delighted everyone.

Bart had become a changed man aboard the sloop. His newfound moral approach to life and the appreciation of the young crew was just what the old sea dog needed. The off duty sailors would listen intently as the old cook told story after story about storms, pirates, and Indians. His physical appearance had changed, also. Bart no longer went unshaven and even took pride in his new navy garb. Lieutenant Mykleburg, a stickler for neatness, had talked the old cook into a haircut. Captain Scott had a way with Bart, too, gently making suggestions, while heaping praise for a job well done. The captain also gave the cook respect, something Bart had never experienced.

The night off Protection Island progressed with no complications, and at first light, main and mizzen sails were hauled up the masts. By mid-morning the black sloop turned south in front of Whidbey Island and entered Puget Sound. A favorable north wind and the addition of more canvas pushed the trim ship at twelve knots. A warm April sun was still high above the western horizon when the *Intense* put over on a long southeast tack to Elliott Bay.

"Captain, that wooded point off the starboard bow is the place we off-loaded those settlers back in November," Matt said, pointing his finger toward Alki Point. "I count two smoke plumes on the point and three over here to port back of the bay. The pioneers must've split up already."

"How's the anchorage off the point, Mister English?" asked Captain Scott.

"It's fine, we should be able to pull within a hundred feet of the shore at low tide," returned the mate.

The captain decided to head for the wooded point, and the course was adjusted slightly. A brand new American flag was run up the mizzen shrouds, and the bright stars and stripes fluttered straight out in the breeze. The sloop passed Bainbridge Island, glided through a pod of small porpoise-like pilot whales, and shortened sail as the cabins on the point came into view.

"Lower the mainsail, drop anchor, Mister Carpenter," commanded the young Captain. "Look smart lads, and there'll be shore leave for most of you."

On shore, the trim warship was making quite a stir among the settlers and Indians. Everyone, especially the Salish, were impressed with the firepower of the little sloop. Young boys pointed at the shiny black guns and fantasized about being naval commanders, making up games that would last for days to come. Andrew seized the opportunity to polish the bow chaser, hoping the gathering on shore would be impressed with the nine pounder and think of him as its gunner.

Both Matt and Andrew were surprised at how the settlement had changed since their last visit. The cabins were expected, but the logging had changed the whole character of the point. Hired Salish loggers were another sight the two sailors found hard to believe, especially after their recent dealings with Northwest Indians.

After the *Intense* was secure at anchor and the last sheet furled and tied down, the ship's cutter was lowered and a rowing party picked to accompany Captain Scott ashore. Both civilian sailors volunteered and were allowed to go. Bart had no desire to leave the ship and stayed in the galley as the cutter rowed away.

Low and Terry were on hand to welcome Captain Scott and, after brief introductions by Matt, the two pioneers and the captain sat down on a rough-hewn bench. They discussed the Indian situation and the captain learned the settlers had experienced no raiding or trouble of any kind. In fact they had not even seen a northern Indian or canoe all winter. The pioneers had heard news of raiding parties in the early fall from Jonas, the old trader, but those incidents occurred before their arrival on Alki Point.

"That would be about right," said Captain Scott. "My orders stated that there were some problems last September, and after we stay the night we will be sailing to Olympia for the full report. You can expect to see more of us in the next three months. We will be patrolling between the Puyallup River and Whidbey Island, and since this location is about mid-Sound we will probably make this a regular anchorage."

"Well, we welcome the security and your company," said Low. "If there is anything we can do for you or your crew just let us know."

The men talked about the prospects of getting more settlers to come to the area and later Mister Low took the captain on a tour of the logging operation. In the meantime Terry asked Matt how he came to be on a naval vessel. Matt recounted the whole story of trading with the Indians and the loss of Chet, and of their hopes to find him alive.

"I remember the boy," said Terry, scratching his chin whiskers. "As I recall, him and the Hill girl, Lucy, became good friends. I don't suppose she'll be too happy to hear the news."

"Yeah, Chet talked of her quite a bit," returned Matt. "We should send word to her. I know the boy told her he would come back to see her some day, and it wouldn't be right havin' her waitin' for nothin'."

The pioneer man said he would see that the girl was given the news and the subject was dropped. That night the rest of the crew came ashore for a makeshift celebration and bonfire on the beach. Some of the settlers from across the bay came over when they saw the sloop anchored and the Salish provided fresh salmon for roasting. Even Bart came ashore and watched as the Indians cooked the salmon whole, split between cedar stakes and roasted by the fire. There was eating, dancing, and card playing well into the night, and the party turned into a celebration of surviving the winter. All the pioneers felt a sense of joy at the coming of spring and the hope for continued prosperity.

Around midnight Captain Scott ordered the men back aboard the sloop and the party on shore started to die down. The officers and crew said goodbyes to their new friends, promising to return soon. Matt reminded the Terrys to let Lucy know about Chet's disappearance, and with that, the cutter left the beach to return to the ship. A drizzly fog greeted the well-rested crew the next morning, but visibility was sufficient to set sail, and before the settlement awoke the little sloop had sailed off to the south.

XX

The day of the potlatch and pole raising grew near. The totem pole was almost finished, and every waking hour the white boy spent was at the pole sanding the carved figures with sharkskin and stone. Swimming Otter had hired skilled men to make the finest pigments of red, white, black and teal green to paint the totems. Some of the family and slaves in *Whale Oil House* were busy making final arrangements for the large amounts of food and gifts that were to be given away. Others were sent to nearby villages to give invitations to the affair. Everyone anticipated a grand potlatch.

Very little had been heard of the rascal Two Skins and his conquered village south of the Hesquiat Peninsula, but words from the few survivors who escaped the massacre told of a harsh rule and warnings that the half-breed had white man's weapons. There was talk of a war with the renegade, but, for the time being, the people of Chahakquot were in a feasting, not fighting, mood.

As Chet sanded the beautiful carving, he thought no piece of art that any white man made could compare to the raw power of the pole. The boy didn't understand the meaning of the sequenced figures, but he recognized bear, frog, whale, eagle, and salmon totems and even marveled at the beauty of the three little watchmen carved with their bark hats on their heads.

The old Haida carver was a master supervisor and planner as well as a master woodworker and the carving detail was magnificent. Wooden Hand saw each worker's strength and knew at what point he could trust each man to finish a carving task. The old man would draw out an area to be adzed and explain its depth.

Chet would have no idea what he was carving when he chipped away with the tool, but as each little section was finished the boy was always amazed at the animal figure produced.

"How much longer will it take to finish the pole carving, old man?" said a disturbed Swimming Otter as he approached the old Haida slave.

"Maybe another day or two," said a surprised Wooden Hand. "I have some refining to finish and then it will be ready to paint. Is there a problem, master? I thought we had over a week before the potlatch and pole raising begins."

Chet was working up the pole a few yards and heard the conversation taking place. Swimming Otter was noticeably upset, and the boy thought that all the pressure of the preparations had made the nobleman more and more on edge as the day drew near.

"No, old slave. There is nothing wrong. You have served me well all these years," said Swimming Otter in a softer tone.

There was no way that Swimming Otter could tell the old man that the re-knewed jealousy of Standing Seal was the only reason Wooden Hand was leaving now instead of when the pole was finished. The nobleman paused and his voice turned hard again.

"But it is time for you to move on. As soon as you have finished here, gather your belongings and report to Standing Seal. Flying Gull can finish whatever is left to be done to the pole."

"Yes, master," returned Wooden Hand, showing no emotion. The old man started to leave then turned back. "Master, what of Cattail Woman?"

"I'm sorry old man. Cattail Women was not asked for."

Chet knew this day was coming but he thought it would be after the pole raising. The white boy watched the master turn and walk away and could feel the sadness in the old man's heart, for he knew Wooden Hand hoped to gain his freedom and leave Chahakquot. Chet lowered his head and began sanding again when he heard his named shouted from the thicket.

"White Clam, you are to go with the old man as well." Swimming Otter turned once more and disappeared down the beach.

257

Chet liked to think the warrior was genuinely sorry to see him leave, but the command was short and abrupt, obviously meant to break any lingering ties between the white boy and his protector of the last six months. The boy felt like he had lost a father as the muscular Indian walked away. Chet put the sharkskin down on the log and walked toward the motionless Wooden Hand.

"Are you all right?" asked White Clam with concern.

The old man just smiled and took the boy by the shoulders.

"White Clam, I have watched you pray to your God many times. Do you not yet know that life is a test and a struggle for those who will go to the promised place after death? Like yours, my God will test me all my life and I will survive. I will feel sorry for myself for a while and then I will be fine. Disappointments are a part of life, but you must never deny your God. Only re-affirm him. Yes, White Clam, I am all right."

Chet understood very little that the old man had spoken, for Wooden Hand said his words in the Haidan language. The smile was something the boy did understand, and it made him feel better. The old man talked with Flying Gull a few minutes, and then walked up the beach away from the village to be alone with his thoughts.

Flying Gull was quick to seize the opportunity and kept the men working, barking orders left and right, displaying confidence and power as though it was he who had supervised the pole all along. Well before dusk Wooden Hand returned and called for Chet to come with him, and, without another word, the two slaves walked away from the project they had worked on for almost two months non-stop.

Whale Oil House was a busy place when they returned, and no one even noticed as they gathered their gear to leave. No one except Cattail Woman, who had already heard the rumors about the move and helped the old man and the boy pack their things. Chet had forgotten about the fat little slave woman who treated him like a son and worried that she might come to some harm without them around. She would surely suffer from the comments of the other women who had been jealous of her in the past. Now that the chief was taking her two providers, things would be harder on Cattail Woman, but the slave woman kept her tears to herself until they left. She was strong and Chet knew he could still make sure she had extra fish and material goods. The white slave would steal them for her if he had to.

Standing Seal was not in his longhouse when the two slaves arrived, but Talking Boy was. The Salish slave was the only one who found any joy in the move, for he now had his two best friends living with him.

Sea Wolf House was larger than *Whale Oil House* and had many more people living in it. Fifty to sixty, Chet thought. The interior was more ornate, with handsomely carved house posts and stacks of boxes containing the massed wealth of the chief. Dozens of inflated sealskin floats hung from the beams, along with many dried foods. In the center of the house was a large gravel and sand dance floor and general gathering place for festivals and feasts. Chet had never really seen the area before, because ever since their return from Nesook he usually chose to stay away from the dances and meetings that were public. There were two huge hearths with large seventy-five gallon cooking boxes on each. The boxes could easily hold a hundred cooking Salmon, and since Swimming Otter would be holding the feast here, Chet would soon see them in use.

Talking Boy took them to a place near the rear of the house where his sleeping niche was located and showed them where they could sleep. The air was foul this far back, but Chet knew it was a place of honor and said nothing. Many of the slaves and common people greeted them and most were happy to see them join the household. A lot of the slaves feared White Clam, for it was well known that the white slave held strong spirits, and they wanted to get on his good side right away. The white boy was happy with the new attention, but Wooden Hand was more distant and colder to the people, keeping to himself.

"Dinner will be started soon," Talking Boy announced. "You both will be like me and not really have to do much of anything for now. We have slave women to cook for us, but, unlike me, you two will have to provide the fish and other goods for them to cook. I can eat at any hearth I choose."

Chet thought Talking Boy sounded a little big-headed, but let the thought pass without a word and set his blankets and gear on the platform floor as close to the wall as he could get. The white boy took his knife and wedged it between two of the wall planks, spreading them for his much needed fresh air. After lying down to try some breathing, he was satisfied with the job.

"Let's go for a stroll before dinner," Chet said. "You want to come, Wooden Hand?"

The old man shook his head and the two boys left for the beach without him.

"I think the old man is not very happy with this arrangement," commented Talking Boy as they left the doorway.

Chet nodded in agreement and they raced down the beach to have one of their stick and rock hitting contests, and for a while they were just two young boys again in a carefree world.

The next few days saw the start of the excavation hole for the new totem pole in front of *Whale Oil House*. Wooden Hand and White Clam had been given specific instructions not to go near Swimming Otter or his house; otherwise they were free to do whatever they chose. Standing Seal wanted everyone to break their ties and wanted the village as a whole to see the two slaves as his property. It was as if the two slaves had never lived at *Whale Oil House*.

Chet went fishing every morning and took long naps on the hillside above the village in the afternoons. He loved lying in the sun almost naked, and soon his body was picking up a deepening tan to match his face and arms. The young man saw to it that Talking Boy took part of his catch each morning to Cattail Woman and unknowingly kept her status high. The other slaves, and common women were afraid of White Clam's power and Talking Boy always made a big deal out of presenting the fish to her, knowing the other women were listening.

Wooden Hand, however, did almost nothing. He wouldn't go anywhere or eat anything. The old man spent hour after hour carving a single piece of cedar wood, using his old stone blade rather than the sharp iron ones. Chet was beginning to worry about the old slave, but Wooden Hand kept re-assuring the white boy that all was fine. Finally, at the boy's insistence the old man ate some fresh salmon, and Chet felt better. It was hard for both of them to forget their old friends down the beach, but though Standing Seal never said much to them he did make it clear that the two were his property and assumed they were satisfied with their higher status.

Another cloudless sky greeted Chet one morning as he shoved the small canoe into the waters of the cove. There wasn't a whisper of wind, and although the morning sun was still far below the mountains to the east the day promised to be the fourth in a row without any rain. The white boy thought that it must be May by now and was upset that he had not kept a calendar ongoing. It would be nice to know for sure. There were already many slaves out fishing, for today would be the day when people started arriving for the potlatch, and extra fish would be needed. This was also the day that Swimming Otter's totem pole would be moved into position in front of the house. The excavation pit was finished to a depth of ten feet in the sand, straight down from the front of the house. A pathway cut at a thirty degree angle led straight away and up from the depth of the pit and would be used to slide the thick base of the pole down into its final resting place the next day. Backfilling with sand and rock would stabilize the pole after placement. Chet did not know that Standing Seal had made Swimming Otter burn off another five feet of base so that the carved part would begin at beach level and lower the overall height a few feet more.

By the time Chet started fishing, a group of women appeared on the beach near the welcome pole. This pole was a human figure with outstretched hands, which served as a greeting of friendship to visitors. The women were decorating it with fresh boughs of cedar. They finished none too soon, for as the first rays of sunlight hit the boy's face he noticed a group of unfamiliar canoes headed toward the village. Almost immediately, a lookout on the cliff beat on a copper shield, and the village prepared for the first of many arrivals.

Chet watched the procession from his canoe as the large black dugouts passed by all morning. Their colorfully painted bows intrigued the boy, and Chet thought he might like to try his hand at painting his own small canoe sometime. Each craft was carrying at least twenty people as it passed by, and all wore painted faces and bodies. Some men had grease and goose down covered heads like Standing Seal and all wore their finest clothing decorated with beads and shells and finery traded from other tribes. Shamans had carved wooden masks depicting ravens and eagles and danced in the bows waving wing-like arms in a flying motion.

Talking Boy was busy this morning, for it was his diplomatic job to greet each canoe and make a formal plea to Standing Seal on behalf of the guest for permission to land. It was all very silly to Chet as he watched from the cove, but the present-giving and speeches and tradition had gone on for a thousand years, so who was he to complain about it? Besides it was a great honor for Talking Boy to have such a job.

The village was in an uproar as old friendships were re-kindled and relatives gave each other hugs and kisses. Games and gambling were started, and soon Chet found himself the only fishing canoe left on the water. Dugouts were still arriving in groups of three and four, and as the sun began to heat the day, Chet decided to take in the festivity from his usual perch on the cliff. No one paid any attention to him as he dropped off his catch and took the bearskin from his sleeping platform. The house was already starting to stink as the huge cooking boxes were boiling with anything that could be fit inside. Fermented herring, salmon, seal, otter, and whale meat were all being prepared, and it was all the boy could do to keep from throwing up. Within minutes he had climbed the hillside and found his usual spot in the sun.

The fresh air revived him and Chet took a few minutes to watch the human wave below. As he looked up and out to sea, the boy noticed a huge seventy-foot canoe round one of the small islets to the west. It was Cod Man's dugout from Yuquot. The most prestigious guest had arrived, and all on the beach knew it almost immediately. Thirty-five men paddled the dugout and the great chief stood in the stern with a bright red flowing wool robe and wooden eagle headdress. The craft looked magnificent and Chet was impressed with its length and size. Now the potlatch could begin in earnest.

Chet had been up since early morning and the warm sun and light wind made his eyes heavy. The soft fur of the bearskin felt good to his tired body, and soon the boy was deep asleep. Below, the festivities gained momentum, and as the late afternoon sun sank into the Pacific, the boy awoke to the sound of chanting and drums beating. Hundreds of people were moving down the beach carrying planks and poles. It was time to unveil the new totem pole and carry it back to *Whale Oil House*. Children ran ahead trying to sneak a peek at the great carving, but younger warriors stationed around the thicket would let none pass until Swimming Otter, Standing Seal, Cod Man, and the lesser chiefs and shaman had their ceremony first.

Chet watched as Salmon Wolf, the shaman, danced around the brightly painted pole, touching it with fresh cedar boughs he held in his hands. Then each chief in turn touched the pole and, finally, Swimming Otter gave the word and all the common people and slaves gathered around and slipped planks and poles under the long totem pole. People on both sides lifted the heavy carving off its chocks. Slowly the pole and the people snaked their way out of the thicket and onto the beach. Everyone tried to get in a little lifting as people rotated in and out, sharing the load, which seemed extremely light because of all the hands that held it.

The white boy felt a bit cheated, especially since he had worked on the carving and was not able to share in the joy of its unveiling. Chet thought of the old Haida slave and how he must feel to give so much to the project, expecting freedom in return, only to have nothing in the end.

Chet climbed back down the hillside and made his way to *Sea Wolf House*. Everyone seemed to be down the beach with the totem pole, but when the boy walked inside, he found a small army of women preparing food. The stench of rotten fish just about gagged him. Chet made it to his platform and quickly fell to the floor with as little motion as possible and stuck his face between the cracks of the wall planks. After a few fresh breaths he sat up and looked around. Wooden Hand was nowhere to be seen. The old man had not left the house in five days and Chet wondered if the wood carver couldn't stand the thought of the pole being moved without him. Better yet, maybe they let him join in. Whatever the reason, Chet just wanted to get some smoked salmon and greens and get back outside. He took a few more breaths from the crack and was getting ready to leave when Standing Seal and Talking Boy came through the door. They made their way to the back of the house with the chief shouting orders all along the way. Standing Seal noticed the white boy and stopped, obviously displeased, and pointed at the boy while yelling something to Talking Boy. Quickly the Salish slave came over.

"White Clam, where have you been all day?" asked Talking Boy. "We have been looking for you. Get out of all your white man's clothes and put on your bark skirt, hat, and Two Skins' bear skin. And smear some of this on your face."

The Salish boy gave Chet a bowl of red grease and nodded a sign of encouragement. Talking Boy already had the smelly stuff on his face and Chet, barely able to stand the stench, had to do the same.

"Why do we have to put this stuff on?" questioned the white boy.

"Chief wants to show you off. Standing Seal wants you to wear Two Skins' robe, so he can take joy in telling the story of how you fooled the half-breed. Now hurry, for the other chiefs will be here shortly."

Talking Boy turned and started walking away, then stopped.
"Where is Wooden Hand?"
"Don't know. I just got back myself," answered Chet.
"Oh, well he'll turn up soon," shrugged the Salish slave. "Standing Seal hasn't asked for him yet."

Chet squatted behind a large box and stripped his clothes off, folding them neatly and putting on the bark skirt. He couldn't bring himself to take off the tattered underpants, but the white slave felt no one would ever know he had them on. After tying the bearskin around his shoulders, the boy, gasping a few more fresh breaths, looked at the red grease near his feet. Chet must have been getting used to the foul smell, for the putrid grease didn't seem so bad. He did take care to keep the red stuff on his cheeks and forehead and not under his nose. Looking like a savage himself, the white boy came out from behind the box.

"White Clam, over here!" called Talking Boy.

Chet walked over to the raised platform in the center back part of the dance floor and took a seat where the Salish slave pointed. The open roof above and the draft caused by the heat and smoke rising from the nearby hearth made the air bearable. Standing Seal came back with a new coating of seal oil and goose down in his hair and approved of White Clam's new look.

Within minutes all the nobles entered *Sea Wolf House* and took their places. Talking Boy sat next to Chet, then Salmon Wolf, Swimming Otter, and Standing Seal in the center, followed by Cod Man on the chief's left and the lesser chiefs scattered around the room. Water bear was some distance away and Chet managed a quick smile at the big fisherman who gave a quick nod in return.

With everyone of importance seated, the highest-ranking common people were allowed to crowd around the periphery, and the feast began. Tray after tray of boiled, smoked, and rotten fish was passed around. Roots, bulbs, and greens were served also, and Chet was able to find enough variety to stuff even his picky stomach.

The eating never stopped all night long, but after awhile the entertainment began, with young men and women dancing while beating drums and cedar planks. Everyone clapped along in time with the singing and dancing and the white boy found excitement in the narration of the ancient stories in the songs and dances. Finally, there was a break in the dancing and Standing Seal got up to address the crowd. This was what Chet had feared. The chief was bragging about the exploits of White Clam and his battles with animal and man. Nods of approval could be seen around the room as the stories of fishing, whaling, and the deception of Two Skins at Nesook were told. But the biggest crowd gasp came when the great chief had White Clam stand with the bearskin on and Cod Man identified the garment as unquestionably being that of the renegade.

Next, Swimming Otter took the center of the floor and talked of his family history and about the totems on his new pole. He put down the half-breed as well, but mostly talked about the pole raising the next afternoon and the feast and gift-giving to follow. When Swimming Otter was finished, more dancing started, but the party took a turn as people started to come and go. Some of the chiefs left to join friends outside or to gamble by firelight and the scene became informal very quickly.

Most of the younger children were already asleep and Chet was able to get Talking Boy alone for a few seconds.

"Talking Boy, I can't stand this smell any longer. I'm going to grab my mats and blankets and slip outside. If you need me I will be up on the cliff sleeping where I usually do in the afternoons."

Talking Boy just laughed but said he didn't think Standing Seal would mind, and helped the suffering white boy carry his bedclothes to the doorway.

"Don't roll off the cliff, my friend," laughed the Salish slave.

Turning his back to the celebration, Chet struggled up the hill, and after some difficulty, found his grassy sleeping spot. Chet placed the mat on the ground and then the wool blankets. It must have been after midnight, but the temperature was moderate and the bearskin was more than enough cover to keep him warm. Even with the noise of merriment below, the boy was fast asleep in minutes.

Chet slept for hours that night. The fresh air, warmth of the bearskin, and the soft grass combined to give him his best night's sleep since his capture. The sky turned cloudy in the early morning, but it didn't feel as if rain would come any time soon. The boy stretched and rubbed his tired eyes with the palms of his hands. He startled himself for a moment when the red ochre grease paint on his face from the night before showed up on his palms. A close inspection of his wool blanket found the oily stuff all over the bedclothes as well. Standing up, Chet walked over to a small spruce tree on the edge of the cliff and surveyed the village below while he relieved himself.

Although it was well along in the day, not a soul could be seen walking the beach. People were asleep in the sand and in dugouts here and there, and a few trickles of smoke rose from the roof vents of some of the houses. A low fog covered the cove, but was not thick enough to hide the islets a half-mile away. The great totem pole was resting on its back it front of Whale Oil House with all the lifting planks and poles still underneath it.

Chet shook himself and yawned. The colder air drove his half naked body back under the bearskin. He wasn't very hungry and the young man could see no use in fishing that day with the surplus of food in the village. He decided to just sleep in some more. This would be a great time to escape, Chet thought to himself. The village was asleep, and with all the commotion he might not be missed for days. If only the boy had a cache of goods like the one at Nesook and the canvas sail, Chet might just slip away into the fog and not stop until he found white settlers.

Wait a minute! Maybe that was what Wooden Hand had done! No one had seen the old carver all day and in the chaos of the potlatch, the Haida slave could have slipped into a small canoe as if he were going fishing and, instead, just kept going.

Chet rose up in his bed. He couldn't sleep now worrying about the old man. The old Haida would never leave without Cattail Woman. The young man wished he could chance a peek into Swimming Otter's house and see if the old lady was missing, too. Chet couldn't do that, but he could check to see if the old slave had returned in the night. Filled with excitement, the boy left his blankets and mat and retreated down the cliff as fast as he could go. There was still no life moving on the beach, but when Chet reached Sea Wolf House, he found people awake inside.

The boy also found a worse stench than the night before. The smell of the fish was bad enough, but mixed with the smell of dozens of overflowing waste buckets, none of which had been emptied all night, was as bad as anything imaginable. Chet picked his way around the sleeping bodies and with anticipation building found Talking Boy sound asleep. And there, right next to him, was the old man. His friend had returned! The white boy grabbed a hunk of smoked salmon from his food box and a wooden bowl and quickly moved back outside to the fresh air. He was glad Wooden Hand was safe, but disappointed at the same time. For a while his own courage soared at the thought of the old slave defying the chief and paddling back to the Queen Charlottes. Chet remembered what Talking Boy had said months before, about wanting to leave but not being able to, and wondered if he would be like the young Salish slave - always planning but afraid to do it.

Chet walked over to the cold, clear stream between the houses and sat down to nibble on the smoked fish. He sat there eating and watching the village wake up. In front of him stood a hundred canoes, and all the white slave could do was wish. Disgusted with himself, the boy dipped the wooden bowl in the stream, took a long cool drink of water, and returned to the cliff to try and sleep some more.

XXI

Drums were beating loudly when the boy next awoke and soon the village was in full gear again. Roaring bonfires lined the beach in the cloudy mid-afternoon as the smell of fresh broiled salmon filled the air. It was then that Chet noticed the cove full of salmon fishermen. He couldn't believe that they had eaten all the fish from the night before, but there they were by the hundreds, fishing, cleaning, splitting and broiling the silver giants as fast as they could get them ashore. It did smell good!

Another hundred men were milling around the totem pole and were setting up a scaffold and beam to help lift the heavy pole upright after it slid into the pit. Groups of men were positioning a half dozen heavy bark cables to guide the pole into the proper position. The two biggest ropes ran across the roof of the house from front to back, with four smaller ropes to the sides and front. Other men were bringing up large stones to backfill the pit and keep the pole stable until the pit could be filled with sand.

Finally, all was ready and the fishing canoes came ashore for the last time with their catch. Chet thought the fresh broiled salmon and wapato bulbs would suit him fine as he descended the cliff once more. The white boy felt out of place with all the partygoers looking at him strangely, pointing and talking as he walked by. Chet soon found his friend Talking Boy and took a big chunk of hot salmon, dripping with oil, for his bowl.

"Brother, you always disappear until the food is ready," said the Salish slave. "And you need to do something about your painted face - it's smeared all over."

"Is that why everyone is looking at me funny?" returned Chet.

"White Clam, they would look at you funny anyway, but the face isn't helping any. Make sure you have someone fix it for you before the feast in *Whale Oil House* tonight. They are going to raise the pole shortly and then at dusk the feast will begin again."

Chet finished his meal and made his way back to his sleeping quarters, where Wooden Hand was still sitting motionless.

"Old friend, I have food to eat," Chet said in Nootkan. "Take food you need eat," the boy continued.

The old man smiled and took the salmon. Chet was so pleased he forgot about the stink, and gathered some additional mats to make a lean-to. It might rain in the night, but the boy had no intention of sleeping inside.

"Wooden Hand, come. Come with White Clam," pleaded the white boy.

Chet wanted the Haida slave to come with him to the cliff and watch the raising of the pole. He felt it might do the old fellow some good to get out.

"White Clam, you silly fool, what are you up to now?" said the old man, still talking in Haidan. "I suppose you will pester me until I give in or I will have no rest. All right, I will go."

The two slaves walked back outside and to the back of the house. The old man wasn't thrilled with having to climb the hill, but went along anyway, and seemed glad he did, for the view of the pole raising was unobstructed. Chet could see the look of pride in the old man's eyes as Wooden Hand looked down upon his creation.

A hundred men were just now climbing the roof of Whale Oil House and taking their places on the two ropes. Swimming Otter gave the signal and the great pole was gently lifted and turned on its carved side. The men on the roof pulled as one and the pole slowly rose skyward. As it rose, the base slid deeper into the pit as men with bracing poles continually supported the front of the pole. The men on the side ropes kept the pole from swaying. After several tense moments of straining and pulling, the people let out a collective, triumphant yell, for the great totem was finally upright and in position.

Wooden Hand and Chet could only see the flat backside of the upright pole as the dancing and drumming started up again. Chet realized he'd been holding his breath, and let it out with a sigh as he turned his gaze toward the sea. Suddenly he noticed a group of three Indian dugouts coming towards Chahakquot from the north. He pointed out the canoes to the old man.

"Latecomers," said Wooden Hand, matter-of-factly. "White Clam, once again I have enjoyed your company, but I grow tired of this place. I will see you later, my son."

Chet watched as the old man made his way down the slope. The white boy's eyes returned to the distant canoes, which were just black dots two miles away but moving closer all the time. The young man picked up a spruce branch and started pulling at the needles, wondering how much time he had before the gift-giving feast would begin. The three canoes slipped behind a small island a mile and a half away and disappeared from sight. Chet waited, counting the seconds to see how long it would take the canoes to reappear. It seemed an extremely long time before the group came into sight, and the boy thought they must have stopped for some reason. Something seemed odd about the group now, and as he looked harder, Chet realized there were four dugouts instead of three. *Could he have counted wrong before?* Chet didn't think so. The last canoe seemed larger and different from the other three, and Chet was bothered by the fact that it had appeared so quickly as though it had been purposely waiting. For a moment the white slave thought he should let someone know what he had seen, but Chet knew lookouts were posted, so he decided not to say anything about it.

The early evening sky was growing darker by the minute. Chet kept his eyes on the approaching canoes as he came down the hill. No one else seemed concerned. Thoughts of Two Skins raced briefly through the boy's head, but he shrugged it off, thinking that not even the half-breed would chance such a bold move as to attack a thousand people with a few canoes.

The newcomers pulled within earshot of the beach and hailed Talking Boy, who was at his station in front of the welcome pole.

It turned out to be a group of distant relatives from Swimming Otter's dead wife's side of the family who lived to the far north near Kwakiutal territory. Since they had the farthest to come, that explained why they came late. They were dressed differently, too, and, except for the last canoe, the dugouts had a different look in their artwork as well.

Swimming Otter greeted the people in the first canoe, and, after introductions, the group moved on to view the pole. Chet came over to get Talking Boy's attention while still keeping an eye on the last canoe that was still not beached.

"Talking Boy, what do you know of these people?" asked Chet suspiciously.

The Salish slave turned and saw his friend.

"White Clam, you're back. Just in time, too. These people are a northern clan with ties to Swimming Otter. Why do you ask?"

"Come over here where you can see better," said Chet.

The boys walked up the slope of the beach toward the houses, and in the growing darkness Chet pointed out the last canoe and its strange crew pulling up to the shore. No one else was paying attention to them and only half of the dozen men in the dugout got out of the craft.

"Talking Boy, see how they do not beach the canoe, but leave it in the shallow water," said Chet. "And see how the men are splitting up, but they don't seem to talk to anyone. They walk through the crowds carrying their heads low as if they are afraid of being recognized. Something is very wrong my friend. You must warn Swimming Otter."

Fresh, dry cedar was thrown on the bonfire in front of *Whale Oil House* and within seconds the flames were shooting upward, illuminating the great pole. The crowds pressed in closer as Swimming Otter and the other chiefs viewed the pole and then began to move inside. Talking Boy was making better time getting through the crowd than Chet, as he had stayed on the higher ground near the houses. The white boy decided to follow the strange men in the crowd, and since he still wasn't sure they were any threat, he said nothing to anyone else. It was a struggle trying to push through the merry crowd. In the darkness he was not recognized as the white boy, otherwise they may have let him pass. It was just as well, for Chet didn't want to draw any attention to himself as he stalked the nearest of the strangers in front of him.

As the boy neared the edge of the crowd around *Whale Oil House*, Swimming Otter quieted the gathering and started giving a speech thanking all who had helped make the pole possible. As the master was speaking, Chet kept his eyes on the tallest stranger less then ten feet away. Something looked familiar about this one, and just as the man raised his head slightly, the logs on the fire shifted, throwing out a momentary bright glow. Chet gasped out loud when he saw the side of the man's face.

There was no doubt now. Chet saw the wicked scar on the side of the man's face as clearly as if it were on his own cheek. It was Two Skins! The white boy froze, not knowing what to do, fear gripping every muscle in his body. Talking Boy had reached the group of chiefs and was waiting for Swimming Otter to finish his speech before telling the warrior what he and White Clam had seen. Chet had to do something but didn't know what.

"Come, my friends, and accept my gifts and my food on this glorious night," said Swimming Otter, turning to go inside.

Before the crowd could react, a loud voice called out.

"Swimming Otter, first, here is a gift from me!" called the uninvited voice.

Two Skins threw back his blanket, revealing an old rifle pointed directly at Swimming Otter's chest. Chet screamed a warning and jumped at the renegade. Two more of the strangers unveiled rifles and took aim at Standing Seal and Cod Man.

"Look out, master!" cried White Clam as he dove for the gun pointed at Swimming Otter. He was too late.

The rifle fired just before the boy hit the half-breed. The bullet slammed into Swimming Otter, sending him falling to the sand bleeding and in shock. Another report hit Cod Man in the chest, but the third rifle misfired, leaving Standing Seal outraged, but unharmed. Everyone seemed rooted in a state of disbelief and limbo while Chet, whose strength and size were no match for Two

Skins, struggled with the scar-faced renegade alone. Two Skins finally knocked Chet to the ground and his steel gray eyes flared hatred as he recognized the white boy. Chet braced for the finishing blow, but the half-breed, fearing for his own life, fled behind the other two renegades through the stunned crowd to the waiting canoe.

The whole attack lasted less then ten seconds, and Chet, still on the ground, could only see legs running to and fro as the canoe disappear into the darkness. Standing Seal yelled orders for men in two small canoes to follow the half-breed immediately while the rest gathered their weapons. Talking Boy was holding Swimming Otter's head in his lap and Water Bear was trying to stop the bleeding with a blanket. Tears were coming from the big man's eyes. The white boy finally got to his feet and ran over to his ex-master. The nobleman had a deep wound high in his right chest and was having trouble breathing, but at least he was alive. The old chief was not so lucky. Cod Man had taken a bullet square in his heart and died instantly. Salmon Wolf, the shaman, danced and chanted to help the great chief's soul in the after-life, and then turned his attention to Swimming Otter.

"Talking Boy, tell Water Bear that I know something of these wounds and I will take care of Swimming Otter!" yelled Chet above the chants of the shaman. "Tell him his brother will live and to go after that bastard, Two Skins!"

Talking Boy told the Nootkan what White Clam had said, and, feeling reassured, the big man left to get his weapons and join the chase. Swimming Otter had heard the words, too, and felt better himself. Chet had him lie on his wounded side and kept pressure on the bullet hole. Chet noticed another hole in the warrior's back where the projectile exited and had the women wrap both wounds with shredded bark dressings. People were crowded around, some crying, others still in disbelief. Still others were arming themselves and setting up defensive positions in case of another attack.

"Master, White Clam says it is good to have two holes from the white man's bullet," explained Talking Boy. "It means that the bullet has passed through you without causing harm to any vital organ or bone."

The nobleman, still in shock, turned to the white boy.

"Thank you, White Clam, for the warning. I owe you my life. If I had not turned, he might have shot my heart and I would be with Cod Man."

"Salmon Wolf, make sure the women keep these bandages on tight and Swimming Otter will probably live. If they don't, I'm holding you responsible," said White Clam in a stern tone.

The shaman had never been spoken to in such a way by a slave before, but being in awe of the boy's spirits, he just nodded and said nothing. Chet adjusted the bearskin robe on his shoulders and dashed off to get his spear.

The white boy rushed through the door of *Sea Wolf House* and ran to his sleeping platform. He searched for his spear, but it was gone. In fact everything Chet owned was gone. His fishing gear, clothes, mats, blankets, food, everything was gone. Puzzled, the young man ran back outside. The beach was still in chaos with people running here and there. As Chet started to leave, a familiar voice called to him from the shadows around the corner of the house. It was Wooden Hand.

XXII

Standing Seal was a man possessed. How dare that renegade attack his village during a day of friendship and kill a great chief! At least thirty canoes gave chase, but for the most part it was a chaotic mess. The clouds were thick, keeping the moon from shining and the chief realized that his only hope would be to get information back from the two tracking canoes ahead. For all Standing Seal knew, the half-breed could stop dead in the water and be right among them. The chief pressed on just the same, hoping the scoundrel would flee for his life.

Torches were lit in the largest canoes, including the chief's, so the pursuers could keep track of each other. The men paddled feverishly for thirty minutes, making almost two miles, then stopped when the first tracking canoe returned. Water Bear, who had just barely made the chief's canoe before it left, moved forward to be with Standing Seal.

"Two Skins heads for the ocean, south along the Hesquiat coast!" yelled one of the young Mowachahts in the small canoe. "The other scouts are staying close."

"He's heading for his village - good," said Standing Seal in a low tone. "Water Bear, we will slow down and be deliberate. Have the canoes spread out so there is no chance we would miss him if he doubles back."

The big Indian bellowed out the orders in a loud voice and the fleet of war canoes settled down to a steady pace. Every so often a smaller canoe would be dispatched to check a cove or islet and then re-join the main body. All night long they paddled southwest in the shadow of the coast until they reached Estevan Point. There

Standing Seal left one large canoe and one small dugout in reserve, rounded the point, and headed northeast into Hesquiat Bay.

As daylight broke, there was no sign of the renegades or the scout canoe. The village was still two miles away when Standing Seal stopped to lay plans and take a head count, which totaled two hundred warriors and twenty-five canoes. With such numbers they decided to just overwhelm Two Skins and his men. They would take their losses from the rifles, but it was agreed that the scar-faced half-breed had to be killed before he could attack again. Besides, there might not be another opportunity to have so many warriors together at one time.

The armada paddled on and spread out to cover the narrowing bay. The smoke from the village rose slowly in the misty air, but as they neared to within a thousand feet, no life could be detected. Finally, a solitary old man came out of the largest house and climbed into a small canoe. He paddled toward the waiting group and Standing Seal maneuvered his craft to intercept the old man.

"We seek Two Skins," announced Standing Seal. "What have you come to say, old man?"

"The scar-faced one is not here, great chief, but some of his men want to surrender to you," the old man said. "My village fears you and wishes no further destruction."

"Tell all your people to come outside and sit in the sand with their backs to us. Tell the warriors to bring their weapons out and place them in a pile. Anyone who does not obey will be killed. Go quickly."

As the old man left, Standing Seal had already sent canoes shoreward to the village flanks. Men were disembarking and running into the woods to surround any would-be escapees. Slowly, the people emerged from the houses. Most of them were women and children, in obvious poor health, less then a hundred altogether. Standing seal gave the order to head for shore and was appalled at the sight he saw there. The people had been greatly abused, and it showed in their faces. Two Skins' men insisted they were against what the renegade was doing and begged forgiveness.

There was little food left in the village, for there were few men to fish or hunt.

After the chief was satisfied that no one else was hiding, fires were built and Water Bear went out with some of the men to fish. The village people slowly warmed to the newcomers when they began to realize they weren't going to be harmed. As the food warmed their bodies, their tongues began moving and the sensitive chief heard horror story after horror story about loss of life, rape, and plunder. While the stories were being told, word reached Standing Seal that his second scout canoe was returning. Within minutes the exhausted crew reported. They had been paddling nonstop all night and could barely stand up.

"What has happened? Where is Two Skins?" Standing Seal asked.

"Master, we followed him far to the south, until the sun rose," the young Indian spokesmen was gasping for breath. "When he saw us following him, he stopped his canoe and we sat there in the waves forty canoe lengths apart for a short time. It was apparent to him that you were not following, so they came toward us and fired the white man's weapon. That is when we fled."

"You did well, my son," the chief said. "Send men to the mouth of the bay and station canoes at intervals across the entrance, in case Two Skins returns. Send word to the men at Estevan point that we are all right, and have the smaller canoe return to Chahakquot to let everyone know that the village has been taken without bloodshed and that the scar-faced one is still at large."

The rest of the afternoon was spent getting the villagers in order. Since the people weren't able to care for themselves, it was decided to take them back to Chahakquot. Those with relatives in other villages that would take the people in would be allowed to go free. Otherwise, they could find homes with Standing Seal's people and serve him with dignity. There was no sign of the renegades, so with darkness approaching and a threat of rain in the air, the large fleet of canoes started its return to Nootka Sound. The scout canoes were called back and the village was left empty, with every usable item taken or destroyed by fire. By nightfall the group was well out of Hesquiat Bay and headed for home.

XXII

Standing Seal was a man possessed. How dare that renegade attack his village during a day of friendship and kill a great chief! At least thirty canoes gave chase, but for the most part it was a chaotic mess. The clouds were thick, keeping the moon from shining and the chief realized that his only hope would be to get information back from the two tracking canoes ahead. For all Standing Seal knew, the half-breed could stop dead in the water and be right among them. The chief pressed on just the same, hoping the scoundrel would flee for his life.

Torches were lit in the largest canoes, including the chief's, so the pursuers could keep track of each other. The men paddled feverishly for thirty minutes, making almost two miles, then stopped when the first tracking canoe returned. Water Bear, who had just barely made the chief's canoe before it left, moved forward to be with Standing Seal.

"Two Skins heads for the ocean, south along the Hesquiat coast!" yelled one of the young Mowachahts in the small canoe. "The other scouts are staying close."

"He's heading for his village - good," said Standing Seal in a low tone. "Water Bear, we will slow down and be deliberate. Have the canoes spread out so there is no chance we would miss him if he doubles back."

The big Indian bellowed out the orders in a loud voice and the fleet of war canoes settled down to a steady pace. Every so often a smaller canoe would be dispatched to check a cove or islet and then re-join the main body. All night long they paddled southwest in the shadow of the coast until they reached Estevan Point. There

Standing Seal left one large canoe and one small dugout in reserve, rounded the point, and headed northeast into Hesquiat Bay.

As daylight broke, there was no sign of the renegades or the scout canoe. The village was still two miles away when Standing Seal stopped to lay plans and take a head count, which totaled two hundred warriors and twenty-five canoes. With such numbers they decided to just overwhelm Two Skins and his men. They would take their losses from the rifles, but it was agreed that the scar-faced half-breed had to be killed before he could attack again. Besides, there might not be another opportunity to have so many warriors together at one time.

The armada paddled on and spread out to cover the narrowing bay. The smoke from the village rose slowly in the misty air, but as they neared to within a thousand feet, no life could be detected. Finally, a solitary old man came out of the largest house and climbed into a small canoe. He paddled toward the waiting group and Standing Seal maneuvered his craft to intercept the old man.

"We seek Two Skins," announced Standing Seal. "What have you come to say, old man?"

"The scar-faced one is not here, great chief, but some of his men want to surrender to you," the old man said. "My village fears you and wishes no further destruction."

"Tell all your people to come outside and sit in the sand with their backs to us. Tell the warriors to bring their weapons out and place them in a pile. Anyone who does not obey will be killed. Go quickly."

As the old man left, Standing Seal had already sent canoes shoreward to the village flanks. Men were disembarking and running into the woods to surround any would-be escapees. Slowly, the people emerged from the houses. Most of them were women and children, in obvious poor health, less then a hundred altogether. Standing seal gave the order to head for shore and was appalled at the sight he saw there. The people had been greatly abused, and it showed in their faces. Two Skins' men insisted they were against what the renegade was doing and begged forgiveness.

There was little food left in the village, for there were few men to fish or hunt.

After the chief was satisfied that no one else was hiding, fires were built and Water Bear went out with some of the men to fish. The village people slowly warmed to the newcomers when they began to realize they weren't going to be harmed. As the food warmed their bodies, their tongues began moving and the sensitive chief heard horror story after horror story about loss of life, rape, and plunder. While the stories were being told, word reached Standing Seal that his second scout canoe was returning. Within minutes the exhausted crew reported. They had been paddling nonstop all night and could barely stand up.

"What has happened? Where is Two Skins?" Standing Seal asked.

"Master, we followed him far to the south, until the sun rose," the young Indian spokesman was gasping for breath. "When he saw us following him, he stopped his canoe and we sat there in the waves forty canoe lengths apart for a short time. It was apparent to him that you were not following, so they came toward us and fired the white man's weapon. That is when we fled."

"You did well, my son," the chief said. "Send men to the mouth of the bay and station canoes at intervals across the entrance, in case Two Skins returns. Send word to the men at Estevan point that we are all right, and have the smaller canoe return to Chahakquot to let everyone know that the village has been taken without bloodshed and that the scar-faced one is still at large."

The rest of the afternoon was spent getting the villagers in order. Since the people weren't able to care for themselves, it was decided to take them back to Chahakquot. Those with relatives in other villages that would take the people in would be allowed to go free. Otherwise, they could find homes with Standing Seal's people and serve him with dignity. There was no sign of the renegades, so with darkness approaching and a threat of rain in the air, the large fleet of canoes started its return to Nootka Sound. The scout canoes were called back and the village was left empty, with every usable item taken or destroyed by fire. By nightfall the group was well out of Hesquiat Bay and headed for home.

XXIII

Wooden Hand was sitting in *Sea Wolf House* pondering his life when he heard the gunfire. He feared the worst, but before the old Haida slave could get outside to see what was happening, common men and slaves came running for their weapons.

"Cod Man is dead and so is Swimming Otter," one man shouted.

The old man had to think fast. He had seen chaos like this before and knew such an opportunity might not present itself again in his lifetime. Wooden Hand had to act quickly, but the old Haida knew he needed help. He hoped the boys would see it his way. The old man returned to the sleeping platform and bundled up White Clam and Talking Boy's belongings, along with his own. He grabbed White Clam's spear and looked like any other man running off to a canoe to do battle. But Wooden Hand didn't go with the others. The crafty slave ran north along the beach to the last canoes in line and stashed the gear in an abandoned sixteen-footer. He quickly returned to the center of the village and saw Chet enter Sea Wolf House. At the same time Cattail Woman came hurrying up and the old man told her to go back for her robe and bring Talking Boy with her to the waiting canoe. Wooden Hand would go after White Clam.

"My son, it is I, Wooden Hand," said the old slave from the shadows.

"Wooden Hand, I cannot find my spear or my clothes!" cried the boy. "I must hurry, for Two Skins has returned."

"I have them, my son. They're in a canoe waiting for you at the end of the beach. Cattail Woman has gone for Talking Boy," said the old man.

Chet was still in shock himself, and in the confusion he did not think to question the old man. The boy thought they were on their way to join the war party. When the two slaves reached the canoe, the boy thought it was odd that Wooden Hand had picked a canoe so far away, but helped him launch it just the same. Talking Boy and Cattail Woman came running up, and Chet was already in the bow calling for the young Indian and the old man to hurry for the others were already leaving.

The white boy didn't notice the old woman get in as well, and soon all of them were paddling into the darkness. It wasn't until some minutes later when Chet saw the torch on Standing Seal's canoe drifting further and further away that the boy became suspicious and turned around to cry out to the others.

"What's going on? You're steering us away from the others!" said Chet, obviously upset. "And what is Cattail Woman doing here? What's going on?"

The other three stopped paddling and sat silently, aware of his confusion.

"Tell him, Talking Boy," the old man finally said.

"Tell me what?" asked Chet, puzzled by the mystery.

"We are not going with the others, my friend. We are leaving. We want you to come with us," the Salish slave said in English.

Chet was stunned by the words. This is what the white slave had been waiting for months, but now that the time was here, he had a hard time accepting it.

"But, what about Two Skins?" Chet asked.

"It is not our fight," continued the Salish slave. "Wooden Hand convinced me days ago that Standing Seal would never let any of us go. We all are too valuable to him."

"What will we eat? Where will we go?"

"You have already decided that for us, my white brother. We'll go to Nesook. There we can hide out for days until they tire of looking for us. You have the white man's sail there, and food, and all the gear you stole and stockpiled in the old house. We can make it."

Chet knew now with a dreadful certainty that he would never have had the courage to leave alone. It took the crucial timing of a disaster and the courage of an old Indian to pull it off. The white boy watched the torches flicker in the distance and took a deep breath.

"Let's do it, then," Chet said. "Let's get out of here so we can get home to our people."

He picked up his paddle and sank it deep into the black water.

The four slaves paddled north through the ring of islets and islands that front the western coast of Bligh Island. Their pace was subdued, for they knew no one would miss them for a day or more, but they paddled all night just the same. The slaves followed the north coast of the island going deeper into Nootka Sound. Chet suggested that they paddle in teams, and although this idea was foreign to Indian slaves, it made sense to conserve their energy.

Sometime in the middle of the night Chet thought the dugout must be close to Fish Egg Island and he was tempted to tell everyone about the Spanish gold, but the boy realized the precious metal meant nothing to the Indians and kept quiet. By daylight the tired group entered the long finger of Nesook Bay, and with their goal in sight all four of them paddled once more. The tide was out and the cedar pole channel markers stood high in the air. The low tide in combination with the spring run made the river a torrent, and the slaves had to get out of the canoe and push it the last fifty yards to the village. The gear was unloaded and the canoe picked up and moved to the back of the first house, where it was flipped over and laid on a wooden rack. Other houses had extra dugouts left on their racks so this one would arouse no suspicion to any would-be pursuers.

"I think we should all get some rest now," said Wooden Hand. "This may be the last day we can sleep safely. I doubt they have missed us yet."

"Talking Boy, tell Wooden Hand I want to check on the stores I've stockpiled and then I'll be back," Chet said.

Chet ran down the deserted riverbank to the old abandoned house and walked inside. Under the pile of old mats, lying undisturbed, were the supplies and food he had stolen and stockpiled. The dugout, net, ropes, and weir were all as the white boy had left them almost three months before. The strong cedar boxes of food were secure as well having survived the probings of raccoons and skunks. Chet opened one of the boxes and removed a piece of smoked salmon before returning to the others.

"Here, everyone, breakfast," the white boy said as he set the fish on a plank. "Let's start a fire and make some herb tea to go with it."

"No fires! At least until dark, and then just a small cooking fire in the corner of the house," said Wooden Hand. "The smoke can be seen for miles during the day."

The old man was right. Chet had not thought of that and settled for silty river water instead. After the light breakfast the tired group rested, and before long all four of them were sound asleep.

When Chet awoke Cattail Woman was outside digging roots and collecting greens. Talking Boy and Wooden Hand were searching the house for any useful items that might have been left behind. It was late afternoon and the skies outside were cloudy, but there was no rain.

"Wooden Hand, Talking Boy, I've got plenty of supplies in the old house. Let's go there first and divide what we already have," said the white boy.

As they walked to the other house, Wooden Hand told how Cattail Woman was searching the best areas for roots, bulbs and any early berries that could supplement their diet. When they reached the old house the Haida slave was still superstitious about going inside, so the boys carried everything outside. Wooden Hand's needs were simple and he took some rope, one extra blanket, a mat for shelter, some fishing gear, and some of the smoked salmon. The old Haida added a bark canoe bailer and a fresh water container made out of a bentwood box.

"White Clam, I had no idea you had become such a thief," the old man laughed. "This water box alone is of excellent quality. I'm sure someone has missed it."

Chet and Talking Boy, with Wooden Hand's help, picked through the other gear, taking only what they absolutely needed in an attempt to keep the escape canoes lighter. Chet took this lesson to heart, for he knew his next stop would bring aboard some extra heavy weight. They carried the spoils back to the first house at the other end of the village and returned for the smaller canoe.

Wooden Hand wanted the little sixteen-foot dugout, not only because it would be easier for Cattail Woman and him to paddle, but also because it was constructed more like the Haida style he loved. Chet, on the other hand, wanted the larger canoe to carry the sail he proposed to put up. The old woman was back when they returned with the canoe and she gave Chet a hug for all the material goods the white boy had gathered. The old woman also gave the boys a supply of cattail bulbs, roots and greens and told them how important it was to only eat a small amount each day to make them last. She also told them how to pick nettles without being stung for making tea and dandelions for greens and to not eat just fish or they would get sick.

"Always eat some greens each day," she repeated.

With only an hour of daylight left, it was time for the boys to retrieve the top foremast and sail hidden in the thicket at the far side of the beach a half-mile away. Since the sailing gear would be awkward to carry, they decided to take the canoe. Armed with two stout cedar poles for getting back up the river, the boys paddled downstream and out into Nesook Bay. Luck was with them, for the tide was high and the empty canoe could navigate the shallow tide flats to within a hundred feet of the beach thicket.

Though wind blown and half covered with sand, the block, tackle, canvas and mast were as they had left them. Chet remembered the cold wet night they had spent there and was glad it was nearing summertime. The thought of spending another freezing night outside didn't appeal to him. Cordage and tackle were placed in the center of the sail and wrapped up in a bundle.

Chet unfastened the boom from the mast and set the two timbers parallel and about a foot apart in the sand. The sail bundle was placed over the boom and mast and both boys lifted the whole affair like a man on a stretcher and carried it back to the canoe. The extra weight in the dugout made it necessary for them to push the craft to deeper water before they could get in and paddle. Before long they were poling up the river towards the village once more.

The old Haida couple had started a fire and were boiling water for cooking when the two young men dumped their schooner gear on the dirt floor. Wooden Hand thought it a waste of energy, but agreed to help Chet rig a support for the mast.

The boy had been thinking about how to attach the mast to a dugout for some time. His lazy afternoons on the cliff the last week gave him ample time to think, and Chet's early morning fishing trips gave him the opportunity to experiment on his small fishing canoe. Chet had settled on wedging a small plank tightly between the gunwales in the bow. The plank would have a hole cut in the center to accept the mast end. With stabilizing shrouds attached, he felt the mast would be strong enough.

When the plan was drawn out in the sand, the old wood worker saw what Chet was trying to do and made some changes. First, Wooden Hand said he would fasten the plank to the topsides of the canoe with bored holes and wooden pegs. Simply wedging the plank would not keep it stable in a wind. The old man also suggested pegging the mast end to a plank just above the floor of the canoe so the base would be stable as well.

With the plan approved, a house plank of suitable size was selected and while Wooden Hand carved pegs, the boys measured and scribed a four-inch circular pattern on the plank. Next, they used the old man's adze to thin the circle and eventually break through it. While Talking Boy refined the hole in the first plank with a metal knife, Chet started the hole for the floor plank. They worked in semi-darkness, deciding it was all right to keep a small fire going one last night. By the time they fell asleep that night, the craftsmen had eight round smooth pegs and two measured planks with neat circular holes in their middles.

"In the morning we will go out and bore the peg holes in the side of the canoe," explained the old man.

Wooden Hand showed them metal augers he had fabricated for drilling holes, each a little bigger then the next, the biggest corresponding to the pegs he had made. As they lay there in the darkness drifting off to sleep, the old man said he would help the boys with the canoe the next day and at dusk he and Cattail Woman would start their long journey north.

"You should travel at dark whenever possible," cautioned the old man, "and only in light seas. You can always take an extra day to get home, but the sea will keep you forever if you give it a chance."

Chet rearranged the bearskin and pulled the soft fur tighter around his face until only a crack of space was left to breath in the fresh air. He was frightened and full of doubts about the escape, but there was no turning back now. If Chet was ever going to see his people again, he had to find the strength to follow through. The white boy thought of his parents in Oregon and how they must be worrying. At least the guys on the schooner will think there's a chance I'm alive. It would be great to have them sail into the Sound tomorrow and meet up unexpectedly. And Lucy. Chet was glad they were going to Puget Sound, to Talking Boy's people. He did so want to see that girl again! He was sure now that he must be in love with Lucy, and he daydreamed of what it would be like to paddle up in a canoe and greet her and the other settlers he'd dropped off seven months before. The young man dreamed his reunion over and over again and finally fell asleep.

The next day dawned bright and sunny, and the temperature rose rapidly. Summer was definitely on its way. The roof planks steamed as the sun's rays touched each house along the riverbank, and Chet rose early to catch some fresh flounder for the day's meal. It felt good having the skills to survive, and after an hour and a half he had plenty of fish for all.

"My son, you are so good to me," said Cattail Woman as the boy gave her the fish.

"Actually," said Chet, "if I was that good I would've cleaned and cooked them too."

He said it in English so she wouldn't understand, but Talking Boy translated it for her and Cattail Woman just laughed.

While the fish were being roasted for breakfast, the work on the twenty-foot canoe began. The planks were set in place five feet behind the bow, and Wooden Hand and Talking Boy started the slow process of boring holes for the pegs. Chet laid out the sail, mast and boom on the sand in order to see what was there and what needed to be repaired or modified. It became obvious that there was more sail and mast than was needed, and the white boy quickly ripped the torn sail the rest of the way, leaving a right triangle shaped sheet with a twelve-foot luff edge and a nine foot boom edge. He cut back the top of the mast with the adze, shortening it to about thirteen feet and the boom to about ten feet. With the metal ring still attached, Chet slipped the wooden pulley block over the mast top and pounded it on with a rock. With the remaining torn piece from the leech side of the sail, Chet thought he could rig a crude jib later.

Cattail Woman helped by hemming the torn leech side of the canvas sail with a whalebone needle and stout bark line. She also repaired the torn canvas around the wooden hank rings that connected the canvas to the mast and boom. Chet, meanwhile, tied four lengths of rope to the top of the mast for use as shrouds and stays, and had Talking Boy bore holes in the stern, bow and topsides to accept them.

By noon the newly formed shipwrights had the mast support planks pegged in place, and were ready to step the mast. With a few practices the boys were able to step the mast, tie down the stays and shrouds, and raise the main sail in five minutes - on land anyway. The Indian dugout with its small main sail that looked more like a storm sail was an unusual sight to see. All that remained were the two items that would allow them to outrun any Indian canoe that might pursue them. A rudder and centerboard.

The rudder was easy, as Chet had found a long paddle behind one of the houses and the simple matter of hacking a deep notch in the transom rail for support did the job nicely. Chet had been thinking he would find some way to lash a vertical board to the side of the canoe for use as a center board, but after seeing how strong the pegged step boards were, the young man had Wooden Hand make two center planks, one for port and one for starboard, with two removable pegs that fit all the way through the sides of the dugout and were held in place with a smaller cotter peg. The side-type centerboards could be removed in a matter of seconds.

By late afternoon the sailing canoe was ready for a sea trial. The two young men and Wooden Hand checked the beach and horizon for any signs of life, and then launched the canoe into the river. As expected, the mast proved harder to step while on the water, but after a certain amount of struggle, they had it up and secure. The sideboards proved harder as well because of the buoyancy of the wood and it took both of them to hold the board down and place the removable pegs. Finally the sailors were ready to haul up the main sheet. While Chet held the boom line, Talking Boy grabbed the halyard and pulled the sail to life. The short stubby sheet caught the light wind, and, to their amazement, the canoe pulled forward.

"It works! Doggone, it works just fine!" exclaimed Chet.

The dugout cut through the light waves at about two knots and the old man laughed as Chet let out the boom trying for more speed. The wind was light enough and the sail short enough to keep the canoe from tipping. The two Indian men were amazed at how the center side boards and rudder made the dugout maneuver so well, and were in shock to see Chet turn the canoe around and close haul it back to the river against the wind, something the Indian sailing canoes could never do.

"This is great. It's not very fast, but it works better than I ever thought," yelled Chet.

"It is too complicated for me," said Wooden Hand. "I'll stay with the paddle."

Chet tacked back and forth up the channel until the river current caught them in a stalemate. They quickly took up the sideboards and lowered the main sail. Leaving the mast up, they poled their way to the village and got out. Filled with new confidence, Chet couldn't wait to get started and made plans to work on the rigging of a jib for the forestay.

His good mood turned sober when Chet noticed Wooden Hand and Cattail Woman starting to load the sixteen-foot canoe. The boy knew they had to leave, but now that it was about to happen he became frightened for their well being and a little frightened for himself. The young man would no longer have the wise old Haida to help him. Chet would no longer have the old man's courage to spur him on.

Talking Boy felt the loss also, and gave the fat little woman a hug. He reached over the side of the canoe and hugged Wooden Hand as well.

"I will miss you, old man," the Indian boy said. "Maybe we can meet in the future. I would love to see your islands someday."

The old woman could not hold back the tears as she said goodbye to the white boy. Chet had a hard time not crying himself as water welled up inside his eyelids.

"Peace be with you all your days, White Clam," Cattail Woman said, hugging him tightly.

"White Clam, don't forget all that I've taught you. Don't forget the cedar," said Wooden Hand. "I will miss you, my son."

They turned and got into the canoe, and the two young men pushed the dugout into the river. The sun was fading as they drifted out to the bay, Chet saw Cattail Woman turn around and heard her call to him.

"White Clam, I love you, my son."

Chet could hold back no longer and felt the tears streak down his cheeks. "I love you, too, Mother," he called back. "I love you."

The words drifted across the water as the tiny craft disappeared behind the sand bar. He and Talking Boy looked at each other. Now they were on their own.

XXIV

The original plan was to stay at Nesook a few days and hide out, letting the Nootkas think they had gone south immediately. Wooden Hand and Cattail Woman were headed north away from Nootka Sound and into Kwakiutl territory, traveling at night only. Their route was less likely to be followed, but was far more dangerous than that of Chet and Talking Boy. The old couple had over four hundred miles, mostly open ocean, to paddle before they could reach their home islands.

The boys had planned to spend the next few days stocking up on fish and practicing with the sailing canoe, but as darkness set in, their courage diminished and their impatience grew. Chet used the last hour of daylight to rummage through the abandoned village once more and found an extra seal bladder water container and an old sealskin whaling float and added them to the stores in the canoe. When he returned the white boy could feel Talking Boy's uneasiness, so he tried to keep a positive attitude. With nothing more to do or say, they decided to put out the fire and turn in early.

"Talking Boy, you still awake?" whispered Chet some minutes later. "Did you hear something?"

"Yes, I'm awake," the Salish boy replied. "I didn't hear anything, but this place is making me nervous tonight."

"This place is givin' me the willies. I got a bad feelin' all of a sudden," returned Chet.

"What do you mean, willies?" asked Talking Boy.

"I mean it's makin' me nervous, too! I don't think we should stay here much longer. In fact, how would you feel about packin' up and gettin' out of here right now?" asked Chet.

"Leave right now, in the dark?"

"Yeah, we've got everything in the canoe except what we're sleepin' on. What do you say?" asked the white boy again. "I'm not ashamed to admit that I'm scared to death."

"Okay," said the Indian. "Let's get out of here."

Chet needed no further encouragement. He jumped up and had his blankets and mat in the canoe in less then a minute. Talking Boy was right behind, and the two frightened runaways quickly pushed the canoe into the river and hopped in.

As they drifted away from shore a dark, shadowy figure emerged from the trees and stood watching them silently. Neither of the boys saw it, for they were busy with the canoe.

The moon wasn't out but the stars were, and the cloudless night made for enough star shine to allow navigation. Both boys felt better after they passed the last channel marker and left the Nesook River behind. With the broadening expanse of the bay and the deepening water, the feelings of being trapped in the dead end village disappeared and they began to relax a little. The wind was almost non-existent, but they raised the small main sail, set the sideboards and found a suitable tack. Chet tied off the boom and the two slaves settled in at a one to two knot an hour pace.

The light winds were a blessing for the two boys, giving them a chance to get the feel of the craft and practice tacking. They also found they had to rearrange their gear for the best balance, and Chet found that he had to lash down the middle of the long paddle-rudder into the notch cut for it, because the wooden blade kept floating out of the water and wouldn't take a deep enough cut to steer the canoe. With the minor changes and the relief of getting on with the escape, the boys sat back and sailed along in silence.

Hours passed and as the two escapees left the eastern channels and headed back into Nootka Sound proper, Chet knew he was getting close to Fish Egg Island, for the landmarks the young man had memorized appeared one after the other. With the island so close, a new crisis became apparent, one Chet had not thought of in the past. He knew Talking Boy would have to be told about the treasure, but for the first time a feeling of greed came over the white boy. Chet wanted the wealth for himself and thought maybe the Indian wouldn't want any of the gold. After all, Indians had no need for it. That was stupid. Of course they had need of it. Chet felt guilty and a little ashamed. He realized for the first time how the greed Lloyd had talked about would drive good men to steal and murder. The white boy would tell his friend about the true value of the stuff and split it with him fifty-fifty. It was the right thing to do.

"Talking Boy, around that next sand bar is Fish Egg Island. I'm going to land there. We are both gettin' tired and we need some rest. There's one other thing, too."

Chet went on to tell the Indian boy about his hunting trip and how he had climbed the hill in the center of the island that day. The young man told about the spear and the ducks and the deer droppings. When the white boy came to the part about the chest of gold, the young Indian needed no lesson on its worth.

"Gold, I know of this gold. The white men on the Nisqually talked about it. I have never seen it, but I know they trade with it and it brings many trade goods for just a few nuggets. I have heard about dollars, too, but I'm afraid I don't understand how it is worth so much."

"Don't worry about that. When we get out of here you'll know all about it in a hurry," said Chet. "Half of it will be yours."

They sailed on until they reached the area where Swimming Otter's family had camped that week. Since the two were going to stay until the following night Chet decided to employ an old trick he had learned from watching Two Skins. The white boy sailed a little farther until they reached the place where the fresh water stream from the marsh in the center of the island fed into Nootka Sound. The boys took up the sideboards and made for the beach. When they hit bottom they got out, and, like Two Skins and his men, the fugitives pushed the canoe up the shallow stream until they reached the thicket behind the sand dunes. There Chet lowered the mast and felt secure that no one would spot them from the water and no one would find any telltale signs in the sand.

It was early in the morning and still dark out as Chet unfolded his mat and blankets next to the canoe. There was a chill in the air and both boys bundled up tightly in their robes, as they prepared to get some sleep.

"I sure feel a lot better being hid out here where nobody will be lookin'," Chet commented.

Talking Boy was already in his blankets and was too tired to say anything but, "Me, too."

"I figure we can sleep till daylight safe enough and then set out for the cave. With any luck we can have the chest back here and be ready to leave again long before dark," Chet continued.

The young man waited for the Indian boy to respond again, but Talking Boy was sound asleep. The long day of physical exhaustion and the relief from mental stress had enabled the boy to relax and Chet was soon fast asleep himself.

As daylight came, thick dew covered the blades of grass around the boy's head as he lay in the shadow of the canoe. His blanket was completely wet and only the trusty bear skin underneath kept Chet dry and warm. The cloudless night had allowed the warmth of day to escape, but the return of the sun as it hit the tops of the trees quickly raised the temperature. Chet was tired and didn't want to get out of his covers, but the thought of the old chest and its treasure of gold got him moving.

"Talking Boy, wake up," shouted Chet as he shook the Indian awake. "Time to get up and get going."

"What? Go where?" asked the Salish boy groggily. "I'm tired. You go."

"Come on, get up. I need your help. The chest weighs a ton," pleaded Chet. "Don't you want some of the gold for yourself, or should I keep it for myself?"

"All right, I'm up," said a grouchy Talking Boy. "What is there to eat?"

There wasn't much to eat at all. The greens and bulbs they had decided to save for dinner each night, and the fresh fish was used up the day before. Chet had some old smoked salmon left over, and, though they both were genuinely sick of it, the two ate a little and washed it down with lots of fresh water from the stream.

"Say, Chet, if this box of gold weighs so much, how are we going to get it back here?" asked Talking Boy, as he licked the salmon oil from his fingers.

"I'm not sure," answered the white boy, "but I figured we'd take some rope and a strong cedar pole and find some way to carry it back."

With the warm sun getting warmer, the boys didn't need their robes, so they left everything in camp except for the pole and rope. It was a much nicer trip up the stream this day than the journey had been a few months earlier. Chet remembered that miserable rainy day and how wet he was before he even got to the marsh, and how the sun broke through and reflected off the sword handle. As the two boys moved upstream, Chet started remembering certain landmarks in the distance, and by the time they entered the near end of the peat bog, the young man had already picked out the spot across the marsh where he thought the game trail would be found.

The boys jumped from peat mound to peat mound, crossing the marsh in a few minutes. Chet could foresee problems on the return trip, for they would not be able to jump around with the heavy chest. They'd have to go around the long perimeter of the bog, where the footing was solid and continuous. When Chet and Talking Boy jumped the last channel at the foot of the hill, the boys separated and looked for the tree that the white slave had blazed, marking the route to the game trail. After a few minutes the white boy found the weathered and darkened cut in the bark of an alder tree, and started up the hill. They soon found another blaze, and then another, until soon the game trail opened in front of them.

Chet's heart was pounding now and the anticipation of what the two were about to experience sent wild thoughts through the boy's head. One minute he was daydreaming about spending money, the next Chet was convincing himself that the treasure would be gone. Finally the large rock next to the trail came into view, with the ledge and rock fall beyond. The young man saw the large blaze he'd left in the tree next to the rock and paused.

"This is it, my friend," Chet called back to Talking Boy, who was following at a distance. "This is the place all right."

Chet waited for the Salish boy to catch up and then began the descent around the side of the cliff and onto the rockslide below. Talking Boy was surprised when they looked back at the ledge and saw the gaping mouth of the cave.

"White Clam, how did you find this place?" asked the Indian as he stared open-mouthed at the wide hole under the ledge.

"Luck, pure luck," returned Chet. "Come on, let's go in and see if it's still there."

Quickly, the two climbed the rockslide and entered the mouth of the cave. The bright sun reflected secondary light inside the cave and it took only a few seconds for their eyes to adjust to the shadows. There, where Chet had left it, was the pile of rock and dirt covering the chest. Without another word they began to uncover the treasure, tossing the rocks aside and scooping the dirt with their hands. The top of the chest came into sight almost immediately, and within seconds Talking Boy was pulling the brilliant sword from its resting place at the side of the chest.

"Here, hold it like this," said Chet, showing the Indian boy how the weapon was used. "You take it like this and then you can hack a guy to pieces swingin' it or just thrust it straight into him."

Talking Boy gave the sword a few practice swings and then turned his attention to the chest as Chet unlatched it and lifted the lid. Each boy took out a solid bar of gold weighing seven pounds each and took them into the sunlight. A light scraping of the bars' tarnished surfaces produced a golden glow, and the boys smiled at each other before returning to the chest.

"Let's put the bars back inside and rig a rope from the chest to the pole," said Chet.

With the gold put away and the lid shut, the boys tried to rig a sling using the handles on the side of the chest, but the years of sitting in the damp cave had decomposed the leather fasteners and the handles ripped away from the brass rivets. Their only hope was to tie the rope around the chest like string around a paper package and hang the whole affair from the middle of the pole, hoping the rope didn't break. With the sling completed, each boy took one end of the pole and gave it a trial lift. The chest came off the ground a few inches with surprising ease, and after tucking the sword between the rope and the side of the chest, the boys lifted it once again and moved to the cave opening.

Lifting the chest and standing in one place proved to be much easier than lifting and walking. As soon as they started out of the cave and around the ledge the chore became a nightmare. The loose rocks and steep grade made it necessary to stop and re-group every few feet. By the time they had climbed the thirty feet to the top, both boys were scraped, bruised, and exhausted from numerous falls, and felt depressed and almost ready to give up. Only the shallow downgrade of the game trail and the promise of better footing gave them renewed hope, so after a short rest they started out again. With frequent rest stops they finally managed to maneuver the chest to the edge of the marsh.

It was well after noon by the time the two boys reached the marsh. The sun had turned hot and they relished the cool water of the bog, taking long drinks and cooling by splashing water on their faces and upper bodies. Their plan was to walk around the perimeter of the bog where the footing looked better, but they soon found that the thick bushes and fallen trees made the travel extremely slow and hazardous. They turned back to try going directly across the bog, crossing between the mounds at the narrowest channels. The going was still slow, but they managed to work their way across the marsh by mid-afternoon. Finally, the peat mounds disappeared and the firm streambed allowed them to travel uninhibited once again.

In all, the three quarters of a mile took four hours to complete, and, when they caught sight of the hidden canoe, the two treasure seekers dropped the chest on the stream bank and walked the last hundred feet, falling on their beds to tired too move.

"I hope this treasure is worth all the trouble," said a doubtful Talking Boy.

"It will be, my friend," returned Chet.

Hunger finally stirred the two escapees to life again, and, throwing caution to the wind, they made a small fire to roast the potato-like bulbs and boil the greens old Cattail Woman had picked for them. They kept the flames going long enough to heat the rocks they would need to cook and then Chet, fearing someone would see the smoke from their fire, kicked the burning sticks off the heated rocks and picked up a bowl of water. Talking Boy tried to stop him with a yell, but it was too late. When Chet unthinkingly poured water on the smoldering sticks, the resulting steam and smoke were ten times more noticeable than the burning wood had been. Chet knew he had made a mistake immediately, and both boys ran to the beach dunes, cautiously peering over the sand mounds to see if anyone was in sight. While the smoke died down, they took turns for the next half hour keeping a close watch on the cove and surrounding channel between the islands and the mainland, but no one was seen. Feeling safe again, they ate their warm meal and decided to pack their things and leave as soon as it was dark.

"Let's get the canoe packed with everything but the gold and get the dugout down to the water," Chet said as he was rolling up his blanket. "Then we can come back and load the chest last. How's that sound?"

Chet, sitting with his back to Talking Boy and the beach waited, a few moments, wondering why the young Indian didn't answer him.

Turning his head, Chet said, "What's the matter? Can't you speak English any mo-." Chet stopped in mid-word; his heart pounding fiercely as fear almost overcame him.

Water Bear was standing perfectly still in front of Talking Boy. Chet leaped to his feet, grabbed the spear, and took a stance at the rear of the canoe. The large man said nothing.

"I'm not going back!" yelled Chet, almost in tears. "Talking Boy, tell him I won't go back without a fight. He will have to kill me first."

"Chet, be reasonable. I have no weapon and you have only that duck spear," pleaded Talking Boy.

"I don't care! Tell him. Tell him I won't go back!"

Chet stood there in a threatening mode with the spear at the ready while the young Salish slave repeated the words to the Mowachaht nobleman.

The Indian boy was shaken and the words came hard. He feared for his friend and his own safety, but could see no point in fighting. Talking Boy had already given up and wished Chet would, too. The large man listened and said nothing, then walked past the Salish boy to the fire pit and kneeled down to sample some of their leftover dinner. This was not the response Chet had expected. The white boy could only stand there and shrug in confusion when he and Talking Boy looked at each other. The last time he'd tangled with Water Bear it was a violent experience. This time the big Indian just sat there eating dinner.

"White Clam, put down the spear. I wish you no harm," the big Indian said between mouthfuls of dandelion greens and smoked salmon. "Come, both of you, sit down, rest."

Talking Boy sat immediately, but though Chet understood the Nootkan words, he continued to stand.

"Why you not mad, Water Bear?" asked Chet in Nootkan. "Why you not tie up like last time?" struggled the white boy.

"White Clam, things are different now," said Water Bear. "You are no longer my brother's slave, and your warning saved his life. He is not without a heart. He sent me ahead of Standing Seal's men to find you and see that no harm came to you. They are only a short distance away, and it is a lucky thing I and not they saw your smoke."

As the big Indian talked, Chet grew more at ease and sat down next to Talking Boy. Water Bear continued talking and told of the capture of Hesquiat and of the poor condition of the people under Two Skins' rule. He told of how the scouts watched as the renegade paddled south into Makah territory and how the Nootkan warriors brought all the people of Hesquiat back to Chahakquot.

"Standing Seal was furious when it became apparent that his slaves were missing, but he wanted you all taken alive. He guessed that you headed for Nesook, for slaves have done that before, fearing the dangerous ocean. Standing Seal knows the old man and woman will travel north through the inland passage towards Tahsis before they turn northwest. Cod Man's people will look for the old ones, but I trust Wooden Hand will stay well hidden," ended Water Bear.

"So what happens now?" asked Talking Boy.

"I will help you get back to the sea and past Chahakquot and then, my friends, you are on your own," said the big man. "If they spot us, I will treat you like my prisoners. Standing Seal has promised me my own household and slaves, made up of the new people from Hesquiat, and I cannot afford to go against him if cornered. Let's get my canoe out of sight and wait for them to pass."

The boys followed Water Bear to the beach and helped him carry the twelve-footer up the stream and into the thicket. With less than an hour of daylight left, the trio returned to the dunes and waited. Before long a pair of dugouts appeared at the head of the channel and split in different directions. One canoe traveled toward the mainland and the other hugged the island shore, their crews looking for signs in the sand. The fugitives stayed low and soon the danger passed without incident. Water Bear suggested they wait another hour and then head west.

The darkness came rapidly and during the wait Chet had been wondering if Water Bear would notice the chest of gold sitting on the riverbank some hundred feet away. Fortunately, the Indian kept his eyes beachward and Talking Boy made no mention of it. Chet wondered how he would explain the heavy chest and where it came from when it came time to leave. As luck would have it, no explanation was needed, because the large Indian told the boys to let him leave first and then follow him when he rounded the point. That way Water Bear could run interference and warn them if any other canoes were sighted, allowing them a chance to sail away undetected.

Chet had showed Water Bear their sail and how it worked, but the big fellow had seen sails before and did not understand the importance of the side centerboards. The three conspirators dragged the two canoes to the water's edge and the large Nootkan launched his canoe and slowly paddled away. The boys waited a minute and then dashed back for the heavy chest. It was quite a feat to lift the chest into the canoe and then to move it so the gold was centered. When they tried to stow their gear, there wasn't enough room left for all of it. They rearranged some gear and still had no room left. So finally, with Water Bear already out of sight, Chet decided to step the mast and put on the sideboards to make more room on the floor of the dugout. The decision was a good one in more ways than one. Not only did they have more room, but also the placement of the heavy chest gave the boat more center ballast and improved the efficiency of the centerboards. Even as light as the wind was, it filled the sail, and, with the increased bite of the side boards, the little dugout shot across the cove on a close reach to the northwest.

Chet realized the difference in the handling of the craft immediately, and at two to three knots an hour, it did not take long to catch up with Water Bear. After a short tack to get back on course the little sail pushed the canoe ever closer to the leading dugout and Chet had to ease off on the boom line to slow the craft so as not to overtake the big Nootkan. The boys felt a little guilty watching their big friend paddle while they just sat back and relaxed, almost falling asleep, but after an hour of short tacks, the wind all but died and the boys had to begin paddling to keep the hundred-yard distance from growing larger.

Hours went by and the glass-like sea passed slowly underneath as the two dugouts continued westward. The expanse of the Sound as they rounded Bligh Island and neared the ocean gave Chet an uneasy feeling. The sights and sounds of the whale hunt raced through his mind and the thought of huge monsters lurking beneath the dugout, able to smash the canoe with one thrust of their flukes, was not comforting. He kept his fears to himself, however, and continued paddling, not wanting to worry Talking Boy as well.

The two canoes were well past the turnoff point for Chahakquot and in among the outer islands of Nootka Sound, when Water Bear turned toward one of the tree encrusted rocks, landing on a small northern beach that had a deep drop-off. The wind had picked up out of the southwest and as the sail started to luff the boys stopped paddling and Chet trimmed the boom and ran close-hauled all the way to the small islet.

The first light of the eastern sky showed its halo above the mountains as the sailing canoe coasted into shore. Water Bear stood on the sand with a confused look on his face, surprised at the way the dugout sailed into a head wind.

"How can you sail into the wind?" asked the big Nootkan, as he pulled the bow of their twenty-foot canoe up on the beach.

Chet didn't understand, so Talking Boy translated what Water Bear had said.

"That's what I was trying to show you back at Fish Egg Island," the boy responded. "Your Indian sails only work when running with the wind. These centerboards and trimming the sails at different angles is the key to running against the wind."

The physics involved were still new to Chet and though he had gained a lot of experience, by trial and error, over the last forty-eight hours, the young man had a hard time explaining the procedure to Water Bear.

The islet where they stopped was about a half-mile square with a high rocky outcrop that hid a small but deep cove. The fifty-foot diameter cove was almost completely closed by the rocky peninsula, leaving a twenty-foot mouth to navigate through. Smaller twisted firs lined the islet, forming a sparse forest that gave shelter to sea birds and protection against the Pacific winds.

The trio moved their canoes into the cove, where they could not be seen by passers-by, and sat down to rest. Water Bear had come to this islet in the past to hunt sea lion and sea otter and always had good luck fishing the waters of the cove. With their food almost gone and knowing the big Indian's appetite, Water Bear and the boys decided to fish through the early morning and sleep later on. Using some of the smoked salmon as bait, and fishing the bottom, it wasn't long before Water Bear had a nice fat sculpin. He took the spiny bottom fish and carefully cut it up into small strips for bait and then the real fishing started.

The little cove had a good population of plump rockfish, and within two hours the three had plenty of fish to last them through breakfast, lunch, and dinner. Since the white meat wasn't good for smoking, they just cleaned the fish and the ones they didn't roast for breakfast were left in a box full of water to be cooked later. The fresh tender fillets were filling and as the warm sun rose higher in the sky, all three of them unrolled their blankets and fell asleep.

Clouds were rolling in from the ocean and the wind had shifted from the southwest to the northwest when Chet awoke in mid-afternoon. Talking Boy was still asleep, but Water Bear was already awake. He had made a cooking fire and was well into his favorite pastime of eating. Chet got up and walked over to the small fire whose smoke was dissipated rapidly by the strong north wind.

"I want to thank you again for helping us," said Chet, not realizing he was speaking English.

"White Clam, your words have no meaning for me," returned Water Bear between mouthfuls.

"Thank you, friend," the boy said in Nootkan. "Will you leave soon?"

"Yes, I'm leaving now. I can make Chahakquot by nightfall, and I don't want to wait any longer. It looks like a storm is coming. You two should wait another day before heading into the ocean," said Water Bear. "Tell Talking Boy I wish him luck."

The large Mowachaht nobleman put his things into the small canoe and turned to Chet shaking him by the shoulders in an act of friendship. The white boy watched as Water Bear got into the dugout and waved to the big man as he paddled out of the cove and east towards Chahakquot. White Clam would miss his Indian friend.

Chet had not thought much of it, but he had not understood all of the Indian's last words, especially the part about the storm and waiting another day until the weather improved. With Talking Boy asleep and not able to translate, the young man thought nothing of the words he missed. The sky was fair to partly cloudy, with a gusty wind, but what the white boy didn't understand was that a storm could come out of the North Pacific at any time. With Water Bear gone, Chet was still planning to leave at dusk.

XXV

With plenty of fish left for dinner and nothing else to do, Chet decided to break out the ripped piece of canvas he had saved and fabricate a small jib. With a whalebone needle and some stout bark twine the boy was able to fold over and stitch the awkward shaped canvas into a rough triangular sail. After another hour of hemming the edges Chet sewed a line to the luff edge, leaving a short end of rope extending on the tack angle and a long lead end for the halyard on the head corner. Another short trim line was tied through a hole he made in the clew angle. All that remained was to secure a loop of rope to the masthead for use as a jib block and the white boy would be ready to hoist the new sail.

Talking Boy had been up for a while and helped Chet lower the mast and attach the loop and jib halyard. They re-stepped the mast and secured the tack corner of the jib to the bow and pulled on the halyard. The loop caused a lot of friction but the two were able to pull the halyard through and the little jib rose to catch the wind.

"This'll give us even more speed," said Chet. We'll be home in no time. Come on, let's cook the fish and greens and get goin'."

They restarted Water Bear's fire and used some of their remaining fresh water to boil the rockfish and dandelion leaves. The sparse clouds continued to let lots of sunshine through and as the boys gathered their things, they failed to notice the darkening clouds to the north. All Chet could think of was the favorable wind and getting home.

"There's not much fresh water left," commented Talking Boy, as he placed the seal-bladder containers on the floor of the canoe.

"At daylight we can find a freshwater stream to land near," returned Chet. "Water Bear said to look for a ravine between two hills and we would always find water."

"He also said not to stray too far from shore when we are paddling at night and to listen for waves breaking," the Salish boy recounted. "What if we smash up in the rocks?"

"If we get that close we'll hear the waves and know it," laughed Chet.

The sun was low in the western horizon as they paddled out of the rocky cove. Center sideboards were put in place and the main sail hauled up. The quartering wind was from the north and Chet set the canoe out on a broad reach to the southwest, out of Nootka Sound and down the Hesquiat Peninsula. When the course was set, the white boy gave the order for Talking Boy to raise the jib. Again the rope loop at the top of the mast made for a hard haul, but the persistent Indian finally got it up and belayed the jib halyard. Grabbing the flapping clew line the Salish boy was able to trim the small sail until it filled completely.

The added canvas and the gusty north wind gave them their first capsize scare as the mast blew over a bit. Chet quickly shifted his weight and eased off on the boom line like Matt English had taught him months before. The Indian boy relished the thrill of sitting on the starboard rail, trimming the jib and watching the water pass by at a steady five knots an hour.

"This is great fun!" yelled Talking boy as the little craft moved farther west into the darkening sunset.

After the first two hours the initial thrill of the long reach to the southwest was lost and with it the need to hand hold the trim lines. Both boys tied off their lines and Chet adjusted the draw of the sails with occasional corrections in course using the rudder paddle. The night was becoming quite dark and the boys were having a hard time seeing the outline of the Hesquiat Peninsula, so Chet steered in a little closer toward shore. Almost without notice the few remaining stars were swallowed up by the unseen clouds overhead, and the mountainous outline was gone. Everything was pitch black.

It was so dark that Chet could no longer make out his Salish friend in the bow. The white boy was getting worried, knowing that some time in the night they would pass Estevan Point at the tip of the peninsula and have to turn southeast to follow the long coast of Vancouver Island to the Strait of Juan de Fuca. To compound matters the wind was picking up and it was a cold wind at that. The sailors had to ease out both trim lines and move back to the rail to keep the mast vertical.

When the rain started, Chet wished he had put on all his clothes, but the young man had no time to dig them out of the boxes as he had his hands full just keeping the dugout on an even keel. Talking Boy didn't think it was fun anymore, especially when the sea started to swell and waves started breaking over the bow.

"Talking Boy," Chet yelled, "I think we need to lower the jib. There's too much wind. And you need to start bailing the water out. It's getting pretty deep back here!"

"All right, I understand," the Indian boy yelled back.

Talking Boy struggled to pull the jib back down, but the rope loop would not loosen in the strong wind. Chet watched him struggle, but could not go forward to help. The canoe was too unstable and the white boy could only sit there frustrated.

"Talking boy," Chet yelled again. "Let the clew line flap in the breeze and lower the main halyard."

The game Salish boy was soaked with spray and his hands were getting numb from the cold water, but somehow he untied the main halyard and the larger sail dropped to the boom. Chet hauled in the boom line and tied it off so it wouldn't swing. When the forward motion of the canoe stopped, the sea began tossing it about at will. Water poured over the sides and the situation turned worse. Something had to be done quickly and Chet, on the verge of panic, remembered the *Exact* and her storm sails.

"Talking Boy, tie off the jib again where you had it before!" screamed Chet.

The Salish slave re-trimmed the jib while Chet steered with the rudder. The resumption of light sail power pushed the craft forward again and stabilized it once more. Chet made course corrections with the paddle while Talking Boy went to work with the cedar bark bailer. Everything was wet, and it was all the Indian could do to keep ahead of the bow spray. All through the night they struggled, keeping the wind to the right quarter and heading southwest, too afraid to turn back toward land and take a chance on going aground on the rocky shore. Talking Boy worked nonstop bailing and Chet helped when he could using the small wooden bait box. The white boy didn't care about the gold anymore and his thoughts of wealth faded the more the troubled craft tossed in the sea. Hour after hour the two young sailors hung on, bailing and steering, soaking wet and numb with the cold. The conditioning on the long canoe journeys paid off as each boy found the strength to keep fighting the sea.

Somehow, they kept the dugout afloat and as the morning sky lightened, the winds subsided and the rain stopped. The sea still had a swell to it, but the waves were small enough to keep from breaking over the sides of the dugout. Exhausted, the two sailors let their numb bodies go limp and rested against the sides of the canoe.

Chet finally lifted his head up again to see if he could recognize any landmarks. There was nothing to see but clouds and water all around, right to the horizon. He had lost the land!

Nothing.

The low clouds promised more rain at any moment, and not really knowing what to do, the white boy moved forward and hauled the main sail up again. He found the wind direction and tied off the boom to run with it. Chet hoped the wind was still blowing out of the northwest, which would take them southeast and back to the coast. He was sure they had to be well out in the ocean and, though it was a gamble, they had no choice but to go with the wind.

A few bites each of soggy smoked salmon and some of the dwindling supply of fresh water was all the two boys allowed themselves for breakfast and they settled in for a long, cold and very wet day at sea.

Rain came in spurts all day long and the wind gusted at times, but held fairly steady. The boys thought of trying to catch a little rainwater to add to their supply, but every time they tried to rig a sealskin bladder as a funnel the salt water from a breaking wave would contaminate what little fresh water they caught. The tiny sailing vessel held her own and any doubts Chet had entertained about the seaworthiness of the Indian canoes were long dismissed.

While Talking Boy tried to sleep, Chet found his stored clothes in a wet basket and put the dripping pants and shirt on. Even though they were miserable next to his skin and never dry, the wool fibers did provide some warmth and with the warmth, his spirits revived too. The young man wondered about his Haida mother and Wooden Hand. He hoped they had not been caught out in the storm and worried about their safety. Surely the old Indian would be smart enough to stay close to shore. After all, they were paddling, not sailing, and the old man knew the weather. Reassuring himself, Chet took a drink of water.

It was almost gone.

After an hour the Salish boy woke up, stiff and sore, and Chet decided to move forward and try to get some sleep. With the boom and canvas it was hard to move past one another, but they succeeded and after some verbal instruction and practice Talking boy was able to keep the sails full and pulling. Chet wrapped the wet bearskin around his head and lay down to sleep in the bow.

XXVI

"Hey Chet, it's about time you were waking up," said Talking Boy as he sat with the rudder paddle tucked under his arm.

The Indian boy was quite pleased at his newfound skill and was happy steering and trimming.

"My friend, when we get home I'm going to buy a sailing ship with my part of the gold and be its captain," said the Salish boy with a big smile on his face.

Chet was glad to see his friend in such good spirits, and as he moved his stiff, wet body into a sitting position, the white boy found he was not as worried as before. The clouds were still low and thick and as darkness fell once more there was no clue as to the direction the sun was setting. The boys switched places once more and ate half of the remaining portion of salmon and drank sparingly from the seal bladders.

"We'll be all right," said Chet after taking his drink. "This weather will break, and even if we don't see any land we'll see the sun and be able to tell which way is east."

"I'm not worried, my friend," returned Talking Boy. "I am free again, and even if we die of thirst, at least we will die free - and rich! We must not forget that."

Before long blackness set in once again, and they prepared themselves for another bad night. Over thirty hours in the canoe made for a lot of stretching of leg muscles and even the occasional standing stretch. They entertained themselves with stories of sea monsters and killer whales and more then once had each other scared to death. Chet kept remembering the huge gray whales and how easily they could have capsized the canoe during the hunt. He felt sorry for the gentle creatures and began to make himself sick again by reliving the bloody hunt and butchering of the huge animals.

Sometime after midnight the sea flattened and the wind stopped to almost nothing. It hadn't rained in hours and the clouds were closing in, forming a thick fog bank. With no sea or swell to keep them busy the boys fell asleep. The gentle lap of the water against the dugout sides and the whisper of the luffing sails combined to block out the cold and wet. Sleep was deep for both.

Sounds of splashing woke Chet and brought him to a sitting position with alarm. At first he thought Talking Boy had fallen in the water but further inspection showed the Indian boy still sleeping soundly. The morning fog engulfed them and visibility was only about fifty yards in any direction. There to starboard and only a few feet away was a huge sea lion playing in the waves. He was a big male and by himself, with a look in his eyes that seemed to say the sea lion was glad to find some companionship. Chet scanned the area for breaks in the fog and could find none. The wind was not blowing at all and the crude little sails hung stoically, dripping large drops of condensed fog onto the contents of the canoe.

Chet wondered why the big mammal was so far out at sea, and then remembered that he wasn't sure how far out they were. The male sea lion must have been seven feet long and five hundred pounds of blubber and fur. Big brown eyes, long black whiskers and canine teeth made him look more like a puppy dog, but when the sea lion flippers showed and that huge body dove, there was no doubt the animal was made for the sea.

Within minutes the big brute let Chet know why he was staying close by the canoe. After an extended dive the fast swimmer returned to the surface with a good sized silver salmon clenched tightly in its jaws. The fat swimmer floated on his back while he systematically ripped the flesh off the struggling fish, keeping the salmon under control with his front flippers.

"There must be a big school of salmon underneath," Chet said aloud. "I wish I had some herring for bait."

The only thing in the bait box before they left were some rockfish strips and they had been dumped out during the storm so the box could be used as a bailer. Chet rummaged around on the floor of the canoe and a few moments later found a mashed strip of white fish with the orange skin and scales still attached.

Opening his gear basket, the boy baited a metal hook and cast the line into the calm sea. Ten minutes later he watched the sea lion make another kill and decided to lower his line deeper. With all the commotion and splashing Talking Boy still snored away sound asleep, unaware of the action going on next to him. Chet fished another ten minutes jerking and jigging without a bite and just as he was about to give up a strong jerk almost pulled the bark line out of his hand. Skillfully, the young man played the fish in and soon had a nice ten-pound salmon flopping in the dugout floor. A smack on the head ended the gleaming fish's struggle and Chet retrieved the hook and as much of the bait as he could.

Well, at least we won't starve, the boy thought, not relishing the idea of eating it raw. He threw the line back in, but try as he could, the boy wasn't able to land another salmon. The bait finally disappeared, so Chet quit fishing. Talking Boy was surprised to see Chet cleaning a salmon when the Salish boy woke and he listened intently to the story of the sea lion, which had since disappeared.

The fog was thick as ever with no break in sight. They ate the rest of the smoked salmon and drank all but the last few mouthfuls of water. The two decided to save the water until nightfall and then finish it. As the day pressed on, the situation turned increasingly grim and the positive moments of the day before turned once again to worry and frustration.

Almost forty-eight hours had passed since they had left the little islet at the mouth of Nootka Sound. The wind was picking up again and the boys trimmed the mainsail and jib for running. At least the chore of sailing the canoe would keep their minds off their hunger and thirst. As the wind continued to increase, the boys noticed patches of clear skies here and there, quick patches of blue overhead, and a lightening of the sky. Almost without warning the canoe broke into sunshine with the western horizon clear as far as the eye could see. Scattered clouds were overhead and the thick fog bank was to port, but there was no doubt as to their bearings now. Chet knew it was late in the day and the sun low in the west was still two hours above the horizon. The wind was out of the southwest and they had been running northeast for the last half hour.

"Talking Boy, get ready to come about!" yelled Chet as he pulled in the boom line.

The white boy dug the rudder paddle deep and braced it tightly against the stern of the canoe and the dugout turned to the west. The Salish boy untied the clew line and pulled the jib in tight until both sails were pulling close-hauled.

"We'll run out away from the fog bank for a few minutes and see what we can see," called Chet. "Then if we don't see a mountain we'll just reach her to the east and take our chances on hittin' a rocky coast."

The dugout raced westward for another ten minutes, then came about again and headed back east. Chet could see nothing above the fog and lined the stern of the canoe up with the setting sun. He hoped the wind would hold steady from the southwest and settled in on a broad reach to shores unknown. After another fifteen minutes they still had not re-entered the fog bank, and half an hour later they were still in the reddening sunshine.

"The wind must be blowing the fog away!" Chet yelled ahead to the Salish boy. "Why don't you stand on the rail and see if you see anything yet!"

The Indian understood and left his rail seat, reaching for the mast. Holding on to the shroud and mast both, Talking Boy stepped up on the raised side of the canoe and peered eastward. He immediately jumped down and turned back to Chet.

"Land, Chet! Land! Maybe an hour away!" screamed the boy. "We can make it. Get ready to cook your salmon."

Chet couldn't believe his ears, and wanted to see for himself, but couldn't move off the tipped rail. They were finally able to steer back on course and their spirits soared. Now that the two were experienced sailors and knew their ship they tightened the trim and pushed the canoe to five knots an hour, tipping the mast as far as they dared without capsizing. After a couple of close calls they eased back on the sails and kept going at a good four knots. Finally, they entered the dissipating fog bank and noticed a rocky islet dead ahead, and then another, and then a real island materialized.

None of the beaches they saw were usable, so they circled the island hoping the eastern shore would afford better anchorage. When they rounded the small island they spotted a larger one a half-mile away with good-sized hills and an inviting coastline. Even though darkness was coming on, the second island was their choice and the two sailors set their sight on a long rocky beach with sand dunes and forest beyond.

The island was called Vargas Island at the southern mouth of Clayoquot Sound some fifty to sixty miles southwest of Nootka Sound. The boys knew nothing of the place and didn't care. As the dugout entered the southern part of the broad western bay, they were happy to find water stretching inland enough to afford a landing on a deep cove protected by a small peninsula.

Chet and Talking Boy raised the center sideboards and let the wind crab them into the beach, dropping the sails as they hit bottom. Their first steps on land for over two days were shaky at best, but nothing had ever felt better to the two weary travelers. The island was bigger than it had looked, being some four miles long and three miles wide, with the forest close to the beach. The boys pulled the canoe as far up on the beach as possible, finished the last of the water, and set out to explore the area in the thickening fog.

Twenty minutes of exploring brought them to their goal, a freshwater creek running into the bay from the forest above the beach. They walked along the bank of the ten-foot wide stream until they were sure they were above the high tide mark and bent over to drink. The water tasted all right but both boys stopped drinking after a few sips and looked at one another.

"Do you feel what I felt?" asked Talking Boy.

"I'm not sure," said Chet. "It tastes a little funny, but is it my imagination or is this water warm? I know I'm cold and wet but this really feels warm."

"I think so, too," said the Salish Boy.

They walked farther upstream, almost to the trees, and this time they waded with bare feet. There was no doubt about it. The water seemed to be getting warmer.

"I know of this kind of place," said Talking Boy. "I have heard Standing Seal talk of special springs hidden in the forest where the water boils from the earth."

Chet was not sure, but he thought the Indian boy was right and they had stumbled upon a hot springs. The white boy had heard the same tales experienced by fur trappers in the Rocky Mountains, but had never actually seen or felt one.

"Let's get the canoe and make this our camp," said Chet.

Talking Boy agreed, and the two boys ran back to the dugout, and none too soon. The tide had been coming in and the dugout was dangerously close to floating away. Only the heavy weight of the gold had kept the bottom of the canoe in contact with the shore. The boys jumped in the dugout and paddled the craft back to where they thought the stream was located. It was getting dark, and the now increasing fog made it hard for the boys to know exactly where they wanted to go. Talking Boy climbed out of the canoe and walked along the last hundred feet of beach until he found the stream.

This time they took the heavy chest, still attached to the pole, out of the canoe and moved it behind the dunes, hiding it in the tall grass. The two adventurers pulled the canoe upstream as far as they could until the bottom dragged, then used a bark rope to tie it to a drift log so the tide could not float it away. The boys packed baskets full of bedding, mats, flint and steel to make a fire, grabbed their salmon and headed upstream. Ten minutes of wading brought them to a small pool where the stream eddied around a fallen spruce log and the temperature of the water was so hot, steam was rising from the surface. A flat rock shelf wide enough to sleep on was adjacent to the pool and the large fir trees beyond provided lots of dry tinder at their bases. The pool itself extended about ten feet between the rocks and the fallen log. The boys left the gear on the rock shelf and took off their wet bearskins.

"I don't know about you," said Chet, "but I'm strippin' down and jumpin' in that bath water."

"Me, too," replied Talking Boy.

After days of numbing cold salt water the feeling of soaking in one hundred degree water was beyond description. The water was so hot Chet had to lower himself gradually to get used to the heat. The young man's legs tingled and then his thighs and back as he lowered himself further into the two-foot deep pool. The white boy hadn't realized how long his hair had become until he dunked himself and the long brown strands hung below his eyes. Talking Boy lay flat in the streambed, letting the warm water flow around him. The water in the stream was slightly cooler, and as they moved from pool to stream and back again, the water in the pool always felt like a hot bath. Chet took the opportunity to sit on the sandy creek bottom and scrub himself from head to foot with sand. The boy wished he had some soap so he could do the job right. It had been almost seven months since he had washed himself properly and it felt good.

The outside air was cold in the fog, and every time they tried to get out and start a fire they would only last a few minutes before jumping back in the hot pool again. Finally Talking Boy braved the cold and found some dry twigs and leaves. Ten minutes later he had a small blaze going, and, with his wet body shivering, quickly jumped back in the pool.

"I started the fire, now you can cook the fish," said the Salish boy as he sank back into the warm water.

Chet had no choice and climbed out on the rock shelf naked. Shivering, he moved fast in the cold air and gathered a modest supply of wood, feeding the small blaze and splitting some dry branches to hold up the salmon. The white boy took the fish and opened the ventral slit, cutting along the backbone so the entire fish would spread apart, exposing the tender pink meat to the flames. After staking it in place, Chet returned to the pool to warm up for a few minutes, then only left for short trips to place more wood on the fire or check the broiling fish.

"You know, Talking Boy, I'm thinkin' of sleepin' right here tonight in the stream," commented Chet, as he placed his head on a chunk of moss and let the rest of his body float. "I bet we could be right comfortable."

"Too bad we don't have planks to make a sleeping platform just under the water. Then we wouldn't have to worry about sinking," laughed Talking Boy.

"Say, you've got an idea there. We don't have a plank but we have those mats and lots of rope. We can make a hammock from the old log across the pool to the first big tree next to the rock shelf," said Chet.

"What is this hammock? I have not heard that word before."

"It'll take too long to explain. I'll just show you what I mean. Wait here."

The white boy grabbed his cold wet underpants, trousers and wool shirt and dunking all of them in the hot pool, put them on for the trip to the beach. He knew the clothes wouldn't stay hot long but it would be better than running naked through the cold fog. Chet put on his moccasins and hurried downstream to the beach and the waiting canoe. Everything was where they had left it, and the tide had risen no further. He grabbed one of the four by eight foot reed mats and a coil of rope and returned upstream to the pool camp. The white boy was freezing when he got back and had to warm up again before starting the hammock construction.

Talking Boy helped Chet lay the reed mat in the pool. Taking two straight branches, the boys weaved the sticks between the strands of reed on both ends, giving them a sturdy support for the rope. A length of rope tied from one end of the upstream stick around a hefty branch on the old fallen log and back to the other upstream end held the first side in place. They tied the other end to the tree on the bank, pulling it tight. Then while Chet held the rope around the tree, Talking Boy carefully sat on the mat. It held his weight sinking a little as the rope stretched. Chet tightened the rope a little more and joined his friend on the mat.

Both of them were able to lie there with their bodies under water and their heads and toes sticking out. The mat seemed sturdy enough and they decided to sleep there after dinner.

The fire was almost out and after stoking it up with more wood, they checked the salmon. The fish was cooked to perfection, and the boys took turns stripping off the broiled pink meat and stuffing themselves until nothing remained. Both of them had forgotten how hungry they had been. With their bellies full the two adventurers took to their hot water bed. It was pleasant enough and though neither one of them slept soundly, they did stay warm, if not dry. During wakeful moments, both boys lay still with their eyes closed, reflecting on the last two days and thankful they were still alive.

Alive at least for now. Underneath the peace and comfort, the thought of Two Skins was ever-present. He was out there somewhere - and Standing Seal probably hadn't given up either.

XXVII

Steam rising off the pool almost fooled Chet into thinking the fog had stayed with them all night, but the bright blue sky above him changed his mind. It was just what the two boys needed. Even though the hot water bed was warm, their wrinkled bodies made them fear that another night in the water might make their extremities fall off. The warm sun would dry their clothes and blankets and allow them to sleep on the ground again.

Chet and Talking boy dried themselves as best they could, put on their bark skirts and took apart the mat hammock, re-using the rope to make a drying line. After hanging up their blankets, robes and Chet's clothes, the boys headed back to the beach, where they first scanned the bay for signs of life and then began to inventory their gear, while checking the canoe for damage. All the boxes and baskets were removed and their contents rinsed in the freshwater stream, then spread on the driftwood logs to dry. The sailing gear came through the storm in decent shape and except for a few loose pegs and shrouds, everything was ship-shape. While Talking Boy took the dip net in search of minnows for bait Chet retightened the rigging on the mast and the sails.

The Salish boy returned shortly with a net full of three-inch minnows taken from a tide pool, and, though they were small, they would do for bottom fish. Chet went through his fishing gear and set up drop lines for himself and Talking Boy. With all of the gear out of the dugout it was an easy task to push the canoe back down the streambed and out into the cove. The young men left the sails furled and paddled away from shore. The water was crystal clear and soon they found a large sandy patch of bottom between kelp covered rocky areas and stopped paddling. Chet searched the cove again for signs of human life, saw none, and checked to see what the sea birds were doing. Back in Chahakquot the birds would let the slave fishermen know where the schools of herring were, but here they saw no mass feeding of birds anywhere.

The first fishing spot produced a few flounder and then nothing but small dogfish shark, which swallowed the hooks and threatened to consume their supply of vital gear, so the fishermen decided to paddle out to a small islet a few hundred yards away. They had better luck at the rocky outcrop, after stopping on the protected eastern side. Soon the boys had a variety of flounder, rockfish, and sea bass, enough to feed themselves for the next two days.

"The bait's all gone. Do you think we have enough fish for now?" asked Talking Boy.

"Yeah, if we catch any more it'll just spoil," said Chet. "Let's head on back and take a nap, I'm fallin' asleep as it is."

Chet pulled in his line, the Salish boy did the same, and within half an hour they were back at the beach pulling the canoe out of sight and cleaning the fish. The sun was extremely warm for May and their blankets and clothes dried quickly on the heated driftwood. After wrapping the clean fish in cold, wet seaweed they placed them in a water tight basket, gathered everything off the beach, and made a sleeping area next to the gold chest that was still hidden from view. A small fire was made to roast some of the fish, and this time Chet smothered the fire with lots of sand so no smoke would be visible. After another visual check of the beach the boys went to sleep on the grassy sand behind the driftwood.

The rest of the day and night were spent catching up on their much-needed sleep, and between naps, eating the fish they had caught that morning. After dark some of the bottom fish was dried over a small fire hidden upstream so neither the smoke nor the flames could be seen. It felt good to sleep on the bearskin on solid ground, and as Chet watched the thousands of stars above his head, the boy couldn't remember a night as clear as this one. He drifted off to sleep wondering what Lucy was doing. He'd dreamed of her so often during his seven-month ordeal, awake or sleeping. The intensity of his feeling worried him. He'd never felt this way about anyone before, and it half-scared him. Was it real? Was she real? Reality and dreams blended until he didn't know. He just knew he wanted to get back to her.

With an uneventful night of sleep behind them and a banner day for sailing ahead, the boys packed up the sailing canoe early and set out once again into the Pacific. They had restocked the water containers, both seal bladder and boxes, and brought along the dried fish and some greens they had found. The young men kept the dip net and fishing gear at the ready in case they ran across some herring or salmon. With supplies and water enough for two days, the two sailors trimmed the main and jib and rounded the southern point of Vargas Island close hauled to the southeast.

The next two days stayed fair and warm with only brief wisps of clouds moving through the sky above two-foot swells and one-foot seas. The southwest wind was hard to sail against, but stayed steady and after spending another night on a small island the two young men reached the northern mouth of Barkley Sound and turned east around Amphitrite Point.

"There must be a hundred islands in that Sound," said Chet as they cleared the point. "Looks like they could be five to ten miles away. Maybe we better find an inlet here on the north side rather then go on."

"I don't think so," said Talking Boy as he pointed his finger back toward Chet and the inlet behind them. "Look at the arm of the sea behind you. There's a village back there. Smoke rising from a half dozen fires. See! A canoe is coming toward us!"

The Salish boy was right. Less then a quarter mile away was a canoe heading for them with at least four people in it and trying to close the distance.

"Guess we got no choice now," said Chet, calmly. "Unless you want to see if they're friendly?"

"Let's see what your sails will do first," said the Salish boy just as calmly.

In fact, both boys felt extremely calm about the outcome as they changed course slightly to stay west of the Sound and skim the western shores of the outermost islands. If the two couldn't shake the pursuers quickly, at least they would be on course to stay in the ocean when night came.

"How much water we got left?" yelled Chet as he trimmed the main sail and leaned over the starboard rail.

"Enough to last until tomorrow afternoon, if we drink one cup tonight and one in the morning," returned Talking Boy.

The race started out even for the first fifteen minutes as the crew in the trailing dugout paddled frantically to close on the sailing canoe. At one point the boys thought of paddling themselves to increase their speed, but it soon became apparent that the strangers were falling behind, and after an hour the trailing canoe changed course to the east and disappeared from view.

Delighted with their craft's performance, but still cautious, the boys sailed on for another two hours, passing many small islands to the east before choosing a larger one. They knew the Indians of Barkley Sound probably just wanted to be friendly and trade, but both boys felt they had made the right decision in not taking a chance.

The island they picked was in the middle of the mouth of the Sound with hundreds of smaller islands and islets all around. Twenty minutes' searching around the two miles of island's shore brought them to what they had wanted. Bubbling away over the raised rocky beach was a small creek emptying into a fairly deep cove. Luck was with them that early evening, for as they dropped the sails and coasted towards the beach, a large blue-green mass moved below them in seven feet of water. Talking Boy didn't make a sound but just grabbed for the dip net, thrusting it deep in the water and lifting it out again in one smooth motion.

"I got the bait," the Indian boy said, as he dumped a dozen flopping ten-inch herring on the dugout floor. "Now you can catch the salmon."

That night on Barkley Sound was just like the previous two nights, clear and warm. Chet was able to catch a couple of salmon and some bottom fish in the early evening, and, after eating a light dinner, the two spent an hour cutting the remaining salmon into strips for smoking. By daylight the boys were restless again, and after a steady west wind started to blow, they decided to fill the water containers and sail the remaining ten miles to the southern mouth of Barkley Sound.

The canoe made good time and a few hours later they rounded Cape Beale, leaving the Sound behind them. The skies were clear and visibility was good, enabling the sailors to see miles ahead. The long coastline looked straight and treacherous with breakers and surf clearly showing for as far as they could see. With the possibility of having no safe beach to land on before dark the boys decided to stay where they were on a protected bay south of Cape Beale. They sailed up the arm of Pachena Bay for another hour until they found a fresh water stream dropping from the hillside and turned to shore.

The two fugitives made a fire and heated some of the salmon for dinner, then sat back and looked at the stars. Before they went to sleep, Chet and Talking boy opened the chest of gold and looked at the yellow fortune. The Indian boy couldn't resist the temptation to pick up the Spanish sword and thrust it around in the darkness cutting down imaginary warriors right and left.

"If old Two Skins were here right now I'd give him this sword right in the belly," boasted Talking Boy.

Chet just shook his head, laughed, and said nothing. He knew his friend was non-violent and probably wouldn't be much use in a real fight, but the young Indian had other qualities that made him more of a man than most and Chet appreciated them. The white boy closed the chest and re-wrapped the rope over the lid. Talking Boy placed the sword alongside the chest and they covered it all up with mats and baskets.

"The center boards are on tight," yelled Chet. "Go ahead and haul up the jib."

It was still dark and early in the morning, but the two adventurers wanted an early start. There was no way to tell how long the beach ahead would be pounded by high surf, so they refilled all the containers with fresh water again and secured their supply of smoked salmon. The young men were prepared to be out as long as two days and nights if need be, but if they found an inlet anytime after noon, they planned to stop for the night.

"Ready to come about," shouted Chet, and Talking Boy switched the clew line on the jib from port to starboard.

The wind was blowing from the southwest as usual and the sleek sailing canoe would have to backtrack on a tack to the northwest to get out of the bay they were in and then swing back to the southeast after the canoe had gained some distance back in the ocean.

When the sun finally did rise the boys found the skies clouding up for the first time in four days with a threat of rain in the air. The seas were choppy on top of a heavy swell that kept the canoe in an up and down motion. The steady wind was cold, forcing the sailors to keep their bearskins on as they settled back for the long haul down the forested coast.

By mid-day Chet was glad they had stopped the night before when they did, for the long flat beach with its high surf was still with them with no let up in sight. The numerous small islands and rocky outcrops of the north were absent here except a very few near the shore, and those were high cliffed affairs with no beaches. Talking Boy rationed out the water and food as if they would be staying in the canoe two days, but both boys were confident an inlet would show itself soon.

Logging two to three knots an hour, the sturdy little craft had been at sea for twelve hours and with early evening at hand Chet was resigning himself to spending the night on the ocean when Talking Boy got his attention.

"Chet! It looks like a break in the coast ahead," shouted the Indian.

Sure enough, the land cleaved, and as the next hour passed a three-mile wide break in the shore developed with a deep bay to the east. The young men didn't know it but they had entered San Juan Bay at the head of the Strait of Juan de Fuca. It was Makah territory, a whaling tribe that inhabited both sides of the Strait, whose people were a transition between the more war-like tribes of the north and the peaceful Salish.

As they turned east into the bay, Chet and Talking Boy kept close to the north shore. From deep in the bay some miles further, the boys thought they could see smoke from a village and they were hesitant to sail any farther inland for fresh water. It would be dark before long and they had to make a decision where to land soon. The young men were scanning the hillside in front of them when all of a sudden there it was, a Makah camp of two canoes and a dozen people.

"Chet, look!" exclaimed Talking Boy as he pointed at the beach just yards ahead.

"I see them," returned the white boy. "What shall we do?"

"You're asking me?" said the Indian. "You're the leader, you decide."

While the two boys argued over who was leader and what they should do, two armed Makah men on the beach with their wives and children extended a greeting, not a warning. Talking Boy did not know the Makah language, but the Makah knew enough familiar words in Salish to communicate. The strange canoe intrigued the men, and although they recognized it as a Nootkan dugout, an enemy of the Makah, they nevertheless did not seem to feel threatened by the two boys. Just the same, Chet, who a short while before had put on his trousers, decided to take out the Spanish sword and place it in his belt as a sign of being armed. That impressed the men at first, but their expressions of awe turned to laughter as Chet tried to sit back down and got the blade stuck on the thwart.

"If you mean us no harm, you are welcome to share our camp," shouted one of the men.

"We come in peace," returned Talking Boy. "I am from the Duwamish and my friend is a white man from Puget Sound."

This seemed to please the two men and they gave their permission to land.

XXVIII

The two Makah families were on a combination berry-picking and fishing trip, and as the two travelers pulled up the center boards prior to touching shore, the curious children gathered around the bow. Some were older and bolder, while the little ones ran back and forth to their mothers. The two oldest were girls not much younger than Chet and they were especially fond of the handsome Indian boy, giggling at his every move.

As the two men approached the canoe, Talking Boy offered them two wool trade blankets, extra ones Chet had stolen at Nesook. The dividends of good will paid off immediately in the form of fresh salmon berries. Chet had eaten dried berry cakes but never the fresh berries, and he was thankful for the change in diet. The plump orange berries looked somewhat like raspberries that grew back on the Willamette, but were larger and not as sweet or tasty. It was still early in the berry season and possibly the fruit had been picked too soon, but Chet relished them just the same.

Sitting, eating berries, and talking, the boys found out the women and children had just returned from berry picking all day and the men had helped them bring in the extra baskets they had picked. That was why there was no fire or people walking around to alert the boys of the presence of the camp. The Makah canoes on the beach just blended in with the drift logs.

The Makah women treated the two adventurers to a real feast that night with broiled salmon steaks, herring oil, greens, roasted bulbs that tasted like water chestnuts, and a different variety of wapato, not to mention more berries. Two of the older daughters waited on Talking Boy hand and foot, almost to the point of embarrassment, but Chet knew the Indian was loving every moment of it. One of the other girls divided her attention between Chet and Talking Boy, giving Chet many sidelong glances and taking every opportunity to touch him when she passed by. He felt himself responding to her attention and was embarrassed when the Makah women laughed and giggled at his discomfort.

After dinner the men discussed the coast ahead and told the boys that the Washington side of the Strait had calmer waters, and beyond the next half-day journey, they could land on any beach, provided the weather didn't turn too windy. After some fun gambling for berries and game playing the group went to sleep for the night under temporary mat shelters. Half afraid the older girls might try to join them and half wishing they would, the boys put up their own mat shelter further down the beach. They felt excited and expectant, and every nuance of sound woke them during the night, but as it turned out, the girls remained with their families.

By morning Chet was glad he and Talking Boy had the shelter.

The rain wasn't heavy but the temperature felt like winter again. As the boys packed their gear into the canoe, only the strong urge to get home as soon as possible made them want to leave their new friends and brave the rainy weather. The three older girls were obviously sad to see them go. The Makah gave them a basket of berries and some more salmon as they left, and with the sails raised the two sailors continued their journey, waving at the little group on shore until they couldn't see them anymore.

There wasn't much wind and what wind there was changed direction every five minutes, so the two-man crew was kept busy tacking and trimming all morning long. The rain gradually turned to off-and-on showers, but thick clouds to the south kept the Washington coast out of view. By early evening they stopped north of a sweeping crescent-shaped bay on a pleasant beach with a small creek and good cover. They had made only twenty miles.

The next day was fair again but the wind still blew sporadically and progress was slow. Chet tried his luck at trolling with some ripe leftover herring, but all he could manage was a dogfish shark and soon gave up for fear of losing his last two hooks. Late in the afternoon the boys passed a deep inlet about a half-mile wide, but the wind had improved and they were making good time so they decided to continue on. As the wind freshened, the clouds cleared and Chet let out a shout.

"Wa-hoo!" the boy shouted, as he saw the snow capped peaks of the Olympic Mountains over his right shoulder. "Look, Talking Boy, the Olympics! That means were almost to Puget Sound! Let's go for it. Let's keep going and make the strait tonight. I remember that shore and there are hardly any bad areas to beach. If we are as far south as I think we are, most of the beaches are sand hooks and shoals."

"Yes, let's go. I don't think I could sleep, anyway," said the Salish boy.

The canoe turned due south as they began the long run across the Strait. Chet could tell that his friend was excited seeing a familiar sight again and knew the Indian boy's years of captivity made his homecoming more intense than his own would be. Neither felt like stopping now. Not for sleep nor food.

The wind seemed to be their friend this evening as the breeze blew down the Strait from the northwest and they sped along at four knots an hour. Before dark they were able to make out the shore and pick out a long sandy spit of land extending a mile or more into the sea. Chet thought it might be Ediz Hook, but since he had only passed it once before, was not sure. It was dark when they made shore on the sand bar and their initial eagerness to keep going gave way to practical thinking. The stars were out with only a few scattered clouds and the next day promised to be sunny again. They ate some smoked salmon and drank a little water, but were too excited to eat much and opted to play their old game of who could hit a rock farther with a driftwood branch.

The morning dawned clear but cold and Chet was glad he had his extra clothes on under the bark skirt. Talking Boy had spent a restless night, but was sleeping now, and Chet almost felt bad waking him. However, his reluctance was tempered by the fact that they needed to get an early start and try to make the mouth of Puget Sound by day's end. Talking Boy was ready to leave as soon as Chet woke him. Neither of them took time to eat and they pushed the loaded canoe into the salt water and paddled for deep water. The early morning wind was light and from the northwest, and the young men soon had the boards out and sails set, making a slow one to two knots.

The two ex-slaves had indeed spent the night on Ediz Hook and most of the sunny morning sailing east toward Dungeness Spit. The wind picked up as the sun rose, and by noon they had rounded the Spit heading for Point Wilson and the mouth of the Sound. To the east the boys could see Whidbey Island, the long branch of land that led into the Sound, and to the south were Sequim and Discovery Bays. It was an exciting afternoon as they sailed closer to their goal over smooth water and sunny skies.

"Chet, let's keep going tonight if the weather stays fair," Talking Boy said as he stretched back over the rail.

Chet knew how the Indian boy felt, for the young white man, too, could not wait to land and see the settlers he had left months before, particularly one of them. He thought of nothing but Lucy all morning and missed the skinny little girl more than ever. Boy, the stories he would be able to tell her about the last seven months!

"As far as I remember there were no shoals to speak of where we might run aground and there isn't a bad beach in the whole inlet," Chet recounted. "I'm game for night sailin'."

Talking Boy was pleased and his excitement was even greater as he watched the long island to the east grow larger with each passing minute. While the Indian boy was looking straight ahead Chet was scanning a medium-sized island to the south about a mile away. A black speck on the horizon in that direction had caught the white boy's attention, and after a few moments he was sure it was moving.

"Hey, is that a canoe heading toward us?" shouted Chet to his friend in the bow. Talking Boy looked in the direction Chet was pointing.

"Yes, it is!" he said, excited. "I can't make out the size yet. It might be a Salish canoe - I might even know them!"

The Indian boy grabbed onto the fore shroud and pulled himself to a standing position, shading his eyes, and staring to the south.

"White Clam, its a big canoe with at least ten men in it. It's not Salish. It might be Makah - No, it's Nootkan! White Clam, it's Nootkan!"

The white boy almost fell overboard when he stood to look for himself. It was definitely a northern-type canoe and at least thirty-five feet long. A dozen men were paddling at top speed as the big dugout flew across the water on an angle that was meant to intercept them. The wind was coming from the north and lighter than it had been for some time and Chet remembered how they had barely outrun the four-man canoe on Barkley Sound a few days ago. They had to do something, and quick, or the canoe would be on them in minutes.

"White Clam, what should we do?" screamed Talking Boy. "I think it's Two Skins!"

The Indian boy thought correctly. It was Two Skins and his men. The group of renegades had paddled south nonstop for several days to make sure they had lost Standing Seal's pursuit. They had taken with them plenty of dried fish and water so they wouldn't have to make landfall until they were well into Makah territory. Their course took them to Neah Bay, a large Makah village on the northwest tip of Washington Territory, just southeast of Cape Flattery. The Makah were cautious of them but let the Nootkas land. The Washington tribe treated the newcomers with reserved courtesy, and kept warriors armed for the length of their stay. Two Skins had told the Makah chief they were on a whaling trip and had strayed south by mistake and thanked the man for his hospitality. In reality, the scar-faced half-breed was checking the village population and vulnerability to attack.

After seeing the security of the Neah Bay Makah village, Two Skins had decided to move into Puget Sound to plunder the easier Salish and maybe try his luck at attacking a white settlement in search of more guns and ammunition. Just the previous night the renegades had attacked a small white outpost on the southwest tip of Whidbey Island, but the settlers, with their newer repeating rifles, were able to hold the raiders in check, and killed one of Two Skins' men. The whites knew there was an American sloop-of-war anchored in Elliot Bay and after darkness the outpost was able to sneak a two-man canoe past the waiting Indians and southward to get help.

Two Skins knew the firepower he faced was great and decided to head north again, away from the white guns. He'd find some Salish to attack. The renegades left well before the American warship was alerted and disappeared into the early morning. When Two Skins' canoe left Puget Sound and rounded Point Wilson, his plan was to head due north, but the crafty Indian changed course when he spotted Chet's sail. The half-breed kept his dugout close to the shore, turning west so the boys would not be able to pick the canoe out of the forested shoreline.

The ploy worked, for the Indian craft crept ever closer until they had to show themselves or fall behind an island. Two Skins screamed the order to attack and the dozen men paddled for all they were worth towards the small sailing vessel and the promise of an easy plunder. As the gap closed between the two vessels, the half-breed was startled and confused by what he saw. He had thought he was chasing a white man in a sailing scow, but it soon became apparent that this was a Nootkan canoe and the renegade had no idea what to make of it. He had never seen this type of sail on a Nootkan canoe.

"White Clam, what do we do?" screamed Talking Boy again. "Chet, I'm afraid they're going to catch us!"

Chet could wait no longer. He knew they couldn't outrun the Indians on their present tack and their only hope was to run with the wind, beach the dugout and flee into the forest. It was only a slim hope, for, unfortunately, running with the wind meant barreling head-on into the oncoming attackers. Chet dug the rudder paddle deep into the water and let out the boom line to catch the north wind.

"What are you doing?" shouted Talking Boy, his face ashen with fear. "We're headed right for them!"

"Trim the jib, and trust me!" yelled back Chet. "Trim the jib, tie it off and lie down when we get close to them."

Talking Boy obeyed the order and clung low in the bow. Chet steered the little canoe straight for the rapidly approaching dugout, holding the boom line at the ready. Even the sea seemed to jump with excitement and Chet could feel the spray of saltwater on his face, but his eyes never left the danger ahead. Talking Boy peeked above the bow and ducked back down as he saw the raiders approaching fast on a collision course less than fifty feet away. Just as the two canoes were about to collide, Chet pulled hard on the rudder and the dugout lurched to starboard. At the same time the white boy pulled in hard on the main boom and kept the wind in the sail. The mast dipped thirty degrees, but the canoe didn't capsize and the two frightened boys sped past the thirty-five foot dugout as though were shot from a cannon.

Chet couldn't resist a look as they sped past and even before he saw the rifle barrels raise in his direction, his eyes locked on the cold pair belonging to Two Skins himself and there was no doubt the Indian recognized Chet. The white boy ducked as he heard the report of three rifles behind him. Knowing he would have a few minutes before they could reload, Chet sat up and turned the canoe straight, easing out the main sail again. The jib that had been luffing during the reach tack, filled as well and the sailing canoe raced away.

Two Skins had let out a scream when he realized who captained the canoe that had just outmaneuvered and avoided him. The scar faced Indian could not believe it at first, but then he began yelling at his men and whipping the nearest ones with a rope end to get them paddling again. Here was a chance to get even with the white boy who had been a thorn in his side for more than half a year. The boy who had humiliated him by stealing his robe, the boy who had foiled his raid on Nesook and warned Swimming Otter at Chahakquot! At last Two Skins would kill this pesky adversary once and for all!

It took some time for the large canoe to get turned around and back to full speed. By then the two boys ahead had opened up a seventy-five yard lead and were holding it. Two Skins guessed what Chet was up to and welcomed it, for he had no wish to chase the small canoe back toward Puget Sound for fear his tired men might not catch them. Better they should land and track the boys down and kill them. Anticipating the pleasure of it, Two Skins' mouth drew back in a maniacal grin.

The sailing canoe headed straight for the middle of the island Two Skins had just left, and for awhile it looked as though they might land on the island's northern shore, but the dugout soon veered to the east and disappeared around the eastern point of the island heading for the mainland. At the same time Two Skins noticed the wind start to fluctuate and die down. He thought his men had been gaining, and now was sure of it, which made him drive them even faster. The small sailing canoe was completely out of sight now and precious minutes passed as the attackers closed in on the eastern point of the island.

Two Skins' canoe finally passed the point and darted out into the channel between the island and the Washington mainland. The half-breed stood in the rear of his dugout and gasped in disbelief, as he saw nothing in front of him. Two Skins yelled at his men to stop as he scanned the shoreline from east to west. Nothing. He quickly looked back at the small island and saw nothing again. The renegade scanned the mile long crescent-shaped beach and saw nothing but sand. They were nowhere to be seen. The sailing dugout had disappeared into the sea.

Chet thought he had recognized the island earlier, but wasn't positive until the sailing canoe rounded the point. He remembered a cold, clear November morning when he and Andrew had climbed the fore and main masts of the *Exact* prior to setting sail and saw the hidden cove that no one else saw from the waterline because of its narrow switched-back inlet channel. Chet remembered Andrew had dubbed it Palmer Cove. Yes, he thought, this was the same place - Protection Island! With the wind failing, the boys sailed into the cove, cutting the bark rope shroud lines with their knives and getting the mast down quickly before Two Skins could see them. As soon as the canoe hit the beach, they jumped out and dragged it into the brush. They hauled the heavy chest and sword into a thicket and covered them with deadfall. Frantically, they gathered more deadfall to camouflage the dugout and used branches to sweep footprints and scrapes from the canoe off the beach. Having hidden everything as best they could, Chet and Talking Boy scrambled up a grassy dune, staying low as they peered over the edge.

There in the southern cove was the enemy canoe, its occupants obviously confused about their disappearance. The two friends knew it was only a matter of time before Two Skins would discover the hidden inlet, so they quickly backed off the ridge and started to race down the inland side of the dune, thinking only of getting as far away from Two Skins as possible.

A loud explosion suddenly rocked their eardrums, stopping them in mid-stride.

"What the heck was that?" exclaimed Chet as he started running back up the dune.

The boys crouched at the top and looked over the edge once more. To their amazement they saw a sight neither could have ever imagined. There to the east on a close-hauled tack was a warship, and as the boys gawked in disbelief, a billow of white smoke shot out from the bow and a few seconds later came the crashing report of the nine-pounder.

The enemy canoe was in a state of shock as the second nine-pound ball hit dangerously close. A defiant Two Skins stood in the stern, calmed his men, and headed the canoe toward the island's sandy shore.

"Ready another round, Mister Jarrell!" shouted Lieutenant Mykleburg, as the sleek warship closed in on the renegades.

"Load another round, men," snapped the ensign.

Matt and Andrew flew through the motions and had the brass cannonade swabbed and loaded in record time.

"Stand by starboard battery. Mister Jarrell fire at will," ordered Mykleburg once again as the rest of the crew stood waiting on the gun deck. The young ensign steadied the sights and locked the swivel.

"Go ahead and pull one off for your friend, Andrew," said the young officer as he stepped aside. "Payback is hell."

The young seaman took the lanyard without hesitation and gave it a jerk. The ball went true to the mark and hit just behind the escaping canoe, lifting the stern five feet out of the water and sending the scar-faced leader and cedar splinters sailing through the air. Two Skins hit the water hard and sank below the surface. The other Indians were shaken, but unhurt, and one of them picked up a loaded rifle and sent a ball sailing past Captain Jordan Scott's head.

"Mister Mykleburg, secure from the batteries and send the marines aloft with rifles," ordered the angry captain. "Mister Carpenter and Mister Jarrell, break out the small boat and small arms and be ready to pick up survivors."

The marines opened fire on the out-gunned Indians, hitting two of them, and within a few seconds the rest gave up, throwing their rifles, bows and spears into the sea.

During this battle the two boys on the beach had stayed well hidden, cheering when they saw Two Skins get blown away. With the outcome of the battle resolved, Chet began taking off his bark vest and skirt, leaving on only his tattered white man's shirt and trousers.

"What are you doing?" asked Talking Boy.

"I'm goin' to run down to the beach and let them know we're here," said Chet.

"I'm going with you," said the Indian boy.

"No, my friend. They might take you for a renegade. Lord knows I look enough like one myself, but with these clothes I should be all right. Stay hidden until I give you the all clear signal."

The two white settlers who had escaped Two Skins' raid on their Whidbey Island village had reached the American sloop of war the day before and Captain Scott had immediately ordered the ship to pursue the Indians. They had a good description of the canoe and its occupants and opened fire when they spotted it. Long before the first cannon fired, Matt English had recognized the scar faced Indian through Captain Scott's glass. Now, the young mate looked hard ahead, as they approached the Nootka war canoe, trying to see a sign of the Indian leader in the water, but the half-breed had obviously drowned.

The seaman's eyes then caught sight of a familiar figure running along the beach. Matt didn't know how the young man got there, but he had no doubt it was Chet waving at them as he ran back and forth on the beach. Bart and Andrew joined Matt at the rail and all three of them waved and yelled at the boy on shore. The rest of the crew was busy dispatching the small boat from their ship to take the disabled Indian canoe and prisoners in tow.

In all the excitement no one noticed a man dragging himself from the shallow water of the cove some hundred yards away from the white boy. The scar faced Indian had survived the blast and was able to swim underwater to shore. Bleeding from half a dozen splinter wounds, the crazed Indian saw Chet and, filled with rage and hate, ran toward him with the thought of killing the boy before he could be killed himself. He ran close by the hiding Talking Boy and the Salish lad stood up in shock, startled to see the bleeding Indian. Two Skins paused, wondering whether to kill Talking Boy first, but when the half-breed took the whalebone club from his belt, the Salish boy turned and ran off. Two Skins let him go and turned his attention to Chet. The white boy had been too busy hailing the ship to notice the menacing figure approach.

The three men at the rail of the *Intense* saw the scar faced Indian and tried to warn the boy of the half-breed's advance, but Chet just thought they were waving and shouting words of jubilation.

"Say, you there, marines! We need a marksman here quick!" yelled Bart.

Lieutenant Mykleburg, taking in instantly what was happening, grabbed a rifle from one of the marines and ran to the rail. Kneeling, he propped the barrel on the wood railing and took aim. But it was too late. Two Skins was upon Chet.

Chet finally sensed that something was wrong and turned around just as the scar faced warrior screamed and lifted his war club. Terrified, the white boy threw up his hands and stumbled, falling backward on the sand, all hope gone as he waited for the crashing blow to come. Seconds seemed like hours as Chet opened his eyes and looked up at the tall half-breed standing over him, clutching a club over his head, his eyes fixed on Chet with a maniacal gleam. Chet braced for the blow. He screamed as the half-breed dropped to his knees and brought the club down on Chet's head with a glancing blow. The club dropped from the Indian's hand just as his heavy weight fell full on Chet. Chet stared horrified at the contorted face not two inches from his own, eyes boring into his, eyes that suddenly turned white as Two Skins reared backward, hands clutching his chest, and rolled off Chet's body. In shock, Chet barely noticed the tip of a silver sword sticking out of Two Skins' chest as the scar-faced Indian gave one last heaving shudder and died. Standing behind him was the ex-slave Talking Boy, shocked at what he had just done.

With Chet staring in disbelief, Talking Boy reached down and pulled the bloody blade out of Two Skins' back and coldly kicked the dead half-breed in the head, the force of the blow exposing a silver and seashell necklace from under Two Skins' vest. Talking Boy knelt down and with a deliberate motion grasped the silver eagle charm firmly in his hand and ripped the necklace off the dead half-breed.

"This was mine," said Talking Boy, holding the necklace aloft as he looked at the shocked white boy. "And now I have it back."

XXIX

The lieutenant put the safety back on his rifle and withdrew his aim. Captain Scott ordered the small boat that had just towed the Indian canoe to the ship to go ashore with Matt, Andrew, and Bart aboard. They found Chet and Talking Boy standing on the beach, hands on each other's shoulders, trying to absorb the ordeal they had just gone through. Both were shaken and in tears as Talking Boy spoke to his friend.

"He killed my father and my family and I did nothing," the Indian boy cried. "I wasn't going to let him kill you, too."

"Talking Boy.....", Chet began to thank his friend.

"No!" the Salish boy said, as he put his hand over Chet's mouth. "It's not Talking Boy anymore. He was a slave. My name is Wikseyah, and I'm a free man."

Two Skins lay on the beach face down, dead. The Spanish sword was stuck upright in the sand next to his body, its golden handle gleaming in the sun.

The boys were aware of the ship's cutter coming to rest on the soft sand of the beach, but they were too shaken to let go of one another. Chet didn't respond at first when the men spoke, until a voice from the past jarred his memory.

"Well, ain't ye a sight," said the old cook. "Damned if ye don't look like a heathen, but I'm one that's sure glad yer alive."

Chet raised his swollen eyes and squinted at the assembled men.

"Bart, is that you?" he asked in amazement. "Matt......Andrew! How did you get here?"

"All in due time, son," said Bart. Let's get ye out of here and on the ship."

"Chet, we thought you were dead," laughed Andrew, shaking his old friend's hand. "Come on, let me help you get in the boat."

"Wait! We've got some gear on the other side of the hidden cove that we can't leave without, and Talking Boy here, I mean Wikseyah, goes with us. He isn't one of these pirate Indians. He's my friend. I want you all to understand that."

"We figured that out already when he skewered that heathen like he was gonna eat him fer dinner," chuckled Bart.

Bosun Carpenter set out a burial detail and the two boys led the others around the cove to the chest of gold. Along the way Matt, Andrew, and Bart told the story of what happened after Chet had been kidnapped. After hearing about Bart's change the boy forgave the old cook on the spot. He was too glad to see them to hold any grudges.

Everyone was amazed at the amount of gold in the chest, and Chet and Wikseyah agreed that everyone on the sloop would get a small share. The crew of the *Intense* was also amazed at the getaway canoe and the ingenuity that had gone into it. Matt couldn't believe the boys had sailed the tiny craft all the way from Nootka Sound. Chet remembered to get Two Skins' bearskin robe and the adze Wooden Hand had given him. The rest of the gear they left in the hidden canoe.

Before sundown everyone was back aboard the *Intense*. Chet and Talking Boy were introduced to Captain Scott and the officers, and the gold was locked away in a cabinet in the captain's quarters. The renegade Nootkans were locked up in the ship's brig below decks and the thirty-five foot war canoe was taken in tow for Wikseyah's people.

"You know the name on this chest looks mighty familiar to me," commented Captain Scott. "Seems to me I remember reading about the earlier times up here when the Spanish claimed all the west coast from South America to Alaska. I think this Jose' Francisco was the Spanish governor of this area back in 1792."

"Spanish Gold," said Bart. "I sure threw in with the wrong crowd. Chet, my boy, yer a rich man."

The sloop wasted no time in setting sail, and, as they turned back to the east and got underway, Bart called to the boys to join him in the galley. When Chet walked in, the smell of real food filled his nostrils for the first time in seven months. The old cook was preparing fresh potatoes, peas, fresh bread, butter and jam, hot tea, biscuits, pork gravy, and a couple of pork loin steaks that the officer's mess had agreed to give up. Chet was in heaven and began stuffing himself with bread and jam. Wikseyah, who was not unfamiliar with white men's food, managed to find the dinner quite pleasing as well and showed better table manners than Chet.

Matt, Andrew, and most of the crew joined the adventurers later and heard the stories of how Chet was captured and how he escaped and made his way back to Chahakquot. Wikseyah, who was rapidly becoming a crowd favorite, used his speaking skills to boast of Chet's mighty deeds, such as catching fish, foiling Two Skins, hunting whales and the like. The talk went on for hours, with the young crew on the edge of their seats listening intently to every adventure.

The sloop made a quick stop so Captain Scott could reassure the settlement on Whidbey Island, then continued on to Olympia, sailing all night. The next morning Chet and Wikseyah accompanied the captain and Matt to the government building, where the gold chest was opened and the bars weighed and tallied. Ten percent of the total was divided among the sloop's crew as a reward for saving the boys and the rest put in bank accounts for the two young men. Matt went to the post office and fired off letters to Lloyd Merrifield and Chet's parents while the two boys signed bank papers.

News of what had happened traveled quickly in the territorial capital and Chet and Wikseyah became overnight celebrities. Each young man took one hundred dollars spending cash for baths, haircuts and new clothes. Chet also stopped at the local hotel cafe and ordered a heaping plate of hotcakes, maple syrup, and bacon, and topped it off with a tall cool glass of milk.

With their financial business complete, the boys returned to the sloop and talked to Captain Scott about taking Wikseyah back to his village.

"After giving the members of the crew their portion of the reward you offered them, I'm sure this ship's company would be glad to take you boys anywhere you wanted to go on the Pacific Coast, let alone Puget Sound," commented the captain. "When do we sail?"

The boys figured the next morning's tide was soon enough to leave so the crew of the *Intense* could spend some of their reward that night. The local merchants were happy they stayed too. Chet and Wikseyah went to dinner on shore with Matt, Bart, and Andrew and they talked some more about their adventures.

"Matt, what are you going to do with the money now that your three months' service time is about up?" asked Chet.

"Well, I'd like to find me a nice schooner to captain," the young mate answered.

"I'd like to buy one some day," interrupted Wikseyah. "Maybe we could make a deal."

"You need to go to school first and learn how to read and write so you can read your bank statement and write checks," laughed Chet.

"If you boys are serious, now's a good time to buy," Matt said. "There are a hundred ships sitting abandoned in San Francisco Bay with their owners back east scramblin' to sell their ships or get new crews to sail um'. Prices are rock bottom."

"What about you, Andrew? What are you going to do?"

"Well, fellas. I sure have takin' a likin' to that nine- pounder. I think the navy might be the life for me," the New England boy said. "I sure liked the way it lifted that war canoe out of the water!"

"Well, boys," began Bart, "if you need a cook on that there schooner, I'm yer man. I figure I'm gettin' too old to be of much trouble and young Captain Matt here can steer me straight iffin' I stray to port. But I won't come cheap!"

They finished their coffee and drinks and returned to the ship for a good night's sleep without Bart getting even a little drunk.

The crew had been given a curfew by the captain and Lieutenant Mykleburg, always the stickler, saw that everyone got back on time and in decent condition.

Chet couldn't fall asleep that night as he relived the last seven months of his life. He wondered about his friends, Wooden Hand and Cattail Woman, and prayed the old couple were doing fine and making it home themselves. Chet wondered about Water Bear and Swimming Otter and Chief Standing Seal. The young man thought he might like to see them again someday and would try to explain why he had left them. Then Chet thought of Lucy. He laughed aloud. Thoughts of her had slipped to the back of his mind during the busy day he'd just completed. He was rich now and could go back to her in style. Every time he thought of her an uncontrollable tingle crossed his body. He wondered if she felt the same. There was only one way to find out.

The cruise up the Sound to Elliot Bay was a pleasant one and when Wikseyah gave directions to his summer village west of Bainbridge Island, Matt wondered if his people were the same tribe that he'd met at Alki Point.

"You know the place, Chet. Alki Point is the name of the spot where we dropped off the settlers and your friend, Lucy." Matt paused. "Say, you know that girl probably thinks you're dead. You'd better find her again quick before some other young buck takes a fancy to her."

Matt turned back to the Indian boy again.

"Anyway, Wikseyah, would your chief be named Sealth?"

"Not only is he my chief but my uncle as well," said the Indian boy.

"Good. We can drop anchor at Elliot bay and find out where the chief is," said Captain Scott. "By the way, young man, you'll be happy to know the pioneers think so much of your uncle they are planning to name their new town after him. They're going to call it Seattle."

The sloop-of-war anchored in the bay late in the afternoon and the small boat took Chet and Wikseyah ashore amid a loud cheer of appreciation from the crew. The Indian boy was told by some Salish people living on the outskirts of the town that his uncle, Chief Sealth, was across the bay at Blake Island.

Chet was recognized by some of his shipboard acquaintances as he shook hands and accepted greetings from well-wishers. The boy asked about the Hill family and especially about Lucy.

"A fine young girl," said one of the ladies. "She comes into town every so often on that horse of hers to see how many newcomers are moving in and to give us a report on the folks in the valley."

Chet was glad to hear that Lucy was healthy and happy and was told how to get to her family's homestead on the Duwamish.

"Chet, my friend, are you coming with me to meet my uncle?" asked the Salish boy. "Matt and I have permission to sail the cutter over to Blake Island."

Chet didn't answer right away, but took his friend aside and spoke to him in low tones.

"I understand, my friend," said Wikseyah. "We can meet again soon. You go and find this one whose name you cried in your sleep, keeping me awake." His eyes twinkled as Chet blushed under his tan.

With that the Indian boy and Matt boarded the cutter and the crewmen rowed away from the beach. Chet watched as they shipped oars and stepped the mast. When the small sail caught air, the white boy chuckled to himself as he watched Talking Boy switch seats with Matt and take the tiller. The young Indian turned one final time and yelled in English.

"So long, **White Clam!**"

The white boy was confused. *What did Talking Boy mean when he said white clam*, Chet thought. *Oh, well. I'll ask him another time.*

Chet asked to borrow a small native canoe, and, after saying goodbye to everyone, took advantage of the last few hours of daylight and headed for the southern part of the bay and the mouth of the Duwamish.

XXX

When Chet had sailed away on the *Exact*, Lucy didn't know if she'd ever see him again. What she did know was that she loved him, heart and soul. When the report came that he was dead, she didn't want to believe it. Death was too final to deal with, so Lucy could not accept it. He had to be alive, for she could not cope with anything less! The news weighed heavily on the girl, and her aunt could tell Lucy was close to breaking down the same way she had when her parents died. Seeing the emptiness in Lucy's eyes, Aunt Lola had taken the girl aside.

"They don't know for sure that he's been killed," the young girl's aunt had said. "He just might turn up some day."

Tears no longer came easily to Lucy after losing both her mother and father, but the thought of losing another loved one was unbearable, and she could hold back no longer. The tears had flowed freely as Lola held Lucy gently in her arms. After a few minutes the girl had felt better.

"I'm all right, aunty. He might not have come back anyway," Lucy said. "I didn't think he would just disappear like this, though."

"You just keep a positive mind and no matter what happens, things will turn out all right," said Lola. "The Lord will see you through."

The next few days had been bittersweet for Lucy, for she felt bad about Chet, but she did like her new life on the Duwamish and kept herself busy working around the farm. As the months passed, the farm grew and the girl tried to move ahead. The emotional upheaval of friendship turning to love for Chet and then losing him, maybe forever, had changed her. That, and her new responsibilities and hard work on the farm caused her to mature much earlier then she might have, had she been living an easier life. She had not only matured, but she was rapidly blossoming into a beauty.

There were several young lads in the area now and Lucy had caught the eyes of most of them. She could have had her pick and did go walking with a few. But there was something special about Chet that Lucy could never keep out of her mind, and images of him and his kiss when he left kept her from getting serious about any of her suitors. Time eased the pain though, and finally the day came when she could smile instead of cry when she thought of him. She was sure Chet would come back to her. Why, she even heard him call her name in her dreams, and she'd wake and stare into the darkness, heart beating wildly!

By the time summer came, Uncle Josh had finished making a small buggy for Lucy to use after training their horse, Candy, to the harness. Lucy's favorite pastime was riding Candy, so she was eager to have an opportunity to work with the small, muscular horse and spend more time with her.

Throughout the early days of June, Lucy worked patiently with Candy, getting her used to the feel and pull of the harness and learning new commands.

Finally, the day arrived when Lucy felt Candy was ready to be harnessed to the new buggy. The horse took to her new role easily, and before long Lucy was recognized around the countryside as the pretty girl in the homemade cart pulled by a smartly stepping little mare.

Summer days in the Pacific Northwest are long, with twilight lasting almost until eleven at night. One late afternoon, toward the end of June, Lucy decided the day was too perfect not to take full advantage of every minute of it, so she quickly finished chores, harnessed the mare to the cart and drove by the cabin where her aunt and uncle were standing at the open front door.

"Aunt Lola, Uncle Josh, I'm going to take Candy across the valley - I'll be back well before dark."

They waved her on, and she started off down the road, waving at her niece and nephew playing in the yard. The two children promptly ran after the buggy laughing and trying to keep up.

Josh watched them for a minute and then called out.

"Mister Jeff and Miss Janie, I have a job for my little darlings. I want each of you to take a bucket, go to the river landing and bring back some water so we can wash up before we go to bed tonight."

"Aw, daddy, do I have to?" pleaded Jeff.

"Yeah, daddy. Do we have to?" added Janie.

"Well I got this here willow switch says you better," grinned their father.

The two young children had been hearing about the willow switch since as long as they could remember, but they'd never seen it. Their gentle father had never used it for anything but a threat, but the threat always worked. They picked up the buckets and grumbled to each other as they walked to the riverbank.

Some weeks before, their father had made a small log landing to keep the canoe on and to fish from. It also worked well for getting water out of the river without getting one's feet wet, and the two children paraded right up the plank walk and onto the deck of the landing. Jeff got on his knees and dipped the first bucket into the slow current, struggling to lift it out.

"Need some help there?" came a call out of nowhere.

The youngsters looked up and saw a young man standing in a Salish canoe poling his way toward them.

"Say, I remember you," said Janie. "You're Chet."

"Yeah, you're Lucy's friend," said Jeff. "Ain't you supposed to be dead?"

"Now that's what they tell me, but it just didn't work out that way," laughed Chet.

The tall boy came alongside the landing and jumped out, tying the canoe to the front post of the deck. Chet took the two buckets and filled them for the children.

"Why don't I carry these for you, while you two run up to the house and tell them I'm here."

"Sure thing," said Jeff, glad to have his work done for him. He turned, running for the house.

Janie just stood there staring at Chet and wondering if he were a ghost, then all of a sudden, she ran away, too. Chet laughed and started up the path, feeling nervous all of a sudden, wondering whether Lucy still liked him.

Josh came running out of the house with Lola right on his heels. They threw their arms around Chet, talking at once and urging him to come inside.

"Chet, my boy, we thought you were dead! How did you get here?"

The young man gave Josh and Lola a quick five-minute overview of his adventures and looked around, wondering where Lucy was.

Lola knew what he was thinking.

"There's a young lady who's going be mighty glad to see you," she said. "I don't mind saying she thinks the world of you. She never believed you were dead - she just wouldn't allow herself to."

"Well, I kind of think a lot of her, too," said Chet. "Is she - is she here?" he stammered, embarrassed.

"She's crossin' the valley yonder," Josh said, pointing to the west.

Chet watched as Lucy drove her horse and buggy up a hill in the distance and stopped at the top to look back at her home. Chet grinned to himself as she squinted, obviously trying to figure out whom the other person was, who was standing with her family. He waved and so did Josh and Lola and she turned Candy around to come back. The horse moved at a fast clip, liking the idea of heading back to the lean-to barn.

When Lucy got close enough and finally recognized Chet, she stopped the cart and just sat there staring at him. Then she jumped out and ran toward him, arms outstretched, laughing and crying all at once. Chet moved toward her, too, unaware he was doing so, completely mesmerized by the vision in front of him. Unseeing of anything but each other, not caring that Josh and Lola and the two children were watching and grinning, the two lovers came together in a close embrace, kissing, touching each other's faces, then kissing again.

"Oh, Lucy, Lucy, you don't know how I missed you," Chet said, half-choking on tears himself. "I don't think I could have stood it if you hadn't been here waiting for me."

"I thought of you every day and every night. I heard you call my name. I knew you'd come back to me," Lucy said, kissing him again and again. "Please don't ever go away."

"I'll never leave you again," Chet said, and kissed her tenderly, holding her, enfolding her, in a forever embrace.

The End

Made in United States
Troutdale, OR
02/25/2025

29307191R00196